From his position above the campsite, Shannow watched the Zealots approach. His pistols leveled on the two men closest to Batik, he squeezed the triggers, and flame blossomed. The first of his targets was hurled from his feet; the second was slammed sideways as a bullet lodged in his brain.

Batik rolled from his blankets, pistol in hand. The third attacker fired, the bullet kicking up dirt some inches to Batik's right. His own pistol thundered a reply, and the man was thrown backward.

Shannow, meanwhile, had turned his guns on the men by his own blanket. He killed one of them, but the second sprinted for the slope. Batik fired twice, missing his target, then lunged to his feet and gave chase.

The Zealot was almost to the foot of the slope when he whirled and fired, the shell whistling past Batik's ear. Batik took aim and pulled the trigger, but there was a dull click.

The Zealot grinned and raised his own pistol . . .

By David Gemmell
Published by Ballantine Books:

LION OF MACEDON
DARK PRINCE

KNIGHTS OF DARK RENOWN

MORNINGSTAR

The Drenai Saga
       LEGEND
       THE KING BEYOND THE GATE
       QUEST FOR LOST HEROES
       WAYLANDER

The Stones of Power Cycle
       GHOST KING
       LAST SWORD OF POWER
       WOLF IN SHADOW
       THE LAST GUARDIAN*
       BLOODSTONE*

*Forthcoming

Wolf in Shadow

The Stones of Power
Book Three

(Formerly entitled *The Jerusalem Man*)

David Gemmell

A Del Rey® Book
BALLANTINE BOOKS • NEW YORK

A Del Rey® Book
Published by Ballantine Books
Copyright © 1987 by David A. Gemmell

http://www.randomhouse.com

ISBN: 0-345-41685-6

Manufactured in the United States of America

First Ballantine Books Edition: February 1997
Second Ballantine Books Edition: June 1997

10 9 8 7 6 5 4 3 2 1

This novel is dedicated to the memory of "Lady" Woodford, who believed in love, courage, and friendship and gave those who knew her fresh insights into the meaning of all three. Sleep well, lady.

And to Ethel Osborne, her sister, for a lifetime of love and care.

Acknowledgments

Nothing is created in a vacuum, and I am grateful to many people for their help in the creation of *Wolf in Shadow*. My thanks to Elizabeth Reeves, my editor, for bringing me out of the mist; to Peter Austin for the wagon master; and to Jean Maund, Stella Graham, Tom Taylor, Ross Lempriere, Ivan Kellham, and Tony Fenelon for invaluable assistance.

Thanks also to Jeremy Wells for loyalty and friendship in a world that rarely understands either.

Prologue

THE HIGH PRIEST lifted his bloodstained hands from the corpse and dipped them in a silver bowl filled with scented water. The blood swirled around the rose petals floating there, darkening them and glistening like oil. A young acolyte moved to kneel before the king, his hands outstretched. The king leaned forward, placing a large oval stone in his palms. The stone was red-gold and veined with thick black streaks. The acolyte carried the stone to the corpse, laying it on the gaping wound where the girl's heart had been. The stone glowed, the red-gold gleaming like an eldritch lantern, the black veins shrinking to fine hairlines. The acolyte lifted the stone once more, wiped it with a cloth of silk, and returned it to the king before backing away into the shadows.

A second acolyte approached the high priest, bowing low. In his arms he held the red ceremonial cape, which he lifted over the priest's bald head.

The king clapped his hands twice, and the girl's body was lifted from the marble altar and carried down the long hall to oblivion.

"Well, Achnazzar?" demanded the king.

"As you can see, my lord, the girl was a powerful ESPer, and her essence will feed many stones before it fades."

"The death of a pig will feed a stone, priest. You know what I am asking," said the king, fixing Achnazzar with a piercing glare. The bald priest bowed low, keeping his eyes on the marble floor.

"The omens are mostly good, sire."

"Mostly? Look at me!" Achnazzar raised his head, steeling

himself to meet the burning eyes of the Satanlord. The priest blinked and tried to look away, but Abaddon's glare held him trapped, almost hypnotized. "Explain yourself."

"The invasion, lord, should proceed favorably in the spring. But there are dangers . . . not great dangers," he added hurriedly.

"From which area?"

Achnazzar was sweating as he licked dry lips with a dry tongue.

"Not an area, lord, but three men."

"Name them."

"Only one can be identified; the others are hidden. But we will find them. The one is called Shannow. Jon Shannow."

"Shannow? I do not know the name. Is he a leader of men or a brigand chief?"

"No, lord. He rides alone."

"Then how is he a danger to the Hellborn?"

"Not to the Hellborn, sire, but to you."

"You consider there is a difference?"

Achnazzar blanched and blinked the sweat from his eyes. "No, lord, I meant merely that the threat is to you as a man."

"I have never heard of this Shannow. Why should he threaten me?"

"There is no sure answer, sire, but he follows the old, dead god."

"A Christian?" spit Abaddon. "Will he seek to kill me with love?"

"No, lord, I meant the old dark god. He is a brigand slayer, a man of sudden violence. There is even some indication that he is insane."

"How do these indications manifest themselves—apart from his religious stupidity?"

"He is a wanderer, lord, searching for a city that ceased to exist during blessed Armageddon."

"What city?"

"Jerusalem, lord."

Abaddon chuckled and leaned back on his throne, all tension fading. "That city was destroyed by a tidal wave three hundred years ago—by the great mother of all tidal waves. A thousand feet of surging ocean drowned that pestilential place, signaling the reign of the master and the death of Jehovah. What does Shannow hope to find in Jerusalem?"

"We do not know, lord."

"And why is he a threat?"

"In every chart, or seer dream, his line crosses yours. Karmically you are bonded. It is so with the other two; in some way Shannow has touched—or will touch—the lives of two men who could harm you. We cannot identify them yet, but we will. For now they appear as shadows behind the Jerusalem Man."

"Shannow must die . . . and swiftly. Where is he now?"

"He is at present some months journey to the south, nearing Rivervale. We have a man there, Fletcher. I shall get word to him."

"Keep me informed, priest."

As Achnazzar backed away from his monarch, Abaddon rose from the ebony throne and wandered to the high arched window, gazing over New Babylon. On a plain to the south of the city the Hellborn army was gathering for the raids of the Blood Feast. By winter the new guns would be distributed, and the Hellborn would ready themselves for the spring war: ten thousand men under the banner of Abaddon, sweeping into the south and west, bringing the new world into the hands of the last survivor of the Fall.

And they warned him of one madman?

Abaddon raised his arms. "Come to me, Jerusalem Man."

◇ 1 ◇

THE RIDER PAUSED at the crest of a wooded hill and gazed down over the wide rolling empty lands beneath him.

There was no sign of Jerusalem, no dark road glittering with diamonds. But then, Jerusalem was always ahead, beckoning in the dreams of night, taunting him to find it on the black umbilical road.

His disappointment was momentary, and he lifted his gaze to the far mountains, gray and spectral. Perhaps there he would find a sign. Or was the road covered now by the blown dust of centuries, disguised by the long grass of history?

He dismissed the doubt; if the city existed, Jon Shannow would find it. Removing his wide-brimmed leather hat, he wiped the sweat from his face. It was nearing noon, and he dismounted. The steeldust gelding stood motionless until he looped the reins over its head, then dipped its neck to crop at the long grass. The man delved into a saddlebag to pull clear his ancient Bible; he sat on the ground and idly opened the gold-edged pages.

"And Saul said to David, Thou art not able to go against this Philistine to fight with him, for thou art but a youth, and he is a man of war from his youth."

Shannow felt sorry for Goliath, for the man had had no chance. A courageous giant, ready to face any warrior, had found himself opposite a child without sword or armor. Had he won, he would have been derided. Shannow closed the Bible and carefully packed it away.

"Time to move," he told the gelding. He stepped into the saddle and swept up the reins. Slowly they made their way

4

down the hillside, the rider's eyes watchful of every boulder and tree, bush and shrub. They entered the cool of the valley, and Shannow drew back on the reins, turning his face to the north and breathing deeply.

A rabbit leapt from the brush, startling the gelding. Shannow saw the creature vanish into the undergrowth and then uncocked the long-barreled pistol, sliding it back into the scabbard at his hip. He could not recall drawing it clear. Such was the legacy of the years of peril: fast hands, a sure eye, and a body that reacted independently of the conscious mind.

Not always a good thing . . . Shannow would never forget the look of blank incomprehension in the child's eyes as the lead ball had cleaved his heart, nor the way his frail body had crumpled lifeless to the earth. There had been three brigands that day, and one had shot Shannow's horse out from under him while the other two ran forward with knife and ax. He had destroyed them all in scant seconds, but a movement behind had caused him to swivel and fire. The child had died without a sound.

Would God ever forgive him?

Why should he, when Shannow could not forgive himself?

"You were better off losing, Goliath," said Shannow.

The wind changed, and a stomach-knotting aroma of frying bacon drifted to him from the east. Shannow tugged the reins to the right. After a quarter of a mile, the trail rose and fell and a narrow path opened onto a meadow and a stone-fronted farmhouse. Before the building was a vegetable garden, and beyond that was a paddock where several horses were penned.

There were no defense walls, and the windows of the house were wide and open. To the left of the building the trees had been permitted to grow to within twenty yards of the wall, allowing no field of fire to repel brigands. Shannow sat and stared for some time at this impossible dwelling. Then he saw a child carrying a bucket emerge from the barn beyond the paddock. A woman walked out to meet him and ruffled his blond hair.

Shannow scanned the fields and meadows for sign of a man. At last, satisfied that they were alone, he edged the gelding out onto open ground and approached the building. The boy saw him first and ran inside the house.

Donna Taybard's heart sank as she saw the rider, and she fought down panic as she lifted the heavy crossbow from the wall. Placing her foot in the bronze stirrup, she dragged back on the string but could not nock it.

"Help me, Eric." The boy joined her, and together they cocked the weapon. She slid a bolt into place and stepped onto the porch. The rider had halted some thirty feet from the house, and Donna's fear swelled as she took in the gaunt face and deep-set eyes shadowed under the wide-brimmed hat. She had never seen a brigand, but had anyone asked her to imagine one, this man would have leapt from her nightmares. She lifted the crossbow, resting the heavy butt against her hip.

"Ride on," she said. "I have told Fletcher we shall not leave, and I will not be forced."

The rider sat very still, then removed his hat. His hair was shoulder-length and black, streaked with silver, and his beard showed a white fork at the chin.

"I am a stranger, lady, and I do not know this Fletcher. I do not seek to harm you—I merely smelled the bacon and would trade for a little. I have Barta coin and—"

"Leave us alone," she shouted.

The crossbow slipped from her grip, dropping the trigger bar against her palm. The bolt flashed into the air, sailing over the rider and dropping by the paddock fence. Shannow walked his horse to the paddock and dismounted, retrieving the bolt. Leaving the gelding, he strolled back to the house.

Donna dropped the bow and pulled Eric into her side. The boy was trembling, but in his hand he held a long kitchen knife; she took it from him and waited as the man approached. As he walked, he removed his heavy leather topcoat and draped it over his arm. It was then that she saw the heavy pistols at his side.

"Don't kill my boy," she said.

"Happily, lady, I was speaking the truth: I mean you no harm. Will you trade a little bacon?" He picked up the bow and swiftly nocked it, slipping the bolt into the gully. "Would you feel happier carrying this around?"

"You are truly not with the Committee?"

"I am a stranger."

"We are about to take food. If you wish, you may join us." Shannow knelt before the boy. "May I enter?" he asked.

"Could I stop you?" the boy returned bitterly.

"With just one word."

"Truly?"

"My faults are many, but I do not lie."

"You can come in, then," said the boy, and Shannow walked ahead with the child trailing behind. He mounted the porch steps and entered the cool room beyond, which was spacious and well constructed. A white stone hearth held a woodstove and an iron oven; at the center of the room was a handsomely carved table and a wooden dresser bearing earthenware plates and pottery mugs.

"My father carved the table," said the boy. "He is a skilled carpenter—the best in Rivervale—and his work is much sought after. He made the comfort chair, too, and cured the hides." Shannow made a show of admiring the leather chair by the woodstove, but his eyes followed the movements of the petite blond woman as she prepared the table.

"Thank you for allowing me into your home," said Shannow gravely.

She smiled for the first time and wiped her hand on her canvas apron. "I am Donna Taybard," she told him, offering her hand.

He took it and kissed her fingers lightly. "And I am Jon Shannow, a wanderer, lady, in a strange land."

"Be welcome, then, Jon Shannow. We have some potatoes and mint to go with the bacon, and the meal will be ready within the hour."

Shannow moved to the door, where pegs had been hammered home. He unbuckled his scabbard belt and hung his side arms beside his coat. Turning back, he saw the fear once more in her eyes.

"Be not alarmed, Fray Taybard; a wandering man must

protect himself. It does not change my promise; that may not be so with all men, but my spoken word is iron."

"There are few guns in Rivervale, Mr. Shannow. This was . . . is . . . a peaceful land. If you would like to wash before eating, there is a pump behind the house."

"Do you have an ax, lady?"

"Yes. In the woodshed."

"Then I shall work for my supper. Excuse me."

He walked out into the fading light of dusk and unsaddled the gelding, leading him into the paddock and releasing him among the other three horses. Then he carried his saddle and bags to the porch before fetching the ax. He spent almost an hour preparing firewood before stripping to the waist and washing himself at the pump. The moon was up when Donna Taybard called him in. She and the boy sat at one end of the table, having set his place apart and facing the hearth. He moved his plate to the other side and seated himself facing the door.

"May I speak a word of thanks, Fray Taybard?" asked Shannow as she filled the plates. She nodded. "Lord of Hosts, our thanks to thee for this food. Bless this dwelling and those who pass their lives here. Amen."

"You follow the old ways, Mr. Shannow?" asked Donna, passing a bowl of salt to the guest.

"Old? It is new to me, Fray Taybard. But yes, it is older than any man knows and a mystery to this world of broken dreams."

"Please do not call me Fray; it makes me feel ancient. You may call me Donna. This is my son, Eric."

Shannow nodded toward Eric and smiled, but the boy looked away and continued to eat. The bearded stranger frightened him, though he was anxious not to show it. He glanced at the weapons hanging by the door.

"Are they hand pistols?" he asked.

"Yes," said Shannow. "I have had them for seventeen years, but they are much older than that."

"Do you make your own powder?"

"Yes. I have casts for the loads and several hundred brass caps."

"Have you killed anyone with them?"

"Eric!" snapped his mother. "That is no question to ask a guest—and certainly not at table."

They finished the meal in silence, and Shannow helped her clear away the dishes. At the back of the house was an indoor water pump, and together they cleaned the plates. Donna felt uncomfortable in the closeness of the pump room and dropped a plate, which shattered into a score of shards on the tiled wooden floor.

"Please do not be nervous," he said, kneeling to collect the broken pieces.

"I trust you, Mr. Shannow. But I have been wrong before."

"I shall sleep outside and be gone in the morning. Thank you for the meal."

"No," she said too hurriedly. "I mean, you can sleep in the comfort chair. Eric and I sleep in the back room."

"And Mr. Taybard?"

"Has been gone for ten days. I hope he will be back soon; I'm worried for him."

"I could look for him if you like. He may have fallen from his horse."

"He was driving our wagon. Stay and talk, Mr. Shannow; it is so long since we had company. You can give us news of . . . where have you come from?"

"From the south and east, across the grass prairies. Before that I was at sea for two years, trading with the ice settlements beyond Volcano Rim."

"That is said to be the edge of the world."

"I think it is where hell begins. You can see the fires lighting the horizon for a thousand miles."

Donna eased past him into the main room. Eric was yawning, and his mother ordered him to bed. He argued as all young people did but finally obeyed her, leaving his bedroom door ajar.

Shannow lowered himself into the comfort chair, stretching his long legs out before the stove. His eyes burned with fatigue.

"Why do you wander, Mr. Shannow?" asked Donna, sitting on the goatskin rug in front of him.

"I am seeking a dream, a city on a hill."

"I have heard of cities to the south."

"They are settlements, though some of them are large. But no, my city has been around for much longer; it was built, destroyed, and rebuilt thousands of years ago. It is called Jerusalem, and there is a road leading to it—a black road with glittering diamonds in the center that shine in the night."

"The Bible city?"

"The very same."

"It is not around here, Mr. Shannow. Why do you seek it?"

He smiled. "I have been asked that question many, many times, and I cannot answer it. It is a need I carry—an obsession, if you will. When the earth toppled and the oceans swelled, all became chaos. Our history is lost to us, and we no longer know whence we come or where we are going. In Jerusalem there will be answers, and my soul will rest."

"It is very dangerous to wander, Mr. Shannow. Especially in the wild lands beyond Rivervale."

"The lands are not wild, lady, at least not for a man who knows their ways. Men are wild, and they create the wild lands wherever they are. But I am a known man, and I am rarely troubled."

"Are you known as a warmaker?"

"I am known as a man warmakers should avoid."

"You are playing with words."

"No, I am a man who loves peace."

"My husband was a man of peace."

"Was?"

Donna opened the stove door and added several chunks of wood. She sat for some time staring into the flames, and Shannow did not disturb the silence. At last she looked up at him.

"My husband is dead," she said. "Murdered."

"By brigands?"

"No, by the Committee. They—"

"No!" screamed Eric, standing in the bedroom doorway in his white cotton nightshirt. "It's not true. He's alive! He's coming home—I know he's coming home."

Donna Taybard ran to her son, burying his weeping face in her breast. Then she led him back into the bedroom, and Shannow was alone. He strolled into the night. The sky was without stars, but the moon shone bright through a break in the clouds. Shannow scratched his head, feeling the dust and grit on his scalp. He removed his woolen jerkin and under-shirt and washed in a barrel of clear water, scrubbing the dirt from his hair.

Donna walked out to stand on the porch and watch him. His shoulders seemed unnaturally broad against the slimness of his waist and hips. Silently she moved away from the house to the stream at the bottom of the hill. There she slipped out of her clothes and bathed in the moonlight, rubbing lemon mint leaves across her skin.

When she returned, Jon Shannow was asleep in the comfort chair, his guns once more belted to his waist. She moved silently past him to her room and locked the door. As the key turned, Shannow opened his eyes and smiled.

Where to tomorrow, Shannow? he asked himself.

Where else?

Jerusalem.

Shannow awoke soon after dawn and sat listening to the sounds of morning. He was thirsty and moved to the pump room for a mug of water. Behind the door was an oval mirror framed in golden pine, and he stood staring at his reflection. The eyes were deep-set and dark blue, the face triangular above a square jaw. As he had feared, his hair was showing gray, though his beard was still dark on the cheeks with a silver fork at the chin.

He finished his drink and moved outside to the porch and his saddlebags. Having found his razor and stropped it for several minutes, he returned to the mirror and cut away his beard. Donna Taybard found him there and watched in mild amuse-ment as he tried to trim his long hair.

"Sit out on the porch, Mr. Shannow. I am expecting some friends today, and I think I should make you look presentable."

With long-handled scissors and a bone comb she worked

expertly at the tangled mess, complimenting him on the absence of lice.

"I move too fast for them, and I swim when I can."

"Is that short enough for you?" she asked, stepping back to admire her handiwork. He ran his hand through his hair and grinned—almost boyishly, she thought.

"That will suffice, Fray Taybard . . . Donna. Thank you. You said you were expecting friends?"

"Yes, some neighbors are coming over to celebrate Harvest. It was arranged before Tomas . . . disappeared, but I told them to come anyway. I'm hoping they will be able to help me with the Committee, but I doubt they will . . . they all have their own problems. You are welcome to stay. There will be a barbecue, and I have made some cakes."

"Thank you, I will."

"But Mr. Shannow, please do not wear your guns. This is still, in the main, a peaceful community."

"As you wish. Is Eric still sleeping?"

"No; he is in the long meadow gathering wood for the fire. And then he must milk the cows."

"Do you have any trouble with wolves or lions?"

"No. The Committee shot the last lion during the winter, and the wolves have moved to the high country. They sometimes forage in winter, but they are not a great problem."

"Life here seems . . . settled," he said, rising and brushing the hair from his shirt.

"It has been. It certainly was when my father was Prester. But now there is Fletcher; we will not call him Prester, and I know that does not sit well with him."

"You said last night that your husband was dead. Is that a fear or a reality?"

She stood in the doorway, her hand on the frame. "I have a talent, Mr. Shannow, for seeing faraway things. I had it as a child, and it has not deserted me. As we speak, I can see Eric in the far meadow. He has stopped gathering wood and has climbed a tall pine; he is pretending to be a great hunter. Yes, Mr. Shannow, my husband is dead. He was killed by Fletcher, and there were three with him: the big man, Bard, and two others whose names I do not know. Tomas' body lies in an arroyo, hastily buried."

"Fletcher desires your lands?"

"And me. He is a man used to obtaining his desires."

"Perhaps he will be good for you."

Her eyes blazed. "You think I will suffer myself to be taken by my husband's killer?"

Shannow shrugged. "The world is a hard place, Donna. I have seen settlements where women are not allowed to pair-bond with a single man, where they are communal property. And it is not strange in other areas for men to kill for what they want. What a man can take and hold, he owns."

"Not in Rivervale, sir," she told him. "Not yet, at least."

"Good luck, Donna. I hope you find a man willing to stand against this Fletcher. If not, I hope he is, as I said, good for you."

She moved back into the house without a word.

Some time later the boy Eric came into view, towing a small handcart loaded with deadwood. He was a slim boy, his hair so fair that it seemed white. His face was set and serious, his eyes sad and knowing.

He walked past Shannow without speaking, and the man wandered to the paddock, where the steeldust gelding trotted to him, nuzzling his hand. There was grass in the pen, but Shannow would have liked to give him grain. The beast could run for miles without effort, but when fed on grain, he could run forever. Five years earlier Shannow had won two thousand Barta coins in three races, but the gelding was too old now for such ventures. Shannow returned to his saddlebags and removed the oilskin gun pouch.

Pulling the left-hand pistol from its scabbard, he tapped out the barrel pin and released the cylinder, placing it carefully on the porch beside him. Then he ran an oiled cloth through the barrel and cleaned dust from the trigger mechanism. The pistol was nine inches long and weighed several pounds, but Shannow had long since ceased to notice the weight. He checked the cylinder for dust and then slipped it back into place, pressing home the wedge bar and replacing the weapon in its scabbard. The right-hand pistol was two inches shorter and brass-mounted with butt plates of polished ivory, unlike the dark applewood of the longer weapon. Despite the difference in barrel length, it was this weapon that fired true, the other kicking to the left and unreliable at anything but close quarters. Shannow cleaned the pistol lovingly and looked up to see Eric watching him closely, his eyes fixed on the gun.

"Will you shoot it?" asked the boy.

"There is nothing to shoot at," said Shannow.

"Does it make a loud noise?"

"Yes, and the smoke smells like the Devil. Have you never heard a gun fire?"

"Once, when the Prester shot a lion, but I was only five. Mr. Fletcher has a pistol, and several of the Committee have long rifles; they are more powerful now than any warmaker."

"You like Mr. Fletcher, Eric?"

"He has always been nice to me. He's a great man; he's the Prester now."

"Then why is your mother afraid of him and his Committee?"

"Oh, that's just women," said Eric. "Mr. Fletcher and my father had an argument, and Mr. Fletcher said the carpenter should live in Rivervale, where the work was needed. The Committee voted on it. Mr. Fletcher wanted to buy the farm, but Father said no; I don't know why. It would be nice to live in Rivervale, where all the people are. And Mr. Fletcher really likes Mother. He told me that; he said she was a fine lady. I like him."

"Did . . . does your father like him?"

"Father doesn't like anybody. He likes me sometimes, when I do my chores well or when I help him without dropping anything."

"Is he the only carpenter in Rivervale?"

"He was, but Mr. Fletcher has a man working for him who says *he's* a carpenter. Father laughs about him; he says the man thinks a dove joint is found on a pigeon's leg!"

Shannow grinned. The boy looked younger when he smiled.

"Are you a warmaker, Mr. Shannow? Truly?"

"No, Eric. As I told your mother, I am a man who loves peace."

"But you have guns."

"I travel through the wild lands, Eric; they are necessary."

Two wagons crested the skyline. "That will be the Janus family and the McGravens," said Eric.

Shannow replaced his guns in their scabbards and moved into the house, hanging the weapons on the hook inside the door.

"Your guests have begun to arrive," he told Donna. The house smelled of fresh-baked bread and cakes. "Is there anything I can do?"

"Help Eric prepare the barbecue fires."

All morning wagons arrived, until more than twenty formed several lines inside the pasture. With three barbecue fires burning and almost fifty people moving about, Shannow felt uncomfortable. He wandered to the barn for a little solitude and found two young people holding hands in the shadows.

"I am sorry to disturb you," he said, turning to leave.

"It's all right," said the young man. "My name is Janus, Stefan Janus. This is Susan McGraven." Shannow shook hands with them and moved outside.

As he stood by the paddock, the steeldust gelding ran to him, and Shannow stroked his neck. "Almost time to leave," he told the horse.

A woman's voice rang out. "Susan! Where are you?" The young girl ran from the barn.

"I'm coming," she answered.

The young man joined Shannow; he was tall and fair-haired, and his eyes were serious, his face intelligent.

"Are you staying in Rivervale?"

"No, I am a traveler."

"A traveler who is uncomfortable with crowds," observed Janus.

"Even so."

"You will find the crowd less hostile when the people are known to you. Come, I will introduce you to some friendly faces."

He took Shannow into the throng, and there followed much shaking of hands and a bewildering series of names that Shannow could not absorb. But the lad was right, and he began to feel more comfortable.

"And what do you do, Mr. Shannow?" came the inevitable question, this time from a burly farmer named Evanson.

"Mr. Shannow is searching for a city," said Donna Taybard, joining them. "He is a historian."

"Oh," responded Evanson, his face portraying his lack of interest. "And how are you, Donna? Any sign of Tomas?"

"No. Is Anne with you?"

"I am afraid not. She stayed with Ash Burry; his wife is not well."

Shannow slipped away, leaving them to their conversation. Children were playing near the paddock, and he sat on the porch watching them. Everyone here seemed different from the people of the south; their faces were ruddy and healthy, and they laughed often. Elsewhere, where brigands rode, there was always tension, a wariness in the eyes. Shannow felt apart from the people of Rivervale.

Toward the afternoon a group of riders came down the hill, six men riding directly toward the house. Shannow drifted back into the main room and watched them from a window. Donna Taybard saw them at the same time and wandered over, followed by a dozen or so of her neighbors.

The riders reined in, and a tall man in a white woolen shirt stepped from the saddle. He was around thirty years old, and his hair was black and close-cropped, his face dark and handsome.

"Good day, Donna."

"And to you, Mr. Fletcher."

"I am glad to see you enjoying yourself. Any word from Tomas?"

"No. I am thinking of going to the arroyo where you left him and marking his grave."

The man flushed deep red. "I don't know what you mean."

"Go away, Saul. I do not want you here."

People were gathering around the riders, and silence settled over the scene.

Fletcher licked his lips. "Donna, it is no longer safe to be so close to the edge of the wild lands. Daniel Cade has been sighted only eight miles south. You must come into Rivervale."

"This is my home, and I will remain here," she said.

"I am sorry, but I must insist. The Committee has voted on this. You will be paid handsomely for your home, and comfortable quarters have been set aside for you and Eric. Do not make this any more difficult. Your friends here have offered to help with your furniture and belongings."

As Donna's eyes swept the group, Evanson looked away and many others stared at the ground. Only Stefan Janus moved forward.

"Why should she go if she does not wish to?" he said.

Saul Fletcher ignored him and moved closer to Donna.

"There is no sense in this, Donna. The Committee has the right to make laws to protect its people. You must leave, and you *will* leave. Now!" Fletcher turned to a huge barrel-chested figure on a large black gelding. "Bard, give Donna a hand with her belongings."

As the big man moved to dismount, Jon Shannow stepped from the shadowed doorway and stood on the porch overlooking the crowd. Bard settled back in the saddle, and all eyes turned to Shannow and the guns he now wore. In turn he studied the men who had just arrived. He had seen men like these all his life: chancers, brigands, warmakers. They all had that look, that stamp of cruelty, of callous arrogance.

"If Fray Taybard wishes to stay," said Shannow, "then that is the end of the argument."

"And who are you, sir?" asked Fletcher, his eyes on the pistols at Shannow's side.

Shannow ignored him and turned to the riders, recognizing two of them.

"How are you, Miles?" he called. "And you, Pope? You are a long way from Allion." The two men sat very still, saying nothing.

"I asked you who you were," said Fletcher, his hand resting on the walnut grip of a double-barreled flintlock sheathed at his waist.

"He's the Jerusalem Man," said Miles, and Fletcher froze.

"I have heard of you, sir. You are a killer and a warmaker. We will not suffer your kind in Rivervale."

"No?" said Shannow mildly. "My understanding is that you are no stranger to murder, and Miles and Pope were riding with Cade only a year ago."

"That is a lie."

"Whatever you say, Mr. Fletcher. I have neither the time nor the inclination to argue with you. You may leave now."

"Just say the word, Saul," shouted Bard. "I'll cut him down to size."

"Yes," agreed Shannow. "Do say the word, Mr. Fletcher."

"Don't, for God's sake!" shouted Miles. "You've never seen him."

Fletcher was far from being a foolish man, and he heard the terror in Miles' voice. He swallowed hard and then moved to his horse, mounting swiftly.

"Too many innocent people could suffer here," he said, "but there will be another day."

"I hope so," Shannow told him, and the riders galloped from the yard.

The crowd remained, and Shannow ran his eyes over them. Gone was the open friendliness, replaced by fear bordering on hostility. Only young Janus approached him.

"Thank you, Mr. Shannow. I hope you will not suffer for your kindness."

"If I do, I will not suffer alone, Stefan," he said, and walked back into the house.

The last wagon left just before dusk, and Donna found Shannow sitting in the comfort chair.

"You shouldn't have done that for me," she said, "but I am grateful."

Eric came in behind her. "What did you mean about Father's grave?" he asked.

"I'm sorry, Eric, but it's true. Fletcher had him killed. I'm sorry."

"It's a lie," he shouted, tears falling freely. "You hated him! And I hate you!" He turned and fled from the house.

"Eric! Eric!" she called, and then began to weep.

Shannow went to her and held her close until the tears and the sobbing eased. He could find no words to comfort her, and Jerusalem seemed so far away.

Shannow sat at the pine dinner table, watching Donna Taybard kneeling at the woodstove as she raked out the ash with even, thoughtless strokes. She was a beautiful woman, and he could see why Fletcher desired her. Her face was strong and finely boned, her mouth full and made for laughter. It was a face of character, of strength in adversity.

"This talent," he said, "of seeing faraway things—how did you come by it?"

"I don't know. My father thought it was the stone, but I'm not sure."

"The stone?"

"The Prester called it the Daniel Stone. It was from the Plague Lands, and when held in the hand it glowed like sunlight behind ice. And it was warm. I played with it often as a child."

"Why should he think the stone caused your talents?"

She brushed ash from her hands and sat back. "Do you believe in magic, Mr. Shannow?"

"No."

"Then you would not understand the stone. When my father held it, the sick would be healed. Wounds would close within seconds, with no scar. It was one of the reasons he became Prester."

"Why was it called the Daniel Stone?"

"I don't know. But one day it refused to glow, and that was an end to it. It is still in my father's old house, where Fletcher now lives. Ash Burry tells me that Fletcher is always toying with it; but it will never work again. The Prester told me its power had departed forever."

"But now you have powers."

"Not of healing, or prophecy, or any real magic. But I can see those close to me even when they are far away."

For a while they sat in silence. Donna added kindling to the stove and lit a fire. Once the blaze was roaring, she closed the iron door and turned to Shannow.

"May I ask you a question?"

"Of course."

"Why did you risk your life with all those men?"

"It was not a great risk, lady. There was only one man."

"I do not understand."

"Where there is a group, there is a leader. Nullify him and the rest count for nothing. Fletcher was not prepared to die."

"But you were?"

"All things die, Donna. And I was pleased to repay your hospitality. Perhaps Fletcher will reconsider his plans for you. I hope so."

"But you doubt it."

"Yes."

"Have you ever had a wife, Mr. Shannow?"

"It is getting late," he said, standing. "Eric should be home. Shall I look for him?"

"I am sorry. Did I offend you?"

"No, lady. My discomfort is my own and no fault of yours. Can you see the boy?"

She closed her eyes. "Oh, God," she said. "They have taken him!"

"Who?"

"Bard and some others."

"Where are they?"

"They are traveling northwest, toward the settlement. They have hurt him, and his face is bleeding."

Gently he pulled her to her feet, then took her hands in his.

"I will find him and bring him home. Rely on it."

Shannow left the house and saddled the gelding, heading him north at a canter. He avoided skylining himself on the crests of the hills, but still he rode with uncustomary speed. He had neglected to ask Donna how many men rode with Bard, but then, the information was immaterial. Two or twenty, the plan would be the same.

He emerged from the trees above the raiding party and sat back in the saddle. There were five men, including Bard; of Fletcher there was no sign. Eric's unconscious body was draped across Bard's saddle. Shannow breathed deeply, trying to stem the red rage swelling within, his hands trembling with the effort. As always he failed, and his vision swam. His mouth was dry, and the Bible text flowed into his mind:

"And David said unto Saul, Thy servant kept his father's sheep and there came a lion and a bear, and took a lamb out of the flock."

Shannow rode down the hill and reined in ahead of the riders. They spread across the trail; two of them, Miles and Pope, were carrying crossbows cocked and ready. Shannow's hands swept up, and smoke and flame thundered from the right-hand pistol. Pope flew from the saddle. The left-hand pistol fired a fraction of a second later, and Miles pitched to the ground, the lower half of his face blown away.

"Step down, Bard," said Shannow, both pistols leveled at the giant's face. Slowly the man dismounted. "On your knees and on your belly." The giant obeyed. "Now eat grass like the mule you are."

Bard's head shot up. "The hell—"

The left-hand pistol bucked in Shannow's hand, and Bard's right ear disappeared in a bloody spray. The big man screamed and ducked his head to the ground, tearing at the grass with his teeth. The other two men sat motionless, their hands well away from their weapons.

Shannow watched them closely, then transferred his gaze to the two corpses.

Then he spoke: *"And I went out after him, and smote him, and delivered it out of his mouth: and when he rose against me I caught him by the beard and slew him."*

The two riders glanced at one another and said nothing. The Jerusalem Man was known to be insane, and neither of them had any wish to join their comrades, living or dead, on the grass.

Shannow edged his horse toward them, and they avoided his eyes, for his face was set and his fury touched them.

"You will put your friends on their horses, and you will take them to a place of burial. You will not, at any time, cross my path, for I will cut you down like deadwood from the Tree of Life. Go collect your dead."

He swung his horse, offering them his back, but neither man considered attacking him. They dismounted swiftly and bundled the corpses across the saddles of the horses standing quietly by. Shannow rode alongside Bard, whose mouth was green and who was vomiting on the grass.

"Stand and face me, man of Gath."

Bard struggled to his feet and met Shannow's gaze. A cold dread settled on him as he saw the eyes and the fanatic gleam. He lowered his head and froze as he heard the click of a pistol hammer. His eyes flickered up, and he saw with relief that Shannow had uncocked the weapons and returned them to their scabbards.

"My anger is gone, Bard. You may live today."

The giant was close enough to pluck Shannow from the saddle and tear him apart bare-handed, but he could not, even though he recognized the opportunity. His shoulders sagged. Shannow nodded knowingly, and shame burned in Bard's heart.

Eric groaned and stirred on Bard's horse nearby.

And Shannow lifted him from the saddle and took him home.

Donna Taybard sat with Eric for over an hour. The boy had been shaken by his ordeal. He had awakened to see Jon Shannow and two corpses, and the smell of death was in the air. The giant Bard had been shaking with fear, and Shannow had seemed an infinitely more menacing figure than Eric could have imagined. He had ridden home behind Shannow, his hands resting on the gun hilts as they jutted from their scabbards. All the way home Eric could see the two bodies, one with half a face missing, the other lying facedown with a huge ragged hole in his back where shards of bone had torn through his shirt.

Now he lay in bed, the aftershock making him sleepy. His mother stroked his brow and whispered soothing, loving words.

"Why did they kill Father?"

"I don't know, Eric," lied Donna. "They are evil men."

"Mr. Fletcher always seemed so nice."

"I know. Sleep now; I'll be just outside."

"Mother!"

"Yes, Eric?"

"Mr. Shannow frightens me. I heard the men talking, and they said he was insane, that he has killed more men than the plague. They said that he pretends to be a Christ person but that all the real Christ people shun him."

"But he brought you home, Eric, and we still have our house."

"Don't leave me alone, Mother."

"You know that I won't. Sleep now. Rest."

Leaning forward, she kissed his cheeks, then lifted the coal-oil lamp and left the room. He was asleep before the latch dropped home.

Shannow sat in the comfort chair, staring at the ceiling. Donna placed the brass lamp on the table and moved to the stove, adding fresh wood to the blaze. As his head tipped forward and he caught her gaze, his eyes seemed unnaturally bright.

"Are you all right, Mr. Shannow?"

"Vanity of vanities, saith the preacher, vanity of vanities; all is vanity. What profit hath a man of all his labors which he taketh under the sun?" Shannow blinked and leaned back.

"I am sorry," she said, placing her hand over his, "but I do not understand you." He blinked once more and smiled wearily, but his eyes lost their glitter and he seemed mortally tired.

"No, it is I who am sorry, Donna Taybard. I have brought death to your house."

"You gave me back my son."

"But for how long, Donna? All my life I have been the rock in the pool. I make a splash, and the ripples rush out, but after that? The pool settles and is as it was. I cannot protect you or Eric from the Committee. I can make no difference to the evil of the world; indeed, sometimes I think I add to it."

She held his hand tightly, forcing him to look at her.

"There is no evil in you, Mr. Shannow. Believe me. I know these things. When you first came, I was frightened, but I have come to know you. You are kind and considerate, and you have taken no advantage of my situation. In fact, the reverse is true; you have risked your life for Eric and me."

"There is nothing to that," he said. "My life is no great treasure; I do not value it. I have seen things in my life that would have cindered another man's soul: cannibals, savages, slavery, and wanton murders. I have traveled far, Donna. And I am tired.

"Last summer I killed three men, and I vowed never to kill again. I have been hired to rid settlements of brigands and warmakers, and I have succeeded. But then the eyes of those who sought me turn on me, and I see the fear in their eyes, and they are glad to see me ride on. They do not say, 'Thank you, Mr. Shannow, stay among us and farm.' They do not say, 'We are your friends, Mr. Shannow, and we will never forget you.' Instead they hand me the Barta coins and ask when I will be leaving.

"And when I go, Donna, the brigands return and all is as it was. The pool settles; the ripples die."

Donna stood and pulled him to his feet. "My poor Jon," she whispered. "Come with me." She led him to a room at the back of the house and in the darkness undressed him, removed her own clothes, and pulled back the blankets on a wide bed. He came to her hesitantly, and where she expected him to cover her with fierce passion, instead he stroked her skin with surprising gentleness. Her arm moved around his neck, pulling his face down until their lips touched. He groaned then, and the fierceness followed.

He was an inexpert and almost clumsy lover, not at all as skilled as Tomas the carpenter, yet Donna Taybard found a fulfillment with Shannow that transcended expertise, for he was giving everything of himself, holding nothing back—and at the end he wept, his tears flowing onto Donna's face.

And she stroked his brow and whispered soothing, loving words—and realized they were the same words she had used to Eric an hour before. And Shannow slept, just as Eric slept.

Donna moved to the porch and washed the sweat from her body with a bucket of cool fresh water. Then she dressed and wandered to the pen, enjoying the freshness of the night.

People would think her a slut for taking a man so soon after her husband's disappearance, but she had never felt less like a slut. Instead, she felt as if she had just come home from a long journey to find all her friends and family waiting with open arms. The Committee could offer no terror tonight. Everything was in harmony.

Shannow's gelding wandered to her, thrusting his muzzle toward her hand. She stroked his face and neck and wished she could saddle and ride him out over the hills, wished he had wings to carry her high in the sky under the moon and over the clouds. Her father had told her wondrous stories of a winged horse from Elder legends and of a hero who rode him to slay demons.

Old John had kept the demons from Rivervale, and when the grateful people had wished to call him leader, he had opted instead for Prester, and no one knew its meaning, except John, and he only smiled knowingly when they asked him. Prester John had gathered the men into a tight military unit and established watch beacons on all high hills, and soon the brigands learned to avoid the lands of Rivervale. Outside, in the wild lands, among the wolves and lions, the new world endured a bloody birthing. But here there was peace.

But the Prester was only mortal, and though he had ruled for forty years, his strength failed him and his wisdom fled, for he allowed men like Fletcher and Bard and Enas to join the Committee.

Tomas had once told Donna that the Prester had died broken-hearted, for in his last days he opened his eyes and saw at last the stamp of the men who would soon replace him. It was even rumored that he had tried to oust Fletcher and that the young man had killed him in his own home. That would never be proved now, but not one of the landsmen would call him Prester, and Rivervale was sliding inexorably back to merge with the wild lands.

Fletcher had recruited many strangers to work his shallow coal mine, and some of them were brutal and versed in the ways of the outside. These Fletcher promoted, and one day—in late autumn the year before—the people of Rivervale awoke to a new understanding.

Able Jarrett, a small farmer, was hanged by Fletcher and four of his men for consorting with brigands. An old wanderer was hanged with him. At first farmers, ranchers, and landsmen got together to discuss ways of dealing with the Committee, but then Cleon Layner, a leading spokesman, was found beaten to death in an alley behind his home, and the meetings ended.

The forty-year mission of Prester John had been undone in less than three seasons.

Donna clapped her hands, and Shannow's gelding ran across the pen. If Shannow felt he was merely a stone in the pool, what would John have felt before he died? she wondered.

She pictured Shannow's gaunt bearded face and haunted eyes and compared him with her memories of Prester John. The old man had been tougher than Shannow, and that made him less deadly, but otherwise there was much about Shannow that John would have liked.

"I miss you, Prester," she whispered, remembering his stories of winged horses and heroes.

◇ 2 ◇

FOR SEVERAL DAYS the little farm received no visitors. The Committee undertook no revenge raid, and Shannow spent his days helping Donna and Eric gather the small corn harvest or picking fruit from the orchard in the west meadow. In the late afternoons he would ride the gelding over the hills and through the high woods bordering the farm to scan the distant skyline for signs of moving men.

At night Shannow would wait until Donna invited him to share her bed, and on each occasion he reacted as if to an unexpected gift.

On the fifth day a rider approached the farm in the hour after noon. Shielding her eyes against the sunlight, Donna recognized the ambling gait of Ash Burry's mule even before identifying the portly saint.

"You will like him, Jon," she told Shannow as the rider approached. "He is another who follows the old ways. There are several saints in Rivervale." Shannow merely nodded and watched warily as the tall, overweight man dismounted. He had wavy dark hair and a friendly open face.

Burry opened his arms and hugged Donna warmly. "God's greeting, Donna. Peace be upon your house." His blue eyes flickered to Shannow, and he held out his hand. Shannow took it; the grip was not firm, and the man's hands were soft.

"And greetings to you, Brother," said Burry with only the trace of a smile.

"Let's not stand in the sun," suggested Donna. "Come inside. We have some apple juice cooling in the stone jug."

27

Shannow remained outside for several minutes, scanning the hills, before joining them.

"There is still no sign of Tomas, I understand," remarked Burry. "You must be very worried, Donna."

"He is dead, Ash. Fletcher killed him."

Burry looked away. "Hard words, Donna. I have heard of your accusation, and it is said to be unfounded. How can you be sure?"

"Trust me," said Donna. "You have known me all my life, and I do not lie. I have a gift of always being able to see those close to me, wherever they are. I watched him die."

"I know of your . . . gift. But once you saw the old Prester lying dead at the foot of a canyon—you remember? Yet he was alive."

"That is not entirely just, Ash. I thought he was dead, for he fell a fair way—and I was right about that."

Burry nodded. "And yet not all gifts are from the Almighty, Donna. I cannot believe that Saul Fletcher would do such a thing."

"He hanged Able Jarrett and some poor wanderer."

"The man was consorting with brigands . . . and it was a Committee decision. I do not condone the taking of life, Donna, but right or wrong, it was in accordance with Rivervale law, the law laid down by Prester John."

"I do not recall the Prester hanging a landsman, Ash."

Shannow pulled up a chair by the window, reversed it, and sat facing the saint, his arms resting on the chair back.

"Mr. Ash, might I inquire the reason for your visit?" he said.

"The name is Burry, sir, Ashley Burry, and I am a longtime friend of the Prester's family. I baptized Donna many years ago, and though she does not follow the faith, I regard her as my godchild."

"So this is merely a friendly visit?" asked Shannow.

"I hope that all my visits are friendly and that all who know me regard them as such."

"I am sure that they do, Mr. Burry," said Shannow, smiling, "but it is a long ride from Rivervale on a hot day."

"Meaning, sir?"

"Meaning that you have something to tell Fray Taybard. Would you be more comfortable if I left you to speak with her?"

Burry rubbed at his chin and smiled to cover his embarrassment. His eyes met Shannow's, and understanding passed between them.

"Thank you for your frankness, Mr. Shannow. Yes, that would indeed be courteous."

After Shannow had gone, Burry and Donna sat in silence for several seconds. The saint refilled his pottery mug with apple juice and then walked around the room, idly examining the furniture he had seen so many times before.

"Well, Ash?" said Donna.

"He speaks well, Donna, but he is a brigand—and a known brigand. How could you allow him to stay?"

"He follows your ways, Ash."

"No, that would be blasphemy. I do not kill wantonly."

"He rescued my son."

"That is not as I have heard it. Bard and the others found the boy lost and were returning him to you when Shannow arrived and killed Pope and Miles."

"Nonsense. My son was beaten and taken from the north meadow, and they were halfway to Rivervale with him. And that was the same day Fletcher tried to force me from my home. Are you blind, Ash?"

"The man is a killer. They say his mind is unhinged."

"Did you find it so?"

"That is not the point. He may be rational now, but he terrified Bard and the others. Did you know he shot off Bard's ear?"

"I wish it had been his head!"

"Donna!" said Burry, shocked. "I think the man is possessed, and I believe that his evil power is affecting your judgment. Saul has spoken to me of you, and I know that he holds you dear. He has no wife, Donna, and he would be a good father to Eric."

Donna laughed. "We talk about judgment, Ash, and then you advise me to marry the man who probably murdered my father and certainly killed my husband! Let's talk of something else. How is Sara?"

"She is well, but she worries about you; we all do. The Committee has passed sentence on Shannow, and they mean to hang him."

"I am going to prepare some food for you, Ash. And while I do it, I want you to find Jon and talk with him."

"What could I say?"

"You can talk about your god, Ash. He at least will be able to understand."

"You mock me, Donna," he said sadly.

"Not by intention, Ash. Go and talk to him."

Burry shook his head and rose from the table. Out in the sunlight he saw Shannow sitting on a white rock and watching the hills. The man was wearing the infernal pistols that had so brutally slain Pope and Miles and God knew how many others, he thought.

"May I join you, Mr. Shannow?"

"Of course."

"When will you be leaving Rivervale?"

"Soon, Mr. Burry."

"How soon?"

"I do not know."

"What do you want?"

"I want for nothing, Mr. Burry."

"It is said that you seek Jerusalem."

"Indeed I do."

"Why?"

"To answer all my questions. To satisfy me."

"But the Book answers all questions, Mr. Shannow."

Shannow smiled. "I have read the Book, Mr. Burry—many, many times. But there are no pistols mentioned. Twelve years ago I saw a picture that had not been painted. It was like a frozen moment in time. It was a city, but it took me a long time to realize it was a city, for the picture was a view from the sky to the ground. There is nothing like it in the Bible, Mr. Burry. I met an old man once who had a special book, very old. In it were drawings of machines with wheels and levers; there were seats in these machines, and men could travel in them without horses. Why are these not in the Bible? The old man said he had once seen a picture of a metal machine that could fly. Why is this not in the Scriptures?"

"It is, Mr. Shannow. You will recall that Elijah ascended to heaven in a chariot of fire. You will also recall that there are many examples of angelic beings in strange machines."

"But no pistols, Mr. Burry. No guns."

"Is that important? We know that Christ told his disciples that the end of the world was nigh, and we know that it happened. The oceans rose, and the world was destroyed. Those of us now living are in the end times."

"But does it not also say, Mr. Burry, that these are the times of the Antichrist, that men would wish they had never been born, and that pestilence, plague, and death would stalk the land?"

"Yes. And that has certainly come to pass."

"And that a New Jerusalem would be built?"

"Yes."

"Then I mean to find it."

"Only God's servants will find Jerusalem, Mr. Shannow. Do you honestly believe you serve the Almighty?"

"No, Mr. Burry, I do not, though I have tried and will go on trying. I was taught that the world is young and that Christ died three hundred years ago and his death caused the oceans to rise. Yet I have seen evidence that the Dark Age of our world lasted much longer than that. You know that there are some who believe that the Lord died two and a half thousand years ago?"

"Heretics," declared Ashley Burry.

"I agree with you, yet I wonder if they are not closer to the truth than you or I. I have seen remnants of old maps that do not even show Israel, or Judah, or Babylon—or even Rome. There are names unheard of in the Book. I need to know, Mr. Burry."

"For what purpose? Are we not advised to ignore the seeking of signs and portents?"

"And yet when the clouds darken, do we not reach for our oilskins?"

"Yes, Mr. Shannow, but what does it matter if the Dark Age after our Lord was long or short? We are here now. Does it matter if machines once flew? They no longer do so. Does not Ecclesiastes say that *'There is nothing new under the sun'* and that everything that ever was will be again?"

"Have you ever heard of England, Mr. Burry?"

"A Dark Age land, I believe. They preserved the Book."

"Do you know where it might be?"

"No. Why is it important to you?"

"I once saw a scrap of paper with a printed verse that said, 'And was Jerusalem builded here, in England's green and pleasant land.' "

"May I offer you some advice, Mr. Shannow?"

"Why not? Most people do."

"Leave this place. Continue your search. If you remain, you will bring only death and despair to this house. The Committee has declared you a brigand and a warmaker; they will hang you, sir."

"When I was a child, Mr. Burry, my parents built a home for my brother and myself. It was by the banks of a beautiful river, and the land was rich and open and wild as sin. My father tamed that land, and it brought forth crops and fed our cattle. Then some men came who wanted fertile land. They killed my father. My mother they abused before cutting her throat. My brother and I escaped, though I was speared and bleeding badly. My brother dragged me to the river, and we swam downstream. We were taken in by a neighboring farmer, a strong man with four strapping sons. No one reproached the brigands who had killed my parents. That was the way life was."

"It is a familiar story," admitted Burry, "but times change."

"Men change them. But I have not finished, Mr. Burry. Both my brother and I were brought up to believe in love and for-giveness. We tried, but the same raiders—growing fat and yet strong—decided they wanted more land. One night they attacked our new home. My brother killed one of them with an ax, and I slew another with an old musket. But still they won. This time it was I who rescued my brother, and we escaped on an old stallion. My brother lost his faith then. Mine became stronger. Two years later I returned to the farm and put the brigands to death.

"Since then I have killed many. I have never stolen or cheated or lied. Nor have I broken the commandment: Thou shalt not do murder. I am not a brigand, but I am a warmaker. I make my war on the evil, and I am no danger to honest landsmen. Only the ungodly need fear me, Mr. Burry, or those who serve the ungodly."

"What happened to your brother, Mr. Shannow? Did he find his faith?"

"We both learned to hate. I hated the brigands and the death dealers, but he came to despise the landsmen who stood by and allowed the brigands to prosper. No, Mr. Burry, he did not find his faith."

"You are a bitter man, Mr. Shannow."

"Indeed I am. But I am content with what I am, and I do not compromise my principles. Now you, Mr. Burry, are a man of God. Yet you come to this house to defend murderers, and you align yourself with the ungodly. Fletcher killed Fray Taybard's husband. His men are a pack of cutthroats. And even now, Mr. Burry, you sit here like the Judas goat, and death is waiting as we speak."

"What do you mean? You are speaking nonsense."

"Am I indeed?"

"Explain yourself."

Shannow shook his head and smiled. "There are three men hiding in the trees to the north. Did they come with you?"

"No, Mr. Shannow, they did not, but you must realize that a sum of fifty Barta coins will be paid to anyone who brings in the body of a known brigand."

"I should have taken the corpses to Rivervale," said Shannow. "Both Miles and Pope were known murderers; they killed a traveling family in Sertace two years ago, and they also rode with Daniel Cade when he was raiding the southwest."

"I do not believe you, Mr. Shannow."

"It is better for your conscience that you do not, Mr. Burry."

* * *

The meal was eaten in silence, and Burry left soon afterward. Eric said nothing as the saint rode away but went to his room, shutting the door behind him.

"I am worried about him," said Donna as she and Shannow cleared away the dishes and plates.

"He fears me, Donna. I do not blame him."

"He is not eating, and his dreams are bad."

"I think your friend Burry is right and I should be moving. But I fear for you. When I am gone, Fletcher will return."

"Then do not go, Jon. Stay with us."

"I do not think you understand the danger. I am not a man any longer; I am a walking bag of Barta coins for any who feel they can collect on me. Even now there are three men in the hills building their nerve to come for me."

"I do not want you to go," she said.

He reached out and lightly touched her cheek. "I want only what you want, but I know what must happen."

He left her then and walked to Eric's room. He tapped on the door, but there was no reply; he tapped again.

"Yes?"

"It is Jon Shannow. May I come in?"

A pause. Then, "All right."

Eric was lying on his bed, facing the door. He looked up at the tall figure and saw that Shannow was wearing his father's shirt; he had not noticed that before.

"May I sit down, Eric?"

"You can do what you like. I can't stop you," said the boy miserably.

Shannow pulled up a chair and reversed it. "Do you want to talk about it?"

"About what?"

"I don't know, Eric. I only know that you are troubled. Do you want to talk about your father? Or Fletcher? Or me?"

"I expect Mother wishes I wasn't here," said the boy, sitting up and hugging his knees. "Then she could be with you all the time."

"She has not said that to me."

"Mr. Burry doesn't like you, and I don't like you, either."

"Sometimes I don't like myself," said Shannow. "That keeps me in the majority."

"Everything was all right until you came," said Eric, tears starting as he bit his lip and looked away. "Mother and me were fine. She slept in here, and I didn't have bad dreams. And Mr. Fletcher was my friend—and everything was fine."

"I'll be gone soon," Shannow told him softly, and the truth of the words hit him like a blow. The pool settled, and the ripples faded, and everything returned to the way it had been.

"It won't be the same," said Eric, and Shannow could offer no argument.

"You are very wise, Eric. Life changes, and not always for the better. It is the mark of a man how he copes with that fact. I think you will cope well, for you are strong, stronger than you think."

"But I won't be able to stop them from taking our house."

"No."

"And Mr. Fletcher will force Mother to live with him?"

"Yes," said Shannow, swallowing hard and keeping the awful images from his mind.

"I think you had better stay for a little while, Mr. Shannow," said Eric.

"I think perhaps I had. It would be nice if we could be friends, Eric."

"I don't want to be your friend."

"Why?"

"Because you took my mother away from me, and now I am all alone."

"You are not alone, but I cannot convince you of that, even though I probably know more about loneliness than any man alive. I have never had a friend, Eric. When I was your age, my father and mother were killed. I was raised for some time by a neighbor called Claude Vurrow; then he, too, was killed, and since then I have been alone. People do not like me. I am the Jerusalem Man, the Shadow, the brigand slayer. Wherever I am I will be hated and hunted or used by 'better' men. That is loneliness, Eric—sitting with a frightened child and not being able to reach out and convince even him—that is loneliness.

"When I die, Eric, no one will mourn for me. It will be as if I never was. Would you like to be that lonely, boy?"

Eric said nothing, and Shannow left the room.

The three men watched Shannow ride from the farmhouse, heading east toward the forests of pine. Swiftly they saddled their ponies and rode after him.

Jerrik took the lead, for he was the man with the long rifle, a muzzle-loading flintlock a mere thirty-five years old. It was a fine gun that had seen three owners murdered for owning it. Jerrik had acquired it as settlement for a gambling debt two years before and had then used it to kill the former owner, who was tracking him to steal it back. It seemed poetic somehow, though Jerrik could not verbalize the reason.

Behind him rode Pearson and Swallow, men Jerrik could rely on . . . so long as all three were poor. The trio had arrived only recently in Rivervale but had swiftly come under Bard's watchful eye. He had recommended them to Fletcher, and this task was their entry to the Committee.

"Hunt down and kill the Jerusalem Man." The long rifle could handle that, given a fixed target, and Swallow was an expert crossbowman. Pearson was more of a knife expert, but he could hurl a blade with uncanny accuracy. Jerrik was confident that the deed could be completed without tears.

"Do you think he's leaving the area?" asked Swallow. Jerrik showed his contempt at the question by ignoring it, but Pearson grinned, showing broken teeth.

"No saddlebags," he said.

"Why don't we wait and hit him when he comes back?" asked Swallow.

"What if he comes back at night?" answered Jerrik.

Swallow lapsed into silence. Younger than the others, he felt a need to be heard with respect, yet every time he spoke, he left himself open to mockery. Pearson slapped the blond youngster on the shoulder and grinned at him. He knew what the lad was thinking, as he knew also the cause of his problem. Swallow was too stupid to *know* that he was stupid. But Pearson liked him, and they were well matched in many ways. Both disliked the company of women; both enjoyed the power that came from a lack of conscience and the godlike joy of holding a life in one's hands before snuffing it out. The only difference lay in the fact that Swallow enjoyed killing men, whereas Pearson found the torture of women to be an exquisite pleasure.

Jerrik was unlike them in that regard. He neither enjoyed nor abhorred killing. It was merely a task—like weeding or felling trees or skinning rabbits, something to be done swiftly. Watching Pearson and Swallow at their work only bored him, and the screams always kept him awake. Jerrik was approaching fifty and felt it was time to settle down and raise children; he had his eye on a farm in Rivervale and the young widow who owned it. With the Barta coins he expected for the Jerusalem Man he would have some woolen clothes made and pay court to the widow. She would have to treat him seriously as a Committee man.

The trio followed Shannow's tracks high into the pine forest, and it was getting toward dusk when they spotted his campfire.

The three dismounted and hobbled their horses, creeping through the undergrowth toward the small blaze. Some fifty feet from the fire Jerrik saw the shadowy outline of the Jerusalem Man sitting with his back against a tree, his wide-brimmed hat tipped down over his eyes.

"You just sit there and think," whispered Jerrik, hunkering down and priming his musket. He directed Pearson and Swallow to the left and right, ready to rush in once the mortal shot was fired. Then the two crept off into the trees.

Jerrik cocked the musket and sat back, resting his elbow on his knee. The gun was leveled at the seated figure . . .

Something cold touched Jerrik's temple.

And his head exploded.

At the sound of the shot Pearson loosed his crossbow bolt. It flashed across the clearing, slicing through Shannow's coat and the bush inside it. Swallow ran up, hurdling the campfire, and his knife followed Pearson's bolt. The coat fell from the bush, the hat toppling with it, and Swallow's mouth fell open. Something hit him a wicked blow in the back, and a hole the size of a man's fist appeared in his chest. He was dead before he hit the ground.

Pearson backed away from the carnage and sprinted to his pony. Loosing the hobble, he leapt to the saddle and booted the animal into a run. The boom of Jerrik's musket came just as Pearson's pony had reached a gallop; the animal fell headlong, and Pearson flew over its neck to land on his back against a tree. He rolled and came up with a knife in his hand.

"Show yourself!" he screamed.

The Jerusalem Man stepped from the screen of trees and moved into Pearson's view. In his hand was the ivory-handled percussion pistol.

"You don't have to kill me," said Pearson, eyes locked on the pistol. "I won't come back. I'll just ride away."

"Who sent you?"

"Fletcher."

"How many others has he sent?"

"None. We didn't think we'd need any more."

"What is your name?"

"Why?"

"So that I can mark your grave. It would be unseemly otherwise."

The knife fell from his fingers. "My name is Pearson. Alan Pearson."

"And the others?"

"Al Jerrik and Zephus Swallow."

"Turn around, Mr. Pearson."

Pearson closed his eyes and began to turn.

He did not even hear the shot that killed him.

Jon Shannow rode into the yard as the moon broke clear of the screen of clouds. He was leading two ponies, and he carried a long rifle across his saddle. Donna stood in the doorway wearing a white blouse of fine wool and a homespun skirt dyed red. Her hair was freshly brushed and glowed almost white in the moonlight. Shannow waved as he rode past and led the ponies into the pen. He unsaddled the gelding and brushed him down.

Donna walked across the yard and took Shannow's arm. He leaned down and kissed her lightly.

"Are you well, Jon?"

"Aye."

"What are you thinking?"

"I was thinking that when I am with you, I understand something that has long escaped me." He lifted her hand and kissed it gently, reverently.

"What? What do you understand?"

"It is a quotation from the book."

"Tell me."

" *'Though I speak with the tongues of men and of angels, and have not love, I am become as sounding brass, or a tinkling cymbal.*

" *'And though I have the gift of prophecy, and understand all mysteries, and all knowledge, and though I have all faith, so that I could remove mountains, and have not love, I am nothing.'* There is more, but I would need the Book to read it."

"It is beautiful, Jon. Who wrote it?"

"A man named Paul."

"Did he write it for a woman?"

"No, he wrote it for everyone. How is Eric?"

"He got upset when he heard the guns."

"There was no danger, Donna," he said softly. "And we have several days together before anyone realizes they have failed."

"You look tired, Jon. Come in and rest."

"Each death lessens me, lady. But still they come."

She led him into the house and trimmed the wicks in the oil lamp. He sat in the comfort chair, and his head dropped back. Gently she removed his boots and covered him with a heavy blanket.

"Sleep well, Jon. Sweet dreams." She kissed him and moved toward her room. Eric's door opened, and he stood there rubbing sleep from his eyes. "Is he back, Mother?" he whispered.

"Yes. He is all right."

"Did he kill all the men?"

"I expect so, Eric. Go to bed."

"Will you come in with me?"

She smiled and led him back to the narrow bed, where she lay beside him. Within minutes he was asleep. But Donna Taybard could not sleep. Outside was a man who in the space of a few days had killed five others, a man living on the edge of sanity, chasing the impossible. He was seeking a city that no longer existed in a land no one could find, in search of a god few believed in—a relic of a world that had passed into myth.

And he loved her, or thought that he did, which was the same thing to a man, Donna knew. And now he was trapped, forced to remain like a magnet drawing death to him, unable to run or hide. And he would lose. There would be no Jerusalem for Jon Shannow and no home with Donna Taybard. The Committee would hunt him down, and Donna would be Fletcher's woman—until he tired of her. Yet even knowing this, Donna could not send Jon Shannow away. She closed her eyes, and his face came unbidden to her mind. She found herself staring at him as he slept in the comfort chair, his face so peaceful now and almost boyish in the lamplight.

Donna opened her eyes back in Eric's room and wished, not for the first time, that the Prester were alive. He always seemed to know what to do. And before advancing years had sapped his judgment he could read men—and women. But he was gone, and there was no one to turn to. She thought of Shannow's fierce god and, remembering Ash Burry's gentle, loving lord, found it incomprehensible that both men worshiped the same deity.

The two men were fleece and flint, and so was their god.

"Are you there, Shannow's god?" she whispered. "Can you hear me? What are you doing to the man? Why do you drive him so hard? Help him. Please help him."

Eric stirred and mumbled in his sleep, and she kissed him, lifting the blanket around his chin. His eyes opened dreamily.

"I love you, Mother. Truly."

"And I love you, Eric. More than anything."

"Daddy never loved me."

"Of course he did," whispered Donna, but Eric was asleep once more.

*   *   *

Shannow awoke in the hour before dawn and opened the door to Donna's room. The bed was still made, and he smiled ruefully. He moved to the pump room and found himself staring once more at his reflection.

"*Quo vadis*, Shannow?" he asked the grim gray man in the mirror.

The sound of horses in the yard made him stiffen, and he checked his pistols and slipped out of the back door, keeping in the moon shadows until he reached the front of the house. Five long wagons drawn by oxen stretched in a line back to the meadow, and a tall man on a dark horse was dismounting by the water trough.

"Good morning," said Shannow, sheathing his pistol.

"Do you mind if we water our animals?" asked the man.

The sun was just clearing the eastern peaks, and Shannow saw that he was in his thirties and strongly built. He wore a black leather riding jacket cut high at the waist and a hat sporting a single peacock feather.

"As long as you replenish it from the well yonder," Shannow told him. "Where are you journeying?"

"Northwest, through the mountains."

"The Plague Lands?" asked Shannow. "No one goes there. I saw a man once who had come from there. His hair fell out, and his body was a mass of weeping sores that would not mend."

"We do not believe it is the land. All sicknesses pass," said the man.

"The man I knew said that the rocks gleamed in the night and that no animals could be found there."

"My friend, I have heard tales of giant lizards, flying pillars, and castles in clouds. I have yet to see any of them. Land is land, and I am sick of brigands. Daniel Cade is raiding once more, and I have a yen for the far mountains where even brigands will not go. Now, I myself have met a man who journeyed there—or said he did. He said that the grass grows green and the deer are plentiful and much larger than elsewhere. He says he saw apples as big as melons and in the distance a city the like of which he had never seen. Now, I am a man who needs to travel, and I mean to see that city."

Shannow's mouth was suddenly dry. "I, too, would like to see that city," he said.

"Then find yourself a wagon and travel with us, man! I take it those pistols are not mere ornaments."

"I have no wagon, sir, nor enough Barta coin to raise one. And I have commitments here that must be fulfilled."

The man nodded and then grinned. "That's why I want you. I'd take no footloose rider straight from the Outlands, and I won't import brigands into Avalon. You are a sturdy soul by the look of you. Do you have a family?"

"Yes."

"Then sell your farm and follow after us. There'll be land waiting."

Shannow left him watering the oxen and walked inside, where Donna was awake and standing by the open door.

"You heard that?" asked Shannow.

"Yes. The Plague Lands."

"What do you feel?"

"I do not want you to go. But if you do, we will go with you if you'll have us."

He opened his arms and drew her to him, too full of wild joy to speak. Behind him the tall man from the yard politely cleared his throat, and Shannow turned.

"My name is Cornelius Griffin, and I may have a proposition for you."

"Come in, Mr. Griffin," said Donna. "I am Donna Taybard, and this is my husband, Jon."

"A pleasure, Fray Taybard."

"You spoke of a proposition," said Shannow.

"Indeed I did. We have a family with us who are not desirous of a risky journey, and it would be that they will part with their wagon and goods in return for your farm. Of course, there will be an extra amount in Barta coin, should the prospect interest you."

* * *

Jon Shannow rode his steeldust gelding down the main street of Rivervale settlement, his long leather coat flapping against the horse's flanks, his wide-brimmed hat shading his eyes. The houses were mostly timber near the roadside, early dwellings of some three or four decades. On outlying hills above the shallow coal mine rose new homes of stone and polished wood. Shannow rode past the mill and across the humpback bridge, ignoring the stares of the workmen and loafers who peered at him from the shadows. Several children were playing in a dusty side street, and a barking dog caused his horse to jump sideways. Shannow sat unmoving in the saddle and rode on, reining in his mount at the steps to the alehouse.

He dismounted and tied the reins to a hitching rail, mounted the steps, and entered the drinking hall. There were some twenty men sitting or standing at the long bar, among them the giant Bard, his head bandaged. Beside him was Fletcher, and both men gaped as Shannow moved toward them.

A stillness settled on the room.

"I am come to tell you, Mr. Fletcher, that Fray Taybard has sold her farm to a young family from Ferns Crossing, a settlement some two months journey to the south. She has given them a bond of sale that should satisfy the Committee."

"Why tell me?" said Fletcher, aware of the spectators, many of whom were known landsmen of integrity.

"Because you are a murderous savage and a brigand, sir, who would lief as not kill the family and pretend they were usurpers."

"How dare you?"

"I dare because it is the truth, and that will always be a bitter enemy to you, sir. I do not know how long the people of Rivervale will put up with you, but if they have sense, it will not be long."

"You cannot think to leave here alive, Shannow," said Fletcher. "You are a named brigand."

"Named by you! Jerrik, Swallow, and Pearson are dead, Mr. Fletcher. Before he died, Pearson told me you had offered him a place on your Committee. Strange that you now have places for known woman killers!"

"Kill him!" screamed Fletcher, and Shannow dived to his right as a crossbow bolt flashed from the doorway. His pistol boomed, and a man staggered back from sight to fall down the steps beyond.

A pistol flamed in Fletcher's hand, and something tugged at the collar of Shannow's coat. The right-hand pistol flowered in flame and smoke, and Fletcher pitched back, clutching his belly. A second shot tore through his heart. Bard was running for the rear door, and Shannow let him go, but the man twisted and fired a small pistol, which hammered a shell into the wood beside Shannow's face. Splinters tore into his cheek, and he pumped two bullets into the big man's throat; Bard collapsed in a fountain of blood.

Shannow climbed slowly to his feet and scanned the room and the men lying facedown and motionless.

"I am Jon Shannow and have never been a brigand."

Turning his back, he walked into the street. A shell whistled past his head, and he turned and fired. A man reared up from behind the water trough, clutching his shoulder; in his hand was a brass-mounted percussion pistol. Then Shannow shot him again, and he fell without a sound. A musket boomed from a window across the street, snatching Shannow's hat from his head; he returned the fire but hit nothing. Climbing into the saddle, he kicked the gelding into a run.

Several men raced to cut him off. One fired a pistol, but the gelding cannoned into the group and sent them sprawling to the dust, and Shannow was clear and over the humpback bridge, heading west to join Donna and Eric . . .

. . . and the road to Jerusalem.

◇ 3 ◇

CON GRIFFIN SWUNG in the saddle and watched the oxen toiling up the steep slope. The first of the seventeen wagons had reached the lava ridge, and the others were strung out like vast wooden beads on the black slope.

Griffin was tired, and the swirling lava dust burned his eyes. He swung his horse and studied the terrain ahead. As far as the eye could see, which from that height was a considerable distance, the black lava sand stretched from jagged peak to jagged peak.

They had been traveling for five weeks, having linked with Jacob Madden's twelve wagons north of Rivervale. In that time they had seen no riders or any evidence of brigands on the move, yet Griffin was wary. He had in his saddlebags many maps of the area, sketched by men who claimed to have traveled the lands in their youth. It was rare for any of the maps to correspond, but one thing all agreed on was that beyond the lava stretch lived a brigand band of the worst kind: eaters of human flesh.

Griffin had done his best to prepare his wagoners for the worst. No family had been allowed to join the convoy unless it owned at least one working rifle or handgun. As things stood there were over twenty guns in the convoy, enough to deter all but the largest brigand party.

Con Griffin was a careful man and, as he often said, a damned fine wagoner. This was his third convoy in eleven years, and he had survived drought, plague, brigand raids, vicious storms, and even a flash flood. Men said Con Griffin was lucky, and he accepted that without comment. Yet he knew that luck was merely the residue of hard thinking and harder work. Each of the twenty-two-foot wagons carried one spare wheel and axle suspended beneath the tailboards, plus sixty pounds of flour, three sacks of salt, eighty pounds of dried meat, thirty pounds of dried fruit, and six barrels of water. His own two wagons were packed with trade goods and spares: hammers, nails, axes, knives, saw blades, picks, blankets, and woven garments. Griffin liked to believe he left nothing to luck.

The people who traveled under his command were tough and hardy, and Griffin, for all his outward gruffness, loved them all. They reflected all that was good in people: strength, courage, loyalty, and a stubborn willingness to risk all they had for the dream of a better tomorrow.

Griffin sat back in the saddle and watched the Taybard wagon begin the long haul up the lava slope. The woman, Donna, intrigued him. Leather-tough and satin-soft, she was a beautiful contradiction. The wagon master rarely involved himself in matters of the heart, but had Donna Taybard been available, he would have broken his rule. The boy, Eric, was running alongside the oxen, urging them on with a switch. He was a quiet boy, but Griffin liked him; he was quick and bright and learned fast. The man was another matter . . .

Griffin had always been a good judge of character, an attribute vital to a leader, yet he could make nothing of Jon Taybard except that he was riding under an assumed name. The relationship between Taybard and Eric was strained, the boy avoiding the man at all but mealtimes. Still, Taybard was a good man with a horse, and he never complained or shirked from the tasks Griffin set him.

The Taybard wagon reached the top of the rise and was followed by the elderly scholar Peacock. The man had no coordination, and the wagon stopped halfway up the slope. Griffin cantered down and climbed up to the driving seat, allowing his horse to run free.

"Will you never learn, Ethan?" he said, taking the reins and whip from the balding Peacock.

He cracked the thirty-foot whip above the ear of the leading ox, and the animal lurched forward into the traces. Slowly the lumbering wagon moved up the hill.

"Are you sure you can't read, Con?" asked Peacock.

"Would I lie to you, scholar?"

"It is just that that fool Phelps can be tremendously annoying. I think he only reads sections that prove his case."

"I have seen Taybard with a Bible—ask him," said Griffin. The wagon moved onto the ridge, and he stepped to the running board and whistled for his horse. The chestnut stallion came at once, and Griffin climbed back into the saddle.

Maggie Ames' wagon was the next to be stopped on the slope, a rear wheel lodged against a lava rock. Griffin dismounted and manhandled it clear, to be rewarded with a dazzling smile. He tipped his hat and rode away. Maggie was a young widow, and that made her dangerous indeed.

Throughout the long hot afternoon the wagon convoy moved on over the dusty ridge. The oxen were weary, and Griffin rode ahead looking for a campsite.

There was no water to be found, and he ordered the wagons stopped on the high ground above the plain, in the lee of a soaring rock face. Griffin unsaddled the chestnut and rubbed him down, then filled his leather hat with water and allowed the horse to drink.

All around the camp people were looking to their animals, wiping the dust from the nostrils of their oxen and giving them precious water. Out there the animals were more than beasts of burden. They were life.

Griffin's driver, a taciturn oldster named Burke, had prepared a fire and was cooking a foul-smelling stew in a copper-bottomed pot. Griffin sat opposite the man. "Another long day," he remarked.

Burke grunted. "Worse tomorrow."

"I know."

"You won't get much more out of these animals. They need a week at least and good grass."

"You see any grass today, Jim?"

"I'm only saying what they *need*."

"According to the map, there should be good grass within

the next three days," said Griffin, removing his hat and wiping the sweat from his forehead.

"Which map is that?" asked Burke, smiling knowingly.

"Cardigan's. It seems about the best of them."

"Yeah. Ain't he the one that saw the body eaters at work? Didn't they roast his companions alive?"

"So he said, Jim. And keep your voice down."

Burke pointed to the fat figure of Aaron Phelps, the arcanist, who was making his way to the wagon of Ethan Peacock. "He'd make a good lunch for them brigands."

"Cardigan came through here twenty years ago. There's no reason to believe the same brigands are still in the area. Most warmakers are movers," said Griffin.

"Expect you're right, Mr. Griffin," agreed Burke with a wicked grin. "Still, I should send Phelps out as our advance scout. He'd feed an entire tribe."

"I ought to send you, Jimmy; you'd put them off human flesh for life. You haven't bathed in the five years I've known you!"

"Water gives you wrinkles," said Burke. "I remember that from when I was a yongen. It shrivels you up."

Griffin accepted the bowl of stew Burke passed him and tasted it. If anything it was more foul than its smell, but he ate it, following it with flatbread and salt.

"I do not know how you come up with such appalling meals," said Griffin at last, pushing his plate away.

Burke grinned. "Nothing to work with. Now, if you gave me Phelps . . ."

Griffin shook his head and stood. He was a tall man, red-haired and looking older than his thirty-two years. His shoulders were broad, and his belly pushed out over the top of his belt despite Burke's culinary shortcomings.

He wandered along the wagon line, chatting to the families as they gathered by their cook fires, and ignored the squabbling Phelps and Peacock. At the Taybard wagon he stopped.

"A word with you, Mr. Taybard," he said, and Jon Shannon set aside his plate and rose smoothly, following Griffin out onto the trail ahead of the wagons. The wagon master sat on a jutting rock, and Shannow sat facing him.

"There could be difficult days ahead, Mr. Taybard," began Griffin, breaking a silence that had become uncomfortable.

"In what way?"

"Some years ago there was a murderous brigand band in these parts. Now, when we come down from these mountains, we should find water and grass, and we will need to rest for at least a week. During that time we could come under attack."

"How may I help you?"

"You are not a farmer, Mr. Taybard. I sense you are more of a hunter, and I want you to scout for us if you will."

Shannow shrugged. "Why not?"

Griffin nodded. The man had asked nothing about the brigands or of their suspected armaments. "You are a strange man, Mr. Taybard."

"My name is not Taybard; it is Shannow."

"I have heard the name, Mr. Shannow. But I shall call you Taybard as long as you ride with us."

"As you please, Mr. Griffin."

"Why did you feel the need to tell me?"

"I do not like living a lie."

"Most men find little difficulty in that respect," said Griffin. "But then, you are not like most men. I heard of the work you did in Allion."

"It came to nothing; the brigands returned once I had gone."

"That is hardly the point, Mr. Shannow."

"What is?"

"You can only show the way, and it is for others to follow the path. In Allion they were stupid; when you have dusted a room, you do not throw away the broom."

Shannow smiled, and Griffin watched him relax. "Are you a Bookman, Mr. Griffin?"

The wagon master returned the smile and shook his head. "I tell people I cannot read, but yes, I have studied the Book, and there is much sense in it. But I am not a believer, Mr. Shannow, and I doubt that Jerusalem exists."

"A man must look for something in life, even if it is only a nonexistent city."

"You should speak to Peacock," said Griffin. "He has a thousand scraps of Dark Age remnants. And now that his eyes are fading, he needs help to study them."

Griffin rose to leave, but Shannow stopped him. "I want to thank you, Mr. Griffin, for making me welcome."

"It is nothing. I am not a weak man, Mr. Shannow. Shadows do not frighten me, nor reputations such as yours. I will leave you with this thought, though: What point is there in seeking Jerusalem? You have a fine wife and a growing son who will need your talents at home, wherever home may lie."

Shannow said nothing, and Griffin wandered back into the firelight. Shannow remained apart, sitting beneath the stars, lost in thought. Donna found him there close to midnight and sat beside him, curling her arm around his waist.

"Are you troubled, Jon?"

"No. I was thinking of the past."

"The Prester used to say, 'The past is dead, the future unborn. What we have is the now, and we abuse it.' "

"I have done nothing to deserve you, lady. But believe me, I thank the Lord for you daily."

"What did Mr. Griffin want?" she asked, suddenly embarrassed by the intensity of his words.

"He wants me to scout for him tomorrow."

"Why you? You do not know this land."

"Why not me, Donna?"

"Will it be dangerous, do you think?"

"I don't know. Perhaps."

"Damn you, Jon. I wish you would learn to lie a little!"

Shannow rode away from the wagons in the hour after dawn, and once they were lost to sight behind him, he removed the Bible from his saddlebag and allowed it to fall open in his hands. Glancing down, he read: *"Behold I create new heavens and a new earth, and the former shall not be remembered, nor come into mind."*

He closed the book and returned it to his saddlebag. Ahead

of him stretched the black lava sand, and he set the gelding off at a canter, angling toward the north.

For weeks now he had sat listening to the petty rows and squabbles of the two scholars, Phelps and Peacock, and though he had gleaned some food for thought, the two men made him think of the words of Solomon: *"For in much wisdom is much grief, and he that increaseth wisdom increaseth sorrow."*

The previous night the two men had argued for more than an hour concerning the word "train." Phelps insisted it was a mechanized Dark Age means of conveyance, while Peacock maintained it was merely a generic term to cover a group of vehicles or wagons in convoy. Phelps argued that he had once owned a book that explained the mechanics of trains. Peacock responded by showing him an ancient scrap of paper that talked of rabbits and cats dressing for dinner with a rat.

"What has that to do with it?" stormed Phelps, his fat face reddening.

"Many books of the Dark Age are not true. They obviously loved to lie, or do you believe in a village of dressed-up rabbits?"

"You old fool!" shouted Phelps. "It is simple to tell which are fictions. This book on trains was sound."

"How would you know? Because it was plausible? I saw a painting once of a man wearing a glass bowl on his head and waving a sword. He was said to be walking on the moon."

"Another fiction, and it proves nothing," said Phelps.

And so it went on. Shannow found the whole argument pointless.

Individually both men were persuasive. Phelps maintained that the Dark Age had lasted around a thousand years, during which time science had produced many wonders, among them trains and flying craft and also pistols and superior weapons of war. Peacock believed the Dark Age to be less than one hundred years, citing Christ's promise to his disciples that some of them would still be alive when the end came.

"If that promise was not true," argued Peacock, "then the Bible would have to be dismissed as another Dark Age fiction."

Shannow instinctively leaned toward Peacock's biblical view but found Phelps to be more open-minded and genuinely inquisitive.

Shannow shook his mind clear of the foggy arguments and concentrated on the trail. Up ahead the lava sand was breaking, and he found himself riding up a green slope shaded by trees. At the top he paused and looked down on a verdant valley with glistening streams.

For a long time he sat his horse, studying the land. There was no sign of life, no evidence of human habitation. He rode on warily, coming at last to a deer trail, which he followed down to a wide pool of fresh water. The ground around the pool was studded with tracks of all kinds: goats, sheep, deer, buffalo, and even the spoor of lions and bears. Near the pool was a tall pine, and ten feet up from the ground were the claw marks that signified the brown bear's territory. Bears were sensible animals. They did not fight each other for territory; they merely marked the trees. When a different bear arrived, he would rear up and try to match the scars. If he could outreach them, he would make his mark, and the smaller bear would depart once he had seen that his adversary was bigger and stronger. If he could not reach the scars, he would amble on in search of new territory. The idea appealed to Shannow, but even here a little trickery could be used.

Back in Allion a very small bear had staked out an enormous territory by coming out of hibernation in the middle of winter and scrambling up the snow banked against the trees, making his mark some three feet higher. Shannow had liked that bear.

He scouted the perimeter of the pool and then took a different route back toward the wagons. At the top of a rise he smelt wood smoke and paused, searching the surrounding skyline. The wind was easterly, and he angled his horse back through the trees, walking him slowly and carefully. The smell was stronger now, and Shannow dismounted and hobbled the gelding, making his way on foot through the thick bushes and shrubs. As he approached a circular clearing, he heard the sound of voices and froze. The language was one he had never heard, though certain words seemed familiar. Dropping to his belly, he eased his way forward, waiting for the breeze to rustle the leaves above him and disguise the sound of his movements. After several minutes of soundless crawling he came to the edge of the clearing and squinted through a break in the leaves. Around a large fire sat seven men, nearly naked, their bodies stained with streaks of blue and yellow dye; by the side of one of the men was a severed human foot. Shannow blinked as sweat stung his eyes. Then a man stood and walked toward him, stopping some yards to his left, where, pulling aside a deerskin loincloth, he urinated against a tree. Through the gap left by the man Shannow could see the charred remains of a body spitted above the fire.

Shannow felt his stomach heave and averted his gaze. By the trees on the other side of the clearing two captives were tied together. Both were children around Eric's age. They were dressed in buckskin tunics adorned with intricate patterns of shells, and their hair was dark and braided. Both children seemed in a state of shock—their eyes were wide, their faces blank and uncomprehending. Shannow forced himself to look at the corpse. It was short and no doubt was another child. Shannow's fury rose, and his eyes took on an almost feral gleam.

Desperately Shannow fought to hold the surging anger, but it engulfed him and he pushed himself to his feet, his hands curling around the butts of his pistols. He stepped into sight, and the men scrambled to their feet, dragging knives and hatchets from their belts of rope and hide. Shannow's guns came up, and then he spoke:

"Thou shalt be visited by the Lord of Hosts with thunder and with earthquake and great noise . . ."

He triggered the pistols, and two men flew backward. The other five screamed and charged. One went down with a bullet in the brain, and a second fell clutching his belly. A third reached Shannow, and the man's hatchet flashed for his head, but Shannow blocked the blow with his right arm and thrust the left-hand pistol under the attacker's chin. The top of his head flowered like a scarlet bloom. A club caught Shannow on the side of the head, and he fell awkwardly; his pistol fired, shattering a man's knee. As a knife blade rose above his face, Shannow rolled and shot the wielder in the chest. The man fell across him, but Shannow pushed the body clear and lurched to his feet. The man with the shattered knee was crawling backward.

"*. . . and great noise, with storm and tempest and the flame of devouring fire.*"

The cannibal raised his arms against the pistols, covering his eyes. Shannow fired twice, the shells smashing through the outstretched hands and into the face beyond, and the man pitched back. Shannow staggered and fell to his knees; his head was pounding, and his vision blurred and swam. He took a deep breath, pushing back the nausea that threatened to swamp him. A movement to his right! He pointed his pistol, and a child screamed.

"It's all right," said Shannow groggily. "I'll not harm you. *'Suffer little children to come unto me.'* Just give me a moment."

He sat back and felt his head. The skin was split at the temple, and blood was drenching his face and shirt. He sheathed his guns and crawled to the children, cutting them free.

The taller of the two sprinted away the moment the ropes were cut, but the other raised a hand and touched Shannow's face where the blood flowed. Shannow tried to smile, but the world spun madly before his eyes.

"Go, boy. You understand! *Go!*"

Shannow tried to stand but fell heavily. He crawled for several yards and found himself lying next to a small clear pool of water. Watching his blood drip to the surface and flow away in red ribbons, Shannow chuckled.

"*He leadeth me beside the still waters. He restoreth my soul.*"

The child came to him, tugging at his arm. "More come!" he said. Shannow squeezed his eyes shut, trying to concentrate.

"More Carns come. You go!" shouted the child.

Shannow slipped his pistols into his hands and knocked out

the barrel wedges, sliding the cylinders from the weapons and replacing them with two fully loaded cylinders from his coat pocket. He fumbled the wedges into place and sheathed the pistols.

"Let them come," he said.

"No. Many Carns." The boy's fingers flashed before Shannow's face. Ten, twenty, thirty, forty . . .

"I get the message, lad. Help me up." The boy did his best, but Shannow was a tall man, and the two made slow progress into the woods. Angry yells and cries pierced the stillness, and he could hear the sounds of many men crashing through the undergrowth. He tried to move faster but fell, dragging the child with him. Forcing himself to his feet, he stumbled on. A blue-and-yellow-smeared body lunged through the bushes, and Shannow's right hand dropped and rose, the pistol bucking in his hand. The warrior vanished back into the undergrowth. The boy ran on ahead and unhobbled Shannow's horse, leaping into the saddle. Shannow staggered forward, caught hold of the pommel, and managed to step into the saddle behind the child.

Three men burst into view, and the horse swerved and took off at a run. Shannow swayed in the saddle, but the boy reached back and grabbed him; he managed to sheathe his pistol, and then darkness overtook him. He fell forward against the boy as the horse raced on toward the west. The child risked a glance behind him. The Carns had given up the chase and were heading back into the trees. The boy slowed the gelding and hooked his fingers into Shannow's belt, holding him upright.

It was not easy, but Selah was strong and owed this man his life.

Donna Taybard screamed once and sat up. Eric hauled on the reins and kicked the brake, and the wagon stopped. The boy climbed over the backrest and scrambled across the bulging food sacks to where his mother sat sobbing.

"What is it, Mother?" he cried.

Donna took a deep breath. "Shannow," she said. "Oh, my poor Jon."

Con Griffin rode alongside and dismounted. He said nothing but climbed into the wagon to kneel beside the weeping woman. Looking up into his powerful face, she saw the concern etched there.

"He is dead."

"You were dreaming, Fray Taybard."

"No. He rescued two children from the savages, and now he is buried deep in the ground."

"A dream," insisted Griffin, placing a huge hand on her shoulder.

"You don't understand, Mr. Griffin. It is a talent I have. We are going to a place where there are two lakes; it is surrounded by pine trees. There is a tribe who paint their bodies yellow and blue. Shannow killed many of them and escaped with a child. Now he is dead. Believe me!"

"You are an ESPer, Donna?"

"Yes . . . no. I can always see those close to me. Shannow is buried."

Griffin patted her shoulder and stepped down from the wagon.

"What's happening, Con?" shouted Ethan Peacock. "Why are we stopping?"

"Fray Taybard is unwell. We'll move on now," he answered. Turning to Eric, he said, "Leave her now, lad, and get the oxen moving." He stepped into the saddle and rode back along the convoy to his own wagons.

"What was the holdup?" Burke asked him.

"It's nothing, Jim. Pass me my pistols."

Burke clambered back into the wagon and opened a brass-edged walnut box. Within were two engraved, double-barreled flintlock pistols. Burke primed them both with powder from a bone horn and gathered the saddle holsters from a hook on the wagon wall.

Con Griffin slung the holsters across his pommel and thrust the pistols home. Touching his heel to the chestnut, he cantered back to Madden's wagon.

"Trouble?" queried the bearded farmer, and Griffin nodded.

"Leave your son to take the reins and join me at the head."

Griffin swung his horse and rode back to the lead wagon. If Donna Taybard was right, his convoy was in deep trouble. He cursed, for he knew without doubt that she would be proved correct.

Madden joined him within minutes, riding a slate-gray gelding of seventeen hands. He was a tall, thin, angular man with a close-cropped black beard but no mustache; his mouth was a thin hard line, and his eyes were dark and deep-set. He carried a long rifle cradled in his left arm, and by his side was a bone-handled hunting knife.

Griffin told him about Donna's fear.

"You think she's right?"

"Has to be. Cardigan's diary spoke of the blue and yellow stripes."

"What do we do?"

"We have no choice, Jacob. The animals need grass and rest. We must go in."

The farmer nodded. "Any idea how big a tribe?"

"No."

"I don't like it, but I'm with you."

"Alert all families—tell them to prime weapons."

The wagons moved on and by late afternoon came to the end of the lava sand. The oxen, smelling water ahead, surged into the traces, and the convoy picked up speed.

"Hold them back!" yelled Griffin, and drivers kicked hard on the brakes, but to little avail. The wagons crested a green slope and spread out as they lurched and rumbled for the river below and the wide lakes opening beside it. Griffin cantered alongside the leading wagon, scanning the long grass for movement.

As the first wagon reached the water, a blue-and-yellow-streaked body leapt to the driver's seat, plunging a flint dagger into Aaron Phelps' fleshy shoulder. The scholar lashed out, and the attacker lost his balance and fell. Suddenly warriors were all around them, and Griffin pulled his pistols clear and cocked them. A man ran at him carrying a club. Griffin shot into his body and kicked his horse into a run. Madden's long rifle boomed, and a tribesman fell with a broken spine. Then the other guns opened up, and the warriors fled.

Griffin joined Madden at the rear of the convoy.

"What do you think, Jacob?"

"I think they'll be back. Let's fill the barrels and move on to open ground."

Two wagoners had been injured in the brief raid. Aaron Phelps had a deep wound in his right shoulder, and Maggie Ames' young son, Mose, had been gashed in the leg by a spear. Four tribesmen had been killed outright. Others had been wounded but had reached the sanctuary of the trees.

Griffin dismounted next to one of the corpses.

"Look at those teeth," said Jacob Madden. They had been filed to sharp points.

Ethan Peacock came to stand beside Griffin and peered at the blue and yellow corpse.

"And idiots like Phelps expect us to agree with their theories of the Dark Age," he said. "Can you see that creature piloting a flying machine? It's barely human."

"Damn you, Ethan, this is no time for debate. Get your barrels filled."

Griffin moved on to Phelps' wagon, where Donna Taybard was battling to stanch the bleeding. "It needs stitches, Donna," said Griffin. "I'll get a needle and thread."

"I am going to die," said Phelps. "I know it."

"Not from that, you won't," Griffin told him. "But by God, it will make you wish you had."

"Will they come back?" asked Donna.

"It depends on how big the tribe is," answered Griffin. "I would expect them to try once more. Is Eric gathering your water?"

"Yes."

Griffin fetched a needle and thread, passed them to Donna, then checked his pistols. He had fired all four barrels yet could remember only one. Strange, he thought, how instinct could overcome reason. He gave the pistols to Burke to load and prime. Madden had taken six men to watch the woods for any sign of the savages, and Griffin supervised the water gathering.

Toward dusk he ordered the wagons out and away from the trees to a flat meadow to the west. There the oxen were unharnessed, and a rope paddock was set up to pen the beasts.

Madden organized guards at the perimeter of the camp, and the travelers settled down to wait for the next attack.

Shannow's dreams were bathed in blood and fire. He rode a skeleton horse across a desert of graves, coming at last to a white marble city and a gate of gold that hurt his eyes as he gazed upon it.

"Let me in," he called.

"No beasts may enter here," a voice told him.

"I am not a beast."

"Then what are you?"

Shannow looked down at his hands and saw they were mottled gray and black and scaled like a serpent. His head ached, and he reached up to the wound.

"Let me in. I am hurt."

"No beasts may enter here."

Shannow screamed as his hand touched his brow, for horns grew there, long and sharp, and they leaked blood that hissed and boiled as it touched the ground.

"At least tell me if this is Jerusalem."

"There are no brigands for you to slay, Shannow. Ride on."

"I have nowhere to go."

"You chose the path, Shannow. Follow it."

"But I need Jerusalem."

"Come back again when the wolf sits down with the lamb and the lion eats grass as the cattle do."

Shannow awoke. He had been buried alive. He screamed once, and a curtain to his left moved to show light in a room beyond. An elderly man crept in to sit beside him.

"You are well; you are in the fever hole. Do not concern yourself. You are free to leave when you feel well enough."

Shannow tried to sit, but his head ached abominably. His

hand went to his brow, fearing that horns would touch his fingers, but he found only a linen bandage. He glanced around the tiny room. Apart from his pallet bed there was a fire built beneath white stones, and the heat was searing.

"You had a fever," said the man. "I brought you out of it."

Shannow lay back on the bed and fell asleep instantly.

When he awoke, the old man was still sitting beside him; he was dressed in a buckskin jacket free of adornments and leather trousers as soft as cloth. He was almost bald, but the white hair above his ears was thick and wavy and grew to his shoulders. The face, thought Shannow, was kindly, and his teeth were remarkably white and even.

"Who are you?" asked Shannow.

"I have long since put aside my name. Here they call me Karitas."

"I am Shannow. What is wrong with me?"

"I think you have a cracked skull, Mr. Shannow. You have been very ill. We have all been worried about you."

"All?"

"Young Selah brought you to me. You saved his life in the eastern woods."

"What of the other boy?"

"He did not come home, Mr. Shannow. I fear he was recaptured."

"My guns and saddlebags?"

"Safe. Interesting pistols, if I may say so. They are copies of the 1858 Colt; the original was a fine weapon as cap and ball pistols go."

"They are the best pistols in the world, Mr. Karitas."

"Just 'Karitas,' and yes, I expect you are right, at least until someone rediscovers the Smith and Wesson .44 Russian or indeed the 1898 Luger. I myself have always held the high-power Browning in great esteem. How are you feeling?"

"Not good," admitted Shannow.

"You almost died, my friend. The fever was most powerful, and you were badly concussed. I am amazed that you remained conscious after being struck."

"I don't remember being hit."

"That is natural. Your horse is being well looked after. Our young men have never seen a horse, yet Selah rode him like a centaur to bring you home. It makes one inclined to believe in genetic memory."

"You are speaking in riddles."

"Yes. And I am tiring you. Rest now, and we will talk in the morning."

Shannow drifted back into darkness and awoke to find a young woman by his bed. She helped him eat some broth and bathed his body with water-cooled cloths. After she had gone, Karitas returned.

"I see you are feeling better; your color is good, Mr. Shannow." The old man called out, and two younger men ducked into the fever hole. "Help Mr. Shannow out into the sunlight. It will do him good."

Together they lifted the naked man and carried him out of the hole, laying him on a blanket under a wide shade made from interwoven leaves. Several children were playing nearby, and they stopped to watch the stranger. Shannow glanced around; there were more than thirty huts in view, and to his right a shallow stream bubbled over pink and blue stones.

"Beautiful, isn't it?" said Karitas. "I love this place. If it wasn't for the Carns, this would be paradise."

"The Carns?"

"The cannibals, Mr. Shannow."

"Yes, I remember."

"Sad, really. The Elders did it to them, polluted the land and the sea. The Carns should have died; they came here two hundred years ago when the plagues began. I wasn't in this area then, or I could have warned them to stay clear. The stones used to gleam at night, and no animal could survive. We still suffer a high incidence of cancer, but the main effects seem to be on the brain and the glandular system. With some, they become atavistic. Others develop rare ESPer powers, while some of us just seem to live forever."

Shannow decided the man was mad and closed his eyes against the pain in his temple.

"My dear chap," said Karitas, "forgive me. Ella, fetch the coca."

A young woman came forward bearing a wooden bowl in which dark liquid swirled. "Drink that, Mr. Shannow." He did as he was told. The drink was bitter, and he almost choked, but within seconds the pain in his head dulled and disappeared.

"There, that's the ticket. I took the liberty, Mr. Shannow, of going through your things, and I see you are a Bible-reading man."

"Yes. You?"

"I have been while you lay ill. It's a long time since I have seen a Bible. I'm not surprised it survived the Fall; it was a best-seller every day of every year. There were more Bibles than people, I shouldn't wonder."

"You are not a believer, then?"

"On the contrary, Mr. Shannow. Anyone who watches a world die is liable to be converted at rare speed."

Shannow sat up. "Every time you speak, I almost get a grip on what you are saying, and then you soar away somewhere. Lugers, Colts, tickets . . . I don't understand any of it."

"And why should you, my boy? Does not the Bible say, *'For behold I shall create a new heaven and a new earth and the former shall not be remembered; nor come into mind'?*"

"That's the first thing you've said that I have understood. What happened to the wagons?"

"What wagons, Mr. Shannow?"

"I was with a convoy."

"I know nothing of them, but when you are well, you can find them."

"Your name is familiar to me," said Shannow, "but I cannot place it."

"Karitas. Greek for love. Though I speak with the tongues of men and of angels and have not karitas—charity, love . . . You recall?"

"My father used to use it," said Shannow, smiling. "I remember. Faith, hope, and karitas. Yes."

"You should smile more often, Mr. Shannow; it becomes

you well. Tell me, sir: Why did you risk your life for my little ones?"

Shannow shrugged. "If that question needs an answer, then I cannot supply it. I had no choice."

"I have decided that I like you, Mr. Shannow. The children here call you the Thundermaker and think you may be a god. They know I am. They think you are the god of death."

"I am a man, Karitas. You know that; tell them."

"Divinity is not a light gift to throw away, Mr. Shannow. You will feature in their legends until the end of time, hurling thunderbolts at the Carns, rescuing their princes. One day they will probably pray to you."

"That would be blasphemy."

"Only if you took it seriously. But then, you are no Caligula. Are you hungry?"

"Your chatter makes my head spin. How long have you been here?"

"In this camp? Eleven years, more or less. And you must forgive my chatter, Mr. Shannow. I am one of the last men of a lost race, and sometimes my loneliness is colossal. I have discovered answers here to mysteries that have baffled men for a thousand years. And there is no one I would wish to tell. All I have is this small tribe who were once Eskimos and now are merely food for the Carns. It is all too galling, Mr. Shannow."

"Where are you from, Karitas?"

"London, Mr. Shannow."

"Is that north, south, what?"

"By my calculations, sir, it is north and sits under a million tons of ice, waiting to be discovered in another millennium."

Shannow gave up and lay back on the blanket, allowing sleep to wash over him.

Mad though he undoubtedly was, Karitas had organized the village with spectacular efficiency and was obviously revered by the villagers. Shannow lay on his blankets in the shade and watched the village life passing him by. The huts were all alike: rectangular and built of mud and logs with roofs slanting down and overhanging the main doors. The roofs themselves appeared to have been constructed from interwoven leaves and dried grass. They were sturdy buildings without ostentation. To the east of the village was a large log cabin, which Karitas explained held the winter stores, and beside it was the wood store, seven feet high and fifteen feet deep. The winter, Karitas told him, was particularly harsh there on the plain.

On outlying hills Shannow could see flocks of sheep and goats, and those he was told were communal property. Life seemed relaxed and without friction in Karitas' village.

The people were friendly, and any who passed where Shannow lay would bow and smile. They were not like any people Shannow had come across so far in his wanderings; their skin was dull gold, and their eyes wide-set and almost slanted. The women were mostly taller than the men and beautifully formed; several were pregnant. There seemed few old people until Shannow realized their huts were in the western sector, nearest the stream and protected from the harsh north winds by a rising slope at the rear of the dwellings.

The men were stocky and carried weapons of curious design, bows of horn and knives of dark flint. Day by day Shannow came to know individual villagers, especially the boy Selah and a young sloe-eyed maid named Curopet, who would sit by him and gaze at his face, saying nothing. Her presence unsettled the Jerusalem Man, but he could not find the words to send her away.

Shannow's recovery was painfully slow. The wound in his temple healed within days, but the left side of his face was numb and the strength of his left arm and leg had been halved. If he tried to walk, his foot dragged and he often stumbled. The fingers of his left hand tingled permanently, and he was unable to hold any object for more than a few seconds before the hand would spasm and the fingers would open.

Every day for a month Karitas would arrive at Shannow's hut an hour after dawn and massage his fingers and arm. Shannow was close to despair. All his life his strength had been with him, and without it he felt defenseless and—worse—useless.

Karitas broached the painful subject at the start of the fifth week. "Mr. Shannow, you are doing yourself no good. Your strength will not return until you find the courage to seek it."

"I can hardly lift my arm, and my leg drags like a rotting tree branch," said Shannow. "What do you expect me to do?"

"Fight it as you fought the Carns. I am not a medical man, Mr. Shannow, but I think you have had a mild stroke—a cerebral thrombosis, I believe it used to be called. A blood clot near the brain has affected your left side."

"How sure are you of this?"

"Reasonably certain; it happened to my father."

"And he recovered?"

"No, he died. He took to his bed like the weakling he was."

"How do I fight it?"

"Bear with me, Mr. Shannow, and I will show you."

Each day Karitas sat for hours, pushing the Jerusalem Man through a grueling series of exercises. At first he merely forced Shannow to raise his left arm and lower it ten times. Shannow managed six, and the arm rose a bare eight inches. Then Karitas produced a ball of tightly wound hide, which he placed in Shannow's left hand. "Squeeze this one hundred times in the morning and another hundred times before you sleep."

"It'll take me all day."

"Then take all day. But do it!"

Each afternoon Karitas forced Shannow to accompany him on a walk around the village, a distance of about four hundred paces.

The weeks drifted by, and Shannow's improvement was barely perceptible, but Karitas—noting everything—would shout for joy over an extra quarter inch on an arm raise, offering fulsome congratulations and calling in Selah or Curopet, insisting that Shannow repeat the move. This was then greeted by much applause, especially from the maiden Curopet, who had, in the words of Karitas, "taken a shine" to the invalid.

Shannow, while recognizing Karitas' methods, was still lifted by the obvious joy the old man gained from his recovery and tried harder with each passing day.

At night, as he lay on his blankets squeezing the leather ball and counting aloud, his mind would drift to Donna and the convoy. He felt her absence but knew that with her talent she could see him every day and would know how hard he was working to be beside her once more.

One morning, as Shannow and Karitas walked around the village, the Jerusalem Man stopped and gazed at the distant hills. The trees were still green, but at the center was a golden shower that shimmered in the sunlight.

"That is wondrous beautiful," said Shannow. "It looks for all the world like a tree of gold coins, just waiting to make a man rich."

"There are many beautiful things to see during autumn here," said Karitas softly.

"Autumn? Yes, I had not thought. I have been here so long."

"Two months only."

"I must get away before winter or there'll be no tracks to follow."

"We'll do our best for you, Mr. Shannow."

"Do not misunderstand me, my friend. I am more than grateful to you, but my heart is elsewhere. Have you ever loved a woman?"

"More than one, I'm afraid. But not for thirty years now. Chines had a baby girl last night. That makes eleven babies this summer for my little tribe. Not bad, eh?"

"Which one is Chines?"

"The tall girl with the birthmark on her temple."

"Ah, yes. Is she all right?"

"Fine. Her husband is disappointed, though; he wanted a boy."

"Your tribe is doing well, Karitas. You are a good leader. How many people are there here?"

"Counting the babes, eighty-seven. No, eighty-eight; I forgot about Dual's boy."

"A sizable family."

"It would be bigger but for the Carns."

"Do they raid often?"

"No; they have never hit the village. They don't want to

drive us away—we are a good source of amusement . . . and food. They usually attack our hunting parties."

"You do not seem to hate them, Karitas. Whenever you mention the Carns, your face reflects regret."

"They are not responsible for the way they are, Mr. Shannow. It was the land. I know you think me a great liar, but when the Carns first came here, they were a group of ordinary farming families. Maybe it was the water, or the rocks, or even something in the air—I don't know. But over the years it changed them. It was a gift from my generation; we were always good at lethal gifts."

"After knowing you for these last months," said Shannow, "I cannot understand why you hold to your preposterous tales. I know you are an intelligent man, and you must know that I am not foolish. Why, then, do you maintain this charade?"

Karitas sat down on the grass and beckoned Shannow to join him. "My dear boy, I hold to it because it is true. But let me say that the land may have affected me, too—it could all be a dream, a fantasy. I think it is true—my memory tells me it is true—but I could merely be insane. What does it matter?"

"It matters to me, Karitas. I like you; I owe you a debt."

"You owe me nothing. You saved Selah. One thing does concern me, however, and that is the direction your wagons are taking. You say you were heading northwest?"

"Yes."

"But was there any intention of turning east?"

"Not that I know of. Why?"

"Probably it is of no matter. It is a strange land, and there are some who live there who would make the Carns seem hospitable."

"That is as hard to swallow as some of your stories."

The smile left Karitas' face. "Mr. Shannow, there was an old legend when I was a boy concerning a priestess called Cassandra. She was blessed with the gift of prophecy and always spoke the truth. But she was cursed also, to be believed by no one."

"I am sorry, my friend. It was thoughtless and rude of me."

"It is not important, Mr. Shannow. Let us resume our walk."

They continued in silence, which Shannow found uncomfortable.

The day was warm; a bright sun was in a blue sky, with only occasional white scudding clouds bringing shade and relief. Shannow felt stronger than he had in weeks. Karitas stopped at a rock pile and hefted a fist-sized stone.

"Take that in your left hand," he said.

Shannow obeyed.

"Now carry it for a second circuit."

"I'll never make it all the way," said Shannow.

"We won't know until we make the attempt," snapped Karitas. They set off, and within a few paces Shannow's left arm began to tremble. Sweat stood out on his forehead, and on the seventeenth step the rock tumbled from his twitching fingers. Karitas took a stick and thrust it into the ground. "That is your first mark, Mr. Shannow. Tomorrow you will go beyond it."

Shannow rubbed at his arm. "I have made you angry," he said.

Karitas turned to him, his eyes gleaming. "Mr. Shannow, you are right. I have lived too long and seen too much, and you have no idea how galling it is to be disbelieved. I'll tell you something else that you will not be able to understand or comprehend: I was a computer expert, and I wrote books on programming. That makes me the world's greatest living author and an expert on a subject that is so totally valueless here as to be obscene. I lived in a world of greed, violence, lust, and terror. That world died, yet what do I see around me? Exactly the same thing, only on a mercifully smaller scale. Your disbelief hurts me harder than I can say."

"Then let us start afresh, Karitas," said Shannow, laying his hand on the old man's shoulder. "You are my friend. I trust you, and no matter what you tell me, I swear I will believe it."

"That is a noble gesture, Mr. Shannow. And it will suffice."

"So tell me about the dangers in the east."

"Tonight we will sit by the fire and talk, but for now I have things to do. Walk around the village twice more, Mr. Shannow, and when you have your hut in sight, try to run."

As the old man walked away, Curopet approached Shannow, averting her eyes. "Are you well, Thundermaker?"

"Better every day, lady."

"May I fetch you some water?"

"No. Karitas says I must walk and run."

"May I walk with you?"

Shannow gazed down at her and saw that she was blushing. "Of course; it would be my pleasure." She was taller than most young women of the village, and her hair was dark and gleamed as if oiled. Her figure was coltish, and she moved with grace and innocent sensuality.

"How long have you known Karitas?" he asked, making conversation.

"He has always been with us. My grandfather told me that Karitas taught him to hunt when he was a boy."

Shannow stopped. "Your grandfather? But Karitas himself could not have been very old at that time."

"Karitas has always been old. He is a god. My grandfather said that Karitas also trained *his* grandfather; it is a very special honor to be taught by Karitas."

"Perhaps there has been more than one Karitas," suggested Shannow.

"Perhaps," agreed Curopet. "Tell me, Lord Thundermaker, are you allowed to have women?"

"Allowed? No," said Shannow, reddening. "It is not permitted."

"That is sad," said Curopet.

"Yes."

"Are you being punished for something?"

"No. I am married, you see. I have a wife."

"Only one?"

"Yes."

"But she is not here."

"No."

"I am here."

"I am well aware of that. And I thank you for your . . . kindness," said Shannow at last. "Excuse me, I am very tired. I think I will sleep now."

"But you have not run."

"Another time."

Shannow stepped into the hut and sat down, feeling both foolish and pleased. He removed his pistols from the saddle-bags and cleaned them, checking the caps and replacing them. The guns were the most reliable he had ever known, misfiring only once in twenty times. They were well balanced and reasonably true if one compensated for the kick on the left-hand pistol. He checked his store of brass caps and counted them; 170 remained. He had enough fulminates for twice that and black powder to match. Karitas entered as he was replacing his weapons in the saddlebags.

"Black powder was a good propellant," said the old man. "But not enough of it burns, and that's why there is so much smoke."

"I make my own," said Shannow, "but the saltpeter is the hardest to find. Sulphur and charcoal are plentiful."

"How are you faring?"

"Better today. Tomorrow I will run."

"Curopet told me of your conversation. Do you find it hard to talk to women?"

"Yes," admitted Shannow.

"Then try to forget that they are women."

"That is very hard. Curopet is breathtakingly attractive."

"You should have accepted her offer."

"Fornication is a sin, Karitas. I carry enough sins already."

Karitas shrugged. "I will not try to dissuade you. You asked about the east and the dangers there. Strangely, the Bible figures in the story."

"A religious tribe, you mean?"

"Precisely, although they view matters somewhat differently from you, Mr. Shannow. They call themselves the Hellborn. They maintain that since Armageddon is now a proved reality and since there is no new Jerusalem, Lucifer must have overpowered Jehovah. Therefore, they pay him homage as the lord of this world."

"That is vile," whispered Shannow.

"They practice the worship of Molech and give the firstborn

child to the fire. Human sacrifice takes place in their temples, and their rites are truly extraordinary. All strangers are considered enemies and either enslaved or burned alive. They also have pistols and rifles, Mr. Shannow, and they have rediscovered the rimless cartridge."

"I do not understand."

"Think of the difference between the percussion pistols you own and the flintlocks you have come across. Well, the cartridge is as far ahead of the percussion cap as that."

"Explain it to me."

"I can do better than that, Mr. Shannow. I will show you."

Karitas opened his sheepskin jerkin, and there, nestling in a black shoulder holster, was a pistol the like of which Shannow had never seen. It had a rectangular black grip, and when Karitas pulled it clear, he saw that the body of the gun was also a rectangle. Karitas passed it to Shannow.

"How does it load?"

"Press the button to the left of the butt."

Shannow did so, and a clip slid clear of the butt. Shannow placed the gun in his lap and examined the clip. He could see a glint of brass at the top, and he slid the shell into his hand, holding it up against the light from the fire.

"That," said Karitas, "is a cartridge. The oval shape at the point is the lead bullet. The brass section replaces the percussion cap; it contains its own propellant and, when struck by the firing pin, explodes, propelling the shell from the barrel."

"But how does the ... bullet get from the clip to the breech?"

Karitas took up the automatic and pulled back the casing, exposing the breech. "A spring in the clip forces the shell up, and releasing the block like so—" The casing snapped back into position. "—pushes the shell into the breech. Now, this is the beauty of the weapon, Mr. Shannow: When the trigger is pulled, the firing pin explodes the propellant and sends the shell on its way, but the blowback from the explosion forces the casing backward. A hook pulls clear the cartridge case, which is then struck from beneath by another cartridge and thrown from the pistol. As the casing springs back, it pushes the next shell into the breech. Simple and superb!"

"What is it called?"

"This, my dear fellow, is the Browning of 1911, with the single-link locking system. It is also the reason why the Carns will not raid where I am."

"You mean it works?"

"Of course it works. It's not a patch on their later models, but it was considered a great weapon in its day."

"I am still to be convinced," said Shannow. "It looks clumsy and altogether too complicated."

"Tomorrow, Mr. Shannow, I shall give you a demonstration."

"Where did you come by these weapons?"

"I took them from the Ark, Mr. Shannow. That is one of the surprises I have in store for you. Would you like to see Noah's Ark?"

◊ 4 ◊

SHANNOW COULD NOT sleep; his mind was full of pictures of Donna Taybard. He recalled her as he had first seen her, standing before her farmhouse with a crossbow in her hand, looking both defiant and delicate. And then, at the dinner table, sad and wistful. And he remembered her in the wide bed, her face flushed, her eyes bright, her body soft.

Images of Curopet crept into his mind, blurring with Donna, and he groaned and rolled over.

Dawn found him irritable and tired, and he dressed swiftly, having first exercised with the leather ball. His left hand was stronger now yet still a shadow of what it had been.

The wind was chilly and Shannow wished he had put on his leather topcoat, but he saw Karitas waiting for him by the rock pile.

"We will put this exhibition to good use," said Karitas. "Pick up a good-sized rock with your left hand and carry it to the flat ground yonder, about thirty paces." Shannow did as he was told, and his arm was aching as he returned.

"Now take another," said Karitas. Six times he ordered Shannow to pick up rocks, and then he told him to watch. The rocks were now in a line, each of them the size of a man's fist. Karitas drew the Browning and cocked it; his arm leveled, and the gun fired with a sharp crack. There was little smoke, and one of the rocks splintered. On the ground by Karitas' feet lay a brass shell, and the weapon in his hand was cocked and ready.

"Now you try, my dear fellow." He reversed the gun and handed it to Shannow. The balance was good, the weight nestling back into his palm rather than forward like the percussion pistols.

He lined up the weapon and squeezed the trigger, and a spurt of dust leapt up a foot behind the rock. Shannow fired once more, and the rock split apart. He was impressed, though he tried not to show it.

"My own pistols could duplicate the accuracy."

"I don't doubt it, but the Browning can be loaded with nine shells in less than ten seconds."

"And you say the Hellborn have these?"

"No, thank God. They have revolvers, copies of the Adams and some Remington replicas. But their craftsmen have evolved the weapons; their level of technology is fairly high."

"Well, they are a problem for another day," said Shannow. "But tell me of Noah's Ark, or is that another joke?"

"Not at all. We will see it in the spring, with the Guardians' permission."

"I will not be here in the spring, Karitas."

The old man moved forward and retrieved his pistol. He uncocked it and slid it back into his shoulder holster. "You are recovering well, but you are not yet strong enough to ride any distance. And there is something else you should know." Karitas' voice was grave.

"What is it?"

"Let us go to your hut and I will explain."

Once inside beside a warm fire, Karitas opened the leather pouch at his hip and produced a round stone, which he passed to Shannow. Warm to the touch and gleaming softly gold in the firelight, it was veined with black streaks and highlighted by tiny specks of silver.

"It is a pretty piece," said Shannow. "But what do you have to tell me?"

"You are holding your life in your hand, Mr. Shannow, for that is a healing stone, and on you it has worked a miracle."

"I have heard of such. The Daniel Stone?"

"Indeed it is. But its significance to you is very great. You see, Mr. Shannow, you are in fact dead. When Selah brought you to me, your skull was smashed. I don't know how you lived as long as you did. But the stone held you . . . as it still holds you. If you travel out of its influence, you will die."

Shannow tossed the stone to Karitas. "Dead? Then why does my heart beat? Why can I still think and speak?"

"Tell me, Mr. Shannow. When you lay in the fever hole and your heart stopped, what did you feel?"

"I felt nothing. I dreamed I sat outside the gates of Jerusalem and they would not let me enter. It was but a dream. I do not believe that I am trapped in this village forever."

"Nor are you. But you must trust me and my knowledge. I will know when you have broken the thread, when you can exist without the stone. Have faith in me, Jon."

"But my wife . . ."

"If she loves you, she will wait. And you say she has power to see great distances. Build your strength."

Day by dreary day Shannow worked: chopping wood, carrying water, scything grass for winter feed. And the autumn passed before the freezing northerly winds piled snow against the huts. Night after night Shannow sat with Karitas, listening to his tales of the New World's birthing. He no longer knew or cared if Karitas was telling the truth; the images were too many and too kaleidoscopic to contain. He listened much as he had when his father had told stories, his disbelief suspended only for the telling time.

Yet though Karitas maintained that he had lived long before the Fall of the world, he would not speak of his society, its laws, or its history, refusing to answer any of Shannow's questions. Strangely, Shannow felt, this gave the old man credibility.

"I would like to tell you, Jon, for it is so long since I spoke of the old world. But I have a fear, you see, that one day man will re-create the horrors of those days. I shall not be a willing party to it. We were so arrogant. We thought the world was ours, and then one day nature put us in our place. The world toppled on its axis. Tidal waves consumed vast areas. Cities, countries, vanished beneath the water. Volcanoes erupted; earthquakes tore the world. It's a wonder anyone survived.

"And yet, now I look back, all the clues were there to see, to warn us of impending disaster. All we needed was to be humble enough to look at it without subjectivity. Our own legends told us that the earth had toppled before. The Bible talks of the sun rising in the west and of the seas tipping from their bowls. And it did. My God, it did!" The old man lapsed into silence.

"How did you survive?" asked Shannow.

Karitas blinked and grinned suddenly. "I was in a magical metal bird, flying high above the waves."

"It was a serious question."

"I know. But I don't want to talk anymore about those days."

"Just one small question," said Shannow. "It is important to me."

"Just the one," agreed the old man.

"Would there have been a black road with diamonds at the center, shining in the night?"

"Diamonds? Ah, yes, all the roads had them. Why do you ask?"

"Would they have been at Jerusalem?"

"Yes. Why?"

"It is the city I am seeking. And if Noah's Ark is on a mountain near here, Jerusalem cannot be far away."

"Are you mocking me, Shannow?"

"No. I seek the Holy City."

Karitas held his hands out to the fire, staring thoughtfully into the flames. All men needed a dream, he knew, Shannow more than most.

"What will you do when you find it?"

"I will ask questions and receive answers."

"And then what?"

"I shall die happy, Karitas."

"You're a good man, Shannow. I hope you make it."

"You doubt I will?"

"Not at all. If Jerusalem exists, you will find it. And if it doesn't, you'll never know, for you'll look until you die. That's how it should be. I feel that way about heaven; it's far more important that heaven should exist than that I should ever see it."

"In my dream they would not let me enter. They told me to come back when the wolf sits down with the lamb and the lion eats grass as the cattle do."

"Get some sleep, Jon. Dream of it again. I went there once, you know. To Jerusalem. Long before the Fall."

"Was it beautiful?"

Karitas remembered the chokingly narrow streets in the old quarter, the stink of bazaars . . . the tourist areas, the tall hotels, the pickpockets, and the car bombs.

"Yes," he said. "It was beautiful. Good night, Jon."

Karitas sat in his long cabin, his mood heavy and dark. He knew that Shannow would never believe the truth, but then, why should he? Even in his own age of technological miracles there had still been those who believed that the earth was flat or that man had been made by a benevolent bearded immortal out of a lump of clay. At least Shannow had a solid fact to back his theory of Armageddon. The world had come close to death.

There had been a lot of speculation in the last years about the possibility of a nuclear holocaust. But next to no one had considered nature herself dwarfing the might of the superpowers. What was it that scientist had told him five years after the Fall?

The Chandler theory? Karitas had a note somewhere from the days when he had studiously kept a diary. The old man moved into the back room and began to rummage through oak chests covered in beaver pelts. Underneath a rust-dark and brittle copy of the London *Times* he found the faded blue jackets of his diary collection, and below those the scraps of paper he had used for close to forty years. Useless, he thought, remembering the day when his last pencil had grown too small to sharpen. He pushed aside the scraps and searched through his diaries, coming at last to an entry for May 16. It was six years after the Fall. Strange how the memory faded after only a few centuries, he told himself with a grin. He read the entry and leaned back, remembering old Webster and his moth-eaten wig.

It was the ice at the poles, Webster had told him, increasing at the rate of 95,000 tons a day, slowly changing the shape of the earth from spheroid to ovoid. This made the spin unstable. Then came the day when mighty Jupiter and all the other major planets drew into a deadly line to exert their gravitational pull on the earth, along with that of the sun. The earth—already wobbling on its axis—toppled, bringing tidal waves and death and a new ice age for much of the hemisphere.

Armageddon? God the father moving from homilies to homicide?

Perhaps. But somehow Karitas preferred the wondrous anarchy of nature.

That night Jon Shannow dreamed of war. Strange riders wearing horned helms bore down on a village of tents. They carried swords and pistols, and as they stormed into the village in their hundreds, the noise of gunfire was deafening. The people of the tents fought back with bow and lance but were overpowered, the men brutally slain. Young women were dragged out onto the plain and repeatedly raped, and their throats were cut by saw-toothed daggers. Then they were hoisted into the air by their feet, and their blood ran into jugs that were passed around among the riders, who drank and laughed, their faces stained red.

Shannow awoke in a cold sweat, his left hand twitching as if to curl around the butt of his pistol. The dream had sickened him, and he cursed his mind for summoning such a vision. He prayed then, giving thanks for life and for love and asking that the Lord of Hosts watch over Donna Taybard until Shannow could reach her.

The night was dark, and snow swirled around the village. Shannow rose and wrapped himself in a blanket. Moving to the hearth, he raked the coals until a tiny flame appeared, then added timber and fresh wood and blew the fire to life.

The dream had been so real, so brutally real.

Shannow's head ached, and he wandered to the window, where, in a pottery jug, the coca leaves given him by Curopet now were. As ever, they dealt with the pain. He pushed open the window and leaned out, watching the snow. He could still see the riders, their curious helms adorned with curved horns of polished black and their breastplates embossed with a goat's head. He shivered and shut the window.

"Where are you tonight, Donna, my love?" he whispered.

Con Griffin had been many things in his life, but no one had ever taken him for a fool. Yet the riders with the horned helms and the casually arrogant manner obviously thought him as green as the grass of the valley.

The convoy, having survived three Carn attacks and a heart-stopping moment when an avalanche had narrowly missed a wagon on the high trail, had come at last to a green valley flanked by great mountains whose snow-covered peaks reached up into the clouds.

At a full meeting the wagoners had voted to put their roots into the soil of the valley, and Con Griffin had ridden with Madden and Burke to stake out plots for all the families. With the land allocated and the first timber felled, the wagoners had woken on a chilly autumn day to find three strange riders approaching the settlement. Each wore a curious helm embossed in black and sporting goats' horns, and by their sides hung pistols the like of which Griffin had never seen.

Griffin strode to meet them while Madden sat on a nearby wagon, his long rifle cradled across his arm. Jimmy Burke knelt beside a felled log, idly polishing a double-barreled flintlock.

"Good morning to you," said Griffin. The leader of the trio, a young man with dark eyes, forced a smile that was at best wintry.

"You are settling here?"

"Why not? It is virgin land."

The man nodded. "We are seeking a rider named Shannow."

"He is dead," said Griffin.

"He is alive," stated the man with a certainty Griffin could not ignore.

"If he is, then I am surprised. He was attacked by a cannibal tribe to the south and never rejoined his wagon."

"How many of you are there?" asked the rider.

"Enough," said Griffin.

"Yes," agreed the man. "We will be on our way. We are just passing through these lands."

The riders turned their horses and galloped toward the east. Madden joined Griffin.

"I didn't like the look of them," volunteered Madden. "You think we are in for trouble?"

"Could be," admitted Griffin.

"They set my flesh crawling," said Burke, coming up to join them. "They reminded me of the cannibals, 'cepting they had proper teeth."

"What do you advise, Griff?" asked Madden.

"If they are brigands, they'll be back."

"What did they talk about?" inquired Burke.

"They were asking about a man named Shannow."

"Who's he?" asked Madden.

"He's the Jerusalem Man," said Griffin, avoiding a direct lie. He had told none of his wagoners Jon Taybard's true name.

"In that case," said Burke, "they'd better hope they don't find him. He's not a man to mess with, by God! He's the one that shot up the brigands in Allion. And he gave Daniel Cade his limp—shot him in the knee."

"Don't mention Shannow to the others," said Griffin.

Madden caught Griffin's expression, and his eyes narrowed. There was something here that remained unsaid, but he trusted Griffin and did not press the point.

That night, just after midnight, fifty riders thundered down on the settlement, riding at full gallop across the eastern pasture. The front line hit the trip wire in the long grass, and the horses screamed as their legs were cut out from under them. Men pitched through the air. The second rank of riders dragged on their reins, stopping short of the wire. Shots exploded from twenty rifles, ripping into the raiders; twenty men went down, plus several horses. A second volley from fifteen pistols scythed through the milling riders, and the survivors galloped away. Several men who had been thrown from their mounts set off at a run. Individual riflemen picked them off in the bright moonlight.

As silence descended, Con Griffin reloaded his pistols and walked out into the pasture. Twenty-nine corpses lay on the grass, and eleven horses were dead or dying. Madden and the other wagoners joined him, collecting pistols from the fallen; they were revolvers and cartridge-fed.

"What will they come up with next?" asked Burke, thrusting a revolver into his belt.

"Look at this," said Griffin, staring down at the corpses. "They are all dressed alike, like an army in the old books. There's something very wrong here." He turned to Madden. "Mount up and follow them. Don't show yourself. And take no chances. I need to know where they are from and how many there are."

Donna Taybard moved alongside Griffin, slipping her arm through his.

"Who are they, Con?"

"I don't know. But they frighten me."

"You think they will be back tonight?"

"No. But if they do come, Jacob will let us know."

"Come home, then. Eric will want to hear all about it; he'll be so proud of you."

Griffin pulled her close and kissed her lightly on the brow. He wanted so desperately not to tell her about Shannow, wanted her to go on believing he was dead. They had become close after Shannow's disappearance, and he had made a special fuss over Eric, which meant he was often invited to eat at the Taybard wagon. One night he had proposed to Donna, expecting a refusal and prepared to wait for her to change her mind. Instead she had accepted, kissed him, and thanked him for his courtesy.

Few men could have been happier than Con Griffin at that moment. For days afterward he had walked with her in the evenings, holding hands in the moonlight, until finally Donna herself had precipitated the move he had longed for. They had walked to a shallow stream, and she had turned to him and put her hands on his shoulders.

"I am not a fifteen-year-old maiden," she had said, loosening her dress.

And they had made love on the grass beside the water.

Since then Con Griffin had slept in Donna's wagon, much to the disgust of old Burke, who did not hold with such flippant behavior. Eric had adjusted well to his new father and seemed relaxed in Griffin's company. For his part Griffin taught him to rope and to track and to name the trees and say which of them grew near water. And they talked man to man, which pleased Eric greatly.

"What should I call you?" asked Eric.

"Call me Griff."

"I cannot call you Father. Not yet."

"It would be nice if you could, but I will not worry about it."

"Will you make my mother happy?"

"I hope so. I will try very hard."

"My father couldn't."

"It happens sometimes."

"And I won't be cruel to you, Griff."

"Cruel?"

"I was very cruel to Mr. Shannow. And he saved my life. I wish I hadn't been; he told me he was very lonely and he wanted to be my friend."

That conversation was in Griffin's mind now as he stood with Donna. He walked her away from the corpses to the canvas-covered wagon beside their home plot.

"Donna, there is something . . . The riders . . ."

"What? Come on, this is not like you."

"Shannow is alive."

"No!"

"I believe that he is. Use your talent—try to see him."

"No, he's dead. I don't want to see him with maggots in his eyes."

"Please, Donna. Otherwise I'll never be able to rest, wondering if the Jerusalem Man is hunting me."

Her head sank down, and she closed her eyes. Immediately

she saw Shannow, limping through a village. Beside him was
an old man, balding, who was smiling and chatting with him.

Donna opened her eyes. "Yes," she whispered. "He is alive.
Oh, Con!"

"I will . . . of course, release you . . . from . . ."

"Don't say it. Don't ever say it! I'm pregnant, Con, and I
love you."

"But you and he . . ."

"He saved me and Eric. And he was very lonely. I didn't
love him. But I never would have done this to him, truly I
wouldn't."

"I know." He took her in his arms.

"There's something else, Con. All the people with Jon are to
die."

"I don't understand."

"I am not sure that I do. But they are all doomed. I saw skulls
floating above all of them and dark shadows in the distance
with horned helmets like those riders there."

"Today's drama has affected your talent," he assured her.
"The important thing is that Jon Shannow is alive. And when
he comes here, he will be looking for you."

"Con, he will never understand. I think he is a little insane."

"I shall be ready."

The following day Shannow rose early, refreshed despite his
troubled night. He pulled on his woolen shirt and a thick
pullover knitted for him by Curopet. Then he added his ankle-
length leather coat and a pair of woolen gloves. He belted on
his guns and hefted his saddle over his right shoulder before
making his way across the village to the makeshift paddock
where the gelding stood. There he rubbed down the horse and
saddled him.

The day was bright and clear as Shannow rode from the
sleeping village. He steered the horse high into the hills to the
north, picking his trail with care on the slippery ground. After
an hour he found a different route and returned to the village,
where he fed the gelding and removed his saddle. He was cold
through and bone-weary. By the time he dumped his saddle

back in the hut, he was ready to drop. Shrugging out of his coat, he picked up the ball of hide and squeezed it two hundred times. Then, tossing it aside, he stood. His hand dropped to his pistol and flashed up, the gun leaping to his hand, cocked and ready. He smiled; not as fast as he had been but fast enough. The rest would follow.

Curopet tapped at his door, and he ushered her in. She had brought a wooden bowl of heated oats and goat's milk. He thanked her, and she bowed.

"I thought you had left us," she said softly, her eyes staring at the floor.

"Not yet, lady. But soon I must."

"To go to your wife?"

"Yes."

She smiled and left him, and he finished his breakfast and waited for Karitas. The old man was not long in arriving, his sheepskin jerkin covered in snow.

Karitas grinned and moved to the fire. "Did you see anything on your ride?"

"Four or five deer to the northeast and some beautiful country."

"And how do you feel?"

"Tired and yet strong."

"Good. I think you are almost mended, Jon Shannow. I heard someone cry out in the night—I thought it was you."

"It could have been," said Shannow, moving to sit beside the fire. "I had a bad dream. I saw men attacking a tent village . . . they were vile."

"They had horned helms?" asked Karitas, staring intently at Shannow's face.

"Yes. How could you know?"

"I had the same dream. It is the land, Jon. As I told you, it grants rare powers. That was no dream; you saw the Hellborn in action."

"Thank the Lord they are not near here!"

"Yes. My little village would be slain. We could not fight them, not even with the Ark weapons."

"One pistol," said Shannow, "would not keep away a small brigand band."

"There is more than one pistol in the Ark, Jon. I will show you in the spring."

"The Hellborn have many riders. There must have been two to three hundred in the attack on the village."

"Would that they had only three hundred. What we saw was one raiding column, and there are more than twenty such. The sexual excesses among the Hellborn mean a plethora of babes, and their tribe grows fast. It was always so throughout history: the migration of nations. Overpopulation causes people to move into the lands of their neighbors, bringing war and death. The Hellborn are moving, and one day they will be here."

"I find it hard to believe that the Lord of Hosts can permit such a people," said Shannow.

"Read your Bible, Jon. Study the Assyrians, the Babylonians, the Egyptians, and the Greeks. Even the Romans. And what of the Philistines, the Moabites, and the Edomites? Without evil there is no counterpoint to goodness."

"Too deep for me, Karitas. I am a simple man."

"I wish that I was," Karitas said with feeling.

For much of the day Shannow chopped firewood, using a long ax with a six-pound head. His back ached, but by dusk he was satisfied that his strength was returning with speed.

That night he dreamed once more of the Hellborn. This time they raided the Carns, and the slaughter was terrible to behold, the blue-and-yellow-streaked savages caught in a murderous cross fire. Hundreds died, and only a few escaped into the snow-covered woods.

At midnight Shannow was awakened by a light tapping at his door. He opened it and saw Curopet standing in the moonlight, a blanket around her slender form.

Shannow stepped aside to allow her in and pushed shut the door. She ran to the fire and added kindling to the coals.

"What is it, Curopet?"

"I am going to die," she whispered.

Her face was strained, and she was close to tears as Shannow moved to kneel beside her in the firelight.

"Everyone dies," said Shannow, at a loss.

"Then you have seen it, too, Thundermaker?"

"Seen what?"

"The horned ones attacking our village."

"No. The Carns have been attacked. Tonight."

"Yes, the Carns," she said dully. "I dreamed of that two nights ago. I am to die. No children for Curopet. No man through the long winter nights. We are all to die."

"Nonsense. The future is not set in stone; we make our own destinies," said Shannow, pulling her to him. The blanket slid away from her shoulders as she moved toward him, and he saw that she was naked, her body glowing in the dancing light of the blaze.

"Do you promise me that I will live?" she asked.

"I cannot promise, but I will defend you with my life."

"You would do that for me?"

"Yes."

"And I am not your wife?"

"No. But you are close to me, Curopet, and I do not desert my friends in their need."

Curopet snuggled into him, her breasts pushing against the bare skin of his chest. Shannow closed his eyes and drew back.

"Let me stay?" she asked, and he nodded and stood. She went with him to his blankets, and together they lay entwined. Shannow did not touch her, and she slept with her body pressed close to him and her head on his breast. Shannow slept not at all.

In the morning Shannow was summoned with all warriors to the long cabin, where Karitas sat on a high chair, the only chair in the village. The warriors—thirty-seven in all, counting Shannow—sat before him.

Karitas looked tired and gaunt. When everyone was seated, he spoke.

"Five of our ESPer women have seen an attack on us by the Hellborn. We cannot run, and we cannot hide. All our stores are here. Our lives are here. And we cannot fight, for they have thunder guns and are many." He fell silent and leaned forward, resting his arms on his knees, his head bent and his eyes staring at the floor.

"Then we are to die?" asked a warrior.

Shannow glanced at the man; he was stocky and powerful, and his eyes glowed fiercely. "It would appear that way, Shonal. I can think of nothing."

"How many are they?" asked Shonal.

"Three hundred."

"And all with thunder guns?"

"Yes."

"Why should they attack us?" questioned another man.

"It is their way."

"Could we not send someone to them?" suggested a third man. "Tell them we will be their friends, offer to share our food?"

"It will avail us nothing; they are killers and drinkers of blood. They have wiped out the Carns, and we are next."

"We must find their camp," said Shannow, standing and turning to face the men. "It is winter, and they must have tents and food stores. We will burn their tents, destroy their stores, and kill many. Perhaps then they will be driven back to their homelands until the spring."

"And will you lead us, Thundermaker?"

"Indeed I will," promised the Jerusalem Man.

With somber faces the men left the cabin to prepare their weapons and bid farewell to their wives and children. Shannow remained with Karitas.

"Thank you," said the old man, his head still bowed.

"You owe me no thanks, Karitas."

"I know you think me a little mad, but I am not stupid, Jon. There is no victory to be gained here. You have made a noble gesture, but my people will still die."

"Nothing is certain," Shannow told him. "When I rode the hills, I saw a number of shallow caves. Fetch the women and children and as many stores as they can carry and take them there. Cover your tracks where you can."

Karitas looked up. "You believe we have a chance?"

"It depends on whether this is an invasion or a raid."

"That I can tell you. It is the ritual of the Blood Feast, where newly ordained warriors gain their battle honors."

"You know a great deal about them, old man."

"Indeed I do. The man who leads them calls himself Abaddon, and I used to know him well."

"It is a name from the Book," said Shannow sharply. "An obscenity named in Revelation as the leader of the Devil's forces."

"Yes. Well, in those days he was simply Lawrence Welby, a lawyer and a socialite. He organized curious parties with nubile young women. He was witty, urbane, and a Satanist. He followed the teachings of a man called Crowley, who preached 'Do what thou wilt is the whole of the law.' Like me he survived the Fall, and like me he appears to be immortal. He believes he is the Antichrist."

"Maybe he is," said Shannow.

"He had a wife back then, a wonderful woman—like light and dark they were. I was a little in love with her myself; still am, for that matter."

"What happened to her?"

"She became a goddess, Shannow."

"Will Abaddon be with the raiders?"

"No, he will be in Babylon. They will be led by seasoned officers, though. I cannot see how my few people can oppose them. Do you have a plan?"

"Yes. I shall prime my weapons, and then I shall pray."

"I think you have your priorities right, at least," commented Karitas.

"They are only men, Karitas. They bleed, they die. And I cannot believe the Lord of Hosts will allow them to succeed."

As Shannow rose to leave, Karitas stopped him. He took the stone from his pouch and offered it to the taller man.

"Without it you may die. Take it with you."

"No. Keep it here. You may need its powers."

"It is almost used up, Shannow. You see, I refuse to feed it."

"How do you feed a stone?"

"With blood and death."

"Do not worry about me, Karitas. I will survive. Just get your people into the hills and keep that pistol primed."

Shannow returned to his hut and loaded his three spare cylinders, stowing them in his greatcoat pockets. Then he took the Bible from his saddlebag and turned to Jeremiah:

"Thus, saith the Lord, Behold, a people cometh from the north country and a great nation shall be raised from the sides of the earth. They shall lay hold on bow and spear; they are cruel, and have no mercy; their voice roareth like the sea, and they ride upon horses, set in array as men for war against thee . . ."

Shannow set aside the section and closed his eyes. In the distance thunder rolled across the heavens.

He rose and left the hut, his saddle on his right shoulder. In the open ground beyond thirty of the warriors awaited him with set faces, their quivers full of arrows.

"I will ride out and scout the land. Follow my tracks and wait for me where you see this sign." He made the sign of the Cross with his arms and then walked past them to the paddock.

Shannow headed east and did not once look back to see the warriors in single file loping behind him.

The country was open, and in places snow had drifted to a depth of more than ten feet. The gelding skirted the drifts and headed on toward the high ground and the distant timberline of the Carns' territory. Shannow had seen the attack on the Carns' village and guessed that the Hellborn would camp there overnight. If he was right, they now had two options: They could rest for the day at the site of their victory, or they could ride on immediately toward Karitas' village. If the former, Shannow's small band stood a chance. If the latter, the two parties would meet on open ground and the villagers would be massacred.

The day was icy cool, and a breeze was blowing from the north. Shannow shivered and gathered his coat at the collar. The gelding pushed on through the morning, and the distant trees grew steadily closer.

The crack of a pistol echoed in the air, and Shannow drew

on the reins and scanned the trees. He could see nothing, and
the distance was too great for the shot to have been aimed at
him. Warily he rode on. Several more shots sounded from the
woods: The Hellborn were hunting the last of the Carns.
Shannow grinned. The first danger was past.

At the foot of the last rise before the woods Shannow dismounted. He gathered two sticks and tied them in a cross,
which he thrust into a snowdrift; it would be many hours
before fresh falls of snow would cover it. Then he guided the
gelding up the rise and into the trees.

A blue-and-yellow-streaked figure hurtled from the snow-
covered bushes, saw Shannow, screamed, and fell as he
attempted to change the course of his flight. Then a horse leapt
the bush. Shannow's pistol fired as the animal landed, and the
helmed rider catapulted from the saddle. Shannow cocked the
pistol and waited, ignoring the cowering Carn, who was gazing
openmouthed at the dead Hellborn. The rider was obviously
alone, and Shannow dismounted, tying the gelding's reins to a
bush. He approached the corpse; the rider could not have been
more than fifteen years of age and was a handsome boy even
with the round hole in his forehead. Shannow knelt beside him,
lifting the boy's pistol. As Karitas had shown him, it was
loaded with cartridges. Shannow opened the rider's hip pouch;
there were more than twenty bullets there, and he transferred
them to his own pockets before thrusting the boy's pistol in his
belt. Then he turned to the Carn.

"Can you understand me?" asked Shannow.

The man nodded.

"I have come to kill the Hellborn."

The man edged close and spit into the dead rider's face.

"Where is your camp?" asked Shannow.

"By tall rocks," answered the savage, pointing northeast.

Shannow tethered the rider's horse beside his own and
moved forward on foot toward the northeast.

Three times riders came close to him, and twice he stumbled
across the bodies of dead Carns. After an hour he found a steep
path winding down into a sheltered glen. There he could see
the huts of the Carns, a picket line, and more than two hundred

horses. The Hellborn were wandering freely around the camp, stopping at cooking fires or talking in groups around larger blazes.

Shannow studied the area for some time and then eased his way back into the trees. Every so often a pistol shot caused him to freeze and drop to the ground, but he made his way back to his horse unobserved. The Carn had gone, but not before ripping out the eyes of the dead Hellborn . . . The boy did not look handsome now. Shannow was cold and sheltered behind the horses, huddled against a bush, waiting for the villagers. After an hour he moved to the edge of the trees and saw the group waiting stoically by the cross. One of them looked up and saw him, and he waved them to join him.

Shonal was the first to arrive. "They are camped?" he asked.

"Yes."

"When do we attack?"

"After midnight." Shonal nodded.

Shannow spotted Selah in the group and summoned him. "You should be back at the village."

"I am a man, Thundermaker."

"So was he," said Shannow, pointing to the corpse.

By dusk the pistol shots had ceased to sound, and Shannow had begun to believe he was freezing to death. The villagers seemed not to notice the cold, and he cursed his aging bones.

The moon rose in a clear sky, and toward midnight the bushes by Shannow's head parted and a warrior stepped into sight. Shannow rolled, his right-hand pistol sweeping up. The man was a Carn, and he squatted beside Shannow.

"I kill Hellborn also," he said.

The villagers were alarmed. Many had weapons in their hands, and several bows were bent and aimed at the newcomer. Shannow sheathed his pistol.

"You are welcome," he said.

The Carn lifted his hands to his lips and blew a soft humming note. All around them Carn warriors appeared, armed with knives and hatchets. Shannow could not count them in the dim light but guessed there were twice as many Carns as villagers.

"Now we kill Hellborn, yes?"

"No," replied Shannow. "We wait."

"Why wait?" asked the warrior.

"Many are still awake."

"Good. We follow you."

Shannow found the man's pointed teeth disconcerting.

Shonal crept to his side. "This is not right," he whispered, "to sit thus with Carns."

The Carn leader hissed and spit, his hand curling around his knife hilt.

"That's enough," said Shannow. "You may resume your war at a later time. One enemy is enough for today."

"I will follow you, Thundermaker, but this turns my stomach."

"He probably feels the same, Shonal. Be patient."

At midnight Shannow called the two leaders to him.

"They will have posted guards, and if they are disciplined, they will change the guard sometime soon. We must wait until the sentries are relieved and then kill those who remain. It must be silent—no screams, no shouts, no war cries. Once the shooting starts, you must flee. Bows and knives are no match for guns. You understand me?" Both leaders nodded.

"Also, we must steal as many of their horses as we can. Shonal, have Selah and several of the younger men assigned to that task. Tell them to head the horses west and wait for us about a mile away."

"What do we do when we have killed the sentries?" asked Shonal.

"We walk into the camp and kill them as they sleep. As each man dies, take his pistol and keep it ready. You know how to fire a pistol?" Both men shook their heads, and Shannow drew his own weapon and eased back the hammer. "Like this; then you point it and pull the trigger, here."

"I understand," said Shonal.

"I also," whispered the Carn.

"Good. Now take your best warriors and seek out the sentries. There should be four, but there might be six, all around the camp perimeter. When you have killed them all, return here with their pistols."

The Carn slid away, and Shonal remained. "It seems . . . unnatural," he whispered.

"I know." The villager vanished into the darkness.

Then began the long wait, and Shannow's nerves were strained to the limits. Every minute that passed he expected to hear a pistol shot or a scream. After what seemed an age the blue-yellow Carn leader appeared through the bushes.

"Eight men," he said, holding up two pistols, both cocked.

"Be careful," said Shannow, gently pushing the barrels away from his face.

He pushed himself to his feet, and his left knee cracked with a sound he felt rivaled the earlier thunder.

"Old bones," said the Carn, shaking his head.

Shannow scowled at him and moved off, the warriors following silently. They arrived at the camp just as the moon vanished behind a cloud. Shannow squatted on the rise above the huts with Shonal and the Carn beside him.

"Split your men into groups of six. It is important that we enter as many huts as possible at the same time. All the men with guns will fade back to that point there, by the stream. Now, at some point someone will wake up, or scream, or shoot. When that happens, run into the woods. Then the men with guns will open fire. But remember that each pistol fires only six times. You understand?" Both men nodded, but Shannow ran through the strategy twice more to ram it home.

Then he drew his hunting knife, and the warriors moved silently down the hill. Starting at the southern end of the village, they split into groups and entered the huts.

Shannow waited outside, eyes scanning the doorways and windows of the other dwellings. Gurgling cries came to him and some sounds of scuffling, but they were muted, and the warriors emerged from the huts bathed in blood.

Dwelling by dwelling the avengers moved on, and the night breeze brought the stench of death to Shannow's nostrils. He sheathed his unblooded knife and drew his pistols; their luck could not hold out much longer.

By the sixteenth hut Shannow's nerves were at the breaking point.

Then disaster struck. A warrior dragged back the hammer of a captured pistol while his finger was on the trigger, and the shot echoed around the camp. In an instant all was chaos as men surged into the night.

Shannow raised his pistols and rained shots into the milling crowd. Men fell screaming, and other pistols flared in the darkness. A shot from behind whistled past his ear, and he turned to see a tribesman vainly trying to recock his weapon. A bullet smashed the Carn from his feet. Shannow fired his left-hand pistol, and a Hellborn warrior toppled to the ground, his head crashing into the coals of the dying fire. With a flash his hair caught light and blazed around his face.

"Back!" shouted Shannow, but his voice was lost in the thunder of shots. He emptied his pistols into the ranks of the Hellborn and then sheathed them, drawing the captured weapon from his belt. He ran back toward the stream, where at least a dozen warriors had remembered his commands. Elsewhere in the camp the Carns had charged the Hellborn and were in among them, shooting their pistols point-blank but hampering Shannow's force.

"Back into the trees," Shannow ordered, but the men continued to fire at the milling mob. "Back, I say!" said Shannow, backhanding a man in the face. Hesitantly the warriors obeyed.

Shots screamed by Shannow as he ran, but none came close. At the top of the rise he stood with his back to a tree, breathing hard. Thrusting the captured revolver back into his belt, he took his own pistols and added fresh cylinders.

Shonal came alongside him. "Most of our men are here, Thundermaker."

"What of the horses?"

"I could not see."

"Without horses they will hunt us down before we are halfway home."

"Selah will have done what he can; the boy is no coward."

"All right," said Shannow. "Get your men out of the woods and head for home. If Selah has done his work well, there should be horses around a mile away. If there are, do not ride straight for the village but head north and then swing back when you reach firmer ground. Try to cover your tracks—and pray for snow."

Shonal grinned suddenly. "Many dead Hellborn," he stated.

"Yes. But was it enough? Go now."

Shannow reached his horse and mounted, wrenching free the reins. A Carn whom he recognized as the leader loomed out of the darkness. "I am Nadab," he said, holding out his hand.

Shannow leaned forward and gripped the man's wrist.

"No more war with the Corn People," said the Carn.

"That is good."

"Shame," corrected the man, grinning. "They taste good!"

"Good luck," said Shannow.

"We killed many, Thundermaker. You think they run now?"

"No."

"I also. It is the end of things for us."

"All things must end," said Shannow. "Why not come west, away from here?"

"No. We will not run. We are of the blood of the lions, and we will fight. We have many thunder guns now."

Shannow reached into his pocket, producing a cartridge.

"The thunder guns fire these," he said, "and you must gather these from the bodies. Pass me your pistol." Shannow took the weapon and flicked open the breech, emptying the spent shells one by one. Then he reloaded the weapon and handed it back.

Swinging the horse's head, Shannow rode to the west.

The Carn watched him go, then cocked the pistol and headed back toward his village.

◇ 5 ◇

SHANNOW RODE SOUTH for an hour before swinging his horse to the northwest. He did not know how many Hellborn had been killed in the night, and now he did not care; he was bone tired, and his muscles ached. He rubbed at his eyes and rode on. Once he could have gone for three days without sleep, but not now. After another hour Shannow began to doze in the saddle. Around him the snow was falling, the temperature dropping. Ahead was a grove of pine trees, and he steered the gelding in among them.

Dismounting near a group of young saplings, he took a ball of twine from his saddlebag. Painstakingly he pulled the saplings together, tying them tightly and creating the skeleton of a tepee. Moving slowly so as not to sweat too heavily, he gathered branches and wove them between the saplings to create a round hut that was open at the top. Then he led the gelding inside and packed snow over the branches until a solid wall surrounded him. Only then did he prepare a fire. His fingers were numb with cold, and the snow fell faster, adding to the walls of his dwelling. Once the fire was under way, he left the shelter and gathered dead wood, piling it across the opening. By dusk he felt strong enough to allow himself to sleep; he added three large chunks of wood to the fire, wrapped himself in his blankets, and lay down.

Far off the sound of gunfire echoed in the air, and his eyes flickered open but closed again almost immediately.

He slept without dreams for fourteen hours and awoke to a dead fire, but the snow had covered his shelter completely and he remained snug and warm in his blankets. He started a fresh fire and sat up. From his saddlebags he took some oatcakes, sharing them with the gelding.

By midday he was once more in the saddle and heading for the village. He arrived to see a smoking ruin and rode on toward the hills, his pistol in his hand.

In the late afternoon he approached the caves and saw the bodies. His heart sank, and he dismounted. Inside the women and children of the Corn People lay frozen in death. Shannow blinked hard and backed away. By the cave mouth he found Curopet, her eyes open, staring up at the sky. Shannow knelt beside her and closed her eyes.

"I am sorry, lady," he said. "I am so sorry."

He walked away from the corpses and remounted, steering the gelding down toward the plain.

There, nailed to a tree with his arms spread, was Karitas. The old man was still alive, but Shannow could not free him, for the nails were too deep. Karitas' eyes opened, and tears welled. Shannow looked away.

"They killed all my little ones," whispered Karitas. "All dead."

"I'll try to find something to cut you loose."

"No, I'm finished. They were looking for you, Shannow."

"Why?"

"They had orders to seek you out. Abaddon fears you. Oh, Jon, they killed my little ones."

Shannow drew his hunting knife and began to hack at the wood around Karitas' right hand, but it was tough and frozen and he could make no impression. Karitas began to weep and sob piteously. Shannow dropped his knife and put his hands on Karitas' face. He could not embrace him.

"Jon?"

"Yes, my friend."

"Read me something from the Book."

"What would you like to hear?"

"Psalm 22."

Shannow fetched his Bible, found the passage, and began to read: *My God, My God, why hast thou forsaken me, why are thou so far from helping me, and from the words of my roaring . . . "* Shannow read on until he reached the verse: *"The assembly of the wicked have inclosed me: They pierced my hands and feet. I may tell all my bones: They look and stare upon me."* Shannow stopped reading, and the tears ran down his cheeks and dropped to the pages.

Karitas closed his eyes, and his head fell forward. Shannow went to him, and the old man rallied briefly, but Shannow watched the light of life go out of his bright eyes. He stumbled to his Bible and lifted it from the snow, brushing it clean. Returning to the old man, he read: *"The Lord is my Shepherd; I shall not want. He maketh me to lie down in green pastures: he leadeth me beside the still waters. He restoreth my soul. He leadeth me in the paths of righteousness for his name's sake. Yea, though I walk through the valley of the Shadow of Death I will fear no evil, for thou art with me . . ."* He could read no more.

Shannow screamed in his anguish, and his voice echoed in the hills. He fell to his knees in the snow and covered his face with his hands.

The boy Selah found him there at dusk, half-frozen and semicoherent. He pulled him to his feet and took him to a small cave, where he lit a fire. After a while Shannow slept. Selah led the horses into the cave and covered the Jerusalem Man with a blanket.

Shannow awoke in the night. Selah was sitting staring into the fire.

"Where are the men?"

"All dead," Selah said.

"How?"

"I took the horses as you said and headed them west. Shonal and the others joined me there, and we went north, as you ordered. There we ran into another group of Hellborn; they must have split up and attacked our women even as we were attacking their camp. They caught us in the open ground, and their guns cut into us; I was at the back, and I wheeled my horse and ran like a coward."

"Dying is a poor way of proving your courage, Selah."

"They have destroyed us, Thundermaker. All my people are gone."

"I know, boy. There are no words to ease the grief."

"Why? Why would they just kill? There is no reason. Even the Carns killed for food. Why should these Hellborn cause such pain?"

"There is no answer," said Shannow. "Get some sleep, lad. Tomorrow we will set out to find my people."

"You will take me with you?"

"If you would like to come."

"Will we hunt the Hellborn?"

"No, Selah. We will avoid them."

"I want to kill them all."

"I can understand that, but one man and a boy cannot change the face of the world. One day they will lose. God will not allow them to persevere and prosper."

"Your God did not protect my people," said Selah.

"No, but he kept you alive. And me."

Shannow lay back, pillowing his head on his arms and staring at the fire shadows on the ceiling of the cave. He recalled Karitas' warning that the Hellborn were looking for him and puzzled at it. Why? What had he done to make them hunt him? Why should an army seek him?

He closed his eyes and drifted into sleep, dreaming that he floated above a great building of stone at the center of a dark, dreary city. Sounds like great hammers on giant anvils boomed in the night, and crowds milled around taverns and squares. Shannow floated down to the stone building and saw statues of horned and scaled demons beside a long stairway leading up to doors of oak. He moved up the stairway, passing through the closed doors and into a hall lined with the carved shapes of dragons and lizards. A circular staircase led to an observatory where a long telescope pointed to the stars and several men in red robes were working with quill and parchment. Shannow floated by them. At another door two guards stood, holding rifles across their chests. Passing them, he entered a room lit with red candles.

There sat a man studying maps. He was handsome, with

dark hair graying at the temples. His nose was long and straight, his mouth full and sensual, and his eyes gray and humorous.

He was wearing a white shirt, gray trousers, and shoes of snakeskin. He stiffened as Shannow floated behind him, and then he rose.

"Welcome, Mr. Shannow," he said, turning and staring directly up at him. His eyes were mocking now, and Shannow felt fear rising toward terror as a dark cloud coalesced around the man and rose toward him. The Jerusalem Man moved back, and the cloud took form. A huge bloated head, horned and scaled, and a cavernous mouth rimmed with pointed teeth gaped before him. Arms grew from the cloud, and taloned fingers reached out toward him . . . He fled to his body and awoke sweating, jerking up from his blankets and stifling a scream. His eyes swept around the cave past the sleeping Selah and the two horses. Fighting down his panic, Shannow drew his right-hand pistol from the scabbard beside his head. The gun was cold in his hand.

He lay back and closed his eyes, and instantly the demon was upon him, its talons tearing at him. Again he awoke, shaking with terror. Calming himself, he prayed long and earnestly; then he sheathed his pistol, crossed his arms, and slept.

Once more he was above the stone building with the demon racing toward him. He raised his hands, and two shining swords appeared there. He sped toward the demon, and the swords flashed into its bloated body. Talons ripped at him, but he ignored them, slashing and cutting in a maniacal frenzy. The beast was forced back, and in its blood-red eyes Shannow saw the birth of fear. Rearing up, the Jerusalem Man plunged his swords into its face. Smoke writhed up from the wounds, and the beast disappeared.

In its place floated the handsome man wearing a robe of purest white.

"I underestimated you, Mr. Shannow," he said.

"Who are you?"

"I am Abaddon. You should know the name."

"The name is in the Book of Revelation," said Shannow. "The angel of the bottomless pit. You are not he. You are merely a man."

"Who is to say, Mr. Shannow? If a man does not die, then he is divine. I have lived for 346 years, thanks to the lord of this world."

"You serve the serpent," stated Shannow.

"I serve the one who conquered. How can you be such a fool, Mr. Shannow? Armageddon is over, and where is the New Jerusalem? Where does the wolf sit down with the lamb? Where does the lion eat straw like the cattle? Nowhere, Mr. Shannow. The world died, and your god died with it. You and I are the opposite extremes of the new order. My land flourishes; my armies can conquer the world. And you? You are a lonely man wandering the world like a shadow, unwelcome and unwanted—just like your god."

Shannow felt the weight of truth bear down on him like a rock, but he said nothing.

"Lost for words, Mr. Shannow? You should have listened to old Karitas. He had the chance to join me over a century ago, but he preferred to live in the woods like some venerated hermit. Now he is dead, quite poetically so, and his grubby people died with him. You will be next, Mr. Shannow, unless you would prefer to join the Hellborn."

"There is no inducement under the stars that could tempt me to join you," answered Shannow.

"Is there not? What about the life of Donna Taybard?"

Shannow blinked in shock and drew back. The handsome man laughed.

"Oh, Mr. Shannow, you are truly not worth my enmity. You are the gnat in the ear of the elephant. Go away and die somewhere." He lifted his hand, and Shannow was catapulted away at dizzying speed.

He awoke and groaned. Reaching for his Bible, by the dawn light he searched in vain for a passage to lift the rock from his soul.

Shannow and Selah rode from the lands of the Corn People,

heading north across a great plain. For weeks they rode and camped in sheltered hollows, seeing no sign of man. Shannow remained silent and subdued, and Selah respected his solitude. The young man would sit in the evenings watching Shannow pore over his Bible, seeking guidance and finding none.

One night Shannow put aside the Book and leaned back, staring at the stars. The horses were hobbled nearby, and a small fire blazed brightly.

"The age of miracles is past," said Shannow.

"I have never seen a miracle," replied Selah.

Shannow sat up and rubbed his chin. Their diet had been meager for over a week, and the Jerusalem Man was gaunt and hollow-eyed.

"A long time ago the Lord of Hosts split a sea asunder so that his people could cross it as dry land. He brought water from rocks, and he sent his Angel of Death against the enemy. In those days his prophets could call upon him, and he would grant them dazzling powers."

"Maybe he is dead," said Selah. "Or sleeping," he added swiftly, seeing the glare in Shannow's eyes.

"Sleeping? Yes, perhaps he is sleeping. Curopet came to me and said she would die. 'No man for Curopet through the long winter nights.' I wanted to save her; I wanted so much to be able to say, 'There, Curopet, the nightmare has been proved false.' I prayed so hard." He fell silent and sat staring at his hands.

"We did what we could," said Selah. "We killed many Hellborn."

"Rocks in the lake," muttered Shannow. "Perhaps she was right. Perhaps it is all predestined and we stalk through life like puppets."

"What does it matter, Thundermaker? As long as we do not know."

"It matters to me; it matters desperately to me. Just once I would like to feel that I have done something for my God, something for which I can feel pride. But his face is turned from me, and my prayers are like whispers in the wind."

Shannow wrapped himself in his blankets and slept fitfully.

At midmorning they spotted a small herd of antelope. Shannow kicked the gelding into a run and brought down a young doe with a shot to the heart. Dismounting, he cut the beast's throat, standing back as the blood drained into the soft earth. Then he skinned and quartered the doe, and the two riders feasted well.

Two days later Shannow and Selah came out of the plain into an area of wooded hills.

To the north was a mountain range taller than any Shannow had ever seen, rearing up into the low scudding clouds. The mountains lifted Shannow's spirits, and he told Selah he would like to see them at close range.

The color drained from the boy's face. "We cannot go there," he whispered. "It is death, believe me."

"What do you know of this place?"

"All the ghosts gather there. And monsters who can devour a herd of buffalo at a single sitting; the earth shakes when they move. My father came close to this place many years ago. No one travels there."

"Believe me, Selah, I have traveled widely; I have seen few monsters, and most of those were human in origin. I am going there."

Shannow touched his heels to the gelding's sides and rode on without a backward glance, but Selah remained where he was, his eyes fearful, his heart pounding. Shannow had saved his life, and Selah regarded himself as a debtor; he needed to repay the Jerusalem Man to be freed from obligation. Yet every ounce of his being screamed against this venture, and the two opposing forces of his intellect and his emotions left him frozen in the saddle.

Without turning, Shannow lifted his hand and beckoned the boy to join him. It was all Selah needed to swing the balance, and he kicked his horse into a run and rode alongside the Thundermaker.

Shannow grinned and slapped him on the shoulder. It was the first time Selah had seen him smile in weeks. Was it a form of madness? Selah wondered. Did the prospect of danger and death somehow bring this man to life?

They rode along a deer trail that wound high into the hills, where the air was fresh with the smell of pine and new grass. A lion roared in the near distance, and Selah could picture it leaping on its prey, for the roar had been the blood-freezing attack cry that paralyzed the victim. Selah's horse shied, and he calmed it with soft words. A shot followed, echoing in the hills. Shannow's Hellborn pistol appeared in his hand, and he steered his gelding toward the sound. Selah tugged Shannow's percussion pistol from his own belt and followed, but he did not cock the pistol, nor had he handled it since Shannow had given it to him on the morning they had left Karitas' grave. The weapon terrified him yet gave him strength, and he kept it in his belt more as a talisman than as a death-dealing thundermaker.

Selah followed Shannow over a steep rise and down a slope toward a narrow glen. Ahead the boy could see a man on the ground, a black-maned lion straddling him. The man's right hand was gripping the lion's mane, keeping its jaws from ripping his throat, while his left hand plunged a knife time and again into the beast's side.

Shannow galloped alongside, dragged on the reins, and, as the gelding reared, fired a shot into the lion's head. The animal slumped over the body of his intended victim, and the man pulled himself clear. His black leather trousers were torn at the thigh, and blood was seeping through; his face had been deeply cut, and the flesh hung in a dripping fold over his right cheek. Pushing himself to his feet, he sheathed his knife. He was a powerful man with wide shoulders and a deep chest, and he sported a forked black trident beard.

Ignoring his rescuers, he staggered to a spot some yards away and retrieved his revolver, which he placed in a leather scabbard at his side. He stumbled but recovered and turned at last to Shannow.

"It was a fine shot," he said, "though had it been a fraction off, it would have killed me rather than the lion."

Shannow did not reply, and Selah saw that his gun was still in his hand and trained on the wounded man. Then the boy saw why. To the man's right was his helm, and on it were the goat's horns of the Hellborn.

Suddenly the man staggered and pitched to the ground. Selah sprang from his horse and ran to him. The wound in the thigh was gushing blood, and Selah drew his knife and cut away the trouser leg, exposing a deep rip almost a foot long.

"We must stop this bleeding," he told Shannow, but the Jerusalem Man remained on his horse. "Give me a needle and thread," said Selah. Shannow blinked, then reached into his saddlebag and passed a leather pouch to the boy.

For almost an hour Selah worked on the wounds, finally pushing back the folds of skin on the man's cheek and stitching them in place. Meanwhile, Shannow had dismounted and unsaddled their horses. He said nothing but prepared a fire within a circle of stones, having first ripped away the grass around it. Selah checked the wounded man's pulse; it was weak but steady.

He joined Shannow by the fire, leaving the man wrapped in his blankets.

"Why?" asked Shannow.

"Why what?"

"Why did you save him?"

"I do not understand," said Selah. "You saved him by killing the lion."

"I did not then know what he was . . . what he is."

"He is a man," stated Selah.

"He is your enemy, boy. He may even have been the man who killed Curopet or nailed Karitas to the tree."

"I shall ask him when he wakes."

"And what will that tell you?"

"If he did attack my village, I shall tend him until he is well and then we will fight."

"That is nonsense, boy."

"Perhaps, but Karitas always taught us to follow our feelings, especially compassion. I want to kill the Hellborn—I said that on the day we found our people. But this is different. This is one brave man who fought a lion with only a knife. Who knows? He might have won without you."

Shannow shook his head. "I don't understand. You went into the Hellborn camp and slew them while they slept. Where is the difference?"

"I did that to save my people. I failed. I have no regrets about the men I slew, but I cannot slay this one—not yet."

"Then step aside and I'll put a bullet in his ear."

"No," said the boy forcefully. "His life is now mine, as mine is yours."

"All right," said Shannow. "I will argue no more. Maybe he will die in the night. Did you at least take his gun?"

"No, he did not," said a voice, and Selah turned to see that the wounded man had raised himself on his elbow with his pistol pointed at Shannow. The Jerusalem Man lifted his head, his eyes glittering in the firelight, and Selah saw that he was about to draw his own weapons.

"No!" he shouted, stepping between them. "Put your pistol down," he told the Hellborn.

Their eyes met, and the man managed a weak smile. "He's right, boy. You are a fool," he said as he slowly uncocked the pistol and lay back. Selah swung toward Shannow, but the Jerusalem Man was walking away to sit on a rock some distance from the fire, his Bible in his hands. Selah, who normally left him alone at such times, approached him warily, and Shannow looked up and smiled gently. Then, under the moon's silver light, he began to read. At first Selah had difficulty understanding certain words, but overall the story fell into place. It seemed that a man was robbed and left for dead and that several people passed him by, offering no help. At last another man came and helped him, carrying him to a place of rest. This last man, Shannow explained, was from a people who were hated and despised.

"What does it mean, then?" Selah asked.

"I think it means that there is good in all men. Yet you have added a fresh twist to the parable, for you have rescued the Samaritan. I hope you do not come to regret it."

"What is the Book?"

"It is the history of a people long dead, and it is the word of God through the ages."

"Does it give you peace, Shannow?"

"No, it torments me."

"Does it give you power?"

"No, it weakens me."

"Then why do you read it?"

"Because without it there is nothing but a meaningless existence of pain and sorrow ending in death. For what would we strive?"

"To be happy, Shannow. To raise children and know joy."

"There has been very little joy in my life, Selah. But one day soon I will taste it again."

"Through your god?"

"No—through my woman."

Batik lay back, feeling the pull of the stitches and the weakness he knew came from loss of blood. He had no idea why the boy wanted him saved or why the man had agreed to it. And yet he lived, and that was enough for now. His horse had reared when the lion had roared, and Batik had managed just one shot as it had leapt. The shot had creased its side, and then he had been catapulted from the saddle. He could not remember drawing his knife, but he recalled with brilliant clarity the arrival of the hard-eyed man on the steeldust gelding, and he had registered even as the gun was aimed that it was a Hellborn pistol.

Now, as he lay under the stars, it was no great work of the intellect to come up with the obvious answer: The man had been one of those who had attacked Cabrik's feasters some weeks back, killing over eighty young men in a single night . . . which made his acquiescence in allowing Batik to live all the more curious.

While he was thinking, the boy Selah approached him. "How are your wounds?"

"You did well. They will heal."

"I am preparing some broth. It will help make more blood for you."

"Why? Why do you do this for me?"

Selah shrugged, unwilling to enter a debate.

"I was not in the attack on your village," said Batik, "though I easily could have been."

"Then you tell me, Hellborn, why they wanted to kill my people."

"Our priests could answer that better than I. We are the chosen people. We are ordered to inhabit the lands and kill every man, woman, and child we find. The priests say that this is to ensure the purity of our faith."

"How can a babe in arms affect your faith?"

"I don't know. Truly. I never killed a babe or a child, though I saw it done. Ask our priests when you meet one."

"It is savagery beyond my understanding," Selah said.

"My name is Batik," said the man. "And you?"

"Selah."

"And your friend?"

"He is Shannow, the Thundermaker."

"Shannow. I have heard the name."

"He is a great soul and a mighty warrior. He slew many of your people."

"And now he is hunted in turn."

"By you?"

"No," said Batik. "But the Lord Abaddon has declared him unholy, and that means he must burn. Already the Zealots are riding, and they have great powers; they will find him."

"When they do, Batik, he will slay them."

Batik smiled. "He is not a god, Selah. The Zealots will bring him down even as they brought me down."

"You are hunted?"

"I need some sleep. We will talk tomorrow."

Batik awoke early, the pain from his wounds pulling him from a troubled sleep. Overhead the sky was clear, and a black crow circled, banking and wheeling. He sat up, wincing as the stitches pulled at the wound in his face. Shannow was awake, sitting still in the dawn light and reading from a leather-covered book with gold-trimmed pages. Batik saw the tension in the man and the way his right hand rested barely inches from the pistol that lay beside him on the rock. Batik resisted the urge to smile; the stitches were too painful.

"You are awake early," he said, lifting the blankets from his legs.

Shannow slowly closed the book and turned. His eyes met Batik's, and the look was glacial. Batik's face hardened.

"I was hoping," said Shannow tonelessly, "that you would die in the night."

Batik nodded. "Before we enter into a prolonged debate on your views, perhaps you would care to know that we are being watched and that within a short time we will be hunted."

"There is no one watching us," said Shannow. "I scouted earlier."

Batik smiled in spite of the pain. "You have no conception, Shannow, of the nature of the hunters. We are not talking about mere men. Those who hunt us are the Zealots, and they ride under the name of the Hounds of Hell. If you look up, you will see a crow. It does not land or scavenge for food; it merely circles us, directing those who follow.

"The lion yesterday was possessed by a Zealot. It is a talent they have; it is why they are deadly."

"Why would you warn me?" asked Shannow, flicking his eyes to take in the crow's flight.

"Because they are hunting me also."

"Why should they?"

"I am not religious, Shannow, and I tried to ruin the midwinter offering. But all that is past. Just accept that I am—as you—an enemy to the Zealots."

Selah groaned and sat up. On a rock a reptilian creature with slavering jaws sat over the body of Shannow. Selah drew his pistol and cocked it. The monster's eyes turned on him, red as blood, as he pointed the pistol.

"What are you doing?" asked Shannow.

Selah blinked as the image shifted and blurred. His finger tightened on the trigger, but at the last second he twisted the barrel. The shot echoed in the hills, and a shell whistled past Shannow's ear. Selah eased back the hammer for a second shot, but Batik had moved behind him. With a swift chop to the neck with the blade of his hand, Batik stunned the boy and retrieved the pistol.

Shannow had not moved. "Is he all right?" he asked.

"Yes. The Zealots work well with the young; their minds are more malleable."

Shannow drew his pistol and cocked it, and Batik froze. The Jerusalem Man tipped back his head, his arm lifted, and he fired. The crow exploded in a burst of flesh and feathers.

Shannow opened the pistol's breech, removed the spent casing, and reloaded the weapon. Then he walked to Selah, kneeling by him and turning him over. The boy's eyelids fluttered and opened; he saw Shannow and jerked.

"You are dead!" he said, struggling to rise.

"Lie still, boy. I am fine."

"I saw a monster over your body. I tried to scare it away."

"There was no monster," Shannow tried to explain, but the boy could not comprehend and Batik stepped in.

"It was magic, Selah. You were fooled by the hunters."

"Magic?"

"Yes. They cast a spell that confused your eyes. It is unlikely they will try again through you, but they may. Be wary and shoot at nothing." He handed the pistol to the boy and then sagged back on the ground, his face gleaming with sweat.

Shannow watched him closely. "You are a powerful man," he said, "but you lost a lot of blood. You need rest."

"We cannot stay here," said Batik.

"From which direction will they be coming?" asked Shannow.

"Northeast," said Batik. "But do not go up against them, Shannow."

"It is my way. How many are there?"

Batik shrugged. "There could be six or sixty. Whatever, they will travel in multiples of six; it is a mystic number."

"Stay here and rest. I will return."

Shannow walked to his saddle and hefted it, making his way toward the steeldust gelding, which was hobbled some thirty feet from the camp. As Shannow approached, he saw horseflies settling on the gelding's hindquarters, yet the animal's tail was still. Shannow slowed his walk, and the gelding dipped its head and watched him. Shannow approached the beast from the left and laid the saddle on its back, stooping to tighten the cinch. The gelding did not move, and Shannow was sweating now. Gripping the bridle tightly in his right hand, he loosed the slipknot hobbling the horse. As the rope fell away, the gelding bunched its muscles to rear and Shannow grabbed the pommel and vaulted into the saddle. The gelding reared up and set off at a dead run, but Shannow maneuvered his feet into the stirrups and held on. The gelding stopped and bucked furiously, but Shannow wrenched its head back toward the camp. Suddenly the horse rolled over; Shannow leapt from the saddle and, as the beast came upright, mounted swiftly.

At the camp Batik watched in admiration as the clash of wills continued. The horse bucked, jumped, twisted, and rolled time and again, but always Shannow held on. As suddenly as it had started, it was over and the gelding stopped, its head down and steam billowing from its nostrils. Shannow walked it back to the camp and dismounted, hobbling the animal once more. He unsaddled the beast and wiped it down, then stroked its neck and ears.

Hefting his saddle, he made his way to Selah's horse and without drama saddled it and headed northeast.

Batik relaxed as Shannow crested the hill and lay back on the grass.

"Whatever else, he is a fine rider."

"He is the Thundermaker," said Selah with pride. "He will return."

"It would be pleasant to think so," replied Batik, "but he has never come up against the Zealots. I have seen their handiwork, and I am under no illusion as to their skill."

Selah smiled and moved to the deer meat, hacking slices for the morning stew. Batik, he thought, was a clever man, but he had never seen Shannow in action.

Six miles to the northeast a small group of riders drew rein and studied the hills ahead. The leader—a slender young man, hawk-nosed and dark-eyed—turned to his companion.

"Are you recovered?" he asked.

"Yes, Donai, but I am exhausted. How could he remain in the saddle? I all but killed the horse."

"He rides well. I wish I knew more about him and his connection with Batik." Donai swiveled in the saddle, his gaze resting on the two corpses draped across their horses' backs. Xenon had possessed the lion, and Cheros the crow. Both had been slain by the long-haired rider.

Donai dismounted. "I will seek guidance," he said. The other three riders sat in silence as their leader knelt on the grass with a round red-gold stone cupped in his hands. For some time he remained motionless. Then he rose.

"Achnazzar says that the man is Shannow, the Jerusalem seeker. He is sending more men, and we are to wait here."

The men dismounted and removed their cloaks of black leather and dark helms.

"Which six are they sending?" asked Parin, the youngest of the riders.

"They are sending six sections; I did not ask which," replied Donai.

"Thirty-six men!" queried Parin. "To tackle two men and a boy?"

"You wish to question Achnazzar's judgment?" Donai asked softly.

"No," Parin replied swiftly.

"No," agreed Donai, "that is very wise. The man Shannow is a great evil, and always there is strength in that. He is unholy and a servant of the old dark god. He must be destroyed. Achnazzar says he carries a Bible."

"It is said that to touch a Bible burns the hand and scars the soul," put in another rider.

"It could be, Karim. I don't know. Achnazzar says to kill the man and his horse and to burn his saddlebags without opening them."

"I have often wondered," said Parin, "how this book survived Armageddon."

"There is evil everywhere," replied Donai. "When the old dark god was destroyed, his body sundered and fell to the earth like rain, and where it touched, it polluted the land. Never be surprised at the places where evil dwells."

"You can say that again," said Karim, a lean middle-aged rider with a gray beard. "I would have staked my life on Batik; there was no finer warrior among the Hellborn."

"Your use of the word 'fine' is questionable, Karim," said Donai. "The man was unholy, but he hid the darkness within himself. But the Lord Satan has ways of illuminating the dark corners of the soul, and I think it was no coincidence that Batik's sister was chosen for the midwinter sacrifice."

"I believe that," said Parin, "but what did he hope to gain by asking Shalea to flee with him?"

"A good question, Parin. He underestimated the holiness of his sister. She was naturally proud to be chosen, and when his evil touched her, she went straight to Achnazzar. A fine woman who now serves the Lord!"

"But how could he underestimate her holiness?" persisted Parin.

"Evil is not logical. He thought she desired an earthly life, and his blasphemy was his unbelief. He thought her doomed and sought to save her."

"And now he is with the Jerusalem Man," remarked Karim.

"Evil invites evil," said Donai.

Toward noon, as the four riders ate an early meal, the sky darkened as heavy black-edged clouds masked the sun. Lightning forked in the east, and thunder cannoned deafeningly across the heavens.

"Mount up!" shouted Donai. "We'll head for the trees."

The men scrambled to their feet, moving toward their horses. Then Donai lifted his cloak and froze. Standing at the edge of their camp, his long coat flapping in the storm winds, was the long-haired rider. Donai dragged his pistol clear of its scabbard, but a white-hot hammer smashed into his chest and drove him back against his horse. Karim, hearing the shot, dived for the ground, but Parin and the other rider died where they stood as Shannow's pistols flowered in flame. Karim rolled and fired, his shot cutting Shannow's collar. The Jerusalem Man dropped to the grass, and Karim fired twice

more, but there was no return fire. Edging sideways, Karim hid
behind Donai's body and closed his eyes. His spirit rose and
entered the mind of his horse. From this high vantage point
Karim scanned the area, but there was no sign of the attacker.
He moved the horse's head and saw his own body lying behind
Donai.

Shannow rose from the long grass behind Karim's body, his
pistol pointed. Karim's spirit flew from the horse straight into
Shannow's mind, and the Jerusalem Man staggered as pain
flooded his brain and bright lights exploded behind his eyes.
Then darkness followed, and Shannow found himself in a
tunnel deep in the earth. Scuffling noises came to him, and
giant rats issued from gaping holes in the walls, their teeth as
long as knives.

On the edge of panic Shannow closed his inner eyes,
blocking the nightmare. He could feel the hot breath of the rats
on his face, feel their teeth tearing at his skin. Slowly he
opened his eyes, ignoring the huge rodents and looking beyond
them. As if through a mist, he could see horses and before them
two bodies. Shannow lifted his hand and aimed his pistol.

The pistol became a snake that reared back, sinking its teeth
into his wrist. Shannow ignored the snake and tightened his
grip on the pistol butt he no longer felt. The gun bucked in
his hand.

Karim fled for his body, arriving just as the second shell
entered his skull. He twitched once and was still.

Shannow fell to his knees and looked around him. Four
corpses littered the grass, and two others were draped across
two saddled horses. Shannow blinked.

*"Do I not hate them, O Lord, that hate thee? And am I not
grieved with those that rise up against thee? I hate them with a
perfect hatred. I count them mine enemies."*

He gathered their weapons and ammunition and then
searched the bodies. Each of the men carried a small stone, the
size of a sparrow's egg, in a pouch around his neck. The stones
were red-gold in color and veined with black. Shannow pocketed them and then led the horses back to his own and returned
to the campsite.

Batik was huddled under his blankets as the rain doused the fire. Shannow called Selah to him.

"Let us get back to the trees and out of this weather," he said as the wind picked up and the sky darkened.

Batik did not move. "What happened out there?" he called.

"I killed them. Now, let's get out of the rain."

"How many were there?"

"Four. Two others were already dead."

"But how can I know that? How do I know you are still Shannow?" The blanket fell away, and Shannow found himself staring down the muzzle of the Hellborn's pistol.

"How can I prove it to you?"

"Name your God."

"Jehovah, Lord of Hosts."

"And what of Satan?"

"The fallen star, the Prince of Lies."

"I believe you, Shannow. No Hellborn could blaspheme like that!"

Beneath the spreading pine on the hillside the strength of the rain lessened, and Shannow struggled to light a fire. He gave up after some minutes and placed his back against a tree.

Batik sat nearby, his face gray, dark rings beneath his eyes. "You are in pain?" asked Selah.

"A little. Tell me, Shannow, did you search the bodies?"

"Yes."

"Did you find anything of interest?"

"What did you have in mind?"

"Small leather pouches, containing stones."

"I took all six."

"Let me have them, would you?"

"For what purpose, Batik?"

"My own was taken from me before I escaped, and without it these wounds will take weeks to heal. It may be that I can use another."

Shannow took the pouches from his greatcoat pocket and dropped them into Batik's lap. One by one the Hellborn took the stones in his hand, closing his eyes in concentration.

Nothing happened until he reached the fifth stone; it glowed briefly, and Batik smiled.

"It was worth a try," he said. "But when you kill the man, you break the power. Still, it eased the pain before it faded." He hurled the stones aside.

"Where do you get those things?" asked Shannow.

"They are birth gifts from Lord Abaddon; the size of the stone depends on your station. We call them Satanseeds."

"Where are they from?"

"Who knows, Shannow? It is said that Satan delivers them to Abaddon at Walpurnacht, the Eve of Souls."

"You believe that?"

"I disbelieve nothing. It's usually safer that way."

Selah picked up a loose stone and twirled it in his hands.

"It's very pretty," he said, "and it feels warm to the touch, but I would prefer a fire."

The wet kindling Shannow had set burst into flames, and Selah leapt back, dropping the stone, which glowed like a lantern.

"Nicely done, boy," said Batik. "Now take the stone and hold it over my wounds." Selah did as he was told, but the glowing faded and the stone grew cold.

"Still, we have a fire," grunted Batik.

Shannow awoke with a start, his heart pounding. He sat up and looked around him. The cave was warm and snug, and a fire blazed brightly against the far wall. He relaxed and settled back.

Cave?

He jerked upright and reached for his guns, but they were not with him. He had gone to sleep alongside Batik and Selah in a wood by a narrow stream. And he had awakened here, weaponless.

A shadow moved, and a man approached the fire and sat down facing him.

It was the handsome, silver-templed Abaddon, Lord of the Hellborn.

"Do not be alarmed, Mr. Shannow. I merely wished to talk."

"We have nothing to talk about."

"Surely that is not true. With my hunters closing in?"

"Let them come."

"Such arrogance, Mr. Shannow. Think you to slay all my men with your pitiful pistols?"

Shannow said nothing, and Abaddon warmed his hands at the fire. He was wearing a dazzling white robe that glistened gold in the firelight.

"A man, a boy, and a traitor," whispered Abaddon, "set against a newborn nation of lusty warriors. It is almost comic." His eyes met Shannow's. "You know, I have lived for almost as long as your friend Karitas, and I have seen many things both in my old world and in this new, squalling infant. There are no heroes, Mr. Shannow. Ultimately we all compromise and secure for ourselves a little immortality, or a little wealth, or a little pleasure. There are no longer any Galahads; indeed, I wonder if there ever were."

"I've never heard of a Galahad," said Shannow.

"He was a knight, Mr. Shannow, a warrior who was said to fight for God. He never succumbed to women or any pleasures of the flesh, and he was allowed to find the Holy Grail. It is a pleasant tale for children, though not Hellborn children."

"What do you want from me?"

"I want you to die, Mr. Shannow. To cease to be."

"Why?"

"On a whim, perhaps. It has been said that you are a danger to me. I cannot see it, but I accept that the evidence suggests some truth to the fear."

"You do not interest me," said Shannow. "You have nothing that I want. Where is the danger?"

"Who knows?" replied Abaddon, smiling smoothly. "You are a thorn in my side, and I need to pluck it out and throw it on the fire."

"Then bring on your demons," said Shannow, rising to his feet.

Abaddon chuckled and shook his head. "I tried that, Mr. Shannow, and you hurt me. Truly. But then, what are my demons compared with yours?"

"I have no demons."

"No? What drives you to seek a buried city? Why do you cling to your superstitions? Why do you fight your lonely battles?"

"I will find Jerusalem," said Shannow softly. "Alive or dead, I will find my way home."

"Home? What did you say to the delightful Fray Taybard? A rock in a lake? The ripples fade, and all is as it was. Yes, you need to find a way home." Abaddon lifted a stick and laid it gently on the fire. "You know, Mr. Shannow, many of my men are just like you, especially among the Zealots. They worship their god with a pure heart, and they would die gladly for him. Men like you are as leaves in the autumn. You are a Bible-reading man. I am surprised you have not yet seen it."

"This is nothing like the Hellborn in my Bible," whispered Shannow.

"Mr. Shannow! Is not lying a sin? I refer you to Joshua and the Israelite invasion of Canaan. Every man, woman, and child in thirty-two cities was slain under the express orders of your god. How are the Hellborn different? Don't bother to answer; there is no difference. I founded the Hellborn two and a half centuries ago, and I have built the nation along the same lines as Israel. I now have a fanatic army and a people fired with a zeal you could not imagine. And they have had their miracles, their parting of the Red Sea, the healings, and the unimaginable wonders of magic.

"In some ways your position is amusing. You are the man of God among a nation of devil worshipers. And yet you are the unholy one; you are the vampire in the night. Stories of you will one day be told to Hellborn children to keep them quiet in their beds."

Shannow scowled. "Everything you say is an obscenity."

"Indeed it is—by your lights. By the way, did you know that Donna Taybard is now living on the edge of my lands?"

Shannow sat very still.

"She and her husband—a worthy man by the name of Griffin—have settled on the lands to the west. Good farmland. They could even prosper."

"Why do you lie?" asked Shannow. "Is it because your master is unable to face truth?"

"I do not need to lie, Mr. Shannow. Donna Taybard, believing you dead, bedded down with Con Griffin. She is now pregnant, though she will not live to see her daughter born."

"I do not believe you."

"Of course you do, Mr. Shannow. I gain no advantage by lying to you. Far from it. Had I left her as your white lady, you would have raced to her side . . . and into my lands. Now you may decide to leave her be, and then I would have a merry job tracking you down."

"Then why tell me?"

"To cause you pain."

"I have been hurt before."

"Of course you have, Mr. Shannow. You are a loser, and they always suffer. It is their lot in this world, as it was in mine. Your god does not bring you many gifts, does he? Have you not realized, Mr. Shannow, that you follow a dead deity? That despite his propaganda and his awful book, he lost?"

Shannow raised his head, and their eyes met. "You are a fool, Abaddon, and I will not debate with you. You were right; Donna's betrayal hurts me. Deeply. Despite it, I wish her only happiness, and if she has found it with Griffin, then so be it."

"Happiness?" Abaddon sneered. "I am going to kill her and her unborn child. She will be my sacrifice in two months. Her blood will flow on the Sipstrassi. How does that sit with you, Jerusalem Man?"

"As I said, you are a fool. Look into my eyes, Abaddon, and read the truth. As of this moment you are dead. Send your Zealots, send your demons, send your God—they will avail you nothing, for I will find you."

"Just words," said Abaddon, but the smile left his face. "Come to me as soon as you can."

"Count on it," Shannow assured him.

Shannow awoke once more, and this time he was back at the campsite by the stream. The fire had died to glowing ash, and Batik and Selah were still asleep. Shannow rose and added sticks to the embers, blowing the fire to life. Then he sat, staring into the flames and seeing only Donna.

Vile as Abaddon undoubtedly was, there was no doubt in Shannow's mind that he had spoken the truth about Donna Taybard and Con Griffin. But he had underestimated the Jerusalem Man's capacity for pain. His love for Donna had been too good, too joyful. Nothing in Shannow's life had ever been that easy. Other men mined pleasure as if it were an everlasting seam, their lives filled with smiles and easy happiness. Shannow panned in a pebble stream that yielded little and vanished swiftly.

And yet he was torn. A part of him wanted to ride swiftly to her, kill Griffin, and take her by force. An even darker thought was to ride, guns in hand, toward the Hellborn and die in a furious battle.

The sky lightened, and the birdsong began in the trees. Batik stirred but did not wake. Shannow stood and wandered up a steep slope to scan the nearing northern mountains. Jagged they were and tall, piercing the clouds, like pillars supporting the sky.

Shannow could never have settled for farm life while the far mountains called him, while the lure of Jerusalem was hooked into his heart.

"I love you, Donna," he whispered.

"It looks to be a fine day," said Batik.

"I did not hear you approach."

"It is a skill, Shannow. What are your plans?"

"I'm not sure. I saw Abaddon last night; he has threatened someone close to me."

"Your woman?"

"No, not mine."

"Then it is not your concern."

"Not in the Hellborn philosophy," said Shannow.

Batik sat down as Shannow outlined his conversation with the Hellborn king and the background to it. He listened intently, seeing far more than Shannow intended.

"You cannot get to Abaddon, Shannow," he said. "I myself have rarely seen him. He is guarded by the Zealots and only occasionally ventures among the people. And anyway, you say the caravan headed northwest, which puts the lands of the Hellborn between you and her. They are preparing for war, Shannow. The Hellborn army will not be turned aside by wagoners and farmers."

"I cannot save her," said Shannow, "but I am pledged to destroy Abaddon."

"It is not possible."

"It may not be possible to succeed; it is certainly possible to try."

"For what purpose? Are you the soul of the world?"

"I cannot explain it to you or to any man. I cannot suffer evil or watch the wicked strong destroy the weak."

"But the strong will always dominate the weak, Shannow. It is the nature of man and beast. You can be either the hunter or hunted. There is no other choice; there is no neutrality. I doubt there ever was, even before the Fall."

"I told you I could not explain it," said Shannow, shrugging, but Batik was not to be diverted.

"Nonsense! At some time in your life you made a decision and weighed up the reasons for your actions. Be honest, man!"

"Honest? To a Hellborn? What do you know of honesty? Or love, or compassion? You were raised under Satan, and you have drunk the blood of innocence. Reasons? Why does a farmer weed his land or hunt wolves and lions? I hunt the wolves among men."

"God's gardener?" Batik sneered. "A sorry mess he must be in if you are all the force he can muster in this broken world."

Shannow's hand flashed down and up, and Batik found himself staring into the black, unwavering muzzle of a Hellborn revolver. He looked up into Shannow's eyes and saw the edge of madness lurking there.

"Insult me if you will," hissed Shannow, "but you will not denigrate my God. This is the only warning I give. Your next foulness will be your last."

Batik grinned wolfishly. "That's good, Shannow. That's very Hellborn. Those who disagree with you die!"

Shannow blinked and uncocked the pistol. "That is not the

way I am," he whispered, slumping down to sit beside Batik. "I am not good in debate. My tongue stumbles into my teeth, and then I get angry. I am trapped, Batik, in a religion I can scarcely comprehend. In the Bible there are many passages I can follow, yet I am not a Christian. My Bible teaches me to smite the enemy hip and thigh, destroy him with fire and sword . . . it also teaches me to love my enemy and do good to him who hates me."

"No wonder you are confused," said Batik. "But then, I have long considered the possibility that man is essentially insane. I believe in no god, and I am happier for it. I don't want eternal life. I want a little joy, a large amount of pleasure, and a swift death once I lose the appetite for either."

Shannow chuckled, and his tension passed. "I wish I could share that philosophy."

"You can, Shannow; there is no charge."

Shannow shook his head and looked toward the mountains. "I shall go there," he said, "and then head west."

"I'll stay with you as far as the mountains, then I head east."

"You think that will take you out of reach of the Zealots?"

Before Batik could answer, the bushes to their left parted and a huge brown bear moved into the open. He saw the men sitting there and rose up on his hind legs, towering to almost eight feet. For some seconds he stood there, then he dropped to all fours and ambled away.

The two men sheathed their pistols.

"You are never out of reach of the Zealots, Shannow," said Batik. Shannow let out a long shuddering breath.

"I felt sure that they had possessed it."

"Next time they probably will," Batik assured him.

◇ **6** ◇

CON GRIFFIN WAS troubled. For most of the day he had worked hard on the new house, laying the foundation wall with care and measuring logs to interlace at the corners. Yet all the while he worked, his eyes would flick to the skyline and the eternal watchers.

Since the first attack there had been no fresh violence, far from it, in fact. The following day six riders had approached the settlement. Once more Griffin had walked to meet them, covered by Madden, and Burke, Mahler, and five other men sporting rifles and guns taken from the dead raiders. The bodies had been removed to a field in the east and hastily buried.

The riders had entered the settlement without apparent fear, and their leader, a slim young man with bright gray eyes, had approached Griffin, smiling warmly.

"Good morning; my name is Zedeki." He extended a hand. Griffin took it and engaged in a short perfunctory handshake.

"Griffin."

"You are the leader here?"

Griffin shrugged. "We don't think of ourselves as needing leaders. We are a group of farming men."

Zedeki nodded and smiled. "Yes, I understand. However, you do speak for the community, yes?"

"Yes."

"Good. You were attacked last night by a group of renegades from our lands, and this grieves us greatly. We apprehended the survivors, who were put to death immediately. We have come to offer our apologies for the incident."

123

"No need for that," Griffin told him. "We dealt with it at no loss to ourselves and gained greatly by it."

"You speak of the weapons," said Zedeki. "In fact they were stolen from our city, and we would like them returned."

"That is understandable," said Griffin smoothly.

"Then you agree?"

"With the principle, yes. Stolen property should be returned to its owners."

"Then we may take them?"

"Unfortunately, there are other principles that must also be considered," stated Griffin. "But perhaps we could sit down and take refreshment."

"Thank you."

Griffin sat down on a felled tree and beckoned Zedeki to join him. The two men sat in silence for some minutes as Donna and two other women brought copper mugs filled with honey-sweetened herb tea. The other riders did not dismount and looked to Zedeki before accepting refreshment.

"You mentioned other principles?" said Zedeki.

"Indeed I did, old lad. You see, where we come from there is a custom that says the spoils of war belong to the victor. Therefore, most of the men here feel they have earned their new weapons. Second, there is the question of reparation. These raiders were your people—unless they also stole the clothes they were wearing. Therefore, my people might feel entitled to some compensation for the terror inflicted on their wives and children, not to mention the cost of the operation in terms of spent ammunition and hard work preparing the trip wires and other devices that happily were not needed."

"So, you are saying that our property will not be returned?"

"No, not at all, Zedeki. I am merely outlining possible objections to such a move. Not being the leader, I can make no prediction as to their individual reactions."

"Then what *are* you saying?"

"I am saying that life is rarely simple. We like to be good neighbors, and we are hoping that we can trade with people living nearby. However, so far we have had few dealings with your people, so perhaps we should both sit back and study each other's customs for a while."

"And then the weapons will be returned?"

"And then we will talk some more," said Griffin, smiling.

"Mr. Griffin, my people outnumber yours by perhaps a thousand to one. We are unaccustomed to being refused our desires."

"But then, I have not refused, Mr. Zedeki. That would be presumptuous."

Zedeki drained his tea and looked around the settlement. His soldier's eye took in the placements of some twenty felled trees that were scattered on the open ground. Each was positioned to provide cover for marksmen and planned in such a way that any raiding force, no matter from which direction it attacked, would come under a murderous cross fire while the enemy would be firing from good cover.

"Did you organize these defensive positions?" asked Zedeki.

"No," said Griffin. "I'm just a humble wagon master. We have several men here skilled in such matters, having dealt with all kinds of brigands."

"Well, let me thank you for your hospitality, Mr. Griffin. I wonder if you would care to join me at my home. It is not a long ride, and perhaps we could discuss further the principles involved."

Griffin's eyes narrowed, but he smiled with apparent warmth. "That is indeed kind of you, and I am pleased to accept, but not at the moment. As you can see, we are currently building our own homes, and it would be impolite of me to accept your hospitality without being able to respond in kind. You see, it is one of our customs. We always respond in kind."

Zedeki nodded and stood. "Very well. I will return when you are more . . . settled."

"You will be welcome."

Zedeki stepped into the saddle. "When I return, I will be demanding our property."

"New friends should not speak in terms of demands," replied Griffin. "If you return peacefully, we can negotiate. If not, then some of your property will be returned to you at a speed you might not appreciate."

"I think that we understand one another, Mr. Griffin, but I do not believe you understand the strength of the Hellborn. We are not a few raiding brigands, as you call them. We are a nation."

As he rode away, Madden, Burke, and a score of the other men clustered around Griffin.

"What did you make of it, Griff?" asked Mahler, a short balding farmer whom Griffin had known for twenty years.

"It is trouble whichever way we look at it. I think we should move on to the west."

"But this is good land," argued Mahler. "Just what we always wanted."

"We wanted a home without brigands," said Griffin. "What we have could be a hundred times worse. That man was right; we are outnumbered. You saw their armor—they are an army. They call themselves the Hellborn. Now, I am not a religious man, but I don't like the name and I dread to think what it implies."

"Well, I'm not running," said Madden. "I have put my roots here."

"Nor I," said Mahler. Griffin glanced around the faces of the other men to see that all were nodding in agreement.

That night, as he sat with Donna Taybard under a bright moon, he felt despair settle on him like a cloak.

"I wanted Avalon to be a land of peace and plenty. I had a dream, Donna. And it is so close to being true. The Plague Lands—empty and open, rich and verdant. But now I'm beginning to see that the Plague Lands could earn their title."

"You fought them off before, Griff."

"I have a feeling they could return with a thousand men should they choose."

Donna moved closer and sat on his lap, draping her arm around his neck. Absently he rested his hand on her swollen belly, and she kissed him lightly on the forehead.

"You'll think of something."

He chuckled. "You have great faith in—"

"—a humble wagon master," she finished for him.

"Exactly."

But the attack he feared did not come to pass, and as the weeks drew by, their homes neared completion. Yet every day the Hellborn riders crested the hills, sitting their dark mounts and watching the settlers. At first it was nerve-racking, but soon the families became used to the skylined riders.

A month had gone by before another incident alarmed the settlement. A young man named Carver had headed into the hills to hunt for fresh meat, but he did not return.

Madden found his body two days later. His eyes had been put out, and his horse slain; all his belongings had been left untouched, but his Hellborn rifle was missing.

The following day Zedeki had returned, this time alone.

"I understand one of your men was killed," he said.

"Yes."

"There are some raiders in the hills, and we are looking for them. It is best if your people stay in the valley for a time."

"That will not be necessary," stated Griffin.

"I should not like to see other deaths," Zedeki said.

"Nor I."

"I see your house is nearing completion. It is a fine dwelling."

Griffin had built in the lee of a hill on a wall foundation of stone topped by timbers snugly fitted under a steep roof.

"You are welcome to join us for our midday meal," invited Griffin.

"Thank you but no."

He had left soon afterward, and Griffin was concerned that he had not repeated his request for the weapons.

Three days later Griffin himself rode from the settlement, a rifle across his saddle and a pistol in his belt. He made for the high ground to the west, where bighorn sheep had been sighted. As he rode, he examined the rifle lent to him by Madden. It was a Hellborn weapon, short-barreled and heavy; the stock was spring-stressed, and Madden had explained that after each shot, when the stock was pulled back, a fresh shell would be slipped into the breech. Griffin disliked the feel and look of the weapon, preferring the clean graceful lines of his flintlock. But he could not argue with the practical applications of a repeating rifle and had accepted the loan readily.

He headed northwest and dismounted in a clearing on a wide ledge that overlooked the valley. To the left and right of him the undergrowth was thick around the base of tall pines, but here, out of the bright sunlight, Griffin looked out over the land and felt like a king. After a little while he heard horses approaching from the north. Picking up his rifle, he levered the stock, then placed the weapon against a rock and sat down.

Four Hellborn riders advanced into the clearing, pistols in their hands.

"Hunting raiders?" asked Griffin pleasantly.

"Move away from the weapon," said a rider.

Griffin remained where he was and met the man's eyes; he was black-bearded and powerfully built, and there was nothing of warmth or friendship in his expression.

"I take it," said Griffin, "that you mean to kill me as you killed young Carver?"

The man smiled grimly. "He talked tough at the start, but he begged and pleaded at the end. So will you."

"Possibly," said Griffin. "But since I am to die anyway, would you mind telling me why?"

"Why what?"

"Why you are operating in this way. Zedeki told me you had an army. Could it be that my settlers frighten you?"

"I would like to tell you," replied the man, "because I'd like to know myself. But the answer is that we are ordered not to attack . . . not yet. But any one of you that strays is fair game. You strayed."

"Ah, well," said Griffin, remaining seated. "It looks like it's time to die."

Shots exploded from the undergrowth, and two riders pitched from their saddles. Griffin snatched up the rifle and pumped three shots into the bearded rider's chest. A shell ricocheted from the rock beside him, and he swung the rifle to cover the fourth rider, but another shot from the undergrowth punched a hole in that man's temple. His horse reared, and he toppled from the saddle. Griffin's ears rang in the silence that followed; then Madden, Burke, and Mahler rose from the undergrowth and joined him.

"You were right, Griff, we're in a lot of trouble," said Burke. "Maybe it's time to leave."

"I am not sure they would let us go," said Griffin. "We're caught between a rock and a hard place. The settlement is well positioned and easier to defend than moving wagons. Yet ultimately we can't hold it."

"Then what do you suggest?" asked Mahler.

"I'm sorry, old lad, but at the moment I'm bereft of ideas. Let us take one day at a time. Strip the ammunition and weapons from the bodies and hide them in the undergrowth. Lead the horses in and kill them, too. I don't want the Hellborn knowing that we are aware of our danger."

"We won't fool them for long, Griff," said Burke.

"I know."

It was after midnight when Griffin slipped silently into the cabin. The fire was dead, but the large room retained the memory of the flames, and he removed his heavy woolen jacket. Moving across the timbered floor, he opened the door to Eric's room; the boy was sleeping peacefully. Griffin returned to the hearth and sat back in the old leather chair he had carried across half the continent. He was tired, and his back ached. He tugged off his boots and stared at the dead fire; it was not cold in the room, but he knelt, prepared kindling, and lit the fire afresh.

"You will think of something," Donna had told him.

But he couldn't. And it galled him.

Con Griffin, the humble wagon master. He wore the title like a cloak, for it served many purposes. All his life he had seen leaders of men, and he had learned early to judge their strengths. Many relied on wit and charisma, which always seemed to be linked with luck. He had never been blessed with charisma and had turned his considerable intellect to creating a different kind of leader. Men who did not know Griffin would see a ponderous, powerful, slow-moving man: a humble wagon master. As the days passed, they would, if they were observant, notice that few problems troubled the big man; troubles seemed to disappear of their own volition as his plans progressed. They would see other men take problems to Griffin and watch their troubles shrink away like mist in a morning breeze. The truly intuitive watcher would then see that Griffin, unlike dashing leaders with golden oratory, commanded respect by being the still center, an oasis of calm amid the storms of the world: rarely provocative, never loud, always authoritative. It was a creation of which Con Griffin was very proud.

Yet now, when he needed it most, he could think of nothing.

He added fuel to the fire and leaned back in the chair.

Donna Taybard awoke from a troubled sleep to hear the cracking of the unseasoned wood on the fire. Swinging her legs from the broad bed, she covered herself in a woolen gown and moved silently into the main room. Griffin did not hear her, and she stopped for a moment, staring at him by the fire, his red hair highlighted by the flames.

"Con!"

"I am sorry; did I wake you?"

"No, I was dreaming. Such strange dreams. What happened out there?"

"The Hellborn killed young Carver—we found that out."

"We heard shots."

"Yes. None of us was hurt."

Donna poured cold water into a large copper kettle and hung it over the fire.

"You are troubled?" she asked.

"I cannot see a way out of the danger. I feel like a rabbit in a snare, waiting for the hunter."

Donna giggled suddenly, and Griffin looked at her face in the firelight. She seemed younger and altogether too beautiful.

"Why do you laugh?"

"I never knew a man less like a rabbit. You remind me of a bear—a great big soft brown bear."

He chuckled, and they sat in silence for several minutes.

Donna prepared some herb tea, and as they sipped it before the fire, the problems of the Hellborn seemed far away.

"How many of them are there?" asked Donna suddenly.

"The Hellborn? I don't know. Jacob tried to attack them on the first night, but they spotted him and he rode away."

"Then how can you plan against them? You don't know the extent of the problem."

"Damn!" Griffin said softly, and the weight lifted from his mind. "Zedeki said there were thousands, and I believed him. But that doesn't mean they are all here. You are right, Donna, and I have been a fool." Griffin tugged on his boots, lifted her to her feet, and kissed her.

"Where are you going?"

"We came back separately in case the watchers remain at night. Jacob should be home by now, and I need to see him."

Slipping on his dark jacket, he stepped out into the night and crossed the open ground to Madden's cabin. The windows were shuttered, but Griffin could see a gleam of golden light through the center of the shutters, and he tapped at the door.

The tall, bearded Madden opened it within seconds. "Is everything all right?" he asked.

"Yes. Sorry to bother you so late," said Griffin, once more adopting the slow, ponderous method of speech his people expected. "But I think it's time to consider our plans."

"Come in," said Madden. The room was less spacious than Griffin's, but the layout was similar. A large table with bench seats was set in the center of the room, and to the right was a stone hearth and two heavy chairs, ornately carved.

The two men sat down, and Griffin leaned forward. "Jacob, I need to know how many Hellborn are close to us. It would also be a help to know something of the land and the situation of their camp and so on."

"You want me to scout?"

Griffin hesitated. Both men knew the dangers involved in such an enterprise, and Griffin was acutely aware that he was asking Jacob Madden to put his life at risk.

"Yes," he said. "It is important. Note everything they do, what kind of discipline they are under, everything."

Madden nodded. "Who will do the work in my fields?"

"I'll see that it's done."

"And my family?"

Griffin understood the unspoken question. "Like my own, Jacob. I'll look after them."

"All right."

"There's something else. How many guns did we take?"

Madden thought for a while. "Thirty-three rifles, twenty-seven—no, twenty-eight—pistols."

"I'll need to know how much ammunition we gathered, but I can check that tomorrow."

"You won't find much more than twenty shells per weapon."

"No. Take care, Jacob."

"You can count on that. I'll leave tonight."

"Good man." Griffin stood and left the cabin. The moon was partially obscured by clouds, and he tripped over one of the defensive logs, bruising his shin. He continued on, passing Ethan Peacock's ramshackle cabin; the little scholar was involved in a heated debate with Aaron Phelps. Griffin grinned; no matter what the perils were, some things never changed.

Back at his own home he found Donna still sitting by the fire, staring vacantly into the flames.

"You should get some sleep," he said, but she did not hear him. "Donna?" He knelt beside her. Her eyes were wide open, the pupils huge, despite the bright firelight. He touched her shoulder, but she did not respond. Not knowing what to do, he remained where he was, gently holding her. After a while she sighed, and her head sagged forward. He caught her and lifted her to a chair; her eyes fluttered, then focused.

"Oh, hello, Con," she said sleepily.

"Were you dreaming?"

"I . . . I don't know. Strange."

"Tell me."

"Thirsty," she said, leaning back her head and closing her eyes. He poured her a mug of water, and she sipped it for several seconds. "Ever since we came here," she said, "I have had the strangest dreams. They grow more powerful with every day that passes, and now I don't know if they are dreams at all. I just drift into them."

"Tell me," he repeated.

She sat up and finished the water.

"Well, tonight I saw Jon Shannow sitting on a mountainside with a Hellborn. They were talking, but the words blurred. Then I saw Jon draw his gun—and there was a bear. But then I seemed to tumble away to a huge building of stone. There were many Hellborn there, and at the center was a man, tall and handsome. He saw me, and smoke billowed from him and he became a monster, and he pursued me. Then I flew in terror, and someone came to me and told me not to worry. It was a little man—the man I saw with Jon at the village when he was wounded. His name is Karitas. It is an ancient name that once meant love, he told me, and the smoke monster could not find us. I drifted then and saw a great golden ship, but there was no sea. The ship was upon a mountain, and Karitas laughed and said it was the Ark. Then all my dreams tumbled on them-selves, and I saw the Hellborn in their thousands riding south into Rivervale and Ash Burry nailed to a tree. It was terrible."

"Is that all you saw?" asked Griffin.

"Almost. I saw Jacob creeping through bushes near some tents, but then I was inside the tent and there were six men seated in a circle—and they knew Jacob was coming, and they were waiting for him."

"It couldn't have been Jacob—he has only just left."

"Then you must stop him, Con. Those men, they were not like the other Hellborn. They were evil, so terribly evil!"

Griffin ran outside across the open ground, but there was no light from within Madden's cabin. Griffin circled the house to the paddock, but Madden's horse was gone.

He could feel panic rising in him and quelled it savagely.

Returning to Donna, he sat beside her and took her hands in his. "You told me you could always see those close to you, wherever they are. Can you see Jacob now?"

She closed her eyes.

Her mind misted, and Jon Shannow's face leapt to her.

He was riding the steeldust gelding along a mountain path that wound down toward a deep valley dotted with lakes. By the sides of the lakes hundreds of thousands of birds splashed in the water or soared in legions into the sky. Behind Shannow rode a Hellborn rider with a black forked beard, and behind him was a dark-haired youngster of perhaps fifteen years.

Donna was about to return when she felt the chill of terror touch her soul. She rose above the scene, floating high above the trees, and then she saw them less than a quarter mile behind Shannow—some thirty men riding tall dark horses. The riders wore black cloaks and helms that covered their faces, and they were closing fast. The sky darkened, and Donna found herself enveloped in clouds that thickened and solidified into leather wings that closed about her.

She screamed and tried to break free, but a soft, almost gentle voice whispered in her ear.

"You are mine, Donna Taybard, to take when I will."

The wings opened, and she fled like a frightened sparrow, jerking upright in the chair.

"Did you see Jacob?" asked Griffin.

"No," she whispered. "I saw the Devil and Jon Shannow."

Selah cantered alongside Shannow and pointed down into the valley, where a cluster of buildings was ranged at the edge of a narrow river. Batik came alongside.

"I must have been dreaming," said Shannow. "I didn't notice them."

Batik looked troubled. "I am sure I scanned the valley. I could not have missed them."

Shannow tugged the gelding and started down the slope, but they had not gone more than a hundred yards when they heard the sound of galloping hooves. Dismounting, Shannow led the gelding behind a screen of trees and thick bushes. Batik and Selah followed him. Above they watched the black-cloaked Hellborn riders thunder by them.

"They should have seen where we cut from the path," mused Batik. "Curious."

"How many did you count?" asked Shannow.

"I did not need to count. There are six sections, and that makes thirty-six enemies skilled beyond our means to defeat them."

Shannow did not reply but swung himself into the saddle and headed the gelding down the slope. The buildings were of seasoned timber, bleached almost white, and beyond them was a field where dairy cattle grazed. Shannow rode into the central square and dismounted.

"Where are the people?" asked Batik, joining him.

Shannow removed his wide-brimmed hat and hung it on the pommel of his saddle. The sun was dipping behind the hills to the west, and he was tired. There were a dozen steps leading to a double door in the building facing them, and Shannow walked toward them. As he approached, the door opened and an elderly woman in white stepped out and bowed low. Her hair was short and iron-gray, and her eyes were a blue so deep that they were almost violet.

"Welcome," she said.

At that moment the trio heard the sound of hoofbeats and swung to see the Hellborn riding down from the hills. Shannow's hands dropped to his guns, but the woman spoke, her voice ringing with authority.

"Leave your weapons where they are and wait."

Shannow froze. The riders swept past the buildings, looking neither right nor left. The Jerusalem Man watched them until they were far away, heading north.

He swung to the woman, but before he could speak, she said, "Join us, Mr. Shannow, for our evening meal." She turned and vanished into the building.

Batik approached him. "I have to tell you, Shannow, that I do not like this place."

"It is beautiful here," said Selah. "Can you not feel it? The harmony. There is no fear here."

"Yes, there is," muttered Batik. "It's all in here," he said, tapping his chest. "Why did they ride on?"

"They did not see us," said Shannow.

"Nonsense. They couldn't have missed us."

"Just as we couldn't have missed these buildings?"

"That makes it worse, Shannow, not better."

Shannow walked up the stairs and into the building, Batik behind him. He found himself in a small room that was softly lit by white candles. A tiny round table had been set with two places, and at the table was the gray-haired woman. Shannow turned, but Batik was not with him. Nor was Selah.

"Sit down, Mr. Shannow, and eat."

"Where are my friends?"

"Enjoying a meal. Be at ease; there is no danger here."

Shannow's guns felt uncomfortable, and he removed the belt and laid them on the floor beside him. He looked at his hands and noticed the dirt ingrained in them.

"You may refresh yourself in the next room," said the woman.

Shannow smiled his thanks and opened an oval door he had not noticed beyond the table. Inside was a metal bath filled with delicately scented warm water. He removed his clothes and climbed in. Clean at last, he rose from the bath to find his clothes gone and in their place a white woolen shirt and gray trousers. He felt no anxiety over the disappearance of his belongings and dressed in the garments he found, which fitted perfectly.

The woman sat where he had left her, and he joined her. The food was plain—seasoned vegetables and fresh fruit—and the clear water tasted like wine.

They ate in silence until at last the woman rose and beckoned Shannow to join her in another room. Shannow followed into a windowless study where two deep leather chairs were drawn up against a round glass-topped table on which sat two cups of scented tea.

Shannow waited for the woman to seat herself, then sat back in a chair and stared at the walls of the room. They seemed to be of stone yet were soft in appearance, like cloth. On the walls were paintings, mostly of deer and horses grazing beneath mountains topped with snow.

"You have journeyed far, Mr. Shannow. And you are weary."

"Indeed I am, lady."

"And do you ride toward Jerusalem or away from her?"

"I do not know."

"You did your best for Karitas. Feel no grief."

"You knew him?"

"I did indeed. An obstinate man but a kindly soul nonetheless."

"He saved my life. I could not return the debt."

"He would not have seen it as a debt, Mr. Shannow. For him, as for us, life is not a question of balances earned and debited. How do you feel about Donna Taybard?"

"I am angry . . . was angry. It is hard to feel anger here."

"It is not hard, Mr. Shannow; it is impossible."

"What is this place?"

"This is Sanctuary. There is no evil here."

"How is this achieved?"

"By doing nothing, Mr. Shannow."

"But there is a power here . . . an awesome power."

"Indeed, and there is a riddle in that for those with eyes to see and ears to hear."

"Who are you? What are you?"

"I am Ruth."

"Are you an angel?"

She smiled then. "No, Mr. Shannow, I am a woman."

"I am sorry that I do not understand. I feel it is important."

"You are right in that, but rest now. We will talk tomorrow."

She rose and left him. He heard the door close and stood. A bed lay by the far wall, and he lay on it and slept without dreams.

Batik followed Shannow into the building and found himself in a round room painted in soft shades of red. On the walls were weapons of every kind, artistically displayed: bows, spears, pistols and rifles, swords and daggers, each of exquisite workmanship.

The gray-haired woman sat at an oval table on which was a joint of red meat that was charred on the outside but raw at the center. Batik moved to the table and picked up a silver carving knife.

"Where is Shannow?" he asked, carving thick slices of the succulent meat.

"He is close, Batik."

"A pleasant room," said the Hellborn, indicating the weapons. "Do they relax you?"

He shrugged. "It reminds me of my home."

"The room bordering the garden of vines?"

"Yes. How did you know?"

"You entertained a friend of mine two years ago."

"What was his name?"

"Ezra."

"I know no one of that name."

"He climbed the wall of your garden while being hunted. He hid among your vines, and when the searchers came, you told them no one was there and sent them away."

"I remember. A little man with frightened eyes."

"Yes. A man of great courage, for he knew great fear."

"What happened to him?"

"He was caught three months later and burned alive."

"There has been a lot of that lately. He worshiped the old dark god, I take it?"

"Yes."

"The Hellborn will stamp out the sect."

"Perhaps, Batik. But why did you help him?"

"I am not a religious man."

"What are you?"

"Just a man."

"You know that if you stay with Shannow you could die."

"We are parting company soon."

"And yet without you he will fail."

Batik lifted a goblet filled with red wine and drained it. "What are you trying to tell me?"

"Do you feel you owe Shannow a debt?"

"For what?"

"For saving your life?"

"No."

"Would you call yourself his friend?"

"Perhaps."

"Then you like him?"

Batik did not reply. "Who are you, woman?" he asked at last.

"I am Ruth."

"Why did the riders not see us?"

"No evil may enter here."

"*I* am here!"

"You saved Ezra."

"Shannow is here."

"He seeks Jerusalem."

"What is this place?"

"For you, Batik, it is alpha or omega, a beginning or an end."

"A beginning of what? An ending to what?"

"That is for you to decide. The choices are yours."

Selah ran up the stairs after his friends and entered a small room. The gray-haired woman smiled and opened her arms.

"Welcome home, Selah."

And joy flooded him.

The following morning Ruth led Shannow into a long hall, past trestle tables set for breakfast, and on into a circular library with shelf upon shelf of books from floor to domed ceiling. At the center of the room was a round table, and the elderly woman sat, gesturing for Shannow to sit beside her.

"Everything you ever wanted to know is here, Mr. Shannow, but you must decide what to look for."

His eyes scanned the books, and an edge of fear touched him, bringing a shiver.

"Are they all true books?" he asked.

"No. Some are fictions. Some are theories. Others are partly true or close to the truth. Most point a way to the truth for those with eyes to see."

"I just want the truth."

"Placed in your hand like a pearl, unblemished and perfect?"

"Yes."

"No wonder you need Jerusalem."

"Do you mock me, lady?"

"No, Mr. Shannow. Everything we do here is to instruct and to help. This room was made for you, created for you. It did not exist before you entered it and will cease to exist when you leave it."

"How long may I stay here?"

"One hour."

"I cannot read all these books in an hour."

"That is true."

"Then why go to all this trouble? How can I use all this knowledge if I have no time?"

Ruth leaned toward him, taking his hand. "We did not create this to torment you, Jon. Far too much effort went into it for that. Sit and think for a while. Be at ease."

"Can you not tell me where to look?"

"No, for I do not know what you seek."

"I want to find God."

Ruth pressed his hand gently. "Do you think he hides from you?"

"That's not what I meant. I have tried to live in a way that does his will. You understand? I have nothing, I want nothing. And yet . . . I am not content."

"I will tell you something, Jon. Even were you to read all these books and know all the secrets of the world, still you would not be content. For you see yourself as Batik saw you: God's gardener, weeding the land, but never fast enough or fully enough or completely enough."

"Do you say it is wrong to defend the weak?"

"I am not a judge."

"Then what are you? What is this place?"

"I told you last night. There are no angels here, Jon. We are people."

"You keep saying 'we,' but I see no one else."

"There are four hundred people here, but they do not wish to be seen. It is their choice."

"Is this a dream?" he asked dully.

"No. Believe me."

"I do believe you, Ruth. I believe everything you say, and it helps me not at all. Outside there are men hunting me, and the woman I love is in terrible danger. There is a man I am pledged to destroy—a man I know I hate—yet here that hatred seems such a small thing."

"You speak of the man who calls himself Abaddon?"

"Yes."

"An empty man."

"His warriors butchered Karitas and his people—women, children."

"And now you will try to kill him?"

"Yes. As the Lord of Hosts told Joshua to kill the unholy."

Ruth released his hand and leaned back. "You speak of the destruction of Ai and the thirty-two cities. *'And so it was that all who fell that day, both of men and women, were twelve thousand, even all the men of Ai. For Joshua drew not his hand back . . . until he had utterly destroyed all the inhabitants of Ai.'*"

"Yes, the very book that Abaddon quoted to me. He said he had based all his methods on the atrocities of the people of Israel."

"This hurt you, Jon, as it was intended to do."

"How could it not hurt me? He was right. If I had lived in those days and seen an invading army killing women and children, I would have fought against them with all my might. What was the difference between the children of Ai and the children of Karitas' village?"

"None," said Ruth.

"Then Abaddon was right."

"That is for you to decide."

"I need to know what you think, Ruth, for I know there is no evil in you. Tell me."

"I cannot walk your path, Jon, and I would not presume to tell you what was right five thousand years ago. I oppose Abaddon in a different way. He serves the Prince of Lies, the Lord of Deceit. Here we answer that with the truth of love—with karitas, Jon."

"Love does not turn aside bullets and knives."

"No."

"Then what good is it?"

"It turns hearts and minds."

"Among the Hellborn?"

"We have more than two hundred converts among the Hellborn despite the burnings and killings. And the numbers grow daily."

"How do you reach these converts?"

"My people go from here to live among the Hellborn."

"By choice?"

"Yes."

"And they are killed?"

"Many of them have died. Others will die."

"But with all your power you could destroy Abaddon and save their lives."

"That is part of the truth, Jon. True power comes only when one learns not to use it. It is one of the mysteries. But now the hour is past, and you must leave on your journey."

"But I have learned nothing."

"Time will tell. The boy, Selah, will remain here with us."

"Does he desire this?"

"Yes. You may see him for your farewells."

"Without him Batik and I would have passed you by just like the Zealots?"

"Yes."

"Because no evil may come here?"

"I am afraid so."

"Then I have learned something."

"Use your knowledge well."

Shannow followed Ruth back to his room, and there lay his clothes, fresh and clean. He dressed and got ready to leave, but the gray-haired woman stopped him.

"You have forgotten your guns, Jon Shannow."

They lay on the floor where he had left them, and he bent to lift the belt. As he touched it, his harmony vanished. He swung the belt around his waist and walked through the door. Batik waited by the horses, and Selah stood by him. The boy was dressed in a robe of white, and he smiled as Shannow approached.

"I must stay," he said. "Forgive me."

"There is nothing to forgive, lad. You will be safe here."

He mounted swiftly and rode from the buildings, Batik beside him. After a while he looked back, and the plain was empty.

"The world is a strange place," said Batik.

"Where did you go?"

"I stayed with the woman Ruth."

"What did she tell you?"

"Probably less than she told you. I tell you this, though: I wish we had never found the place."

"Amen to that," said Shannow.

The two men skirted a great lake edged with pine forests, and the ground beyond the water rose into a section of rock hills. Shannow drew rein and scanned the area.

"If they are there, you wouldn't see them," Batik pointed out.

Shannow moved the gelding forward, and they rode with care to the crest of the hill. Below them the last section of the plain stretched to the foothills of the mountain range. There was no sign of the Zealots.

"You know their methods," said Shannow. "What would they have done once they lost us?"

"They're not used to losing trails, Shannow. They would have possessed an eagle or a hawk and quartered the land looking for a sign. Since they couldn't see the buildings, they would have then perhaps split up into their own sections and spread out for a search."

"Then where are they?"

"Damned if I know."

"I don't like the idea of heading out into open ground."

"No. Let's just sit here on the skyline until they spot us!"

Shannow grinned and urged the gelding down the hill. They rode for an hour over the undulating plain, discovering deep gullies that scored the ground as if giant trowels had scooped away the earth. In one of those gullies they came across a huge curved bone some fifteen feet in length. Shannow dismounted and left the gelding grazing. The bone was at least eight inches in diameter; Batik joined him, and the two men lifted it.

"I wouldn't have wanted to meet the owner of this while he walked," said the Hellborn.

They dropped the bone and searched the ground. Jutting from the earth was a second bone, and then Batik found a third, just showing in the tall grass ten paces to the right.

"It looks to be part of a rib cage," said Shannow. Thirty paces ahead Batik found an even larger section with teeth attached. When the two men dug it clear, the bone was shaped like a colossal V.

"Have you ever seen anything with a mouth that big?" asked Batik. "Or heard of such a thing?"

"Selah said there were monsters here; he said his father had seen them."

Batik looked back. "It must be thirty feet from head to rib cage. Its legs must have been enormous." They searched for some time but found no evidence of such limbs.

"Maybe wolves took them," suggested Batik.

Shannow shook his head. "The leg bones would have been twice the thickness of the ribs; they must be here."

"It's mostly buried; maybe the legs are way below ground."

"No. Look at the curve of the bone jutting from the grass. The creature died on its back; otherwise we would find the vertebrae on the surface."

"One of life's mysteries," said Batik. "Let's move on."

Shannow dusted the dirt from his hands and mounted the gelding.

"I hate mysteries," he said, staring down at the remains. "There should be four legs. I wish I had time to examine it."

"If wishes were fishes, poor men wouldn't starve," said Batik. "Let's go."

They rode up out of the gully, where Shannow dragged back on the reins and swung the gelding.

"What now?" asked Batik.

Shannow rode back to the edge and looked down. From there he could see the giant jaw and the ruined ribs of the creature. "I think you have answered the mystery, Batik. It is a fish."

"I am glad I didn't hook it. Don't be ridiculous, Shannow!

First, it would be the great mother of all fishes, and second, how did it get into the middle of a plain?"

"The Bible talks about a great fish that swallowed one of the prophets; he sat in the belly of it and lived. Ten men could sit inside that rib cage. And a fish has no legs."

"Very well; it's a fish. Now that you've solved it, we can go."

"But as you said, how did it get here?"

"I don't know, Shannow. And I don't care."

"Karitas told me that in the Fall of the World the seas rose and drowned many of the lands and cities. This fish could have been brought here by a tidal wave."

"Then where is the sea? Where did it go?"

"Yes, that's true. As you say, it is a mystery."

"I'm delighted we've solved that. Now can we go?"

"Do you have no curiosity, Batik?"

The Hellborn leaned forward on his saddle. "Indeed I have, my friend. I am curious as to the whereabouts of thirty-six trained killers; you probably find it strange that I seem so preoccupied."

Shannow lifted his hat and wiped the sweat from the brim. The sun was high overhead—it was just past noon—and the sky was cloudless. A speck caught his eye. It was an eagle circling high above them.

"For much of my life, Batik," he said, "I have been hunted. It is a fact of my existence. Brigands soon became aware of me, and my description was well circulated. I have never known when a bullet or an arrow or a knife might come at me from the shadows. After a while I became fatalistic. I am unlikely to die in my bed at a grand old age, for my life depends on my reflexes, my keen eyesight, and my strength. All will fade one day, but until that day I will retain an interest in things of this world, things that I do not understand but that I sense have a bearing on what we have become."

Batik shook his head. "Well, thank you for sharing your philosophy. Speaking for myself, I am still a young man, in my prime, and I have every desire to be the oldest man the world has ever seen. I am beginning to think that Ruth was right. If I stay in your company, I am sure to die. So I think this is the time to say farewell."

Shannow smiled. "You are probably right. But it seems a shame to part so swiftly. Up there looks to be a good campsite. Let's share one last evening together."

Batik's eyes followed Shannow's pointing finger to where, high up on a slope, there was a circle of boulders. The Hellborn sighed and kicked his horse into a run. The ground within the circle was flat, and at the back of the ledge was a rock tank full of water. Batik dismounted and unsaddled his horse. Tomorrow, he decided, he would leave the Jerusalem Man to whatever fate his dark god intended.

Just before dusk Shannow lit a fire despite Batik's protestations concerning the smoke and brewed some tea. Then he wrapped himself in his blankets against a rock wall and laid his head on his saddle.

"For this you wanted my company?" asked Batik.

"Go to sleep. You've a long ride tomorrow."

Batik lifted his blanket around his shoulders and settled down beside the fire. A loose rock dug into his side, and he pried it loose. After a while he dropped into a light sleep.

The moon rose over the hills, and a solitary owl swooped down over the camp and back up into the night. An hour passed, and six shadows moved slowly up the slope, pausing at the edge of the rocks. The leader stepped into the campsite, pointing to the far rock face. Three men crept silently forward while the others stealthily approached Batik at the fire.

From his position twenty feet above the campsite, wedged behind a jutting finger of rock, Shannow watched the men approach. His pistols leveled on the two men closest to Batik, he squeezed the triggers, and flame blossomed, the guns bucking in his hands. The first of his targets was hurled from his feet, his lungs filling with blood; the second was slammed sideways as a bullet lodged in his brain.

Batik rolled from his blankets, pistol in hand. The third attacker fired as he moved, the bullet kicking up dirt some inches to Batik's right. His own pistol thundered a reply, and the man was lifted from his feet and thrown backward.

Shannow, meanwhile, had turned his guns on the men by his own blanket. Two of them had fired into what they thought was his sleeping body, and a ricochet from one of the rocks hidden there had slashed a wound in a Zealot's thigh. Now the man was kneeling and trying to stanch the blood gushing from the wound. Batik ran forward, dived, and rolled to come up on one knee, firing as he rose. Shannow killed one of the men, but the second sprinted for the slope. Batik fired twice, missing his target, then lunged to his feet and gave chase.

The Zealot was almost to the foot of the slope when he heard Batik closing on him. He whirled and fired, the shell whistling past Batik's ear. Batik took aim and pulled the trigger, but there was a dull click. He cocked the pistol and tried again. It was empty. The Zealot grinned and raised his own pistol . . .

A small hole appeared at the center of his forehead, and the back of his head exploded.

As the Zealot tumbled to the ground, Batik spun around to see Shannow kneeling at the top of the slope, his pistol held two-handed. Batik cursed and ran back to the camp.

"You son of a slut," he stormed. "You left me like a sacrificial goat!"

"I thought you needed your sleep."

"Don't give me that, Shannow; you planned this. When did you climb that damned rock?"

"About the time you started snoring."

"Don't make jokes; they don't become you. I could have died tonight."

Shannow moved forward, the moonlight glinting from his eyes, giving them a feral look.

"But you didn't, Batik. And if you want the lesson spelled out for you, it is this: While you were berating me, you failed to notice an eagle circling above us for over an hour. You also missed the reflection of sunlight on metal west of us before we found the bones, which is one of the reasons I was happy to stay hidden in the gully. You are a strong man, Batik, and a brave warrior, but you have never been hunted. You talk too much and see too little. Dead if you remain with me? You won't live a day *without* me!"

Batik's eyes blazed, and he raised his pistol.

"Load it first, boy," Shannow told him, moving toward his saddle and blankets.

◇ 7 ◇

JACOB MADDEN CROUCHED on the hillside above the Hell-born camp and watched the men below getting in line for the evening meal. There were almost two hundred men already in the camp, and over the last two days he had estimated that a further fifty were scattered over the surrounding countryside.

Griffin had asked him to study the discipline in the camp, and Madden had to accept that it was good. There were twenty-eight tents set in two rows on the banks of the river. A latrine trench had been dug downwind, and earthworks had been thrown up around the camp to a height of around four feet; they were patrolled at night by six sentries working four-hour shifts. The horses were picketed in three lines north of the latrine trench, while the cooks' tents were set at the other end of the camp. Madden was impressed by the organization.

A skilled hunter himself, Madden had had no problems avoiding contact. His horse was well hidden, and the bearded farmer had never approached within sixty yards of the camp. His scouting had been conducted with patience and care.

But this morning six men had ridden into the camp, and from the moment of their arrival Madden had felt an increasing sense of disquiet. In appearance they seemed little different from the other Hellborn riders, with dark armor emblazoned with a goat's head, black leather cloaks, and high riding boots. But on their heads they wore dark helms that covered their faces, all but the eyes. For some reason Madden could not pin-point they had made his flesh crawl, and he was filled with an unreasonably burning desire to move to their tent and find out more about them.

With infinite patience Madden bellied down and dragged his long, lean frame into a tight circle of bushes to wait for nightfall. As he lay overlooking the camp, he worried about the riders. One of them had swung his head and seemed to be staring up at the hidden farmer. Madden had frozen in place, allowing not a flicker of movement, yet he was convinced the man had seen him. Common sense—a commodity Madden possessed in quantity—told him he must have been virtually invisible, but still . . .

He had waited for the inevitable pursuit, but nothing had happened. The man could not have seen him, yet the notion would not desert him.

He ignored the growing discomfort as the damp soil seeped into his clothing and thought back to his farm near Allion. It had been a good site, and his wife, Rachel, had given birth to their first son there. But brigands had driven them out, just as they had from his other four homes.

Jacob Madden was a tough man, but strength was not enough against the wandering bands of killers that moved across the lands like locusts. Two of his homes had been burned out, and the third had been taken over by Daniel Cade and his men. Burning with shame, Madden had packed his belongings in an old wagon and headed north.

He would have taken to the hills for a guerrilla war, but he had had Rachel and the boys to consider. So he had run and had tried not to notice the disappointment in the eyes of his sons.

Now he would run no more. Griffin had sold him on the idea of Avalon, a land without brigands, a land rich and verdant, with soil so fertile that the seeds would spring to life as they touched the ground. His boys were older now, almost ready to stand alone against the savage world, and Madden felt it was time to be a man again.

The moon rose, bathing the hillside with silver light. Madden looked to his left, where a rabbit was sitting staring at him. He grinned and snapped his fingers, but the rabbit did not move. Madden turned his attention back to the camp, where the sentries were out now, patrolling the earthworks. He eased himself into a sitting position and stretched his back. The rabbit remained, and Madden picked up a small stone and flicked it at the little creature. It jumped aside, blinked, saw him, and scampered away into the bushes.

A rustling in the tree branches over his head caused him to look up. A brown owl was sitting on a branch above. No wonder the rabbit had run, thought Madden.

It was close to midnight, and he eased himself from the bushes, ready for the descent to the river camp. Suddenly a shimmering figure appeared before him. Madden leapt back. The figure became a small man dressed in white, his face round and kindly, his teeth almost too perfect.

Madden drew his pistol and cocked it. The figure pointed at Madden, looked at the camp, then shook its head.

"Who are you?" whispered the farmer. In response the figure pointed to the east of the camp; Madden followed his direction and saw a black-cloaked man creeping into the woods. The little old man then pointed west, and Madden saw two other Hellborn warriors moving into the shadows.

They were surrounding him. He had been right all along; they *had* seen him.

The spectral figure vanished, and Madden moved back and started to run toward the hollow where he had hidden his horse. He leapt boulders and fallen trees, panic rising with every step.

"Be calm!" said a voice whispering in his mind. He almost fell but righted himself and stopped by a thick oak tree, resting his hand on the bark. His breath came in great gulps. He could hear little above the beating of his heart and the roaring in his ears.

"Be calm," said the voice once more. "Panic will kill you." He waited until his breathing steadied. His hat had fallen from his head, and he bent to retrieve it.

A shot spattered wood splinters from the oak, and Madden dived to the ground and rolled into the bushes. He moved forward on his elbows to a safer position, hidden in the undergrowth. A second shot sliced his ear.

"Kill the owl," whispered the voice.

Madden rolled to his back to see above him the brown owl perched on a tree branch. He pulled his pistol clear and aimed it, and the bird leapt into the air. Madden blinked. The bird had known! Another shot came close. Madden crawled to a tree trunk, anger rising in place of his panic and fear.

He had been pushed around and threatened for years by brigands of every sort. Now they thought they had him, just another farmer to torture and kill. Madden moved around the tree, then ducked low and sprinted from cover. Two shots came from his left, and he hit the ground, rolled, and fired to the left and right of the gun flashes. A man screamed. Madden was up and moving even as other guns opened up. A wicked blow hit his thigh, and he went down. A black figure leapt from the undergrowth, but Madden shot him in the face and the attacker disappeared. Pushing himself to his feet, Madden dived into the undergrowth. Above him the owl silently swooped to a thick branch, but Madden had been waiting for it. His shot blew it apart, and feathers drifted down to where he lay.

"Get to your horse," whispered the voice. "You have less than a minute."

With a groan Madden levered himself upright. His thigh was bleeding badly, but the bone was not broken. He limped to the hollow and pulled himself into the saddle. Ripping the reins loose, he swung the horse and thundered from the hollow. Then a bullet took him low in the back, and pain seared him. Leaning forward over the saddle, he urged the horse into a full gallop toward the west.

His eyes drifted closed.

"Stay awake," came the voice. "To sleep is to die."

He could not sit upright because of the pain in his back and could feel the blood drenching his back and leg. Doggedly he hung on until he crested the last hill, seeing the settlement spread out below him.

The horse galloped on, and Madden passed into darkness.

Shannow and Batik stripped the corpses of ammunition and supplies, but when the Jerusalem Man started to transfer the Zealots' dried meat to his own saddlebags, Batik stopped him.

"I do not think you would find it to your taste," he said.

"Meat is meat."

"Indeed, Shannow? Even if it is stripped from the bodies of young children?"

Shannow hurled the meat aside and swung on Batik. "What kind of a society do you come from, Batik? How could this be allowed?"

"It is meat from the sacrificial offerings. According to Holy Law, the flesh, when absorbed by the pure Zealots, brings harmony to the departed spirit of the victim."

"The Carns were at least more honest," said Shannow.

Taking his knife, he cut hair from the tails of the Hellborn horses and began twisting it into twine. Batik ignored him and moved to the outer circle of rocks, staring out over the plain.

He felt humbled by Shannow's outburst after the attack; he felt young and stupid. The Jerusalem Man was right; he had no experience of being hunted and would be easy prey for the Zealots. Yet if Ruth was right—and he believed she was—then to stay with Shannow meant death anyway. Foolish and arrogant he might have been, but Batik was not without intellect. At present his chances of survival rested with Shannow; the real trick would be timing the moment of their parting to give him a chance at life. Perhaps if he observed the Jerusalem Man long enough, some of his innate skill would rub off on the young Hellborn.

He scanned the plain for signs of movement, but there was nothing suspicious. No birds flew, and no deer moved out on the grass. As dawn lightened the sky, Shannow and Batik rode from the rocks, veering east along the mountain's foothills. After an hour they came to a curling pass cutting through the peaks, and Shannow urged the gelding up over the scree and into the narrow channel. Batik swung in the saddle to study the back trail. His eyes widened—just short of the far horizon twelve riders were galloping their horses.

"Shannow!"

"I know," said the Jerusalem Man. "Take the horses into the pass. I'll join you later."

"What are you going to do?"

Without answering, Shannow slid from the saddle and clambered into the rocks high above the pass.

Batik rode on, leading Shannow's horse. The trail widened into a bowl-shaped valley edged with forests of spruce and pine. Batik led the horses to a stream and dismounted; Shannow joined him almost an hour later.

"Let's move," he said, and the two men rode across the valley, scattering a herd of heavy-horned buffalo and crossing several small streams before Shannow called a halt. He glanced at the sun, then turned his horse to face the west. Batik joined him, saying nothing. It was obvious that Shannow was listening and concentrating. For some time nothing happened, then a gunshot split the silence. Two more followed. Shannow waited, his hand raised, three fingers extended. Another shot. Shannow seemed tense. A fifth shot.

"That's it," said Shannow.

"What did you do?"

"I set up trip wires and wedged five Hellborn pistols into rocks overlooking the trail."

Batik smiled. "They'll rue the day they started hunting you, Shannow."

"No, they'll just get more careful. They underestimated me. Now let's hope they overestimate my talents. It will give us more time."

"I wonder if we hit any of them," said Batik.

"Probably one. The other shots might have hit horses. But they'll proceed now with caution. We will ride through every narrow channel we can, whether it be between rocks or trees or bushes. They will have to stop and check every one for a possible ambush, and they won't catch us for days."

"Aren't you overlooking something?"

"Like what?"

"Like we are heading west, back into Hellborn country. They'll have patrols ahead of us."

"You are learning, Batik. Keep at it."

Toward dusk Batik spotted some buildings to the north, and they swung their horses and cantered down a gentle slope toward them. They were of white stone and spread over three acres. Some were more than single-story, with outside stair-cases winding up to crenellated marble towers. Shannow eased his gun into his hand as they closed on the town, but there was no sign of life. The streets were cobbled, and the iron horse-shoes clattered on the stones.

The moon came out from behind dark clouds, bathing the scene in silver light, and suddenly the town took on a ghostly look. As the two men rode into a central square, Shannow drew rein alongside a statue of an armored warrior wearing a plumed helmet; his left arm was missing, but in his right he held a short broad-bladed sword.

On the other side of the square was a broad avenue lined with statues of young women in flowing robes; it led to a low palace with a high oval doorway.

"There is no wood anywhere," said Batik, riding up to the doorway and running his hands over the stone.

Both men dismounted and tethered their horses, and Shan-now stepped inside the palace. Statues ringed the central hall, and moving to each in turn, he studied them. Some were regal women, and others were young men of lofty bearing. Still more were older men, heavy-bearded and wise. On the far wall, past a raised dais, was a mosaic in bright-colored stones showing a king in a golden chariot followed by an army of plumed warriors bearing long spears and bows.

"I have never seen clothes like these," said Batik. "The war-riors appear to have worn skirts of wood or leather studded with bronze."

"They could be Israelites," said Shannow. "This might be one of the old cities. But why no wood?"

Batik wandered to another wall, then called Shannow to him. In an alcove, piled against a corner, were crushed goblets and plates of solid gold. Flowing script had been engraved on the goblets, but Shannow could not read it. Near a doorway he found a golden hilt, but with no dagger attached. He pressed his finger inside the hilt and withdrew it; the faintest red stained his skin.

"Rust," said Shannow. "No wood, no metal. Only stone."

"I wonder why no one lives here," said Batik. "It wouldn't take much to restore this place."

"Would you live here?" asked Shannow.

"Well . . . no. It is a little sinister."

Shannow nodded. The bright moonlight shone through an upper window in a shaft of silver, illuminating a broad staircase. Climbing it, Shannow found himself in a round room open to the sky. The stars were bright, and at the center of the room, an equal distance apart, were four golden eagles, each flat on one side. Shannow lifted one, and a golden screw fell from a small hole in a wing.

"I think it was a bed ornament," said Shannow.

"The king's bedchamber," said Batik. "A little chilly."

They returned to the main hall, and Shannow noticed that Batik was sweating heavily. "Are you all right?"

"No. My vision keeps blurring, and I feel dizzy."

"Sit down for a moment," said Shannow. "I'll get some water."

Leaving Batik, he started to walk toward the horses but missed a step and staggered, his vision misting. Reaching out, he took the arm of a statue and held himself upright. When he looked up into the blank stone eyes, Shannow heard a roaring in his ears. Taking a deep breath, he staggered to the doorway, nausea rising to choke him.

He fell heavily on the outer step. Bright sunlight bathed him, and he looked up. People were moving in the square, the men clad in bronze armor and leather kilts, the women in flowing robes of silk or cotton.

Flower sellers thronged the streets, and here and there children gathered to play on the shiny stones. Suddenly the sky darkened, clouds racing across the heavens. The sun flashed away toward the east, and in the distance a colossal black wall moved toward the city. Shannow screamed, but no one heard him. The wall advanced, blotting out the sky to thunder across the city. Water filled Shannow's lungs, and he clung to the doorposts, choking and dying . . .

His eyes opened to the moon and the silent city. Shaking, he rolled to his knees, took the canteen of water from his horse, and returned to Batik.

"Did you see it?" asked Batik, his face gray, his eyes haunted.

"The tidal wave?"

"Yes, this whole city was under the sea. That's why there was no wood or metal. And your giant fish—you were right; it was dumped here."

"Yes."

"What the hell is this place, Shannow?"

"I don't know. Karitas said the world was destroyed by the sea. But as you said, where did the sea go? This city must have been under water for centuries for all the wood and metal to disappear."

"There is another thought, Shannow," said Batik, sitting up. "If all the world was destroyed by the sea and yet this city is above the ocean, perhaps there have been two Armageddons."

"I do not understand you."

"The Fall of the World, Shannow. Perhaps it happened twice."

"That could not be."

"You told me yourself that Karitas talked about an Ark of Noah; you told me about a great flood that covered the earth. That was before Armageddon."

Shannow turned away. " '*The thing that hath been, it is that which shall be, and that which is done is that which shall be done, and there is no new thing under the sun.*' "

"What is that?"

"The words of Solomon. And very soon after that he writes, '*There is no remembrance of former things, neither shall there be any remembrance of things that are to come with those that shall come after.*' "

Batik chuckled and then laughed aloud, the sound echoing in the dead palace.

"What is amusing you?"

"If I am right, Shannow, it means we are now sitting on what was once the floor of the ocean."

"I still do not see what is amusing."

"It is you. If what was sea is now land, what was land is now sea. So, Shannow, you will need gills to find Jerusalem!"

"Only if you are right, Batik."

"True. I wonder what this city was. I mean, look at the statues; they must have been great men. And now no one will ever know of their greatness."

Shannow studied the closest statue in the moonlight. It was of an old man with a tightly curled white beard and a high domed forehead. His right hand was held across his chest, and it carried a scroll. In the left he had what looked like a tablet of stone.

"I don't think," said Shannow at last, "that he would have minded about immortality. He has a look of contentment, of wisdom."

"I wonder who he was."

"A lawmaker. A prophet. A king." Shannow shrugged. "Whatever, he must have been a great man—his statue stands higher than all the others."

"He was Paciades," said a voice. Shannow rolled to his right, and his pistol leveled at a tall figure standing in a doorway to the left. The man advanced into the hall, holding his hands out from his body. He was some six feet tall, and his skin was as black as ebony.

"I am sorry to startle you," he said. "I saw your horses."

"What in heaven's name are you?" asked Shannow, rising to his feet and keeping the gun trained on the man.

"I am a man."

"But you are black. Are you of the Devil?"

"It is strange," the man said without rancor, "how the same prejudices can cling to the minds of men no matter what the circumstances. No, Mr. Shannow, I am not of the Devil."

"How do you know my name?"

"Ruth contacted me and asked me to look out for you."

"Are you armed?"

"No, not as you would understand it."

"If you have come peacefully, I apologize," said Shannow, "but we are being hunted and I will take no risks. Batik, search him."

The Hellborn approached the man cautiously and ran his hands over the gray tunic and black leggings. "No weapons," he reported, and Shannow sheathed his pistol.

"I'll check outside," said Batik.

"If it's clear, gather some kindling for a fire," asked Shannow, beckoning the stranger to sit.

The black man stretched himself out and smiled. "You are a careful man, Mr. Shannow. I like to see that; it shows intelligence, and that appears to be a rare commodity in this new world of ours."

"Why would Ruth contact you?" Shannow asked, ignoring the statement.

"We have known each other for some years. We may disagree on points of theology, but in the main we seek the same ends."

"Which are?"

"The reestablishment of a just society—a civilization, Mr. Shannow, where men and women can live together in harmony and love without fear of brigands or Hellborn."

"Is such a thing possible?"

"Of course not, but we must strive for it."

"What is your name?"

"Samuel Archer."

Batik returned with an armful of dried wood, complaining that he had had to ride from the city to find it. As the fire crackled to life, Shannow asked the black man about the statue.

"I have studied this city for about eighteen years," said Archer. "There are some remarkable writings inscribed on gold foil; it took four years of effort to translate. It appears that old man was Paciades, the uncle of one of the kings. He was an astronomer—a student of the stars—and through his work people knew exactly when to plant for the best harvests. He also discovered the instability of the earth, though he didn't understand the awesome significance for his world."

"Did he live to see the end?"

"I have no idea. His death is not recorded anywhere that I have found."

"When was the city destroyed?" asked Batik.

"About eight thousand years ago."

"Then for some seven and a half thousand years this *was* ocean?"

"True, Batik. The world is much changed."

"What was this city?"

"My research shows it was called Balacris. It is one of supposedly thirty cities that made up the nation of Atlantis."

Batik fell asleep long before midnight, and Shannow and Archer walked together along the statue-lined avenues of Balacris.

"I often come here," said Archer. "There is a tremendous sense of peace to be found in a dead city. And often the ghosts of previous times join me on my walks." He glanced at Shannow and grinned. "Do you think me mad?"

Shannow shrugged. "I have never seen a ghost, Mr. Archer, but I have no reason to doubt their existence. Do you speak with them?"

"I tried when I first saw them, but they do not see me. I do not believe they are spirits at all; they are images, much like the one you and Batik saw this afternoon. This is a magic land, Mr. Shannow. Come, I will show you."

Archer led the way up a winding hill and down into a bowl-shaped hollow where great stones had been raised in a circle around a flat altar. The stones were black and towered over twenty feet high. Each was six feet square and polished like ebony.

"The sea smoothed them for thousands of years. Occasionally you can still see the hairline traces of carved inscriptions," Archer told him, moving into the circle and stopping by the altar. "Watch this," he said, removing a Daniel Stone the size of a thumbnail from his pocket. Immediately, all around them, Shannow saw swirling figures, translucent and shining; women in silken shifts twirled and danced, while men in tunics of many colors crowded between the stones to watch them. "And this," said Archer, covering the stone. The dancers vanished. He moved the stone a fraction of an inch and removed his hand; three children appeared, sitting by the altar and playing with knucklebones. They were oblivious to the visitors. Shannow knelt beside them and reached out, but his hand passed through them and they disappeared.

Archer returned the stone to his pocket. "Interesting, isn't it?"

"Fascinating," said Shannow. "Do you have an explanation?"

"A theory. I have now transcribed some two hundred thousand words of the Rolynd language, that is to say, Atlantean. They called themselves Rolynd—'the People of Heaven' would be a loose translation. I myself prefer 'the People of Fable.' " Archer sat down on the altar. "Are you hungry, Mr. Shannow?"

"A little."

"If you could choose an impossible food, what would it be?"

"A rich honey cake. Why do you ask?"

"I ask because I am a showman." Archer stood and moved out onto the grass by the altar, stooping to lift a fist-sized rock. He took the Daniel Stone from his pocket and touched it to the rock. Then he handed a honey cake to Shannow.

"Is it real?"

"Taste it."

"There is trickery, though, yes?"

"Taste it, Mr. Shannow." Shannow bit into the cake, and it was soft and honey-filled.

"How? Tell me how?"

Archer returned to the altar. "The People of Fable—they had a power source unlike any other. I don't know how they came upon it or whether they created it, but the stones were the secret of Atlantean culture, and with them they could create anything the mind could conceive. When you were a child, Mr. Shannow, did your mother tell you stories of magical swords, winged horses, sorcerers?"

"No, but I've heard them since."

"Well, Atlantis is where all fables begin. I found an inventory at the palace that listed presents to the king on his one hundred eighty-fifth birthday. Each of the gifts mentioned Sipstrassi—stones. Swords had Sipstrassi set in the handle, a crown with a central stone for wisdom, armor with a stone above the heart for invincibility. Their entire society was

founded on magic, on stones that healed, fed, and strength-
ened. One hundred eighty-five and he still wore armor! Think
of it, Shannow."

"But they did not survive despite all their magic."

"I am not sure about that, either. But that's a story for
another day. Let's get some sleep."

"I am not tired. You go on. I need to think."

"Of Jerusalem, Mr. Shannow?"

"I see Ruth has indeed spoken of me."

"Did you doubt me?"

"I still do, Mr. Archer. But I am not a man of hasty
judgment."

"Because I am black?"

"I will admit that it makes me uneasy."

"It is merely a pigment in the skin that separates us, Mr.
Shannow. But may I refer you to your own Bible and the Song
of Solomon. *'I am black but comely, o ye daughters of
Jerusalem.'* He was writing of the queen of Sheba, which was
a country in Africa where my ancestors were undoubtedly
born."

"I'll walk back with you," said Shannow.

At the top of the hill he turned and stared back at the ring of
black stones, remembering the words of Karitas. Blood and
death fed them. The altar stood stark at the center of the circle
like the pupil of a dark eye.

"Ruth spoke well of you," said Archer, and Shannow swung
his gaze from the altar.

"She is a remarkable woman. She showed me my life,
though I did not recognize it."

"How so?"

"She conjured a library all around me and gave me but a
single hour to find the truth. It was impossible, just as my life
is impossible. The truth is all around me, but I don't know
where to look and there is so little time to seek it."

"Surely that is a discovery in itself," said Archer. "Tell me,
why did you first decide to seek Jerusalem?"

"It is an act of faith, Mr. Archer—no more, no less. No high-
blown philosophical reasons. I live by the Bible, and to do that

a man must believe, implicitly believe. Seeking Jerusalem is my way of dealing with doubt."

"Chasing the Grail," said Archer softly.

"You are the second man to mention this grail. I hope you are not friends."

"Who was the first?"

"Abaddon."

Archer stopped walking and turned toward Shannow. "You have met the Satanlord?"

"In a dream. He taunted me with Galahad."

"Do not let it concern you, Mr. Shannow. There are worse things to be than a knight in search of the truth. I would imagine Abaddon envies you."

"There is little to envy."

"If that were really true, I would not have sought you out, nor would Ruth have asked me to."

"I could not see the buildings of Sanctuary."

"Nor I," said Archer ruefully. "There is great power there ... awesome. Ruth can turn energy to matter—and without a stone. I sometimes think she is on the verge of immortality."

"How did she become so powerful?" asked Shannow.

"She claims, and I have no reason to doubt her, that the clue is in the Bible. Non-use of power makes you stronger."

"In what way?"

"It's hard to explain, but it goes something like this: If a man strikes you on the right cheek, your desire is to strike back. Marshaling that desire and holding it in check makes you stronger.

"Think of it in these terms: You have an empty jug. Each time you get angry or feel violent or emotional, the jug gains water. If you vent your anger, the water disappears. The more you control your feelings, the more full the jug. When the jug is full, you have power—all the power you did not use when you first felt the need to strike back. Ruth is very old and has been practicing this art for many years. Her jug is now like a lake."

"But you do not quite believe it?" said Shannow.

"Yes and no. I think she has a strong point, but these are the Plague Lands, Mr. Shannow, and much happens here that defies rational explanation. This area was once a dumping ground for chemical weapons, weapons so deadly that they were sealed in drums and dropped from the decks of ships to harbor their venom on the bottom of the ocean. Added to this, during the Fall there was a great deal of radiation—like a plague, Mr. Shannow—which killed whomever it touched. The land was polluted beyond anything you could imagine. It still is. Where we now sit the radiation level is a hundred times greater than that which would have killed a strong man before the Fall; this in itself has caused mutations in people and animals. There are more ESPers per head of the population than ever there were in the old days. Far to the east there are tribes of people with webbed hands and feet. To the north there is a people who are covered in hair; their heads are long and wolflike. There are even tales of people with wings, but these I have never seen.

"I think Ruth has discovered part of the truth, but her talents have been vastly enhanced by the Plague Lands.

"You mentioned a library. She probably created it just for you—out of thick air, reassembling molecules to the shape of that which she desired."

Shannow sat silent for a moment, then he said, "God has very little place in your thinking, Mr. Archer."

"I have no idea what God is. The Bible says he created everything, and that includes the Devil. A big mistake! Then he created man—a bigger mistake. I can't follow someone who makes errors on such a colossal scale."

"Yet Ruth, with all her power and knowledge, believes," said Shannow.

"Ruth is almost on the verge of creating a god," responded Archer.

"To me that is blasphemy."

"Then forgive me, Mr. Shannow, and put it down to ignorance."

"You are not an ignorant man, Mr. Archer, and I do not think you are an evil one. Good night to you."

Archer watched the Jerusalem Man walk back to the palace, then sat back and let his eyes roam the star-filled sky. Ruth had told him that Shannow was a haunted man, and Archer felt the truth of her diagnosis.

Less of a Galahad than a Lancelot, thought Archer. A flawed knight in a flawed world, unstable yet unyielding.

"Good night, Shannow," whispered Archer. "I find no evil in you, either."

Ruth's image flickered in front of him, forming into flesh as she sat beside him.

"Stones into cakes, indeed! You are incorrigible, Samuel."

He grinned. "Did you divert the Zealots?"

"Yes. They are riding west, with Shannow and Batik just in sight."

"You were right, Ruth. He is a good man."

"He is strong in the broken places," said Ruth. "I like him. How is Amaziga?"

"Well, but she nags me constantly."

"You're a man who needs a strong wife. And how is life at the Ark?"

"You should visit and see for yourself."

"No, I do not like Sarento—no, don't tell me again what a good administrator he is. You like him because he shares your fascination for the dead cities."

Archer spread his hands. "Admit it. You would like to see the home of the Guardians."

"Perhaps. Will you take Shannow to Sarento?"

"Probably. Why is he important to you?"

"I can't say, Sam—not won't, *can't*. The Hellborn are moving, death is in the air, and the Jerusalem Man sits in the eye of the hurricane."

"You think he plans to kill Abaddon?"

"Yes."

"Not a bad thing for the world, surely."

"Perhaps, but I sense there are wolves in the shadows, Sam. Keep Shannow safe for me."

She smiled, touched his arm in farewell . . .

And vanished.

* * *

The Hellborn invasion of the southlands began on the first day of spring when a thousand riders swept into Rivervale, killing and burning. Ash Burry was captured at his farm and crucified on an oak tree. Hundreds of other families were slain, and refugees took to the hills, where the Hellborn riders hunted them down.

And the army continued ever south.

Forty miles from Rivervale, in the foothills of the Yeager mountains, a small band of men gathered in a sheltered hollow, listening to the tale of a refugee who had lost his whole family. The listeners were tough brutal men, long used to the ways of brigandry, but they listened in growing horror to the stories of butchery, rape, and naked blood lust.

Their leader, a thin, almost skeletal man, sat on a rock, his gray eyes unblinking, his face emotionless.

"You say that they have rifles that fire many times?"

"Yes, and pistols, too," replied the refugee, an aging farmer.

"What should we do, Daniel?" asked a youth with sandy hair.

"I need to think, Peck. They're doing us out of our trade, and that's not right—not by a long haul. I thought we was doing all right what with the three new muskets and the five pistols Gambion brought back. But repeating rifles . . ."

Peck pushed his hair from his eyes and scratched at a flea moving inside his stained buckskin shirt. "We could get ourselves some of them guns, Daniel."

"The boy's right," put in Gambion, a huge misshapen bear of a man who was heavily bearded and bald as a coot. He had been with Daniel Cade for seven years and was a known man with knife or gun. "We could hit them Hellborn damn hard, gather ourselves some weapons."

"It may be true," said Cade, "but this problem is a little larger than just getting guns. We survive off the land, and we spend our Barta coin in towns that don't know us. These Hellborn are killing off the farmers and merchants and burning the towns. There will be nothing left for us."

"We can't take on an army, Dan," said Gambion. "There ain't but seventy men among us."

"You can count me in," said the farmer. "By God, you can count me in!"

Cade pushed himself to his feet. He was a tall man, and his left leg was permanently straight and heavily strapped at the knee with tight leather. He ran his hand through his thick black hair and then spit on the grass.

"Gambion, take ten men and scour the countryside. Any survivors you come across, direct them to Yeager. If you find a group that don't know the mountains, escort them in."

"Men and women?"

"Men, women, children—whatever."

"Why, Daniel? There's not enough food for our own selves."

Cade ignored him. "Peck, you take a dozen men and round up any stray stock—horses, cattle, sheep, goats; there's bound to be plenty. Drive them back into the Sweetwater canyon and set a pen across the entrance. There's good grass there. And I don't want any of you tackling the Hellborn. First sign of the bastards and you run for it. Understand?"

Both men nodded and Gambion made to speak, but Cade lifted his hand.

"No more questions. Move!"

Cade limped across the hollow to where Sebastian sat. He was a short, sallow-faced youth barely nineteen years old but a scout more skilled than any Yeager mountain man.

"Take a good horse and get behind the Hellborn. They must have supplies coming in, ammunition and the like. Find me the route."

Cade turned and twisted his knee. He bit back an angry oath and gritted his teeth against the blinding pain. Two years had passed since the incident, and there had not been a day during that time when the agony had been less than tolerable.

He could still recall with crystal clarity the morning when he, Gambion, and five others had ridden into the market town of Allion to see a lone figure standing in the dusty main street.

"You are not wanted here, Cade," the man had told him. Cade had blinked and leaned forward to study the speaker. He had been tall, with shoulder-length graying hair and piercing eyes that looked right through a man.

"Jonathan? Is it you?"

"Hell, Daniel," said Gambion, "that's the Jerusalem Man."

"Jonnie?"

"I have nothing to say to you, Daniel," said Shannow. "Ride from here. Go to hell, where you belong."

"Do not judge me, little brother. You have no right."

Before Shannow could reply, a youngster riding with Cade—a foolish boy named Rabbon—pulled a flintlock from his belt and cocked it. Shannow shot him from the saddle, and the main street became a bedlam of rearing horses and gunshots, screaming men and the cries of the dying. A stray shot smashed Cade's knee, and Gambion, wounded in the arm, grabbed the reins of Cade's horse and galloped clear. Behind them lay five dead or dying men.

Three weeks later the good people of Allion had sent Shannow packing, and Cade had returned with all his men. By heaven, they had paid for his knee!

He had not seen his brother since that painful day, but one day they would meet again, and meanwhile Cade dreamed of the sweetness of revenge.

Lisa, his woman, moved alongside him. She was a thin, hollow-eyed farm girl Cade had taken two years before. Normally he discarded his women within weeks, but there was something about Lisa that compelled him to keep her, some inner harmony that brought peace to Cade's bitter heart. She would cock her head to one side and smile at him; then all his aggression and violence would fade and he would take her hand, and they would sit together, secure in each other's company. The single undeniable fact of Cade's nomadic life was that Lisa loved him. He did not know why, and he cared less. The fact was enough.

"Why are you doing this, Daniel?" she asked, leading him to their cabin and sitting alongside him on the leather-covered bench he had made the previous autumn.

"Doing what?" he hedged.

"Bringing refugees into Yeager."

"You think I shouldn't?"

"No; I think it is a good thing to save lives. But I wondered why."

"Why a brigand wolf should lead the lambs into his den?"

"Yes."

"You rule out the milk of human kindness?"

She kissed his cheek and tilted her head and smiled.

"I know you have a kind side, Daniel, but I also know you are a cunning man. What do you see in this for you?"

"The Hellborn are destroying the land, and they will leave no place for me. But if I oppose them alone, they will crush me. So I need an army."

"An army of lambs?" she asked, giggling.

"An army of lambs," he conceded. "But bear in mind that the reason the brigands prosper is that the farmers can never link together to oppose us. There are brave men among them— skillful men, tough men. Together I can make them a force to be reckoned with."

"But what do *you* get out of this?"

"If I lose . . . nothing. If I win? I get the world, Lisa. I will be the savior. Ever thought of being a queen?"

"They'll never stand for it," she said. "As soon as the battle is over, they'll remember what you were and turn on you."

"We shall see, but from now on there will be a new Daniel Cade, a caring, kind, understanding leader of men. The Hellborn have given me the chance, and damned if I'm not grateful to them."

"But they'll come after you with all their terrible weapons."

"True, little Lisa, but they have to come up the Franklin Pass, and a child could hold that with a catapult."

"Do you really think it will be that easy?"

"No, Lisa," he said, suddenly serious. "It will be the biggest gamble of my life. But then, my men are always telling me they would follow me into hell. Now's their chance to prove it!"

Shannow could not sleep. He lay back with his head on his saddle, his body warm in the blankets, but images flashed and swirled in his mind: Donna Taybard, Ruth and the library, Archer and his ghosts, but most of all Abaddon.

It had been an easy threat to utter, but this was not some brigand chief hiding in a mountain lair. This was a general, a king, a man who could command an army of thousands.

Donna had asked him once how he had the nerve to face a group of men, and he had told her the simple truth: Take out the leader and nullify the followers. But could that hold true in this case?

Babylon was some six weeks ride to the southwest. Walpurnacht, according to Batik, was less than a month away. He could not save Donna, as he had not been able to save Curopet.

All he could exact was vengeance. And for what?

His eyes burned with weariness, and he closed them, but still sleep would not come. He felt burdened by the size of the task ahead. At last he fell into a fitful sleep.

He dreamed he walked on a green hill, beneath a warm sun, where he could hear the sea lapping on an unseen shore and the sound of horses running over grass. He sat beneath a spreading oak and closed his eyes.

"Welcome, stranger," said a voice.

Shannow opened his eyes to see a tall man sitting cross-legged in front of him. He was bearded and wore his shoulder-length hair in three braids; his eyes were sky-blue, his face strong.

"Who are you?"

"Pendarric. And you are Shannow the questor."

"How is it you know me?"

"Why should I not? I know all who dwell in my palace."

The man was wearing a light blue tunic and a thick cloth belt braided with gold thread. By his side hung a short sword with an ornate hilt, and the pommel was a Daniel Stone the size of an apple.

"Are you a ghost?"

"An interesting point for discussion," said Pendarric. "I am as I always was, whereas you are not truly here. So who is the ghost?"

"This is a dream—Archer and his games."

"Perhaps." The man drew his sword and thrust it into the ground. "Take a long look, Shannow. Be sure you will recognize it again."

"Why?"

"Call it a game. But when you see it, in whatever form, reach out for it and it will be there."

"I am no swordsman."

"No, but you have a heart. And you are Rolynd."

"No, I am not one of your people."

Pendarric smiled. "The Rolynd is not a race, Shannow; it is a state of being. Your friend Archer has it wrong. A man cannot be born Rolynd or even become Rolynd. It is what he is or what he is not.

"It is an apartness, a loneliness, a talent. You have not survived this far on skill alone; that within you guides you. You have a sense for danger that you call instinct, but it is far more. Trust it . . . and remember the sword."

"You think I can win?"

"No. What I am telling you is that you are not merely a lone warrior set against an impossible enemy. You are Rolynd, and that is more important than winning."

"Are you also Rolynd?"

"No, Shannow, though my father was. Had I been so lucky, my people would not have died so terribly. I killed them all. And that is why I brought you here. No one understands the power of the Sipstrassi. It can heal, and it can kill. But in the main it enhances, transmutes dreams to reality. You wish to heal the sick? The Sipstrassi will do it until its power is no more. You wish to kill, and the stone will do that, too. But here there is a terrible power, for the stone will feed on death and grow in strength. It will gnaw the soul of the wielder, enhancing his evil. In the end . . . ? My people could tell you about the end, Shannow. The world almost died. We ripped apart the fabric of time and buried our world under an ocean. Tragic as that was, there was one great virtue: the Sipstrassi was buried, too. But now it has returned, and the terror waits."

"Are you saying the world will fall again?"

"Within a year."

"How can you be sure?"

"Have you not heard my words? I caused it once. I conquered the world; I built an empire across the center of the lands, from Xechotl to Greece. I opened the gateways of the universe and gave your people the myths they carry to this day: dragons and trolls, demons and Gorgons. What man can imagine, the Sipstrassi will create. But there is a balance to nature that must not be changed. I tore the thread that held the world."

Shannow saw the anguish in Pendarric's face. "I cannot stop the spread of evil. I can only kill Abaddon. He will be replaced, and I cannot change the fate of the world."

"Remember the sword, Shannow."

The sun sank, and darkness covered Shannow like a blanket.

He opened his eyes and was once more within the ruined palace.

Batik was preparing a fire. "You look well rested," said the Hellborn.

Shannow rubbed his eyes and threw aside his blankets. "I think I'll scout for sign of the Zealots."

"Archer says they headed west."

"I don't give a damn what Archer says!"

"You want company?"

"No." Shannow tugged on his boots, then hefted his saddle to his shoulder and left the palace. Saddling the gelding, he rode from the city and for three hours scanned the lands bordering the mountains, but there was no trace of the hunters. Confused and uncertain, he returned to the city.

Batik had killed two rabbits and was roasting them on a spit when Shannow entered the palace. Archer was asleep by the far wall.

"Find anything?"

"No."

Archer stirred and sat up. "Welcome back, Mr. Shannow."

"Tell me of Pendarric," said the Jerusalem Man, and Archer's eyes widened.

"You are a man full of surprises. How did you come by the name?"

"What does it matter? Tell me."

"He was the last recorded king, or at least the last I have found. It seems he was a warlord. He extended the Atlantean empire to the edges of South America in the west and up to England in the north; heaven knows how far south he went. Is there a reason for these questions?"

"I am becoming interested in history," said Shannow, joining Batik at the fire.

The Hellborn sliced some meat from the cindering carcass and placed it on a half-crushed gold plate. "There you go, Shannow. Now you can eat like a king."

Archer moved over and sat beside Shannow. "Tell me, please: how did you learn of Pendarric?"

"I dreamed the name and woke up with it on my mind."

"That is a shame; he is my last great mystery. Ruth considers me obsessed."

Outside the palace, the sky darkened and thunder rumbled. The winds picked up, and soon lashing rain scoured the dead city.

"Hardly worth traveling today," observed Batik.

Shannow nodded and turned to Archer. "Tell me more about the Sipstrassi."

"There is very little of certainty. The name means 'stone from the sky,' and the Rolynd took it to be a gift from God. I've discussed this with my leader, Sarento. He believes it could have been a meteor."

"Meteor? What's he talking about, Shannow?" asked Batik.

Shannow shrugged. "Archer has been studying the stones, the ones you call Satanseeds. And I've never heard of a meteor, either."

"Put simply," said Archer, "it is a giant rock spinning in space, among the stars if you like. For whatever reason, it crashed into the earth. Now, such a collision would cause an immense explosion, and the Rolynd legend says that the sky was dark as night for three days and there was no sun or moon. Sarento suggests that the impact would have hurled thousands of tons of dust up into the atmosphere, blocking the sun. The meteor itself would have burst into millions of fragments, and these are the Sipstrassi.

"Apart from obvious myths, there is no valid record of the first use of the stones. Even now, after much research, we understand little about them. With each use their power fades by a fraction, until at last they are merely small rocks. The black veins within the stones swell, obliterating the gold; when the stone becomes black, it is useless."

"Unless you feed it blood," put in Shannow.

"I'm not sure that's true, Mr. Shannow. Blood-fed stones become dull red and cannot be used for healing or the creation of food. Sarento and I carried out experiments using small animals—rabbits, rats, and the like. The stones retain power, but they are altered. My own findings show that Blood Stones have a detrimental effect on their users. Take the Hellborn, for example; their ruthlessness grows, and their lust for blood cannot be sated. Tell me, Batik, when you lost your stone."

"How do you know I lost it?"

"Carrying a Satanseed, you would never have been allowed into Sanctuary. So, when you lost the stone, how did you feel?"

"Angry, frightened. I could not sleep for almost a week."

"How often did you feed the stone?"

"Every month, with my own blood."

"And were I to offer you a stone now, would you take it?"

"I . . . yes."

"And yet you hesitated."

"I seem to feel more alive without one. But then again, the power . . ."

"Yes, the power. In another year, Batik, if you live that long, you will not hesitate. And that, Mr. Shannow, is why I am fascinated by Pendarric. His laws were just in the early years, but he it was who discovered the obscene power of the Blood Stones. And within five years he was a merciless tyrant. But as yet I can find no end to his story. Did he succumb totally, or did he prevail? Or did the seas wash away all his deeds?"

Shannow was about to answer when he froze. An edge of fear touched him. "Get away from the fire," he hissed.

Batik was already moving, but Archer remained. "What . . . ?"

The door burst open, and two Zealots leapt inside, pistols blazing. Shannow dived to his right and rolled, shells shrieking around him.

Archer disappeared in a plume of red smoke. Another Zealot opened fire from the upper balcony, and the shell exploded shards of mosaic from the floor by Shannow's head. His own pistol came up and fired, and the Zealot spun from sight.

Batik wounded the nearest Zealot and pinned down the other one behind a white statue. Shannow rolled to his back in an alcove and leveled both pistols at the door to the rear.

The door exploded inward and three men raced into sight, only to be cut down in the rolling thunder of Shannow's guns. The one remaining Zealot made a run for the door but was pitched from his feet as Batik's shell smashed a hole in his temple.

Batik reloaded his pistol and crept through the shadows toward the man he had wounded.

"Down!" yelled Shannow, and Batik dived to the floor as the Zealot's pistol was leveled. The Jerusalem Man fired twice, and the would-be assassin slumped back. Shannow reloaded his pistols and waited, but only silence surrounded them.

"How the Devil did you do that, Shannow?" asked Batik, moving across the mosaic floor. "I heard nothing."

"I used to think it was instinct, but now I am not sure. Where is Archer?"

"Here," said the black man. He was sitting by the fire, staring at a small black pebble in his palm. "All used up. Shame! I was rather fond of that little stone."

"They were supposed to be far from here," snapped Batik.

"Put not your faith in magic, boy," Shannow told him, smiling. Together the two men searched the bodies, gathering ammunition, while Archer added wood to the blaze.

"I don't think we should stay much longer," said Shannow. "I hate to sit here like a target."

"I'll take you to the Ark," said Archer. "You'll be safe there."

"I need to be heading southwest, to Babylon."

"To kill the Satanlord?"

"Yes."

"I don't think that's what Ruth has in mind for you."

"Archer, it doesn't matter what she has in mind; I am not her servant. And despite her beliefs, surely she can see that the world would be a better place without him."

"Perhaps. But then, in the case of Abaddon, there is a link between them that is stronger than blood."

"What link?"

"Ruth is Abaddon's wife."

◇ 8 ◇

SAMUEL ARCHER STOOD in the doorway as the two warriors dragged the corpses out into the open, dumping them by a low wall. There was no dignity in death, he realized, seeing that the dead had fouled themselves and that the stench carried even through the rain.

There were some among the Guardians who were considered soldiers, men of action. Yet none whom Archer could bring to mind could match the chilling quality possessed by the Jerusalem Man. How he had heard the approach of the assassins amid a storm baffled Archer. And without the stone to mask him with invisibility, Archer himself would have died sitting at the fire. Neither Shannow nor Batik had mentioned the plume of red smoke, which Archer had been quite proud of—a distraction for the Zealots, giving the warriors time to react. He decided he would mention it himself when the opportunity arose.

The palace hall smelled of cordite and death, and Archer wandered up the long steps to the balcony. There was a pool of blood by the rail, and the black man recalled how Batik had walked there earlier and heaved the body to the stones below, where it had landed with a crunching thud.

Shannow came in out of the rain and removed his leather coat. He knelt for a few seconds at the fire, warming his hands, then took his Bible from his saddlebag.

"Clues as to the whereabouts of Jerusalem?" asked Archer, sitting beside him.

"No, I find reading eases my mind." He shut the Bible. "I saw Pendarric in a dream last night. He said he caused the world to drown by using Blood Stones, and he warned me that it is about to happen again."

"Through the Hellborn?"

"Yes, I believe so. Do you have anything in the Ark that could help me bring down Abaddon?"

"It's not my field, Mr. Shannow. I am a researcher into things arcane. But there are weapons there."

"And knowledge?"

"Indeed, there is knowledge."

"I will ride with you, Archer. Now leave me to read in peace."

Archer wandered to the door and looked out into the rain. Batik joined him.

"You can't talk to him when the dark moods are upon him, and for a religious man he is in no hurry to share his God."

"He has much on his mind, Batik."

"I don't care about that, just so long as he hears the killers in the night. He's a remarkable man. All my life I have been taught to fear the Zealots as the greatest warriors in the world, but they are like children compared with him."

"Will you stay with him?"

"For a little while, Archer. I have no intention of returning to Babylon and following Shannow as he charges the palace single-handed."

"A strange attitude for a friend to take."

"We are not friends, Archer. He has no friends—he does not need friends. Look at him, sitting there like a rock. I am a warrior, yet I am still shaking over the attack. I wonder how many other enemies are closing on us as we speak. Him? He reads his Bible."

"But if he needed you, would you go?"

"No. What do I care if Abaddon conquers the world? I made one mistake, Archer, when I tried to save my sister. Otherwise I would probably now command a company and be invading the southlands myself."

"You think he will succeed alone?"

"I don't know. But I tell you this: I would not want him hunting me even if I sat in a fortress surrounded by guards.

There is something inhuman about him; he is unable to recognize impossible odds. You should have seen him when the Zealots attacked just now; he turned and trained his guns on the rear door long before the other three came in. He knew they were coming, but all I could hear was gunfire and all I could see were the men before me. If I were Abaddon, I would not be sleeping well."

"He does not know Shannow as you do."

"No, but he will be counting the bodies."

Archer glanced back. Shannow was no longer reading; his head was on his saddle, his blankets drawn around him, but his right arm was uncovered.

And in his hand was a pistol.

"Fine way to sleep," said Batik. "Whatever you do, don't make a sudden noise in the night!"

Shannow was awake, and the words of the two men carried to him like whispers on the wind. How little Batik understood him. But then, why should he? Shannow had long since learned that in loneliness there was strength. A man who needed to rely on others left a gap in his defenses. A lonely man sat within walls.

A need for friends? No man could have it all, Shannow knew. It was all a question of balance, and nature was always miserly with gifts. A long time earlier Shannow had known a runner. To maintain his strength the man forsook all the foods he desired and trained daily. It was so with Shannow the hunter. Alone, he was a rock, relying on nothing and no one to defend his back.

For a while he had tasted the other life with Donna. And it had been good . . .

Now he was back where he belonged.

And Jerusalem would have to wait.

He heard his companions settle in their blankets, then sat up.

"You think it advisable that we all sleep?" he asked Batik.

"You are suggesting that I stand watch?"

"Better than waking up dead."

"I'll not argue with that."

Shannow closed his eyes once more and fell into a dreamless sleep, waking as Batik crept toward him three hours later.

"I swear you could hear an ant break wind," said Batik. "It's all quiet out there."

Shannow sat up and stretched, then took his place by the door. The night was still, and the rain had passed. He walked from the palace, scanning deserted buildings that gleamed in the moonlight. In the distance he heard the coughing roar of a hunting lion and the far-off howl of a mountain wolf.

The whisper of leather on stone saw him swivel, his hand sweeping up and his pistol cocked. Archer spread his hands in alarm.

"It is only me," he whispered. "I couldn't sleep."

Shannow eased the hammer into place and shook his head. "You are a fool, Archer. The difference between life and death for you just then was too small to be measured."

"I apologize," said Archer, "though I don't know why. You were in no danger."

"No, that is not true. I once killed someone who just happened to be behind me at the wrong moment. It is not something I wish to do again. But understand this: Had you been a Zealot, that fraction of hesitation would have killed me. And the next time I hear a noise, I might just wonder if it is you being stupid or an enemy coming closer. Then I might die. You understand that?"

"No need to belabor the point, Mr. Shannow. I shall never again approach you without warning."

Shannow sat back on a low wall and sheathed his pistol. He grinned suddenly, his face becoming boyish. "Forgive me, Archer; that was terribly pompous. I am on edge, but it will pass. How long will it take us to reach the Ark?"

"Two days. Three. You can relax there, and I'll show you a library that is not conjured from air."

"Will it show me the way to Jerusalem?"

"Who knows?" replied Archer. "I can certainly show you images of the Jerusalem that once was. Then at least you'll know it when you see it, that is, if God used the same architect."

A flash of annoyance darkened Shannow's features, but he forced it to pass. "I expect that he did, Mr. Archer." His eyes swept the buildings and the land to the south and east.

"You think there are more of them out there?" asked the Guardian.

"Of course. We have been lucky this far. Their arrogance has betrayed them, but I think they will be more careful now."

"I wish I had not lectured Batik about his stone. You have no idea how much I miss mine; I feel like a child in the dark."

"There is a positive side to fear," said Shannow. "It sharpens the senses, keeps you alert."

"I think you rather enjoy the danger."

"Do not be taken in by appearances. I am not inhuman, as Batik thinks. I, too, shook after the attack. That's why I read my Bible—to take my mind from the fury and the fear. Now, get some sleep, Mr. Archer, and be assured that nothing will disturb your slumber. If you like, you can borrow one of my spare pistols."

"No, thank you. I don't believe I could ever kill a man."

"I wish more people felt like you. Good night."

Soon after dawn the three men saddled their mounts and left the city, heading northwest. To the east of them a pride of lions was slumbering beneath a gnarled oak. Nearby the carcass of a buffalo was gathering flies. The lions were content and sleepy.

Suddenly the leader, a great beast with a red-gold mane, jerked as if stung. Then he stood and turned toward the west, and five other young males rose with him.

In the distance three horsemen were riding slowly toward the mountains.

The six lions padded silently after them.

Abaddon stood on the tower ramparts above his palace and stared out over the city below him, listening to the steady rhythmic pounding of the weapons factory machines and watching the thick black smoke belching from the three mud brick stacks above it.

Dressed in a black robe embroidered with a golden dragon,

Abaddon felt almost at peace above the nation he had cultivated for so long.

Only one nagging doubt assailed his peace of mind.

The high priest, Achnazzar, approached, bowing low.

"They have located Shannow, sire, and the renegade Batik. They are traveling with a Guardian," said the hawk-nosed priest, his bald head shining with sweat.

"I know this," said Abaddon.

"Do you wish them all dead?"

"It is necessary."

"You have said, sire, that we should leave the Guardians be."

"I know what I have said, Achnazzar."

"Very well, sire. It will be as you command."

"It was you, priest, who brought me the first word on Shannow; you said he was a danger. He was to have been killed in Rivervale, but instead he killed our man there. He was to have died at the camp of Karitas, but no, he led a raid that saw scores of our young men butchered as they slept. And how many Zealots has he slain? No, don't bother me with the arithmetic. But tell me this: If I cannot rely on you to kill one man, how can I rely on you to build me an empire?"

"Lord," said Achnazzar, falling to his knees, "you can rely on me to death and beyond. I am your slave."

"I have many slaves, priest. What I need from you is results."

"You shall have them, sire. I promise on my life."

"Indeed you do," whispered Abaddon.

Achnazzar blanched and backed away from the ferocious gleam in Abaddon's gray eyes. "It will be done, sire."

"And we need Donna Taybard on the high altar on Walpurnacht Eve. Have you rechecked the star charts?"

"I have, sire."

"And are the results the same?"

"Yes, sire. Even more promising, in fact."

"There must be no error with her. She must not be harmed in any way until that night. The power contained in her must be harnessed for the Hellborn."

"It will be, sire."

"So far I have heard many promises."

"The army is sweeping south, and there is little resistance."

"You hesitated on the word 'little,' " noted Abaddon.

"It seems that twenty of our men were ambushed near the Yeager mountains. But a punitive force has been dispatched to deal with the attackers."

"Who were they?"

"A brigand named Daniel Cade. But he is not a problem, sire, I assure you."

"Find out all you can about the man. He intrigues me."

Daniel Cade looked down at the gathering of men and women on the mountainside below him. At the last count there were 670 refugees, including 84 children. Cade had brushed back his hair and cleaned his black frock coat with the wide leather lapels. Leaning on a handsomely carved stick, he cast his eyes over the crowd. He could see suspicion on many faces and blank open hatred on others.

He took a deep breath and cleared his throat.

"You all know me," he said, his voice deep, clear, and resonant in the mountain air. "Daniel Cade. Cade the brigand. Cade the killer. Cade the thief. Many of you have cause to hate me. And I don't blame you; I have been an evil man."

"You still are, Cade," shouted a voice from the crowd. "So get on with it! What do you want from us?"

"Nothing. I want you to be safe."

"What is it going to cost us?" asked another man.

"Nothing. Let me speak, and then I will answer all your questions. Ten days ago something happened to change my life. I was on that mountain yonder, just short of the snow line, when a voice came to me out of the sky and a bright light struck my eyes, blinding me. 'Cade,' it said, 'you are an evil man, and you deserve death.' "

"It was damned right about that!" came the shout.

"Indeed it was," agreed Cade. "I don't mind admitting that I lay there on that mountain begging for life. I knew it was God talking to me, and I knew I was done for. All the evil deeds came flooding back to me, and I wept for the trouble I'd caused. But then he says to me, 'Cade, the hour has come for your redemption. My people, whom you've sore beset, have come upon tribulation. And a people of the Devil have come to the borders like angry locusts.'

" 'I can't do nothing, God,' I said. 'I can't fight armies.'

"Then he says, 'I took the people of Israel from out of Egypt against the power of the Pharaoh. I took Joshua and gave him the Promised Land. I took David and gave him Goliath. To you I will give the Hellborn.'

" 'I can't do it,' I said. 'Take my life. End it here.'

"But he refused. 'Save my lambs,' he told me. 'Bring them here to the Yeager mountains. Suffer the little ones to come unto safety.'

"And then the blindness lifted from my eyes, and I said to him, 'But all these people hate me. They'll kill me.'

"And he said, 'They hate you with good reason. When I have led you to conquer the Hellborn, you will make amends to all the people you have made to suffer.'

"I stood up then and asked him how we could beat the Hellborn. And his voice came down—and I'll never forget it to my dying day—and said, 'With their own weapons ye shall strike them down.' And he told me that there was a convoy of wagons to the north, and I sent Gambion and forty men. And they captured that convoy and brought it here. And do you know what it contains? Rifles and pistols and bullets and powder. Two hundred weapons!

"And they are yours. For nothing. I ask nothing—only that you allow me to obey my God and lead you against the spawn of Satan."

Cade waved Gambion forward, and the huge man shuffled to the front of the crowd, carrying several rifles, which he passed to the men in the front line.

A young farmer Cade recognized but could not name took a rifle and asked Gambion how to cock it. The bearded brigand showed him, and the farmer swung the rifle on Cade, his eyes burning with anger.

"Give me one good reason, Cade, why I shouldn't kill you. And don't bother with talk of God, because I ain't a believer."

"There's no reason, Brother," said Cade. "I am a man who deserves death, and I'll not complain."

For several seconds Cade ceased to breathe, but he stood his ground. The man handed the rifle to Gambion. "I don't know about you, Cade, but it seems to me that any man so unafraid of dying ought to be sincere. But if you ain't . . ."

"Trust in the Lord, Brother. You'll have no reason to doubt my sincerity. And here's the proof: The Lord came to me yesterday and said: 'Three hundred riders are bearing down on your mountains, Cade, but I will deliver them into your hands.' How many of you will come with me to destroy the Devil's people?"

The air came alive with waving arms, and a roaring cry echoed in the mountains.

Cade limped away to where Lisa sat with a canteen of water. She wiped his face with a towel and was surprised to see the sweat on his features.

"You look like you've been through hell," she said, kissing his cheek.

"You don't know the half of it. When that boy pointed the rifle, I thought it was all over. But I got them, Lisa. By God, I got them!"

"I wish you hadn't lied about God," said Lisa. "It frightens me."

"There's nothing to be frightened of, girl. Who's to say? Maybe God *did* come to me. Maybe it was his idea that I should tackle the Hellborn. And even if it wasn't, I'm sure he won't mind me smiting the bastards hip and thigh. Where's the harm?"

"It mocks him, Daniel."

"I didn't know you were a believer."

"Well, I am, and don't you mock me."

He took her hands and smiled. "No mockery, I promise. But I was reading the Bible all last night, and I tell you there's power in it. Not miracles and suchlike but the way one man can bind a people together merely by telling them he's God's mouthpiece. And it seems they'll fight like devils if they think God is with them."

"But it wasn't God who told you about the convoy; it was Sebastian."

"But who led Sebastian to the convoy?"

"Don't play with words, Daniel. I am afraid for you."

He was about to reply when Lisa placed her fingers on her lips in warning. He turned to see Sebastian climbing the hill. The young man squatted down beside him.

"Was it true, Dan?"

"What, lad?"

"About God and the convoy?" His eyes were shining, and Cade glanced at Lisa, suddenly ill at ease.

"Of course it was true, Sebastian."

"Dammit, Daniel. Damn it all to hell," Sebastian said happily. He smiled at Lisa and then sprinted away over the mountainside.

"Would you believe that?" said Cade.

"No, but he did."

"What does that mean?"

"Didn't you look at his face, Daniel? He was overjoyed. He looks up in the sky now and sees God smiling down on him."

"Is that so bad?"

"I don't think you realize the full power of such a deceit."

"Power is what I want, Lisa. And it won't hurt Sebastian to think that God loves him."

"I'm not sure that is true," said Lisa, "but let's wait and see. I am more worried about you. What will you tell them when things go wrong? How will you explain when God lies to you?"

Cade chuckled. "That was all in the Bible, too, Lisa. It's a smart book. When things go right, God did it. When they go wrong, it was because he was disobeyed, or the people were unholy, or it was a punishment. He never loses, and neither will I. Me and God, we understand one another. Trust me."

"I trust you, Daniel. I love you. You're all I have, all I want."

"I'll give you the world, Lisa. Wait and see."

* * *

Two days later Cade and Gambion sat their horses on the plain before the Yeager mountains, watching the column of Hellborn bearing down on them.

"Time to run, Daniel?"

"Not yet," said Cade, pulling clear his long rifle and cocking it. Leaning forward, he sighted the weapon on the lead rider and gently tightened the trigger. The rifle bucked against his shoulder, and the rider tumbled from the saddle.

Shells whistled around their ears.

"Now, Daniel?"

"Damn right!"

They wheeled their horses and thundered toward the pass.

Cade cursed, knowing he had left it a little late. A shot killed his horse, and the animal pitched headfirst to the ground, catapulting Cade from the saddle. He landed hard and screamed as his knee cracked against a rock. Gambion was almost clear; and he dragged his mount back, drew his pistol, and charged back toward Cade. By some miracle he was not hit, and his hairy hand grasped Cade's collar, hauling him across the saddle.

Gambion's horse was hit twice but gamely stuck to its run into the pass; then, with blood pumping from its nostrils, it sank to the ground. Gambion leapt clear, pulled Cade across his shoulders, and ran for the rocks. Bullets screamed close, and the Hellborn bore down on them.

Hidden in the rocks all around the pass, the riflemen of Yeager took careful aim. But they could not fire, for Gambion and Cade were virtually in the midst of the enemy.

Gambion shot two riders from their mounts before a bullet struck his shoulder, knocking him back. He fell heavily, pitching the stunned Cade to the ground.

Cade rolled and came up on his knees to find himself staring into the black muzzles of the Hellborn rifles and pistols. His eyes raked the warriors with their shining black breastplates and curious helms.

"God damn you all!" he said.

A rifle shot broke the silence, and Cade winced, but the shell came from the pass and smashed a Hellborn from the saddle.

Suddenly the air was alive with a merciless hail of bullets that shrieked and screamed into the massed ranks of the enemy. The noise echoed in the mountains like the wrath of God, and when the smoke cleared, the dozen or so Hellborn survivors were racing from the pass.

Cade limped back to Gambion. The big man was alive, the wound high in his chest having cut the muscle above his collarbone.

He gripped Cade's arm. "I never seen nothing like it, Daniel," he whispered. "Never! I thought you was lying to them farmers, but now I've seen it with my own eyes. Them Hellborn couldn't shoot you, and you on your knees and unarmed. And then you called on God . . ."

"Lie there, Ephram. Rest and I'll stop that bleeding."

"Who would have believed it? Daniel Cade, chosen by God!"

"Yes," said Cade sadly. "Who could believe it?"

The spirit of Donna Taybard soared out of control in a blur of speed and light that caused her mind to spin. Her thoughts were incoherent, and a thousand voices lashed at her like whips of roaring sound.

Stars sped by like comets, and she hurtled through the hearts of many suns, feeling neither heat nor cold in her mad race to escape the voices in her mind.

A hand touched hers, and she screamed, but the hand held on, pulling her, and the voices faded.

"Be calm, child. I am with you," said Karitas.

"I can't endure this anymore. What is happening to me?"

"It is the land, Donna. As your child grows within you, so, too, does the power."

"I don't want it."

"It is not a question of want; you must conquer it. You will never overcome fear by running away from it."

Together they floated above a peaceful blue planet and watched the swirling clouds below.

"I cannot cope with it, Karitas. I am losing all sense of reality."

"It is all real—both the life of the flesh and the power of the spirit. This is real. Con Griffin is real. Abaddon is real."

"He covered me with black wings and talons. He told me he could take me whenever he chose."

"He is a princely liar. Who knows where your power will lead you?"

"I can't control it, Karitas. I was sitting at home looking after Jacob, dressing his wounds, when he opened his eyes and could not see me. And I realized that my body was asleep in a chair before the fire and I had come to him as a spirit. And I did not even know!"

"But you *will*," he said soothingly. "I promise you. And I will help you."

"What have I become, Karitas? What am I becoming?"

"You are a woman, and a very pretty woman. Were I a couple of hundred years younger and not dead, I would pay court to you myself!"

She smiled then, and some of the tension eased from her.

"What are the voices?"

"They are the souls of sleepers, dreamers. Imagine yourself in a river of souls; they are just random voices, not directed at you. You must learn to screen them out as you screen out the noise of the wind in the trees."

"And my pregnancy is the cause of this?"

"Yes and no. The babe and the land, working together."

"And will she be harmed by what is happening to me? Will she be changed?"

"She?"

"It is a girl . . . she is a girl."

"I do not know, Donna. We'll see."

"Will you take me home?"

"No. You must find your own way."

"I can't. I am lost."

"Try. I will follow you."

Donna flashed toward the blue planet, skimming mountains and crossing wide glistening lakes and rolling prairies. There was nothing she recognized. She saw settlements of tents, homes of stone—cabins, huts, and even cave dwellings. She crossed an ocean and watched ships with triangular sails battling storms and reefs, until at last she came to a world of ice and glaciers, like palaces, tall and stately.

"I cannot find my way," she said.

"Close your eyes and think yourself home."

She tried, but when she opened them, she was below the sea, watching sharks gliding around the spiked head of an enormous statue. She panicked and flew, and Karitas caught her.

"Listen to me, Donna. Fear and panic are your enemies. Look on them with loathing as the servants of Abaddon and dismiss them from your mind. Your home is a warm cabin where your husband and your son wait for you. Be drawn by their love and their need; you can explore sunken cities at any time."

She closed her eyes once more and thought of Con Griffin, but Jon Shannow's face came to her mind. She shut him out and saw the redheaded Griffin sitting beside her sleeping form. He had her hand in his, and his face was troubled. She closed on the scene and opened the eyes of her body.

"Con," she whispered.

"Are you well?"

"I am fine." She lifted her hand to touch his face, and he recoiled.

Both her hands were in her lap, and she had touched him with her spirit. Tears welled in her eyes.

"I cannot control it," she said. "There are no chains anymore holding me to my body."

"I don't understand. Are you sick?"

"No." She concentrated on standing and felt loose inside her body, as if her soul were liquid and her flesh a sponge that could not contain it. He helped her to her bed. In the other room Madden's wife, Rachel, sat by him as he slept.

Madden stirred. He had lost a great deal of blood, but his strength was returning. He opened his eyes to see Rachel's careworn face.

"Don't worry about me, lass. I'll be back on my feet in no time."

"I know that," she said, patting his hand.

He fell asleep once more, and Rachel lifted the blankets to his chin and left him for a while, moving to sit beside Griffin at the woodstove.

"What's happening to us, Con?" she asked.

He looked at her lined, troubled face and pictured her as she must have been a decade before, a slim pretty woman with huge brown eyes that veiled the strength hidden behind them. Now her hair was graying, her skin had the texture of worn leather, and dark rings circled her eyes.

"These are not the best of times, Rachel. But we are still alive, and there's plenty of fight left in us."

"But we didn't come here to fight, Con. You promised us Avalon."

"I am sorry."

"So am I."

He poured her some tea. "Are you hungry?"

"No," she said. "I'd best be going. How soon do you think we can move him home?"

"In a day or two."

"How is Donna?"

"Sleeping."

"Be careful with her, Con. Pregnancy often disturbs a woman's mind."

"Often?"

She looked away. "Well, no, not often, but I have heard of it before."

"There is nothing wrong with her mind, Rachel. Had it not been for Donna's powers, Jacob would now be dead."

"Had it not been for you, Jacob would not have been shot at all!"

"I cannot deny that, but I wish you wouldn't hate me for it."

"I don't hate you, Con," said Rachel, standing and smoothing her heavy skirt. "I just see you as less of a friend."

He saw her to the door and returned to the fire.

Events seemed to be moving out of control, leaving Griffin feeling like a leaf in a storm. Donna was caught in the grip of something Griffin could not begin to understand, and the Hell-born had sealed the valley tighter than sin.

But why did they not attack? What did they want?

Griffin rammed his fist down on the arm of the chair.

He had offered the people Avalon . . .

And he had brought them to purgatory.

An hour out from the ruined city a fresh storm broke over the riders. Driving rain lashed their faces, and a howling wind raged before them like an invisible wall. Shannow dragged his long leather coat from behind his saddle and swung it over his shoulders; it billowed like a cape as he struggled to don it. The gelding ducked its head and pushed on into the fury of the storm. Shannow tied a long scarf over his hat as the wind continued to increase in power.

A tree nearby exploded with a tremendous crack as lightning ripped through it, and Shannow tried to ignore the weight of the metal he carried in his pistols and knives. Batik turned in the saddle and shouted to him, but the words were torn away and lost in the wind.

The trail wound slowly upward, narrowing to a rocky ledge. Riding at the rear, Shannow found his left stirrup grazing the cliff face while his right hung over the edge. There was no going back now, for there was nowhere for a horse to turn.

Lightning flashed nearby, the gelding reared, and Shannow fought to calm it. In the eerie light of the lightning's afterglow the Jerusalem Man glanced down to the raging torrent some two hundred feet below, where white water raced over jagged rocks. Lightning flashed again, and some instinct made him turn in the saddle and look back down the trail.

Behind him six lions were charging out of the storm like demons. His cold hand dropped to his pistol, but it was too late and the lead lion—a giant beast with a red-gold mane—leapt to land with terrible force on the gelding's back, its talons raking through flesh and muscle. Shannow's pistol pressed against the lion's head, and the bullet entered its eye just as the gelding leapt from the ledge in pain and terror.

The pistol shot alerted Batik; he drew his weapon and emptied it at the remaining beasts, which turned and ran. With no room to dismount, the Hellborn leaned in the saddle and stared down into the torrent far below.

There was no sign of the Jerusalem Man.

As Shannow's gelding leapt, the Jerusalem Man kicked himself from the saddle and spread his arms to steady his fall. Below him the rocks waited like spear points, and he tumbled through the air, unable to control his movements. Down, down he fell, bringing his arms over his head, struggling to stop the dizzying spin. He hit the water at a deep section between rocks, and the air was smashed from his lungs. He fought his way to the surface, sucked in a deep breath, and was swept below the water once more. His heavy coat and pistol belt dragged him down; rocks cracked against his legs and arms as he battled the dreadful pull of the swollen river. Time and again, as he felt his lungs had reached the bursting point, his head cleared the surface, only to be dragged below once more.

Grimly he fought for life until he was hurled out into the air over a waterfall some thirty feet high. This time he controlled his dive and entered the water cleanly. The river there swirled without violence, and he struck out for the shore, dragging himself from the water with the last of his strength. He grasped a tree root and hung on, gasping for breath, his legs still under water. Then, having rested for some minutes, he eased his way up into thick undergrowth. Exhausted, he slept for over an hour and then awoke cold and shivering, his arms cramped and painful. Forcing himself to a sitting position, he checked his weapons. His left-hand pistol had been torn from his grasp after he had killed the lion, but the other gun was still in its scabbard, the thong over the hammer saving it. His gelding lay dead some forty paces to his right, and he staggered to the body, pulling clear his saddlebags and looping them over his shoulder.

A dead lion floated by, half-submerged, and Shannow smiled grimly, hoping that the Zealot who had possessed it had died with the beast.

With the storm still venting its fury over the mountain, Shannow had no idea in which direction to travel, so he found a limited shelter in the lee of a rock face and huddled out of the wind.

He could feel bruises beginning to swell on his arms and legs and was grateful for the heat the throbbing caused in his limbs. Fumbling inside his saddlebags for his oilskin pouch, he removed six shells, then emptied his pistol and reloaded it. Looking around, he gathered some twigs from the ground close to the rocks. It was drier there, and he carefully built a pyramid of tiny sticks. Breaking open the shells he had discarded, he emptied the black powder from the brass casings into the base of the pyramid and then reached into his shirt pocket to take out his tinderbox; the tinder within was drenched, and he threw it aside, but wiped the flint clean and worked the lever several times until white sparks flashed. Holding the box close to the base of the pyramid, he ignited the powder. Two sticks caught, and he crouched down, blowing gently and coaxing the flame to life. Once the fragile blaze had taken, he gathered thicker branches and sat beside the fire, feeding it constantly until the heat drove him back. Then he pulled off his coat and laid it over a nearby rock to dry.

A shimmering light grew before him, coalescing into the form of Ruth. At first she was translucent, but then her flesh became solid and she sat beside him.

"I have searched for you for hours," she said. "You are a tough man."

"Are the others all right?"

"Yes, they are sheltering in a cave twelve miles from here. The Zealots fled after you went over the ledge. I think their main purpose was to kill you; Batik is a much lesser prize."

"Well, they failed, but not by much," said Shannow, shivering as he added wood to the blaze. "My horse is dead, poor beast. Best I ever had. He could run from yesterday into tomorrow. And he had heart. If he could have turned, he would have driven the lions away with his hooves."

"What will you do now?"

"I'll find the Ark and then Abaddon."

"And you will try to kill him?"

"Yes, God willing."

"How can you mention God in the same breath as murder?"

"Don't preach at me, woman," he snapped. "This is not Sanctuary, where your magic fills a man's mind with flowers and love. This is the world, the real world—violent and uncertain. Abaddon is an obscenity to both God and man. Murder? You cannot murder vermin, Ruth. He has forsaken all rights to mercy."

"Vengeance is mine, saith the Lord?"

"An eye for an eye, a tooth for a tooth, a life for a life," Shannow countered. "Do not seek to debate with me. He chose to visit death and destruction upon the woman I loved. He taunted me with it. I cannot stop him, Ruth; a nation separates us. But if the Lord is with me, I shall rid the world of him."

"Who are you to judge when a man's life is forfeit?"

"What are you to judge when it is not? There is not this debate when a mad dog kills a child. You kill the dog. But when a man commits the blackest sins, why must we sermonize and rationalize? I am sick of it, Ruth. I've lost count of the number of towns and settlements that have called for me to rid them of brigands. And when I do, what do I hear? 'Did you have to kill them, Mr. Shannow?' 'Was there a need for so much violence, Mr. Shannow?' It is a question of balance, Ruth. If a man throws his food on the fire, who will have pity on him when he runs around shouting 'I'm starving'? So it is with the brigand. He deals in violence and death, theft and pillage. And I give them no pity. I don't blame you, woman; you're arguing for your husband. But I'm not listening."

"Do not patronize me, Mr. Shannow," Ruth said without anger. "Your arguments are simplistic, but they carry weight. I am not, however, arguing for my husband. I have not seen him in two and a half centuries, and he does not know I am alive, nor would he care greatly if he did. I am more concerned with you. I am not a prophet, yet I feel that some terrible catastrophe looms, and I sense that you should not pursue this current course."

Shannow leaned back. "If I am not mad, Ruth, and it was not just a dream, then I can tell you the danger that awaits. The world is about to fall again."

He told of his dream of Pendarric and the doom the Blood

Stones carried. She listened in silence, her face set; when he had finished, she looked away and remained silent for some minutes.

"I am not omnipotent, Mr. Shannow, but there is something missing. The catastrophe fits with my fears. But the Blood Stones of the Hellborn? Small fragments of minuscule power. To tear the fabric of the universe would require a mountain of Sipstrassi and a colossal evil."

"Do not seek to fit the facts to your theories, Ruth. Examine the facts as they stand. Pendarric says blood and death unleashed the power of the stones. Abaddon has sent his armies into the south. Where else can the evil lie?"

She shrugged. "I don't know. I only know I feel very old. I was married eighteen years before the Fall, and I was not a young bride. I had such dreams, such romantic dreams. And Lawrence was not evil then.

"He was an occultist, but he was witty and urbane and very welcome at select parties. We had a daughter, Sarah. Oh, Shannow, she was a lovely child." She lapsed into a silence Shannow did not disturb. "She was killed at the age of five in an accident, and it broke Lawrence, cut him so deeply that no one could see the scar. I just cried out my pain and learned to live with it. He delved more deeply into occult matters, finding Satanism just before the Fall.

"When the earth toppled, we survived with some three hundred others, and before long, in the sea of mud that was the new world, people started dying. It was Lawrence who bound the survivors together; he was wonderful, charismatic, understanding, strong, and caring.

"For three years we were almost happy, and then the dreams began—the visions of Satan talking to him, making him promises. He left us for a while to go into the wilderness. Then he returned with a Daniel Stone, and the Hellborn age began.

"I stayed for another eight years, but one day when Lawrence was away on some blood-filled raid, I walked from the settlement with eight other women. We never looked back. From time to time I heard of the new nation and the madman who called himself Abaddon. But the real disaster came eighty years ago, when Abaddon met a man who gave him the key to conquest. He was another survivor from before the Fall, and though his early years had been spent in another career, his abiding hobby had been weapons—pistols and rifles. Together he and Abaddon reconstructed the science of gun making."

"What happened to the gun maker?"

"Sixty years ago he rivaled Abaddon in evil. But he repented, Mr. Shannow, and fled the vileness he had helped to create. He became Karitas and tried to build a new life among a peaceful people."

"And you think I should spare Abaddon in case he has just such a repentance? I think not."

"Why do you mock? You think God cannot change a man's heart? You think his power so limited?"

"I never question his power or his actions," said Shannow. "It is not my place. I don't care that he wiped out men, women, and children in Canaan or that he caused Armageddon. It is his world, and he is free to do as he likes without criticism from me. But I cannot see Abaddon walking the Damascus road, Ruth."

"What about Daniel Cade?"

"What about him?"

"Can you see him walking the Damascus road?"

"Speak plainly, Ruth; this is no time for games."

"The brigand chief is now leading the people of the south against the Hellborn. He says he is being led by God, and he is performing miracles. People are flocking to him. What do you think of that?"

"Of all the things you could have told me, lady, that gives me the most joy. But then, you do not know, do you? Daniel Cade is my elder brother. And believe me, he will not be preaching forgiveness; he'll smite the Hellborn hip and thigh, as the Good Book says. By heaven, Ruth, they'll find him harder to kill than me!"

"It seems I am preaching a lost cause," Ruth said sadly. "But then, throughout history love has taken second place. We will talk again, Mr. Shannow."

Ruth turned away from him . . .

And vanished.

Daniel Cade received a number of shocks in that early-spring
campaign, the first being that he became a man apart. People
would approach him with disquieting deference, even men he
had known for years. When he approached campfires, bawdy
tales would die in an instant and the tellers would look away
embarrassed. When men swore in his presence, an apology
would be instantaneous. At first he had been amused, thinking
that such displays would cease after a few days or perhaps a
week. But far from it.

The second shock came from Sebastian.

Cade was in his shack with Lisa when he heard the shouts
and emerged into bright sunshine to see men streaming down
the slope toward a small party of refugees. His knee was
paining him, and he used his cane to help him as he limped
toward them. In the lead was a middle-aged woman, followed
by four adolescent girls and some dozen children. They were
leading a horse, across the saddle of which lay a body.

When the gray-haired woman saw him, she ran forward and
threw herself to her knees. Around Cade the crowd drew back.
Many were farmers who still retained some suspicion of the
former brigand, and they fell silent as the woman wept at his
feet. Cade stepped forward and self-consciously raised her, and
her eyes met his.

"You are free from trouble, Sister," Cade told her.

"But only through you and the hand of God," she answered,
her voice trembling.

"What happened to you, Abigail?" asked a man, pushing
forward.

"It is you, Andrew?"

"It is. We thought you were lost to us."

The woman sank to the ground, and the man knelt beside
her. Cade felt lost and curiously alone standing at the center of
the circle, but Lisa joined him and took his arm.

"We had taken the children into the high hills for a picnic,"
said Abigail, "when the riders descended on the valley. We

knew we could not return, so for days we hid in the caves on the north side, eating berries and roots and nettle soup. In the end young Mary suggested trying for the Yeager mountains.

"For two days we moved only at night, but on the third we took a chance and struck out across the wide meadows. That's where the riders found us—evil men, cold-eyed and vile. Six of them there were, and I swear they were not human." The woman lapsed into silence; all the onlookers were seated around her in a wide circle, except for Cade, whose stiff knee prevented him from stretching out on the grass.

"Our terror was great, too great even for tears. One of the children passed out in a faint. The riders climbed down from their horses and removed their black helms, but instead of lessening the fear, it increased it. For here were human faces so bestial that they froze the blood.

"One of them struck me, and I fell to the ground. I will not tell you what they then did to certain of us, but I do tell you there was no shame in it for those who suffered, for we were incapable of fighting back.

"Then one of them drew a long knife; he told me that they were going to cut the throats of the children and that if we wanted to live, we must drink the blood and swear an oath to their demon god. I knew they lied; it was in their faces.

"I begged for the children's lives, and they laughed at me. Then we heard hoofbeats. The six of them swung around, and we saw a rider thundering toward us. There were two loud explosions, and—blessed be God—both shots hit home and two of our attackers collapsed to the grass. Then the other four opened fire, and the rider was hit in the chest and hurled from the saddle.

"You know, they did not even check their fallen comrades. The leader turned to me and said, 'Your death will be very slow, you crone.'

"But there was another shot, and the young man, blood pouring from his body, came staggering forward. The Hellborn shot him again and again, but still he fired back, and each shot claimed another victim. It was so swift, and yet in my mind's eye I can see each second as if it were an hour—his young body pulled and torn, his teeth clenched against the pain, holding off death until we were safe. The Hellborn leader was the last to die, shot through the heart by the last bullet in the young man's pistol.

"I ran forward and had to close my eyes against the sight of the boy's wounds. His back was open, his ribs had spread like broken wings, and blood was gurgling in his throat. But his eyes were clear, and he smiled at me like he was happy to be lying there like a torn doll.

"It was hard to see through my tears as he spoke. 'Daniel Cade sent me,' he whispered.

" 'How did he know we were here?' I asked him.

" 'We're the army of God,' he said, and he died there. And his face was so peaceful and full of joy. I counted his wounds and saw there were fourteen, and there was no way a man could have lived through that unless the Almighty had touched him.

"We lifted him to his horse, and he weighed no more than a child. We came here then, as we had always planned, and not a soul opposed our path. We saw the dark riders on their patrols, but they did not see us although we did not hide. We all knew we were protected by the spirit of that young man; he rode with us, to be buried here among his folk.

"But we don't even know his name." She stopped and looked at Cade.

Cade cleared his throat. "His name was Sebastian, and he was nineteen." He turned away and made as if to leave, but a farmer's voice stopped him.

"There's more to tell than that," he said, and Cade faced him, unable to speak. "The boy was a killer," said the man, "a rapist and a thief. I knew his people, and I can tell you he never did an honest deed in his life."

"That cannot be so," cried Abigail.

"By God I swear it," said the farmer, "but I'll help dig his grave and be proud to lift the shovel." He turned to the silent Cade. "I cannot explain all this, Cade, and I've never believed in gods or devils, but if a boy like Sebastian can give his life, there must be something in it. I'd be grateful if you'd have me at your next prayer meeting."

Cade nodded, and Lisa led him away to the cabin. He was shaking when they arrived, and she was surprised to see tears streaking his face.

"Why?" he said softly. "Why did he do it?"

"You heard her, Daniel. He was a part of God's army."

"Don't you start that," he snapped. "I didn't tell him there was a woman and children. I just told him to scout for refugees."

"What you said, Daniel, to impress him, was that God had told you to send him west to look for refugees."

"What's the difference? I didn't tell him they were *there*."

"For a man so sharp and quick-witted, you surprise me. You might send a man out on a half chance, but for God there are no half chances. In Sebastian's mind the refugees had to be there, and they were. And he was needed. And he came through, Daniel. Shot to pieces, he came through."

"What's happening to me, Lisa? It's all going wrong."

"I don't think so. What are you going to do about the prayer meeting?"

"What prayer meeting?"

"You didn't hear it, did you? The farmer asked if he could be present, and there must have been fifty other men who showed agreement. They want to hear you speak; they want to be there when God talks through you."

"I can't do it—you know that."

"I know it. But you have to. You began this charade, and you must live it. You've given them hope, Daniel. Now you have to find a way to nourish it."

Cade slammed his hand down on the chair arm. "I'm not a damned preacher. Christ! I don't even believe in it."

"That hardly seems to matter now. You're Daniel Cade the prophet, and you are about to bury your first martyr. There's not a man or a woman in Yeager who will miss your funeral oration."

Lisa was right. That evening Gambion came to Cade and told him they would be burying Sebastian on a high hill overlooking the plain. He asked Cade to say a few words, and when the former brigand walked out onto the hillside, with the sun beginning to die in fire beyond the western mountains, some six hundred people were gathered silently on the grass around the newly dug grave. Cade carried his Bible to the graveside and took a deep breath.

"Way back," he said, "the Lord Jesus was asked about the last days when the sheep would be separated from the goats. And his reply was something that Sebastian would have liked to hear. For it don't say a damned word about being good all your life—which is just as well, for he was a hot-tempered boy, and there's some deeds behind him he'd just as soon have forgotten.

"But when the Lord came to the people chosen for fire and damnation, he said, 'Be on your way from me, you who have been cursed, into the everlasting fire prepared for the Devil and his angels. For I became hungry, but you gave me nothing to eat, and I got thirsty, but you gave me nothing to drink. I was a stranger, but you did not receive me hospitably; naked, but you did not clothe me; sick and in prison, but you did not look after me.'

"Then they answered with the words, 'Lord, when did we see you hungry or thirsty or a stranger, or naked or sick and in prison, and did not minister to you?' Then he answered them, 'Truly I say to you, to the extent that you did not do it to one of these little ones, you did not do it to me.'

"You want to know what that means?" asked Cade. "If you do, then ask it of your own hearts. Sebastian knew; he saw the little ones in danger, and he rode into hell to bring them back. He rode to the borders of death, and they couldn't stop him. And right now, as we speak and as the sun sets, he's riding on to glory.

"And when he gets there and someone says, as they surely will, that this man has been evil, he has killed and stolen and caused grief, the Lord will put his arm around Sebastian's shoulder and say, 'This man is mine, for he took care of my little ones.' " Cade stopped for a moment and wiped the sweat from his face. He had finished the speech he had so carefully rehearsed, but he was aware that the men were still waiting and knew that something had been left unsaid. Raising his arms, he called out: "Let us pray!"

The whole congregation sank to their knees, and Cade swallowed hard.

"Tonight we bid farewell to our brother Sebastian and ask the Lord Almighty to take him into his house forever. And we ask that soon, when the dark days fall upon us, the memory of Sebastian's courage will lift the heart of every man and woman among us. When fear strikes in the night, think of Sebastian. When the Hellborn charge, think of Sebastian, and when the dawn seems far away, think of a young man who gave his life so that others could live.

"Lord, we are your army, and we live to do your bidding. Be with us all evermore. Amen."

Three men lifted Sebastian's body on a blanket and laid him gently in the grave, covering his face with a linen towel. Cade stared down at the body, fighting back tears he could not understand. Gambion gripped his shoulder and smiled.

"Where to now, Daniel?"

"Nowhere."

"I don't understand."

"The enemy is coming to us. In their thousands."

◇ 9 ◇

SHANNOW'S IRRITATION GREW with the pain in his feet. Like most riding men, he abhorred walking, and his knee-length boots with their thick wedged heels made his journey a nightmare. By the end of the first day his right foot was blistered and bleeding. By the third day he felt as if both boots contained broken glass.

He was heading north and west, angling toward the mountains, where he hoped to find Batik and Archer. His belly was empty, and the few roots and berries he had found did little more than increase his appetite. Despite his switching the saddlebags from shoulder to shoulder, the skin on his neck was being rubbed raw by the leather.

His mood darkened by the hour, but he strode on. Occasionally herds of wild horses came into sight, grazing on the hills. He ignored them. Without a rope, any pursuit would be doomed to failure.

The land was wide and empty, the surface creased and folded like a carelessly thrown blanket. Hidden gullies crossed his path—some quite steep—forcing him to take a parallel route, often for miles, before he could scramble down and go up the other side.

An hour before dusk on the third day Shannow came upon the tracks of shod horses. He scanned the land around him and then dropped to one knee to examine them more closely. The edges were frayed and cracked, and the imprints were crisscrossed with insect traces. Several days had passed since the horses had ridden this way. Slowly he examined all the imprints until he was satisfied there were seven horses. This

204

gave him some small relief; he had dreaded the thought that there might be six and that the Zealots were once more on his trail.

He walked on and made a dry camp in a shallow arroyo out of the wind. He slept fitfully and set off again soon after dawn. By midday he had reached the foothills of the mountain range but was forced to move northeast, looking for a pass.

Three riders approached him as he angled back down toward the flatlands.

They were young men dressed in homespun cloth, and they carried no guns that he could see.

"Lost your horse?" asked the first, a heavily built man with sandy hair.

"Yes. How far from your settlement am I?"

"Walking? I'd say about two hours."

"Is there a welcome for strangers?"

"Sometimes."

"What is this area called?"

"Castlemine. You'll see when you get there. Is that a gun?"

"Yes," said Shannow, aware that all three were staring at his weapon intently.

"Best keep it hidden. Ridder allows no guns in Castlemine except those he keeps for his men."

"Thank you for the warning. Is he the leader there?"

"Yes, he owns the mine and was the first to settle the ruins. He's not a bad man, but he's run things for so long, he kind of thinks he's a king or a baron, or whatever they had in the old days."

"I'll keep out of his way."

"Be lucky if you do. Are you carrying coin?"

"Some," Shannow said warily.

"Good. Keep most of that hidden, too, but keep three silver coins handy for the inspection."

"Inspection?"

"Ridder has a law about strangers. Anyone with less than three coins is a vagrant and subject to indenture, that is, ten days' work in the mine. But it ends up more like six months when they add on the transgressions."

"I think I get the message," said Shannow. "Are you always so free with advice for strangers?"

"Mostly. My name is Barkett, and I run a small meat farm north of here. If you are looking for work, I can use you."

"Thank you, no."

"Good luck to you."

"And to you, Mr. Barkett."

"You're from way south, I see. Out here it is Meneer Barkett."

"I'll remember that."

Shannow watched them ride on and relaxed. Lifting his saddlebag to a rock, he removed his gun scabbards and hid them alongside his Bible. Then he removed his small sack of Barta coins, looped the thong over his head, and swung the sack down behind his collar. He glanced back along the way Barkett and the other two had ridden, made one more adjustment, and walked on with his hands thrust deep into his coat pockets.

Hoofbeats made him turn once more to see that Barkett was returning alone.

Shannow waited for him; the man was smiling as he approached.

"There was one other thing now that you've removed your guns," said Barkett, producing a small, black single-shot pistol. "I'll relieve you of the Barta coins."

"Are you sure this is wise?" asked Shannow.

"Wise? They'll only strip it from you in Castlemine. You'll soon earn it back working in Ridder's mine—well, in a year or three."

"I'd like you to reconsider," said Shannow. "I'd like you to put the gun away and ride on. I do not think you are an evil man, just a little greedy—and you deserve a chance to live."

"I do?" said Barkett, grinning. "And why is that?"

"Because you obviously intend only to rob me; otherwise you would have shot me down without a word."

"True. Now hand me your money and let's make an end to this."

"Do your friends know you are engaged in this venture?"

"I didn't come here to debate with you," said Barkett, cocking the flintlock. "Give me the saddlebag."

"Listen to me, man; this is your last chance. I have a gun in my pocket, and it is trained on you. Do not proceed with this foolishness."

"You expect me to believe that?"

"No," said Shannow sadly, pulling the trigger. Barkett crumpled and pitched sideways, hitting the ground hard, his flintlock firing a shot that ricocheted from the rocks. Shannow moved closer, hoping that the wound was not fatal, but Barkett was dead, shot through the heart.

"Damn you!" said Shannow. "I gave you more chances than you deserved. Why did you take none of them?"

Barkett's two companions came riding into view, both carrying hand weapons. Shannow drew the Hellborn pistol from his coat pocket and cocked it.

"One man is dead," he called. "Do you wish to join him?"

They drew their reins and stared down at the fallen man, then pocketed their weapons and rode forward.

"He was a damned fool," said the first rider, a dark-eyed young man with a slender tanned face. "We had no part in it."

"Put him across the horse and take him home," said Shannow.

"You are not going to take the horse?"

"I'll buy one in Castlemine."

"Don't go there," said the man. "Most of what he told you was true, except the part about the three coins. It no longer matters what you are carrying; they'll take it as tax and make you work the mine, anyway. It's Ridder's way."

"How many men does he have?" asked Shannow.

"Twenty."

"Then I'll take your advice, but I'll buy the horse. What is the going rate?"

"It's not my horse."

"Then give the money to his family."

"It's not that easy. Just take the beast and go," said the young man, his face reddening.

Shannow understood. He nodded, slung his saddlebags across the horse's back, and stepped into the saddle.

If the riders returned with cash, that would mean they had faced the killer of their friend without exacting revenge and would brand them as cowards.

"I did not desire to kill him," said Shannow.

"What's done is done. He has family, and they'll hunt for you."

"Best for them that they do not find me."

"I don't doubt it."

Shannow touched his heels to the horse and moved on. Turning in the saddle, he called back, "Tell them to look for Jon Shannow."

"The Jerusalem Man?"

He nodded and pushed the horse into a canter. Behind him the young men dismounted, lifted the dead body of their erstwhile friend, and draped it across the back of one of the horses.

Shannow did not glance back. The incident, like so many in his life, was filed and forgotten. Barkett had been given a chance at life and had spurned it. Shannow did not regret the deed.

He carried only one burning regret . . .

And that was for a child who had been in the wrong place at the wrong time and who had touched the orbit of death around the Jerusalem Man.

Shannow rode for an hour and his new horse showed no sign of fatigue. It was a chestnut stallion some two hands taller than his gelding and was built for strength and stamina. The horse had been well cared for and grain-fed. Shannow was tempted to run it hard to gauge the limits of its speed, but in hostile country that temptation had to be put aside.

It was coming up to nightfall before Shannow saw the lights of Castlemine. There could be no doubt of the identity of the settlement, for it sprawled against the mountains beneath a granite fortress with six crenellated towers. It was an immense structure, the largest building Shannow had ever seen, and below it the shacks and cabins of the mining community seemed puny, like beetles beside an elephant. Some larger dwellings had been constructed on either side of a main street that ran to the castle's arched main gate, and a mill had been built across a stream to the left of the fortress.

Lights shone in many windows, and the community seemed friendly under the gentle moonlight. Shannow was rarely deceived by appearances, however, and he sat his horse, quietly weighing the options. The young rider had advised him to avoid Castlemine, and in daylight he would have done so. But he was also short on supplies and from his high vantage point could see the town's store nestling beside a meeting hall or tavern house.

He checked his pistols. The Hellborn revolver was fully loaded, as was his own ivory-handled percussion weapon. His mind made up, he rode down the hillside and tethered his horse behind the tavern house. There were few people on the streets, and those who were about ignored the tall man in the long coat. Keeping to the shadows, he moved to the front of the store, but it was bolted. Across the street was an eating house, and Shannow could see that it sported around a dozen tables, only half of which were in use. Swiftly he crossed the street and entered the building. The eight diners glanced up and then resumed their meals. Shannow sat by the window facing the door, and a middle-aged woman in a checkered apron brought him a jug of cool water and a pottery mug.

"We have meat and sweet potatoes," she told him.

He looked up into her dull brown eyes and detected an edge of fear. "That sounds fine," he told her. "What meat is it?"

She seemed surprised. "Rabbit and pigeon," she said.

"I'll have it. Where can I find the storekeeper?"

"Baker spends most evenings in the tavern. There is a woman there who sings."

"How will I know him?"

The woman glanced anxiously at the other diners and leaned close.

"You are not with Ridder's men?"

"No, I am a stranger."

"I'll fetch you a meal, but then you must move on. Ridder is short of workers since the lung fever massacred the Wolvers."

"How will I know Baker?"

The woman sighed. "He's a tall man who wears a mustache but no beard; it droops to his chin. His hair is gray and parted at the center; you'll not miss him. I'll fetch your food."

Although the meal was probably not as fine as Shannow's starved stomach told him it was, he ate with gusto. The gray-haired woman came to sit beside him as he finished the last of the gravy, mopping it with fresh-baked bread.

"You look as though you needed that," she said.

"I did indeed. It was very fine. How much do I owe?"

"Nothing—if you leave now."

"That is kind, but I came to Castlemine for supplies. I shall leave when I have seen Baker."

The woman shrugged and smiled. Years ago, thought Shannow, she must have been strikingly attractive. Now she was overweight and world-weary.

"Do you have a death wish?" she asked him.

"I don't think so."

The other diners left, and soon Shannow found himself alone. The woman locked the door and cleared away the plates, and a thin man emerged from the kitchen, removing a stained apron. She thanked him and gave him two silver coins.

"Good night, Flora," he said, and nodded in Shannow's direction.

The woman let him out, then moved around the large room, extinguishing the lamps before rejoining Shannow. "Baker will be leaving the hall around midnight. You are welcome to sit here and wait."

"I am grateful. But why do you do this for me?"

"Maybe I'm just getting old," said Flora, "but I'm sick of Ridder and his ways. He was a good man once, but too many deaths have hardened him."

"He is a killer?"

"No, although he has killed. I meant the mine. Ridder produces silver for the Barta coin. There is a river sixty miles north that goes to the sea, and he ships his silver to many settlements in exchange for grain, iron, salt, and weapons—whatever he needs. But that mine eats people. Ridder used to pay for miners, but they died or left. Then he began trapping Wolvers and using them. But they can't live underground; they sicken and die."

"What are these Wolvers?"

"You've never seen them? Then you must have traveled from a far place. They are a little people, covered in hair; their faces are stretched, their ears pointed. It is said that they once looked like us, but I do not believe it."

"And there is a tribe of them?"

"There are scores—perhaps hundreds—of tribes. They tend to gather in small packs within the tribes and are pretty harmless. They live on rabbits, pigeons, turkeys—any small animal they can bring down with their bows and slings. Ridder says they make fine workers while they live. They're docile, you see, and do as they're told. But since the lung fever Ridder has been desperate for workers. Now any stranger will end up in Castlemine. He even has men scouring the countryside. Sometimes we see wagons driven into the castle with whole families doomed to the shafts and tunnels. It used to be that a man could work his way out in two or three months, but now we never see them."

"Why is he allowed to do this?" asked Shannow. "It is a big settlement; there must be three, maybe four hundred people here."

"You don't know much about people, do you?" said Flora. "Ridder is the main source of wealth. Those of us who live beneath the castle need have no fear of brigands or raiders. We live comfortable lives; we have a school and a church. Life is good."

"A church?"

"We are a God-fearing people here," she said. "The pastor sees to that."

"And how does your pastor react to Ridder's methods?"

She chuckled. "Ridder *is* the pastor!"

"You are right, lady. I do not know much about people."

"Ridder quotes the Bible with every other sentence. The

verse that always seems to surface is 'Slaves, obey your master.' "

"It would," said Shannow. His eyes were fixed on the door of the hall, which opened as a tall gray-haired man stepped onto the porch.

"Is that Baker?" he asked.

"Yes."

Shannow removed a shiny Barta coin from his pocket and placed it on the table. "My thanks to you, lady."

"It is too much," she protested.

"The laborer is worthy of the hire," he told her. Flora let him out through the front door, and he crossed the street swiftly, moving up behind the storekeeper. The man was a little unsteady on his feet.

"Good evening, Meneer Baker."

The man turned his watery blue eyes toward Shannow. "Good evening." He blinked and rubbed his eyes. "Do I know you?"

"Only as a customer. Would you be so kind as to open your store?"

"At this time of night? No, sir. Come back when the sun is up."

"I am afraid that will not be convenient, but I shall pay you well for the privilege."

"I suppose you want hunting goods," said Baker, fishing in his pocket for the key to the store.

"Yes."

"I would have thought Ridder would have been well pleased today."

"How so?"

"With the pair Riggs brought back. I shouldn't have thought you would need to rush out in the dead of night."

The storekeeper pushed open the door, and Shannow followed him inside.

"Well, choose what you need. I'll put it on Ridder's bill."

"That will not be necessary. I have coin."

Baker seemed surprised but said nothing, and Shannow took

salt, dried oats, sugar, herb tea, and a sack of grain. He also bought two new shirts and a quantity of dried meat.

"You are a friend of Riggs, I see," said Baker, pointing to the Hellborn pistol at Shannow's side.

"He has one of these?"

"He took it from the man they captured today—not the black man, the other one with the forked beard."

Ruth stared from her study window at the students taking their midday break on the wide lawns below. There were thirty-five young people at Sanctuary, all willing to learn and all yearning to change the world. Usually the sight of these young missionaries lifted Ruth's spirits, gave her renewed belief. But not today.

The evils of men like Abaddon she could withstand, for they could be countered by the love at Sanctuary. But the real dangers to the new world, she knew, were men such as Jon Shannow and Daniel Cade—dark heroes, understanding the weapons of evil and turning them on their users, never realizing they were merely perpetuating the violence they sought to destroy.

"You are an arrogant woman, Ruth," she told herself aloud, turning from the window. The parable of man was there to be seen within the Sipstrassi Stones, a gift from the heavens that could heal, nurture, and feed. But in the hands of men that was never enough; it had to be turned to death and despair.

Ruth could feel herself slipping from harmony, so she took a deep breath and prayed silently, drawing the peace of Sanctuary deep into her soul. The bay window disappeared as she closed the study to all intrusion. Pine-paneled walls surrounded her. The carved oak chair shimmered and became a bed. A stone hearth with a glowing log fire appeared, and Ruth lay back and watched the flames.

She felt the presence of another mind, and her defenses snapped into place as she sat up and tentatively reached out her thoughts.

"May I enter?" came a voice. Power emanated from the source of the sound, but she could sense no evil there.

She lowered the defensive wall, and a figure appeared within the room. He was tall and bearded, with blue eyes and braided hair. Upon his brow was a circlet of silver, at the center of which sat a golden stone.

"You are Pendarric?" she asked.

"I am, my lady."

"The Lord of the Blood Stones."

"Sadly true." A divan appeared beside him with braid-edged cushions of down-filled satin. He lay on his side, resting on one elbow.

"Why are you here?"

"To make amends, Ruth."

"You cannot undo the evil you sired."

"I know that; you are not the world's only source of wisdom. You are still mortal, lady. I was overwhelmed by the power of the stones, and I would argue against judging me. At the end my own strength triumphed, and I saved many thousands of my people. Abaddon is not so strong."

"What are you saying?"

"He is lost to the Sipstrassi. Nothing remains of the man you wed; he is not the father of the evil he sires any more than I was. He has lost the balance, even as you have."

"I am in harmony," Ruth told him.

"No, you are mistaken. In obliterating the desires of self, you have lost in your struggle. Harmony is balance; it is understanding the evil we all carry but holding it in stasis by the good we should desire. Harmony is achieved when we have the courage to accept that we are flawed. Everything you have achieved here is artificial. Yes, Sanctuary is pleasant. But even you, when you leave to travel the world, find that your doubts have grown. Then you fly back like a moth to the purifying candle. The truth should remain even when Sanctuary is gone."

"And you understand the truth?" she asked.

"I understand true harmony. You cannot eradicate evil, for without it how would we judge what is good? And if there is no greed, no lust, no baleful desires, what has a man achieved who becomes good? There would then be no mountains to climb."

"What do you suggest that I do?"

"Take the swan's path, Ruth."

"It is not time."

"Are you sure?"

"I am needed. There is still Abaddon."

"And the wolves in the shadows," said Pendarric. "If you need me, I will be with you."

"Wait! Why did you appear to Jon Shannow?"

"He is Rolynd. And only he can destroy the wolf you fear."

After he had gone, Ruth sat alone, once more staring into the flames. For the first time in many years she felt lost and uncertain and reached out, seeking Karitas and drawing him to her. His power was fading, his image drifting and unclear.

"I am sorry, Ruth, I will not be here to help you much longer. The ties that hold me to this land are weakening by the hour."

"How is Donna Taybard?"

"Her power is too great for her, and it grows at a frightening pace. Abaddon plans to sacrifice her on Walpurnacht, and then her power will soak into the Blood Stone. You must stop it, Ruth."

"I cannot."

"You have the strength to destroy the entire Hellborn nation."

"I know what power I have," snapped Ruth. "Do you believe the thought has not crossed my mind? Do you not think I was tempted when I saw the Hellborn bearing down on your village? I cannot help her in the way you desire."

"I shall not argue with you, Ruth," he said, reaching out a spectral hand, which she took into her own. "I have not the time. I love you, and I know that whatever you do will be for the best as you see it. You are a rare woman, and without you I would probably still be Hellborn. But you saved me."

"No, Karitas. You were strong enough to seek me out. It took great courage to see yourself as you were and struggle to change."

For one brief moment the image of Karitas glowed like fire, then it was gone. Ruth reached out, but nothing remained.

Loneliness settled on her, and she wept for the first time in more than a century.

Con Griffin had trouble controlling his temper. The Hellborn officer Zedeki had ridden into the settlement alone and asked to speak to the community's leaders. Accordingly, Griffin had assembled Jacob Madden—still weak from his wounds—Jimmy Burke, Ethan Peacock, and Aaron Phelps to listen to Zedeki's demands.

What Griffin heard made him tremble with fury.

"We will leave you in peace in return for one hostage who will accompany us to our city and meet our king. We want Donna Taybard."

"Or else?" said Griffin.

"I now have a thousand men. My orders are to destroy you if you do not comply."

"Why do you want my wife?"

"She will not be harmed."

"She is pregnant and cannot travel."

"We know this, and there is a comfortable wagon being prepared. Believe me, Mr. Griffin, we wish to see no harm come to the child."

"I will not do it," declared Griffin.

"That is your choice. You have until tomorrow at noon." With that he left them, and Griffin was dismayed to see that none of his friends would meet his eyes when he returned to the table.

"Well?" he asked them.

"They ain't left us many choices, Con," said Burke.

"You don't mean you agree?"

"Hold on, Griff," put in Madden, "and think it through. We can't survive against them in a war, and you've done us right proud so far. But we've all got families to care for . . . and they said no harm would come to her."

"You believe that, Jacob? Look at me, damn you! You believe that?"

"I don't know," he admitted.

"She's one of us," said Peacock. "We can't let them take her; it's not Christian."

"What is Christian about starting a war where we all get wiped out?" asked Aaron Phelps, his fat face streaked with sweat.

"Let's sleep on it," said Madden. "We've got till noon."

They agreed on that and left Griffin sitting by the cold woodstove and staring at the ceiling. As the last one left, the bedroom door opened and Eric walked across to Griffin.

"You won't let them take my mother, will you, Con?"

Griffin looked at the boy, and tears fell suddenly, streaking his face. Eric ran forward, throwing his arms around Griffin's neck.

The following day dawned bright and clear, but in the west dark clouds gathered with the promise of storms. The committee met once more, and Griffin forced a vote to include the whole community in the decision. Zedeki rode into the settlement with a wagon and waited for the votes to be cast.

One by one the settlers filed past the wooden box; even the children had been allowed to vote. Toward noon the Hellborn army came into sight, ringing the high ground at the valley's entrance and sitting their dark horses in chilling silence.

Madden and Peacock were detailed to count the votes, and they carried the box into the scholar's small cabin. Ten minutes later Madden called for Burke, and the oldster joined them. Then he moved among the men, and the crowd dispersed to their homes.

Griffin could barely contain himself.

Zedeki glanced up at the army and smiled. What a preposterous charade this was. He could see that Griffin knew the outcome, as did he, but the lengths to which ordinary people would go to preserve their pride remained a source of great amusement.

Madden emerged from the cabin and walked past Griffin, who half rose only to be waved back. The farmer made his way to the wagon.

"Might as well be on your way," he said. "We ain't giving her up."

"Are you insane?" asked Zedeki, his arm sweeping up to point to the armed riders. "Do you think you can withstand them?"

"Only one way to find out," said Madden. All around the settlement men and women were moving from their homes, weapons ready, to crouch behind the log screens.

Zedeki swallowed hard. "You are condemning the settlement to death."

"No," said Madden. "You're the man for that job. I don't trust you, Zedeki; I've seen your kind before. Your word ain't worth ant spit. You want Donna, you ride in and take her."

"We will," said Zedeki, "and you won't live long enough to regret your decision."

Madden watched as Zedeki swung the wagon and toyed with the idea of killing him. Instead, he merely stood and waited as the wagon lumbered up the rise. He drew his pistol and cocked it as Griffin joined him.

"Thanks, Jacob."

"Don't thank me. I voted for letting her go."

"Thanks, anyway."

As the wagon cleared the skyline, the Hellborn riders turned their mounts and disappeared. For an hour or more the settlers waited for the attack, but it never came. At last Madden and Griffin saddled their horses and rode up the rise. The Hellborn had gone.

"What's going on here, Con?"

"I don't know. They weren't frightened, that's for sure."

"Then why?"

"It's got something to do with Donna. They want her badly, but I think they want her alive."

"For what reason?"

"I don't know. I could be wrong, but it's the only thing that fits. I have a strong feeling that had we given her up to them, they would have butchered the settlement. But they're frightened Donna might get hurt."

"What do we do?"

"We've no choice, Jacob. We wait."

*   *   *

Donna watched it all from the seeming sanctuary of the spirit sky. Her body lay in a virtual coma, but her spirit rose unchained to soar free between the gathering clouds and the green valley. She saw the settlers vote to fight for her and was both gladdened and saddened, for she also saw the treachery in the heart of Zedeki.

The settlement was doomed.

Unable to face stark reality, Donna fled in a tumbling blur where colors swirled around her and stars grew as large as lanterns. There was no time there, no feeling for the passing of seconds or hours or days. At last she stopped and floated above a blue sea where gulls wheeled and dived around coral islands. It was peaceful there and beautiful.

Calm came to her, and peace filled her like the coming of dawn after the sleep of nightmare.

A woman appeared alongside her, and Donna felt tranquillity flowing from the newcomer. She was middle-aged, with iron-gray hair and a face of ageless serenity.

"I am Ruth," she said.

"They are going to kill my son," said Donna. "My boy!" There were no tears, but there was anguish, and Ruth felt it.

"I am sorry, Donna. There are no words."

"Why do they act in this way?"

"They have a dream that has haunted men since the dawn of time. Conquest, victory, virility, power—it is evil's most potent weapon."

"I'm going home," said Donna. "I want to be with my son."

"They want you as a sacrifice," said Ruth. "They need to draw power from your death; they need you to feed their evil."

"They won't have me."

"Are you sure?"

"My strength has grown, Ruth. Abaddon cannot take me. I will take my soul and my strength far from him and let my body die like a shell."

"That will take great courage."

"No," said Donna, "for then I will be with my son and my husband."

Donna began the long journey home. This time she traveled

without panic, and the swirling colors became events, a kaleidoscopic history of a world touched with insanity. Caesars,
princes, khans and kings, emperors, lords, dukes and thanes—
all with a single purpose. She saw chariots and spears, bows
and cannon, tanks and aircraft, and a light that shone over cities
like a giant torch. It was all meaningless and insurmountably
petty.

It was dark when she descended into the valley. Madden and
Burke were standing guard, waiting with grim courage for the
attack they knew was imminent. She floated above Eric's bed;
his face was peaceful, his sleep soothing.

Karitas appeared beside her.

"How are you faring, Donna?" His voice was strangely cold,
and she shivered.

"I cannot stand to see them die."

"They do not have to die," he said. "We can save them."

"How?"

"You must trust me. I need you to return to your body, and
then we will leave the valley. The settlers will be in no danger
if you are not here, and I will take you to a place of safety."

"My son will live? Truly?"

"Come with me, Donna."

She was unsure and hesitated. "I must tell Con."

"No. Speak to no one. When it has all blown over, you may
return. Trust me."

Donna fled to her body and saw Con Griffin asleep in the
chair beside her bed. He looked so tired. She settled back into
herself and concentrated on rising, but once more she was
liquid within a sponge.

"Picture your body as a thin sheet of copper," Karitas
advised. "Believe it to be metallic."

It was easier now, and she half rose, then fell back.

"Concentrate, Donna," urged Karitas. "Their lives depend
on you."

She rose and dressed in silence. "Dark clothes," said Karitas. "We must avoid the guards." She could no longer see him,
but his voice came as a cold whisper in her mind.

She slipped out of the door and into the shadows. Madden

and Burke had their eyes fixed on the surrounding hills, and
she moved away into the darkness unobserved. Moving from
shrub to boulder to tree-shrouded hollows, she slowly climbed
the rise. At the top she stopped.

"Over there," said Karitas, "by that circle of rocks, you will
find something to help you. Come."

She moved to the rocks, and there, gleaming in the moonlight, lay five silver circlets.

"Place two over your ankles, two on your wrists, and the last
on your brow. Quickly, now!"

She clipped them into place. "Now try to leave your body."

She relaxed and tried to soar, but there was nothing: no
movement, no dizzying flight.

"Now what, Karitas?"

Six Zealots moved out of hiding and approached her. She
tried to run, but they caught her easily. She fought to tear the
circlets from her wrist, but they pinned her arms. Then another
voice entered her mind.

"You are mine, Donna Taybard, as I promised," hissed
Abaddon.

Sanity spun away from her, and the world faded into blessed
darkness.

Griffin stumbled from the cabin, pistol in hand.

"Jacob!" he screamed, and Madden leapt to his feet.

"What is it, Con?"

"She's gone. Donna. Oh, my God!"

Suddenly Burke shouted, and Madden's gaze followed his
pointing finger. The Hellborn army sat once more on the crest
of the rise. A single trumpet blast shrieked out into the dawn
air, and the riders swept toward the settlement. Men and
women ran from their cabins with weapons at the ready and
took up positions behind the log screens.

Madden called for Rachel to bring him his rifle, and she
ducked into the house and came out cradling the Hellborn
weapon. She ran toward him, but the first shot of the battle took
her low in the chest. Madden saw her stumble and raced to her
side, catching her as she fell.

"Something hit me, Jacob," she whispered . . . and died.

Madden snatched up the rifle, levering a shell into the breech just as the rolling thunder of hooves was upon him. He swiveled and fired twice, pitching two riders from their saddles. A third fired a pistol, and dust mushroomed by Madden's feet. His return shot all but tore the man's head from his shoulders.

Griffin threw a rifle to Eric and ran from the cabin. He saw Madden down and riders sweeping toward him. Coolly Griffin leveled his pistol, sending six shots into the mass.

Burke and some twenty men managed to get to the eastern log screen, sending volley after volley into the riders. But the Hellborn rode through the field of fire and leapt from their horses to engage the settlers in hand-to-hand combat.

Griffin rammed fresh shells into his pistol and ran from the cabin toward Madden. A rider bore down on him, and he dived clear of the horse's hooves. His gun thundered, the bullet taking the horse in the head; the beast went down, hurling the rider headfirst to the ground. Griffin was up and running when a bullet smashed into his back; he turned, but another shell caught him in the chest. Seeing Griffin's plight, Madden swung his rifle and emptied two saddles. A shell struck his temple, and he fell face forward into the dust. As Griffin struggled to rise, he saw Eric move into the open with the rifle in his hands. He tried to wave the boy back. The rifle fired twice, then a score of guns were turned on the boy and blasted him from sight.

Aaron Phelps sat trembling in the back room of his cabin, listening to the shots and the screams and the thunder of hooves. His pistol was pointed at the door. Someone's shoulder crashed against the wood, and Phelps fired. Then the door exploded inward. He did not see the Hellborn crowded there; he pushed the barrel of his pistol into his mouth and blew out his brains.

Outside the Hellborn had overcome all but one man. Jimmy Burke, blood seeping from a dozen wounds, had staggered into his cabin and slammed the door shut, dropping an oak bar in place. He reloaded his pistols and crawled to a chest by the rear wall, from which he took an old blunderbuss. He charged it with a double load, then poured a measure of tack nails into the barrel.

The Hellborn began pounding against the door, and an ax blade crashed through. Burke switched his gaze to the wooden shutters of the window; a shadow blocked the sunlight at the center and he sent a bullet punching through. A man screamed, and Burke grinned. More axes swung against the door, smashing a head-sized hole above the bar. An arm reached through, and Burke aimed the pistol and waited. As the man began to lift the bar, he exposed his neck; then Burke's pistol bucked in his hand, and blood gushed to stain the wood of the door. Suddenly the window crashed inward. A bullet took Burke in the chest, and he winced as his lungs began to fill with blood. Taking up the blunderbuss, he swallowed hard and waited.

"Don't take too long, you bastards," he muttered. Another arm reached through the hole in the door, and Burke cocked his weapon. The bar slid clear, booted feet kicked open the door, and the Hellborn surged inside.

"Suck on this!" screamed the old man. The blunderbuss exploded with a deafening roar, and a half pound of nails ripped into their ranks, scything them down. Burke dropped the weapon and reached for his pistol, but two more shots from the window ended his defiance.

Silence fell on the valley, and the Hellborn collected their dead and rode from Avalon.

A westerly wind drove the storm clouds over the settlement, and lightning speared across the valley. As the rain began, Griffin groaned and tried to move, but pain ripped through him and he rolled to his side. His weapons were gone, and the ground below him was soaked with his blood.

"Come on, Griffin," he told himself. "Find your strength."

Pushing his arms beneath him, he forced himself to a sitting position. Dizziness swept over him, but he fought it back. Madden was lying twenty yards to his right, and he crawled through the rain to his friend's body. Madden's face was covered with blood, and beyond him lay Rachel, her dead eyes staring up at the lowering sky.

"I'm sorry, Jacob," said Griffin. When he placed his hand on his friend's shoulder, Madden moved. Griffin lifted his arm, feeling for a pulse. It was there and beating strongly. Examining the head wound, he found that the bullet had glanced off Madden's temple, tearing the skin but not piercing the skull. He tried to lift the wounded man, but his own injuries had sapped him and he sat helpless in the rain.

The storm passed as he waited, the sun beaming down on the desolated settlement. Madden moaned and opened his eyes, seeing Griffin sitting beside him.

"Did we drive them off?" he whispered. Griffin shook his head.

"Rachel? The boys?"

"I think they killed everyone, Jacob."

"Oh, God!"

Madden sat up and saw Rachel. He crawled to her and shut her eyes, leaning forward to kiss her cold lips.

"You deserved better than this, my girl," he said. Griffin swayed and fell as Madden stood and stared at the skyline.

Somewhere out there the Hellborn were riding, and Madden sent his hatred out after them in one bloodcurdling scream of frustrated rage and despair. He moved to Griffin and half carried, half dragged him into the nearest cabin, where the body of Burke lay beside an open chest. Madden managed to maneuver Griffin to a bed and opened his shirt. There were two wounds, one high in the shoulder at the back and the second low on the left side of the chest, close to the heart. Neither showed an exit wound. Madden plugged the holes with linen and covered the unconscious man with a blanket.

Leaving the cabin, he found his boys together near the paddock behind his cabin. From the blood on the grass around them, they had made a fight of it. Pride and sorrow vied in Madden's mind as he turned away from the corpses and moved through the settlement, checking body after body. All had been slain.

Back in his own cabin Madden pulled the bed from the wall

and lifted the sack he had hidden there. Inside were two Hell-born pistols and around thirty shells. He loaded the pistols and strapped them to his side.

All dead. All the dreams gone down to dust.

"Well, you didn't kill me, you sons of bitches! And I'll be coming after you. You want hell? I'll give you hell!"

◇ **10** ◇

SHANNOW STOOD OUTSIDE the store with his supply sack over his shoulder, gazing up at the white marble fortress. There were six cylindrical towers, two of them flanking the high arched gate. There appeared to be no sentries. The store-keeper, Baker, had locked the door and wandered away into the shadows, and Shannow stood alone, pondering his course of action.

Somewhere in or below that vast fortress Batik and Archer were prisoners. Yet was it any concern of his? What did he owe them? Would either of them come riding to his rescue? More to the point, *could* he rescue them?

Ridder had twenty men, and Shannow did not know their disposition or the layout inside the fortress. Riding inside would be a futile gesture, achieving nothing. He returned to his horse and mounted, riding out into the main street and up toward the black-shadowed gateway.

The white towers loomed over him, and he had the feeling that he was riding into a massive tomb, never to see the sun rise again. A man stepped into his path; he was carrying an old rifle.

"What's your business?" he asked.

"I've come to see Ridder."

"He expecting you?"

"Can you think of another reason I should be here at this time of night?"

The man shrugged. "I'm just told to watch for runaway Wolvers; nobody tells me anything else. Still, it's better than the mine, by God."

Shannow nodded and touched his heels to the horse, riding on as if he knew where he was going. The gate arch led to a cobbled courtyard; straight ahead was a wide set of marble steps leading to a double door of oak, while to the right lay a narrow alleyway. Shannow chose the alley and soon found himself in a yard housing a row of stables. A young lad moved out of the shadows, scratching his head, and Shannow dismounted and handed him the reins.

"Don't unsaddle him. I'm leaving shortly."

"All right," said the boy, yawning.

Shannow slipped him a silver coin. "Give him some oats and a rubdown."

"I will," promised the lad, the brightness of the silver dispelling all thoughts of sleep.

"Where will I find Meneer Ridder?"

"In his rooms this time of night."

"How do I get there?"

"You new?"

"Yes."

"Go back out into the courtyard, past the steps, and you'll see a staircase on the outside of the wall. Climb that, pass the first two doors, and go in through the third. The sentry there will take you the rest of the way."

"Thank you."

Shannow left the boy and returned to the main courtyard, waving to the sentry as he passed. He found the spiral stair and climbed to the third story, pausing outside the timber door. Then he removed his coat and folded it across his arm before opening the door. Inside was a corridor hung with rugs and lit by oil lamps. Stepping into the light, Shannow forced a smile for the sentry who was sitting with his feet on a small marble statue of a snarling dog. The man swung his legs clear and stood.

"What do you want?" he whispered. "You ain't my relief."

"True," said Shannow, moving casually toward him. The coat slipped from his arm to reveal the black muzzle of the Hellborn pistol. He cocked it, and the noise seemed to echo in the corridor like cracking bones. The man's eyes widened as Shannow moved closer, pushing the muzzle up under his chin.

"Which room is Ridder's?" he whispered.

The sentry pointed over Shannow's shoulder.

"Tell me," Shannow said, without following the man's shaking finger.

"Two doors down on the left."

"And where are the prisoners who were brought in today?"

"I've no idea. I've only just come on. I've been asleep all day."

"Would they be kept in the mine?"

"Probably."

"How do I get there?"

"Jesus, man, I couldn't tell you that. There's a score of staircases and corridors and a pulley lift. You could lose yourself in this place."

"What's through the door behind you?"

"It's a storeroom."

"Be so kind as to open it."

"Don't kill me—I've a wife . . . children."

"Get inside." The man turned and opened the door; Shannow followed him in and struck him savagely on the back of the neck, and the sentry fell forward without a sound. Shannow searched the room for cord but found none, so he removed the man's belt and tied his hands behind his back. Then he gagged him with a linen kerchief, which he stuffed into his mouth, binding it with a piece of torn curtain.

Stepping out into the corridor, he moved silently to Ridder's room, cursing softly when he saw a light showing under the door. He opened it and stepped inside, finding himself facing a small altar before which knelt a slim man with a shock of white hair. The man turned. He was around fifty years old, with round dark eyes and a hatchet face that bore no trace of humor.

"Who in God's name are you, sir?" exclaimed Ridder, surging to his feet, his thin face reddening.

"You can ask him yourself," said Shannow, leveling the pistol.

All color fled from Ridder's face. "You can't mean to kill me."

"Just so, pastor."

"But why?"

"On a whim," snarled Shannow. "I have no time for brigands."

"Nor I. I am a man of God."

"I think not." Shannow moved forward swiftly and with his left hand took hold of the lapels of Ridder's black jacket, pulling the man to him. "Open your mouth."

The terrified man did so, and Shannow slid the muzzle of the pistol between his teeth.

"Now listen to me, pastor, and note every word. You are going to take me to the two men you brought in here today, and then we are going to leave together, all four of us. It is your only chance for life. You understand?"

Ridder nodded.

"Now, in case you think that once we are away from here your men will help you, bear this in mind: I am not a man who is afraid to die, and I will take you on the journey to hell with me."

Shannow withdrew the pistol and sheathed it. "Wipe the sweat from your face, pastor, and let us go."

Together the two men walked into the corridor and down several flights of stairs. Shannow was soon lost within the maze of the building as they passed one shadow-haunted corridor after another. The air was musty, and several times they passed sentries who stood to attention as Ridder went by. At last they emerged into a dimly lit hall where six men sat at a table dicing for copper coins. All were armed with handguns and knives.

"Prepare the lift," said Ridder, and the men moved swiftly to a series of pulleys and ropes beside an open shaft. A burly man with huge forearms cranked an iron handle, and after a few seconds a large box rose into view. Ridder stepped inside, and Shannow followed; within the box was a handbell on a rope. With a sickening lurch the box descended into darkness;

Shannow blinked sweat from his eyes as the lift continued its descent.

After what seemed a lifetime they reached another level, and Ridder rang the handbell. The lift stopped, and the two men emerged into a dimly lit tunnel filled with the stench of human excrement.

Shannow gagged and swallowed hard. Ridder gestured toward a series of bolted doors.

"I don't know which one they are in, but they'll be here somewhere."

"Open every door."

"Are you mad? We'll be torn limb from limb."

"How many people are down here?"

"About fifty people. And maybe sixty Wolvers."

Shannow's jaw tightened, for there were only six doors. "You keep twenty people locked up in each of these? And you call yourself a man of God?" Shannow's rage exploded, and he struck Ridder on the side of the head, hurtling the man from his feet. "Get up and open the doors—every God-cursed one of them!"

Ridder crawled to the first, then turned. "You don't understand. This whole community needs the mine. They're my responsibility—caring for my flock. I wouldn't have used people if I hadn't been forced to. I used Wolvers, but the lung fever killed scores of them."

"Open the door, pastor. Let's see your flock."

Ridder pushed the bolt clear and swung the door open. Nothing moved in the darkness within.

"Now the others."

"For God's sake . . ."

"You talk of God down here?" shouted Shannow.

A dark shape moved into the half-light, and he stepped back in shock. The creature was maybe five feet in height and covered with fur; its face was long, caricaturing a wolf or dog, but its eyes were human. It was naked and covered with sores. More creatures came into sight, ignoring the two men. They limped to a chest by the far wall and stood apathetically, staring at nothing.

"What's in the chest?" asked Shannow.

"Their tools. They think it's work time."

"All the doors, Ridder!" The white-haired pastor stumbled from one dungeon to the next. From the last room but one the bloodied face of Batik could be seen above the smaller Wolvers.

"Shannow?"

"Over here, man. Quickly!"

Batik pushed his way through the milling slaves, and Shannow handed him his percussion pistol.

"Stay down here with that creature," he said, pointing at Ridder. "I'll send the lift back. Try to get all of them to understand that they're free."

"They'll only be rounded up again. Let's get out while we can."

"Do as I say, Batik, or I'll leave you here. Where's Archer?"

"Unconscious. They beat him badly, and we'll have to carry him out."

"Get something arranged," said Shannow, stepping into the lift.

"Easy for you to say," snapped Batik. "I'll just stay down here with the wolf beasts and arrange a stretcher!"

"Fine," said Shannow, ringing the handbell. The lift lurched upward, and once more the journey seemed interminable, but finally he came into the light where the six men labored at the winch and stepped out.

"Where's Meneer Ridder?" asked the burly man with the huge arms.

"He'll be along," said Shannow, producing his pistol. "Lower the lift."

"What the hell is this?"

"This is death, my friend, unless you do exactly as you are told. Lower the lift."

"You think you can take us all?"

Shannow's gun exploded, and a man was smashed back into the far wall, a bullet through his heart.

"You think I can't?" he hissed.

The burly man turned the winch as if his life depended on it . . .

Which it did.

Within an hour most of the slaves had been lifted to the next level, but as Batik pointed out, several of the Wolvers had refused to leave, sitting silently staring at the tool chest. Batik was not even sure they had understood his urgings.

Shannow went below and saw them, crouched in a half circle around the chest. It was not locked, and he opened it; inside were a dozen pick handles and a stack of blades. He handed them to the waiting Wolvers, who stood and moved into a line facing the black tunnel that led to the mine. Shannow went to the hunched figure at the front of the line and gently took him by the shoulders, turning him to face the lift. When the Wolver moved obediently toward the shaft, the others followed.

Shannow rang the handbell and waited below as the box moved out of sight. Then he checked the six dungeons. In one he found seven bodies, small and emaciated; in another two corpses had begun to rot, and the stench was almost overwhelming. He forced himself to check the other rooms, and in the last he found Ridder crouching against the wall.

"It's not my fault," said Ridder, staring down at the body of a child of around eleven.

"How long is it since you visited these cells?"

"Not for a year. It's not my fault. The mine had to work. You see that, don't you? Hundreds of people rely on it."

"Get up, pastor. It's time to go."

"No, you can't take them away. People will see them, and they'll blame me. They won't understand."

"Stay here, then," said Shannow. He left the man squatting in a corner and moved back into the tunnel. Batik had sent down the lift, and he stepped inside and rang the bell.

On the upper level Batik had disarmed the guards and had laid Archer's unconscious body across the table the men had used for their dice game. Shannow examined the black man's swollen features; he had been beaten badly.

"Who did this?" he asked Batik.

"The man Riggs and a half dozen others. I tried to help him, but he wouldn't help himself; he just stood there and took it. It seemed to make them more angry, and when he fell, they started kicking him."

"Why did they do it?"

"He simply told them that he wouldn't work for them, that he would sooner just starve to death."

Shannow moved to the guards. "You," he said, pointing to the burly man, "lead us out of here. The rest of you can help carry my friend."

"Are you going to let them live?" asked a man, pushing himself through the milling Wolvers. Shannow turned to see a wasted scarecrow of a figure with a matted blond beard streaked with filth. He was naked but for a stained leather loincloth, and his upper body was a mass of sores.

"We need them, my friend," said Shannow softly. "Hold your anger."

"My son is down there—and my wife. They died in that black hole."

"But we're not free yet," said Shannow. "Trust me."

He took the man by the arm and led him to Batik, collecting a double-barreled flintlock pistol the Hellborn had taken from one of the guards and pressing it into the man's hand.

"We may have to fight our way out. Take your revenge then."

Shannow looked around the room and saw that there were close to ninety people packing the chamber. He signaled the guards to lift Archer and then led the way into the tunnel beyond. Batik was at the rear. Shannow cocked his pistol and walked behind the guard he had chosen to lead them. Slowly the column of slaves moved through the bowels of the castle, the air freshening as they climbed toward the light. Finally they came into a high-walled corridor where far above them the dawn light shone in majestic shafts through arched windows. A chittering noise broke from the Wolvers, who raised their skinny arms, hands stretching toward the golden glow.

Ahead was a double door of studded oak, and the guard began to move more swiftly.

"Stop!" said Shannow, but the man merely dived for the floor, and the doors began to open.

"Down!" bellowed Shannow, dropping to his knees, his pistol coming up as the muzzles of several rifles appeared in the open doorway. Shannow fired, and the first rifleman pitched from sight. The corridor was filled with deafening explosions. Shells whistled past Shannow, and his own gun boomed twice more; then there was silence. He flicked open the cylinder guard and reloaded his pistol, then ran forward, hugging the wall. A rifleman stepped into sight, and Shannow put two shots in his chest.

Behind Shannow the guard who had been leading them reached into his boot and produced a long-bladed knife. He rose silently and launched himself at the Jerusalem Man, but a shot rang out and he staggered. Shannow twisted and fired, and the man slumped to the floor.

Batik sprinted along the other side of the corridor.

"Nice pistol," he said. "Pulls a little to the left."

Shannow nodded and pointed to the right of the doorway, and Batik sighed and cocked his pistol. Moving forward at a run, he dived through the doorway and rolled on his shoulder. Behind the door a crouching rifleman swung his weapon, but Batik shot him in the head before he could bring the barrel to bear. Shells ricocheted off the marble floor, shrieking past Batik's head. He glanced up and saw that he was in a huge hall edged by a wide inner balcony where other marksmen were kneeling, covering the door. He scrambled to his feet and hurled himself back into the corridor.

"Any other ideas?" he asked Shannow.

"Not at the moment."

"That's just as well!"

Behind them four of the Wolvers were down and dying; the others were crouching around them, keening softly.

"Can you climb?" asked Shannow.

Batik glanced up at the high windows. "I'll break my neck."

"All right, we'll just sit here and wait for a miracle."

"I thought your God was good at those."

"He helps those who help themselves," said Shannow dryly.

Batik exchanged pistols with Shannow and pushed the fully loaded Hellborn gun into his belt. The wall below the window was constructed of solid marble blocks about two feet square; between the blocks were cracks that allowed a tentative grip. Batik placed his foot on the first block and began to climb. He was a powerful man, but before he had climbed more than fifteen feet, his fingers were aching with the effort; at thirty feet he began to curse Shannow. At forty feet he slipped. His feet scrabbled for purchase, and all his weight hung on the three fingers of his right hand. Sweat dripped into his eyes, and he fought down panic, moving his foot slowly into position to take his weight. His arms began to tremble, but he took a deep breath and pushed on, hooking his arm over the ledge of the arched window. Light blinded him, and he blinked rapidly; he was overlooking the main courtyard and could see men running from the walls to the steps below, heading into the hall.

Swiftly he straddled the ledge and leaned out. As he had feared, there was no easy way to the windows above the hall balcony, and now the drop was even worse. With a whispered curse he lowered himself to the first foothold and started to traverse the outer wall. He had moved some ten feet when a musket ball hit the stone beside his head and screamed off above him. Glancing over his shoulder, he saw a man on the gate turret hastily reloading his weapon.

Batik moved on. How long would it take to reload? Thirty seconds? A minute? His heart was pounding furiously as he reached the window and clamped his hand on the secure ledge. He risked another glance and saw the man aiming the rifle. Batik swung out, hanging by his right arm as the shot hit the ledge, chipping stone fragments that stung his hand. He hauled himself over the ledge and tumbled onto the balcony. Two men were kneeling there watching the doorway below, and they both turned as Batik fell. The Hellborn threw himself at them, knocking aside a musket barrel. The weapon fired. Batik cracked his fist against the man's chin and kicked out at the second rifleman, catching him in the chest and knocking him flat. The first man drew a knife and leapt forward; Batik blocked the man's knife arm with a chopping blow, grabbed his hair, and with a tremendous surge of power hurled him over the balcony wall. The man's scream was cut off as he hit the marble floor.

Batik pulled his pistol clear and swung on the second man, who was sitting motionless with his hands above his head. He was a youngster, maybe sixteen, with wide blue eyes and an open face too pretty to be called handsome.

Batik shot him between the eyes.

Across the hallway other riflemen had seen the action and opened fire. Batik dived to the floor and scrambled toward a stone pillar at one corner of the hall. From that position he had two fields of fire and could also see the stairwell that led to the balcony. He glanced at the riflemen opposite; there were three of them, each armed with a musket.

"Shannow!" he called. "There's only three. You want me to kill them?"

At the other end of the hall Shannow grinned. "Give them a chance to surrender," he shouted.

Batik waited for several seconds. "They haven't surrendered," he said.

"Wait!" came a cry from the balcony. "We don't want any more killing."

"Throw the muskets over the edge," Batik called, and three weapons clattered to the stone. "And any pistols." More weapons crashed to the floor. "Now stand up where we can see you."

The men did so. Batik would have killed them, but he had only five shots left and knew there were more enemies in the courtyard below. "Bring them out, Shannow," he yelled, and then ran for the stairs, taking them two at a time and emerging into the shadowed doorway of the main entrance. Outside, several men were crouching behind hastily built barricades constructed of water barrels and grain sacks.

"What now, General?" Batik asked as Shannow moved alongside him in the shadows.

"Now we talk," said Shannow, and moved forward. "Hold

your fire," he called, descending the steps and moving slowly toward the crouching riflemen.

"That is far enough," called a voice.

Shannow stopped. "Inside there are seven dead men; some of them were probably friends of yours. Eight others surrendered, and tonight they will be with their families enjoying supper. You decide what you want to do. Batik! Bring them out."

The Jerusalem Man stood calmly before the riflemen as the first of the Wolvers stumbled into the daylight. One by one the guards put down their rifles and stood. Batik led the former slaves through the gates and out into the main street of the town, where the Wolvers huddled together behind the black-garbed Hellborn.

Back in the courtyard a terrible scream tore through the air as the skeletal, bearded widower ran into the open, clutching the flintlock pistol. He looked at Shannow and the guards and then ran out into the street behind the Wolvers, stopping only when he saw the crowds lining the buildings. He screamed again and fell to his knees, staring down at his filthy body and the pus-filled sores on his skin.

His wild eyes raked the crowd. "You took it all!" he shouted, lifting the pistol under his chin and pulling the trigger. Blood gushed from his throat, and he toppled forward.

Shannow rode from the castle, leading two horses. He paused by the body and then looked at the silent crowd. There were no words to convey his contempt, and he rode on. The guards had carried Archer to the porch by the store; the black man was coming around, but he could not stand.

"Take him inside somewhere," ordered Shannow. "Find him a bed."

"Bring him to my place," said Flora. "I'll see to him."

Shannow nodded to the woman. The Wolvers were sitting in the center of the street, some of them still holding their pick-axes. Shannow dismounted and moved to Batik. "Get some food from the store for them. Clothes, supplies ... Jesus! I don't know. Get them anything they need."

The storekeeper, Baker, walked out onto the street.

"Who is going to run the mine?" he asked.

Shannow hit him, and the man fell to the dust.

"There was no need for that," whimpered Baker.

Shannow took a deep breath. "You are correct, Meneer Baker, and I cannot begin to explain it." He left the man and walked to the Wolvers, moving in to kneel among them.

"Can any of you understand me?" he asked.

They looked at him but did not speak; their faces were cowed, their eyes dull. Flora approached, bringing with her the young boy who had stabled Shannow's horse.

"They do understand you," she said. "Robin here has lived with them."

"We are going to get you some food," Shannow told them. "Then you are free to return to the plains or the mountains or wherever you call home."

"Ree?" said a small dark figure to the right, his head tilting, his eyes fixed on Shannow's. The voice was piping and high, almost musical.

"Yes. Free."

"Ree!" The creature blinked and touched one of its comrades on the shoulder. Shannow saw it was a female. It placed its arms around her shoulders, and their faces touched. "Ree," the Wolver whispered.

"Archer wants to see you," sàid Flora.

Shannow stood and followed her through the eating house and up a flight of rickety wooden steps to a bedroom above the kitchen.

Archer was dozing when Shannow entered, but he awoke when the Jerusalem Man sat on the bed beside him.

"Nicely done, Shannow," he whispered.

"I was lucky," said Shannow. "How are you feeling?"

"Strange. Light-headed, but there's no pain. I'm so glad to see you, Shannow. When you went over that ledge, I had a sinking feeling in my heart." The black man leaned back and closed his swollen eyes; his face was badly cut and gashed, and his words were badly slurred.

"Rest now," advised Shannow, squeezing his shoulder. "I'll come back later."

"No," said Archer, opening his eyes, "I feel fine. I thought for a while that Riggs and his friends were going to kill me, and I knew Amaziga would be so angry. She's a fine woman and a wonderful wife, but nag? She's always telling me to take a weapon with me. But then, how many enemies does a man meet in a dead city? You'll like her, Shannow; she made me wait eight years before agreeing to marry me—said that I was too soft, that she wasn't going to risk falling in love with a man who would be killed during his first hostile encounter. She was nearly right. But my charm won her in the end. Tough lady, Shannow . . . Shannow?"

"What is it?"

"Why has it gone dark? Is it so late already?"

The sun was shining brightly through the open window.

"Light a lamp, Shannow. I can't see you."

"There is no oil," Shannow said desperately.

"Oh, well, never mind. I like the dark. Do you mind sitting here with me?"

"Not at all."

"I wish I had my stone. Then these bruises would be gone in seconds."

"There'll be another at the Ark."

Archer chuckled. "How could you attack a fortress?"

"I don't know; it seemed like a good idea at the time."

"Batik told me you are unable to comprehend impossible odds, and I can quite believe him. Did you know that Ridder was a priest?"

"Yes."

"Strange religion you have, Shannow."

"No, Archer. Just that some very strange people are attracted to it."

"Including you?"

"Including me."

"Why are you sounding so sad? It's a fine day. I never thought to get out of there alive—they just kept kicking me. Batik tried to stop them, but they beat him down with staves. Staves . . . I'm very tired, Shannow. I think . . ."

"Archer . . . Archer!"

Flora moved forward and lifted the man's wrist. "He's dead," she whispered.

"He can't be," protested Shannow.

"I'm sorry."

"Where is Riggs?"

"He was in the meeting hall."

Shannow strode from the room and down the stairs, emerging into the sunlight, where Batik was passing out food among the Wolvers. Batik saw the expression on his face and moved to join him.

"What's happened?"

"Archer is dead."

"Where are you going?"

"Riggs," Shannow said tersely, pushing past him.

"Wait!" Batik called, grabbing Shannow's arm. "He's mine!"

Shannow turned. "What gives you the right?"

"Poetry, Shannow. I'm going to beat him to death!"

Together the two men entered the meeting hall. There were two dozen tables and a long bar running the length of the room. At the back sat three men, all of them armed. As Shannow and Batik moved forward slowly, two of the men eased themselves to their feet and edged away from the third.

The man hurled the table away and stood. Riggs was over six feet tall and powerfully muscled, his face flat and brutal, his eyes small and cold.

"Well?" he said. "What's it to be?"

Batik handed the pistol to Shannow and moved forward unarmed.

"You must be insane," said Riggs.

Batik hit him with a crashing right-hand blow, and he staggered and spit blood from his mouth. The fight began. Riggs was heavier, but Batik moved with greater speed and landed more blows; the punishment each man took was appalling to Shannow's eyes.

Grabbing Batik in a bear hug, Riggs lifted him from his feet, but Batik hammered his open palms into Riggs' ears and broke free. Riggs kicked Batik's legs from under him and then leapt feetfirst at his head. The Hellborn rolled and rose to his feet; then, as Riggs rushed at him, he ducked under a left hook and hammered a combination of punches to Riggs' belly. The big man grunted and backed away, and Batik followed, thundering blows to Riggs' chin. Both men were bloodied now, and Batik's shirt was in tatters. Riggs tried to grapple, but Batik swung him around and tripped him. The bigger man landed on his face, and Batik leapt on his back, grabbing his hair and chin.

"Say good-bye, Riggs," he hissed, then wrenched the chin up and to the right. The sound of the snapping neck made Shannow wince. Batik staggered to his feet, then moved to a nearby table, where Shannow joined him.

"You smell awful," said Shannow, "and you look worse!"

"Always words of comfort from you just when they're needed."

Shannow smiled. "I'm glad you are alive, my friend."

"You know, Shannow, after you went over that ledge and Archer and I raced clear of the lions, he talked about you. He said you were a man to move mountains."

"Then he was wrong."

"I don't think so. He said you would just walk up to a mountain and start lifting it a rock at a time, never seeing just how big it was."

"Maybe."

"I'm glad he lived long enough to see you attack a castle single-handed. He would have enjoyed that. Did he tell you about Sir Galahad?"

"Yes."

"And his quest for the Grail?"

"Yes. What of it?"

"Are you still planning to kill Abaddon?"

"That is my intention."

"Then I'll come with you."

"Why?" Shannow asked, surprised.

"You might need a hand lifting all those rocks!"

Ruth floated above the fabled palaces of Atlantis, gazing in wonder at the broken spires and fractured terraces. From her

position just below the clouds she could even see the out-
lines of wide roads beneath the soil of the rolling prairies.
Around the center of the city was a flat uninspired wasteland
that once must have housed the poorer quarters of Atlantis,
where the homes were built of inferior stone long since eroded
by the awesome might of the Atlantic Ocean. But now, once
more, the gleaming marble of the palaces glistened beneath a
silver moon.

She wondered what the city must have been like in the days
of its glory, with its terraced gardens and vineyards, its wide
statue-lined ways, its parks and colosseums. Part of the city to
the north had been destroyed by a volcanic upheaval, and now
a jagged mountain range reared above the ruins.

Wishing herself downward, she floated gently to an open
terrace before a gaunt and shadowed shell that once had been
the palace of Pendarric. Wild grass and weeds grew everywhere, and a tree had taken root against a high wall, its roots
questing like skeletal fingers for a hold in the cracked marble.

She stopped before a ten-foot statue of the king, recognizing
him despite the artificially curled beard and the high, plumed
helm. A strong man—too strong to see his weakness before it
was too late.

A sparrow settled on the helm and then flew off between the
marble pillars of a civilization that once had stretched from the
shores of Peru to the gold mines of Cornwall. The land of
fable!

But even the fable would fade. For Ruth knew that in centuries to come her own age of technology and space travel
would become embroiled in myth and legend to which few
would give credence.

New York, London, Paris . . . all synonymous with the fiction of Atlantis.

Then one day the world would topple once more, and the
survivors would stumble upon the Statue of Liberty protruding
from the mud, or Big Ben, or the pyramids. And they would
wonder, even as she did, what the future held now.

She turned her gaze to the mountains and the golden ship

lodged in the black basaltic rock five hundred feet above the ruins.

The Ark. Rust-covered and immense and strangely beautiful, it lay broken-backed on a wide ledge. Within its thousand-foot length the Guardians labored, but Ruth would not go among them. She wanted no part of the old world or the knowledge they so zealously guarded.

Ruth returned to Sanctuary and her room. As always, when her mood was somber, she created a study without doors or windows, lit only by candles that did not flicker.

For a while she sat and remembered Sam Archer, praying silently for the soul of the man. Then she called for Pendarric.

He came almost at once and stood by the far wall, which opened to become a window looking out on Atlantis in its glory. People thronged the winding streets and marketplaces. Chariots drawn by white horses clattered along the statue-lined main avenue.

Ruth joined him. "As it was?" she asked.

"As it is," he answered. "There are many worlds that overlap our own and many gateways to them. In the last days before the oceans drank my empire I led my people through. But there are other gateways, Ruth, to darker worlds. These Abaddon has discovered; they must be closed."

"I will close them if I can."

"Shannow will close them—if he lives."

"And what can I do?"

"I told you, lady. Take the swan's path."

"I am not ready to die. I am afraid."

"Donna Taybard has been taken. Her settlement is destroyed; her son is dead. Believe me, Ruth, if the woman is sacrificed, the gateways will be ripped asunder. Worlds within worlds will be drawn together, and the resulting catastrophe will be cosmic in scale."

"How would my dying aid the world?"

"Think on it, Ruth. Find the answer."

Madden prepared a grave for Rachel and the boys, laying them side by side and covering them with wildflowers of purple and yellow. For a long while he sat by the grave, not having the energy or the inclination to fill it. Robert's arm had flopped across his mother's breast, and it seemed to Madden that he was hugging her. He had always been her favorite, and now they would lie together for eternity.

His eyes misted, and he swung his gaze to the mountains, recalling the joy he had felt as he had stood near this spot on their first day in Avalon. Rachel had been fussing about the size of cabin they would need, and the boys had charged off into the woods above the valley. Everything had been peaceful then, and the dream had seemed as solid as the rocks around them.

Madden's wounds still pained him and the right side of his face was heavily bruised, but he stood and lifted the shovel and slowly filled the grave. He had intended to cover it with more flowers, but he was too tired to gather them and returned to the cabin to check on Griffin.

The man was asleep, and Madden fueled the woodstove and prepared some herb tea. He sat in a wide chair staring at the dusty floor, his mind drifting back to all the times when he had quarreled with Rachel or caused her to cry. She had deserved so much more than he could ever offer her, yet she had stuck by him through savage winters and dry summers, failed crops and brigand raids. It was she who had convinced him they should follow Griffin's dream. Now the wagoner was probably dying, and Madden would be alone in a strange land.

He sipped his tea and moved to the bedside. Griffin's pulse was erratic and weak; he was lying facedown, and Madden cut away the bandages to examine his wounds. About to turn him, he noticed a bulge near the swollen purple bruise on Griffin's side and touched it with his finger. It was hard, and it moved as he felt it. Removing his knife from its sheath, Madden pressed the razor edge to the skin, which parted easily, spurting blood on his fingers as the misshapen shell popped into his hand. It must have hit one of Griffin's ribs and been redirected to his back, whereas Madden had feared the bullet was lodged in Griffin's stomach. Moving to the other side of the bed, he examined the second wound in Griffin's back; it was healing well, but there was no sign of the bullet. He stitched the knife cut and returned to his chair.

The wagon master would either live or die, and there was nothing more the bearded farmer could do for him. Madden ate some food—a little bacon and some stale bread—and left the cabin. Bodies littered the ground, but he ignored them and walked on toward the foothills of the mountains. There he picked flowers until dusk. Then he returned to the graveside, where he sprinkled the blooms over the freshly turned earth and dropped to his knees.

"I don't know if you're there, God, or what a man has to do to have the right to talk to you. I keep being told there's a paradise for them that believes, but I'm sort of hoping there's a paradise for them that don't know. She wasn't a bad girl, my Rachel; she never done evil to anybody, ever. And my boys didn't live long enough to learn what evil was, not until it killed them. So maybe you'll just overlook their disbelief and let 'em in, anyway.

"I ain't asking nothing for myself, you understand. I ain't got much time for a God who allows this sort of thing to happen in his world. But I'm asking for them, because I don't want to think about my girl just being food for worms and suchlike.

"She deserves better than that, God. So do my boys."

He pushed himself to his feet and turned. There, at the edge of the paddock, was Ethan Peacock's dapple-gray mare, and Madden walked slowly over to her, speaking in a soft gentle voice. The mare's ears pricked up, and she wandered toward him. He stroked her neck and led her into the paddock; she must have jumped the fence when the shooting started.

Back in the cabin he found Griffin awake.

"How you feeling?" he asked.

"Weak as a day-old lamb."

Madden made some fresh tea and helped Griffin to a sitting position.

"I'm sorry, Jacob. I brought you to this."

"Too late for sorries, Con. And I don't blame you, so put it from your mind. We got us a horse and guns. I figure to go after them bastards and at least get Donna back."

"Give me a day, maybe two, and I'll ride with you."

"I'll find you a horse," said Madden. "There must be more than one that the Hellborn didn't take. I'll scour the western valleys. You feel up to eating?"

Madden lit two oil lamps and cooked bacon and the last three eggs on the griddle iron of the stove. The smell of the frying bacon made Griffin acutely aware of his hunger.

"I reckon you might live," said Madden, watching the wagon master wolfing the food. "No dying man would eat like that."

"I've no intention of dying, Jacob. Not yet, anyhow."

"Why did they do it, Con? Why did they hit us?"

"I don't know."

"What did they gain? We must have killed a couple of hundred of them, and all they took was the guns. It don't make no sense. It's not as if they wanted the land; it was just killing for the sake of it."

"I don't think there *are* answers for people like them," said Griffin. "It's like the brigands. Why don't they farm? Why do Daniel Cade and others like him move around the land killing and burning? We can't understand them or their motives."

"But it must be *for* something," insisted Madden. "Even Cade could argue that he gains by his evil . . . stores, coins, weapons."

"There's no point in even wondering at it," said Griffin. "They are what they are: plain evil. Sooner or later someone is going to give it back to them."

"You ever hear of an army, Con? There ain't nobody to stop them."

"There's always somebody, Jacob. Even if it starts with you and me."

"Two wounded men, one horse, and a couple of pistols? I don't think we'll put much of a scare into them."

"We'll see," said Griffin.

The grizzly had found the beehive in a rotting tree trunk and was busy tearing away the wood when the Zealot struck into its brain. The beast reared in anger and pain, settled down, and ambled away to the south, toward the wooden homes of the Yeager men.

The bear was the undisputed monarch of the high country, weighing more than a thousand pounds, and even the lions crept from his path. Wisely he had avoided the haunts of man, and even more wisely the hunters of Yeager had steered clear of the grizzly, for it was well known that a large bear could soak up musket balls as if they were bee stings, and no one wanted any part of a wounded grizzly.

It was an hour before dawn when the bear moved into the settlement, heading unerringly for the cabin of Daniel Cade. Mounting the porch, it reared up before the door; then its huge paw swept down, splintering the wood.

Cade awoke and scrambled from his bed. His captured Hell-born pistol hung in its scabbard from the bedpost, and he whipped the gun clear. The bear moved into the room beyond, smashing a table. When it reached the bedroom door and crashed it inward, Lisa screamed and Cade cocked the pistol, aiming it at the bear's head. The Zealot, his work all but done, fled the bear's mind and returned to his own body in the camp before the pass.

Back in the cabin Cade shielded Lisa with his body and watched as the grizzly dropped to all fours, shaking its great head. Cade reached slowly for the jar on the shelf by the bed. Inside were flat sugar biscuits Lisa had made the day before, and he tossed one to the floor. The bear growled and backed away, confused and uncertain. Then it sniffed at the biscuit, savoring the sweetness. Finally it licked out, lifting the biscuit to its mouth and noisily devouring it. Cade threw another and another, and the grizzly settled down on its haunches.

"Climb out of the window," Cade told Lisa. "But move slow—and don't let any fool shoot the damned bear."

Lisa opened the catch and stood on the bed. The bear ignored her, its eyes on Cade and the jar. She climbed over the ledge and ran to the front of the house, where Gambion, Peck, and several others were waiting with rifles in their hands.

"Daniel says not to shoot the bear."

"What the hell is he doing in there?" asked Gambion.

"He's feeding it biscuits."

"Why don't he climb out and let us kill it?" asked Peck. Lisa spread her hands and shrugged.

Inside, Cade was down to the last four biscuits. Slowly he stood and tossed one of them over the bear's head and into the room beyond. The grizzly sat looking at him.

Cade grinned. "No more till you get that one," he said. The bear growled, but Cade was beginning to enjoy himself. "No use you losing your temper." He tossed another over the shaggy head, and the bear turned and ambled into the room. Cade followed and threw the third biscuit into the doorway. The bear lumbered after it and came face-to-face with the men beyond, who scattered in fear. Peck threw his rifle to his shoulder.

"Don't shoot it!" screamed Lisa.

The bear moved to the porch. It was frightened by the sudden noise and moved off at an ambling run toward the hills as Cade appeared in the doorway.

"What's the matter with you people?" he asked. "Never seen a bear before?"

"It's no joke," said Gambion.

"You're right about that. It only left me two biscuits!"

Gambion climbed the porch. "I mean it, Daniel. A bear don't just come out of the hills and smash its way into a man's home. It's not natural. I don't know how, but the Hellborn are behind it; they were trying to kill you."

"I know. Come inside."

Cade sat down by the ruined table, and Gambion pulled up a chair.

"They've tried frontal attacks on the pass, and they know it's suicide," said Cade. "Now they'll be more cagey. They'll be scouting north and south, and it won't be long before they find Sadler's Trail—and then they'll be behind us."

"Did God tell you this?"

"He didn't need to; it's plain common sense. We need the trail held. I've sent a rider south for help, but I don't know if there'll be any. I want you to take thirty men and hold Sadler's."

"It's pretty open, Daniel. Any big attack will win through in the end."

"You may be lucky. I only need ten days to get everyone back into the Sweetwater valley. Now, there's only one way in there, and we can hold that for damn nigh a year."

"If we had supplies," put in Gambion.

"One day at a time. We've food enough for at least a couple of months, but we're running low on ammunition. I'll fix that. But you pick your men and hold Sadler's Trail."

"Will God be with me, Daniel?"

"He'll be as much with you as he is with me," promised Cade.

"That's good enough for me."

"Take care, Ephram. And no heroics. I don't need another martyr. I just need ten days! With luck you won't see any action at all." The sound of distant gunfire came to them, but neither man was unduly alarmed. Every day the Hellborn tried some action in the pass, and always they were beaten back with losses.

"Better be going," said Gambion.

"Evanson is already there, with Janus and Burgoyne—good men."

"We're all good men now, Daniel."

"Damned right about that!"

After Gambion had left, Cade dressed and rode to the rim of the pass, where down on the rocks there were four Hellborn corpses. Cade dismounted and limped to the first defender, a youngster called Deluth.

"How we doing, boy?"

"Pretty good, Mr. Cade. They tried just the once, and we burned 'em good. Must have hit five or six more, but they rode out."

"Where's Williams?"

Deluth pointed to a ledge some forty feet away.

"Go get him for me. I don't think I can make that climb."

The boy left his rifle, bent double, and ran along the rock line. Shots spattered close to him, but he moved too fast for the Hellborn snipers to catch him in their sights. Cade hefted the boy's rifle and sent a shot toward the telltale powder clouds on the far side of the pass. He hit nothing, but it kept their minds from the running Deluth.

Within minutes the maneuver was repeated with Williams running the gauntlet of shots; a short stocky man of forty-five, he was breathing hard as he slumped down beside Cade.

"What is it, Daniel?"

"I'm pulling everyone back to the Sweetwater."

"Why? We can hold them here till the stars burn out."

Williams was a farmer, and his knowledge of the mountain range was limited. Most people believed the Yeagers were impenetrable but for the pass.

"There's another way in; it's called Sadler's Trail after a brigand that rode these parts forty . . . fifty years ago. It starts in a boxed canyon, and unless you're real close, you'll miss it. It cuts up through the range and onto the Sweetwater. Sooner or later the Hellborn will stumble on it, and I can't take the risk. It would put them behind us, and we've not the numbers to hold on two fronts."

Williams cursed and spit. "How do we know they ain't found it already?"

"I've got people watching it. And anyway, I figure once they find it, they'll stop these frontal assaults. That'll tell us they feel they're on to a better bet."

"What do you want me to do?"

"Nothing. I just wanted you to know in case you saw us moving and felt you'd been left here."

"Well, would you believe that?" said Williams, pointing over Cade's shoulder. He turned to see a small doe rabbit squatting several feet from the talking men. "You surely do have a way with animals, Daniel." The rabbit shook its head and darted away . . .

In the tents of the Hellborn a young warrior opened his eyes, a look of triumph on his face.

"There is another way in," he told the hawk-faced young officer beside him. "It's called Sadler's Trail, and it starts in a boxed canyon; it must be to the south. The entrance is hidden, but it backs onto an area called Sweetwater, and Cade is trying to get his people there before we find a way behind them."

"Fine work, Shadik. I will tell the general."

"It is their first mistake," said Shadik.

"May it also be the last. I shall have the attacks stopped at once."

"No, sir. That's what Cade is waiting for."

"He has a cunning mind, that one. Very well."

The officer walked down the line of tents until he reached a dwelling of white silk and canvas. Before it were two guards; they saluted him, and he ducked under the tent flap.

Inside, working at a folding desk, was the general Abaal, said to be one of the great-grandsons of Abaddon. Many claimed that distinction, since it could not be proved, but in Abaal's case he could point to the special favor his family always received from the king.

"I take it, Alik, you have some good news for me?"

"Yes, Lord General."

"The bear killed him?"

"No, lord. The man lied. It seems he departed from the beast at the moment Cade pointed his pistol."

"And what did the brigand do? Pat it and send it on its way?"

"He fed it with sugar biscuits, Lord General."

"Then your other news had better be good."

"The man has been put to death, but another of my brothers has, I think, redeemed the situation. There is another way into the valley."

"Where is this place? The other pass?"

"In a boxed canyon; to the south, I believe. We scouted it last week, but the entrance is said to be hidden; this time we will find it."

"Take three hundred men."

"You are giving me the command? Thank you, Lord General."

"Do not thank me, Alik. If you fail, you will die. How long will it take Cade to get his people back into this Sweetwater?"

"A week, ten days. I'm not sure."

"You have six days to get behind him. If you have not breached the pass in that time, hand over the command to Terbac and take your life."

"Yes, Lord General. I shall not fail."

◇ 11 ◇

GAMBION ARRIVED TWO hours after dusk and advised his thirty men to make a cold camp while he scouted the entrance to Sadler's Trail. He took Janus and Evanson with him, leaving Burgoyne to point out the best campsites. Janus appeared to be in his early twenties, blond and lean, while Evanson was maybe ten years older and running to fat. The older man was soft-eyed, and Gambion had no faith in him, but the younger had the look of eagles about him: sharp, sure, and confident.

"They came about six days ago," young Janus told them, "but they missed the entrance to the pass. We were all set up, and there were only ten of them; we could have stopped them. It's unlikely they'll be back."

"If Cade asked me to come here, then they'll be back," said Gambion. "Count on it."

"Was it a message from heaven?" asked Evanson.

"Cade says no, but I'm not sure anymore." He told them about the bear that had smashed its way into Cade's cabin only to leave with a few biscuits.

"And you saw it happen?" asked Janus.

"As true as I'm standing here," answered Gambion. He wiped a piece of toweling across his shiny bald pate. "Damn, but it gets hot here."

"The sun reflects off the white rock, especially at dusk. It'll be mighty cool in a few minutes," said Janus. "The men can fix a fire; no one could see it from the pass."

"Well, the three of you can go back into Yeager," said Gambion. "You'll be glad to see your folks, I don't doubt."

"The other two can go," declared Janus. "I'll stay here. I know this land."

"Pleased to have you."

"If it's all right with you, I'll leave now," said Evanson, and Gambion nodded, dismissing the man from his mind.

Janus watched the big man, noting the catlike movements and the sureness with which he carried himself.

"What are you staring at?" asked Gambion, sensing the other's hostility.

"I'm looking at a man who drove people from their farms," said Janus evenly. "And I was wondering why God would choose you."

"Because I was there, son," said Gambion, grinning. "You don't fight the Hellborn with a plow, and this here's the work of men who know weapons."

"Maybe," said Janus doubtfully.

"You don't have to like me, boy. Just stand beside me."

"Have no fear on that score," said Janus. "I'll stand as firm as any man."

"I know that, Janus—I'm a good judge. Show me the killing ground."

Together they strolled down the narrow slope that led to the cleft in the cliffs, opening onto the rich plain that flared from the mountains into the canyon. Once they were beyond the cleft, Gambion glanced back and the entrance had all but disappeared.

"The mountains are young," said Janus, "probably volcanic in origin, and the cleft was made by lava flow."

"But a few men could hold it for quite some time," responded Gambion.

"Depends on how anxious the enemy was to take it."

"What does that mean?"

"Well, if they charge, they can ride through the gap in a couple of seconds. Sure, we could catch them in a murderous cross fire, but once they're through, they can spread out and circle us."

"Then we don't let them get through," stated Gambion.

"Easy to say."

"Son, we don't have no choice. Daniel needs ten days to get all the people back into Sweetwater. He said ten days to me, and I promised it. Ten days is what he'll get."

"Then you better hope they don't find us," said Janus.

"Whatever it is, it will be the way God planned it."

"Yes? Well, I don't believe in God."

"After all you've seen?" asked Gambion, amazed.

"What have I seen? A band of brigands and a lot of death. If you don't mind, Gambion, I'll put my faith in this here rifle, and God can keep the hell out of my way."

The young man strode back to the campsite and ordered Burgoyne to watch the pass. Burgoyne refused, saying he was going back to Yeager, and Janus turned to Gambion.

"Any of your men who can be counted on not to fall asleep?"

"Peck!" called Gambion. "Take the first watch. I'll relieve you in four hours."

"Why me?"

"Because I told you to, you son of a bitch."

"Nice line in discipline you have," said Janus, sitting down and wrapping his blankets around himself.

"Move yourself, Peck!"

"I'm going."

"And don't go to sleep. Daniel is relying on us."

"I hear you."

"I mean it, Peck."

"Have a little faith, Ephram."

Gambion lay back in his own blankets for about two hours, but he could not sleep. Finally he got up and moved off toward the pass, where he found Peck curled up and fast asleep between two boulders. He grabbed the man by his shirt collar and hoisted him upright; then he hit him in the mouth, smashing two front teeth. Three more blows and Peck was unconscious, his face bloody and swollen. Gambion took away his rifle and pistol and sat until dawn, watching the plain.

Janus joined him there as the sun was rising. He stopped to look down at the unmoving Peck.

"Heavy sleeper?" he asked.

"Shut it, Janus. I'm not in the mood."

"Calm down, big man. Go and get some rest. I'll take it for a few hours."

"I'm all right. I don't need much sleep."

"Do it anyway. If they come, there'll not be much time for rest during your 'necessary' ten days."

Gambion had to admit that Janus was right and that he was beginning to feel bone-weary. He passed Peck's rifle and pistol to Janus and hoisted the unconscious Peck to his shoulder, walking off without a word.

Janus remained where he was, watching a distant herd of antelope grazing on the plain. It was so peaceful there, he thought, so hard to imagine a war with blazing guns and sudden death. He had been working on his father's farm when the Hellborn had struck, and his father had gone down almost at once, his head blown away. His mother had followed as she ran from the house. Then Janus had picked up his father's gun—a single-shot musket—and downed the first rider. The man had flown from the saddle. Janus had dropped the rifle and, as the horse swept past, grabbed the pommel and vaulted onto its back, galloping away across the fields with bullets shrieking past him. The horse had been hit twice, but by the time it had died under him, he was into the woods and away.

Alone now, he could not even consider the future. He had wanted to marry Susan McGraven, but she and all her family were dead, so he was told, killed by the same raiders who had struck his farm. Everything he knew was gone; everyone he had loved was dead.

He was nineteen years old, though he looked older, and he saw no future except to kill or be killed by the Hellborn. He had no faith in Daniel Cade and his visions. What little he knew of the Bible and its teachings negated any belief in Cade. Would God use a man like him, a killer and a thief? He doubted it, but then, he doubted God. So what do you know, Janus? he asked himself.

Two hours later a sullen young man relieved him, and Janus moved off the ridge and down to the campsite. On the way he passed a dozen men digging a broad trench across the trail and piling the earth in front of it. He saw Gambion directing operations and approached him.

"What's the idea?"

"If they get through the pass, they'll be riding hard. This line ought to separate the men from the boys."

"True, but there's nowhere to run to. If you don't stop them here, you'll be cut to pieces."

"I wasn't sent here to run, Janus," said Gambion, turning back to the trench.

"Why are you doing this?"

"Why do you think?"

"I haven't a clue, Gambion."

"Then I can't explain it to you."

"I mean, what do you get out of it?"

Gambion leaned on his shovel, his heavy face showing signs of strain. He scratched his thick black beard and thought for a moment. "I joined Cade a lot of years ago, and I never thought too much about what we were. Then God spoke to Cade, and I realized it's not too late to change. It's never too late. Now I'm part of God's army, and I'm not going back. Not for plunder, nor Barta coin, nor goddamn Hellborn. Daniel says to stand here, so here I'll stand. They can send men, beasts, or demons, but they won't pass Ephram Gambion—not as long as there's life in this old body. That make it clear to you, farmer?"

"It's clear, Ephram, but would you mind a suggestion?"

"Not at all."

"Dig a second trench up there and put a few men in it. That way, if you are overrun, they can give you covering fire while you withdraw."

Gambion followed the direction and saw a natural screen of rocks and undergrowth rising some twenty feet above their present position.

"You've a good eye, son. We'll do it."

"How's your man Peck?"

Gambion shrugged. "He went and died on me. But that's life, isn't it?"

"It's not an easy life in God's army, Ephram."

"Not by a long haul. We've no time for shirkers."

"You mind if I get some sleep?"

"You go right ahead."

Janus left them and wandered on. He was hungry and ate some dried fruit before settling back into his blankets.

The day passed without incident, but just before noon on the second day three hundred Hellborn riders entered the canyon. The man on watch, a youngster named Gibson, ran to fetch Gambion. Janus came with him.

"They're not just scouting," said Janus. "They're looking for something."

"I agree," muttered Gambion. "I'll get the men set."

"How are you going to place them?"

"Fifteen in the two trenches, the rest with us here."

"A suggestion?"

"Go ahead."

"They won't be geared to charge straightaway, and they'll probably ride in slowly the first time. Put every man we have overlooking the entrance; that way we'll hit them hard. The next time we'll have men in the trenches for when they really put the spurs in."

Gambion chewed his lip for a while, then nodded. "Sounds good."

He spread the men evenly across the pass, telling them not to fire until he did but then to pour it on like there was no tomorrow. Afterward he returned to squat beside Janus as the Hellborn moved across the canyon.

Within the hour a scout had discovered the cleft and was riding through it while the main body of horsemen waited outside. The Yeager men kept their heads down as the dark-armored rider mounted the first slope. If he rode much farther, he would come in sight of the trenches, but he stopped and removed his helm. He was young, about the same age as Janus, and from where Gambion lay he could see that his eyes were blue. The rider wheeled his horse and rode back to the canyon, and the Hellborn began to move. Gambion pumped a shell into the breech and waited, his mouth dry. Beside him Janus nestled the rifle stock into his shoulder and took a deep breath, willing himself to relax. With half the riders inside Gambion sighted on the leader and took in the slack on the trigger.

"Not yet," whispered Janus, and Gambion froze. The Hellborn moved on, and Gambion could hear the laughter from some of the riders, who were obviously sharing a joke.

"Now," said Janus.

Gambion's rifle thudded back against his shoulder, and then he was up on his knees, pumping shot after shot into the rearing, bucking ranks of the enemy. The pass was alive with gunfire as rider after rider was swept from the saddle. Horses went down screaming, and the Hellborn turned and galloped from the pass. Volleys swept through them, and then there was silence. Gambion rose to charge down the slope, but Janus grabbed his arm. "They're not all dead. Get the men to hold back."

"Back to your positions!" yelled Gambion.

Most of the men obeyed him, but one youngster, oblivious to the commands, raced down the slope. A fallen Hellborn rolled and fired his pistol at point-blank range, and the youngster stopped dead, gripping his belly. A second shot exploded his head. Janus lifted his rifle and killed the Hellborn.

Outside the pass Alik regrouped his men. He knew he should lead them straight back, but fear gnawed at him and he dithered. He did not want to risk such slaughter again so swiftly.

"How many lost?" he asked his deputy, Terbac.

The man cantered his horse along the line, returning some minutes later. "Fifty-nine, sir."

"We'll go in on foot."

"With respect, a charge could carry us past them."

"On foot, I said."

"Yes, sir."

The men dismounted and tethered their horses.

Back in the pass Janus watched them, his brow furrowed.

"They're coming in again," he said, "but without horses."

"What are they playing at?" asked Gambion.

"They probably mean to secure the entrance and push forward slowly."

"Can they do it?"

"It's possible but unlikely. Move the men on the far side about thirty paces to the right." Gambion shouted his orders, and the men moved into position.

"What now?"

"Now we wait and take as many as we can. If they've got sense, they'll wait till nightfall. But I don't think they will."

The first Hellborn reached the cleft and ran for the rocks. He didn't make it.

But the third did, and that gave the enemy a chance to return fire. Gambion crept along the ridge and shot the marksman. The Hellborn retreated back to the canyon.

Gambion moved back alongside Janus, looking at him expectantly. The young man knew then that the command had passed to him, and he grinned ruefully.

"Ask your God for a cloudless night," he said.

"I'll do that. But what if it isn't?"

"A man will have to stay down there, someone with sharp ears."

"I'll do it."

"You're the leader; you can't do it."

"You're the leader here, Janus. I'm not too pigheaded to see that."

"But your men don't know that. Send someone else."

"All right. You don't think they'll come again today?"

"Not with any serious intent. I think we were lucky, Ephram. I think there is a coward leading them."

"You call being outnumbered ten to one lucky?"

"It's only eight to one now, and yes, I'd call that lucky. If they'd started with a charge, they could have cut through us and been on their way into Yeager by now."

"Well, you keep on outthinking them, son, and I'll be forever in your debt."

"I'll do my best, big man."

Two days out from Castlemine, having found a gap in the mountains that allowed them to move west, Shannow and

Batik found themselves in a cool valley edged with spruce and pine.

They stopped at the shores of a lake that sheltered beneath tall peaks and watered their horses. Shannow had said little since they had buried Archer, and Batik had left him to his solitude.

As the afternoon drew on, Batik saw a rider bearing down on them from the west. He stood and shaded his eyes against the falling sun, and as he neared, Batik's eyes widened in shock.

"Shannow!"

"I see him."

"It's Archer!"

"It can't be."

The rider approached and slid from the saddle. He was a black man over six feet tall and was wearing the same style of gray shirt Archer had sported.

"Good afternoon, gentlemen," he said. "I take it you are Shannow?"

"Yes. This is Batik."

"I am pleased to see you. My name is Lewis, Jonathan Lewis. I have been sent to guide you in."

"Into where?" asked Batik.

"Into the Ark," he replied.

"You are one of the Guardians?" Batik asked unnecessarily.

"Indeed I am."

"Archer is dead," said Shannow, "but then, you knew that."

"Yes, Mr. Shannow. But you made his passing more easy, and for that we are grateful. He was a fine man."

"I see you are armed," said Batik, pointing to the flapped scabbard at Lewis' waist.

"Yes. Samuel could never see the point . . ." He did not need to finish his sentence. "Shall we go?"

They followed Lewis for more than two hours, turning into a wide canyon flanked by black basaltic rock.

Ahead of them lay another ruined city, larger than the first they had found before meeting Archer. But it was not the city that caused the breath to catch in Shannow's throat. Five hundred feet above the marble ruins lay a golden ship, glowing in the dying sunlight.

"Is it truly the Ark?" whispered Shannow.

"No, Mr. Shannow," said Lewis, "though many have taken it to be so, and in the main we do not disenchant them."

The trio rode into the ruins along an overgrown cobbled street to the foot of the mountain. There Lewis dismounted, beckoning the others to follow. He led his horse to the rock and stopped to turn a small handle set within it. A section of the rock face then moved sideways, leaving a rectangular doorway seven feet high and twelve feet wide. Lewis entered, with Shannow and Batik leading their horses behind. Two men waited within the tunnel; they took the horses, and Lewis led Shannow and Batik to a steel doorway that slid open to reveal a room four feet square and seven feet high. With the three men inside, the door whispered shut.

"Level twenty," said Lewis, and the room shuddered.

"What's happening here?" Batik asked, alarmed.

"Wait for a moment, Batik. All will be well."

The door opened once more, this time to a bright hallway, and Shannow stepped out. It was lighter than day there, yet there were no windows. All along the walls were glowing tubes; when Shannow reached up and touched one, it was faintly warm.

"You must have many stones to produce this much magic," said Shannow.

"We do indeed, Mr. Shannow. Follow me."

Another door opened before them, and the three men entered a round room at the center of which was a white desk in the shape of a crescent moon. Behind it sat a white-haired man, who stood and smiled at their approach. He was more than six feet six, and his skin was golden, his eyes slanted and dark. His hair was long, sweeping out from the scalp like a lion's mane.

Lewis bowed. "My Lord Sarento, the men you wished to meet."

Sarento moved around the table and approached Shannow.

"Welcome, my friends. For my sins I am the leader here,

and I am delighted to welcome you. Lewis, fetch chairs for my guests."

With Batik and Shannow seated and Lewis having been sent to bring refreshment, Sarento leaned back on the table and spoke. "You are a remarkable man, Mr. Shannow. I have followed your exploits for a number of years: the taming of Allion, the hunting down of the brigand Gareth, the attack on the Hellborn, and now the liberation of Castlemine. Is there nothing that can stop you, sir?"

"I have been fortunate."

"Fortune favors the Rolynd, Mr. Shannow. Have you come across the name?"

"Archer mentioned it, I believe."

"Yes, dear Samuel . . . I cannot tell you how much his death depresses me. He more than anyone is responsible for the growth in Guardian wisdom. But I was speaking of the Rolynd. A wondrous race were the Atlanteans; they conquered mysteries that still baffled our elders eight thousand years later. They were the fathers of magic, and they understood the gifts men carried. Some could heal, others could grow plants, still others could teach. But the Rolynd were special, for they were lucky; they carried luck like a talisman, a personal god who would step in whenever needed. And with the Rolynd warriors it was needed often. Warriors like you, Mr. Shannow, who could somehow hear a stealthy assassin creeping upon them in the midst of a storm. The Atlanteans believed the gift was linked to courage. Perhaps it is. But whatever the cause, you have the gift, sir."

Lewis returned and served a goblet of white wine to each of the men, then laid the pitcher on the table and left the room.

"You have great power here," said Shannow.

"Indeed we do, sir. With knowledge comes power, and we guard the secrets of the old world."

"But you also have the stones."

"What is the point you are making?"

"With all this power, why do you not stop the Hellborn?"

"We are not meddlers, Mr. Shannow, though we have tried to guide this world for more than three hundred years. Men like

Prester John Taybard and the man you knew as Karitas have been sent from here to educate the people of this continent, to lead them toward an understanding of what they are and whence they come. I have no army, and even if I did, I have no God-given right to change the destiny of the Hellborn. On the other hand, since the battle is unequal, I am willing to help you."

"In what way?"

"I can give you weapons to take to Daniel Cade."

"How will that help me kill Abaddon?"

"It will help you do more than that; it will help you beat him."

Shannow looked into Sarento's dark eyes and stayed silent.

"What sort of weapons?" asked Batik.

Sarento gave an order to one of his men, who opened a hidden door in the far wall to reveal a firing range. At the farthest end of the first line was a wooden statue dressed in the armor of the Hellborn. Sarento stepped onto the range and lifted a bulky black weapon almost three feet long, which he handed to Batik. "Pull back the bolt on the left, then aim it—but hold it steadily; it may surprise you."

Batik sprang the bolt and pulled the trigger. The rolling explosion deafened them momentarily, and the statue disappeared, its upper torso smashed beyond recognition. Batik laid the weapon gently to rest.

"Five hundred bullets a minute, moving at three thousand miles per hour," said Sarento. "Hit a man in the upper leg with just one, and the hydraulic shock will drag his blood from his heart and kill him. You can destroy an army with ten of these, and I'll give you fifty."

"I'll think about it," said Shannow.

"What is there to think about?" argued Batik. "We could ride in and take Babylon itself with these."

"Probably, but I'm tired. Is there somewhere I can rest?" Shannow asked Sarento.

"Of course," was the reply, whereupon he opened a door, which Lewis entered. "Show our guests to suitable quarters. I will see you both in the morning."

The Guardian took them to another level and into a T-shaped room containing two beds, a table, four chairs, and a wide window looking out on a gleaming lake. Shannow moved to the window and tried to open it, but the lock would not shift.

"It does not open, Mr. Shannow. It is not a window at all but a light picture, what we call a mood-view." He moved to a dial on the wall and turned it. The view mellowed into dusk, evening, and finally moonlit night. "Set it as it pleases you. I shall have food sent to you."

Once the Guardian had left, Shannow lay back on the first bed, his head pillowed on his arms.

"What's bothering you, Shannow?" asked Batik.

"Nothing. I am just tired."

"But those weapons ... Even your god would be hard-pressed to come up with a better miracle."

"You are easily pleased, Batik. Now leave me to think."

Batik shrugged and wandered around the room until Lewis returned with food. For Batik he brought a huge rare steak and green vegetables. For Shannow there was cheese and black bread. When they had consumed the food, Lewis rose to leave.

"Is there no water anywhere?" asked Shannow. "I would like to clean the dust from my body."

"How foolish of me," said the Guardian. "Look over here." As he spoke, he slid back the wall by the mood-view to reveal a cubicle of glass. Lewis reached inside and pressed a switch, at which point warm water jetted from a nozzle in the wall. "Soap and towels are in here," said Lewis, opening a wall cupboard.

"Thank you. This place is like a palace."

"It was constructed from plans that existed before the Fall."

"Did the Guardians build this place?"

"After a fashion, Mr. Shannow. We used the stones to re-create the magic of our forefathers."

"Where are we now?"

"You are inside the shell of the Ark. Once we harnessed the Sipstrassi, we rearranged the interior to house our community. I think that was some three centuries ago; there have been some modifications since."

Shannow sipped a glass of clear wine. He was bone-weary, but there was much he needed to know.

"I never really had a chance to talk to Archer about what you guard. Would you mind explaining?"

"Not at all. Our community exists to gather and hoard the secrets of Pre-Fall in the hope of one day bringing it back. We have a library here with over thirty thousand books, most of them technical. But there are also four thousand classics in eleven languages."

"How can you bring back what is past?" asked Batik.

"That is a question for Sarento, not for a soldier."

"And you believe you can help bring back civilization with guns that can kill five hundred men a minute?" said Shannow softly.

"Man is an inventive animal, Mr. Shannow. Any weapon of death will be improved. Would you not sooner have the guns than the Hellborn? Sooner or later their gunsmiths will perfect them."

"How many of you are there?"

"Eight hundred, including the women and children. We are a fairly stable community. Tomorrow I will show you around. Perhaps you would agree to meet Amaziga Archer. It will be painful, but I know she wants to hear of her husband's last hours."

"He spoke of her at the end," said Shannow.

"Perhaps you would be kind enough to tell her that."

"Of course. Were you a friend of Archer's?"

"Very few people disliked Sam. Yes, we were friends."

"His stone turned black," said Batik. "It was very small."

"He always overused it; he treated it like a magic bauble. I shall miss him," Lewis said with genuine regret.

"Was he the only Guardian with a love of Atlantis?" asked Shannow.

"Very much so. He and Sarento, that is."

"An interesting man. How old is he?"

"Just over two hundred eighty, Mr. Shannow. He is very gifted."

"And you, Mr. Lewis? How old are you?"

"Sixty-seven. Sam Archer was ninety-eight. The stones are wondrous things."

"Indeed they are. I think I will rest now. Thank you for answering my questions."

"It was a pleasure. Sleep well."

"One last question."

"Ask it."

"Do the stones create your food for you?"

"They used to, Mr. Shannow, but we needed the power for other and more important things. We now run a sizable herd of cattle and sheep, and we grow most of our vegetables."

"Thank you again."

"Not at all."

Shannow lay awake long after Batik had fallen asleep. The mood-view was set to moonlight, and he watched as clouds drifted across the sky, the same clouds time and again in relentless regularity. He closed his eyes and saw once more the sundered statue, picturing a real man lying there with his entrails around him like torn ribbons.

Had Karitas possessed weapons such as these, the Hellborn would never have destroyed his village and young Curopet would still be alive.

Shannow rolled over and lay on his stomach, but sleep evaded him despite the softness of the bed. He was uneasy and tense. He swung his legs from the bed and moved to the water cubicle, stepping into the shallow basin and turning on the spray. In a tray to his right was a bar of scented soap, and he scrubbed his skin, reveling in the heat of the shower. Toweling himself down, he returned to the mood-view and on impulse switched it to day and watched the sun hurtle into the sky.

He sat at the table and poured a glass of water. All his life he had been both hunter and hunted, and he trusted his instincts. There had to be a cause for his uneasiness, and he was determined to find it before his next meeting with Sarento.

Sarento. He did not like the man, but that was no reason to judge him harshly. Shannow liked few men, and the Guardian leader had been pleasant enough. Despite his words, he had not seemed unduly distressed by Archer's death, but then, the man had merely been a follower and Shannow knew that the emotions of men whom the world thought great rarely ran deep. Humanity invariably ran a poor second to ambition.

Shannow relaxed his mind. In hunting one used peripheral vision to spot movement, and it was the same with a problem. Staring at it head-on often blurred the perspective. He let his thoughts roam . . .

Karitas leapt from his subconscious, kind, gentle Karitas.

Hellborn Karitas, the father of guns.

Sent out by Sarento?

To serve Abaddon?

Shannow's jaw tightened. He knew little of Karitas' background, but had not Ruth told him that he had given Abaddon the secrets of firearms? And had not Sarento claimed he was a Guardian sent to instruct?

What game was being played here?

And why did the Guardians need cattle when their stones could create such a palace of miracles within a ghost ship? Lewis said they needed the power for more important things. What was more important than feeding a colony?

Sarento had said that Shannow was Rolynd, which meant that his knowledge of Atlantis was greater than Archer's. Why had he not shared it with the Guardian?

And lastly there was Cade—Cade the brigand, Cade the killer—throwing his hat into the ring of war.

What right-thinking man would supply him with the weapons of empire?

Shannow had told Ruth that he was happy to hear of Daniel's actions, and that was true. Blood was thicker than water, but Shannow knew Cade better than any man alive. His brother was tough and merciless. And if he had taken on the mantle of leadership, it would not be for altruistic reasons. Somewhere within the horror of war Cade had seen the chance for profit.

He switched the mood-view to night and returned to his bed. With his thoughts more settled, he fell into a deep sleep. When he awoke, Batik was already dressed and sitting with Lewis at the table. Before the Hellborn was a plate stacked high with eggs and bacon. Shannow dressed and joined them.

"Would you like some food, Mr. Shannow? I am afraid Batik ate your ration."

"I am not hungry, thank you."

Lewis glanced at a rectangular bracelet on his wrist. "Sarento is ready to meet you."

Batik belched and rose. "How are we going to get those guns to Cade?" he asked.

Shannow smiled and ignored the question. "Shall we go?" he said to Lewis.

Once they were in the glowing corridor, Shannow slipped the retaining thong from the hammer of his right-hand pistol. Batik noticed the surreptitious movement and silently freed his own pistol. He asked no more questions but dropped back a pace, keeping Lewis ahead of him.

Inside the meeting room Sarento rose and greeted his guests with a warm smile.

"Did you sleep well?"

"We did indeed," said Shannow. "Thank you for your hospitality, but we must be leaving."

"It will take time to prepare the guns for the journey."

"We will not be taking the guns."

The smile left Sarento's face. "You are not serious?"

"Indeed I am. You misread me, sir. There is only one dream in my life: to find Jerusalem. Sadly, I must first kill Abaddon. It is a question of pride and revenge. I am not part of the Hellborn war. If you wish guns to go to Cade, send some of your men."

"Is that not a little selfish, Mr. Shannow?"

"Good-bye, Sarento." Shannow turned his back on the Guardian leader and moved to the door. Behind him Batik spread his hands and backed out into the corridor. Shannow stood by the elevator, Lewis joined them, and the journey to the canyon floor was made in silence.

The horses were brought out, and Lewis walked out into the bright sunlight with the two men.

"Good luck in your quest, Mr. Shannow."

"Thank you, Mr. Lewis."

Shannow mounted and swung the stallion's head to the south. Batik cantered alongside him, and the two rode in silence to the rim of the hills overlooking the ruined city and the golden Ark.

"What was that about, Shannow?" Batik asked as the men reined their mounts. "I would have thought you would leap at the chance of using those guns."

"Why? You think I am in love with killing?"

"For Cade, to beat the Hellborn."

"I will not be used, Batik, in another man's game." Shannow drew his pistol. "With this gun I have slain many Hellborn. But is it mine? No, I took it from the body of an enemy. Tell me, Batik—how long before the Hellborn capture one of those disgusting rifles? How long before they dismantle one and learn to make their own? They are not an answer to the war; they merely enlarge it. I am not a child to be mesmerized by a pretty toy."

"You think too much, Shannow."

"All too true, my friend. I think the Guardians are playing their own game. I think they created the Hellborn weapons and took them to Abaddon. And I think we were lucky to leave there alive."

"Why did they allow it?"

"Surprise. They did not expect us to refuse."

"How many more enemies do you expect to make in this quest of yours?"

Shannow grinned, and his expression softened as he leaned over and grasped Batik's shoulder. "Let me tell you this: One friend is worth a thousand enemies."

Above them the spirit of Ruth soared away, her joy golden. She sped to the south and west, passing Babylon and searching for the wagon carrying Donna Taybard, which she located in the foothills some four days journey from the city. Donna lay in the back of the wagon with silver bands around her brow, wrists, and ankles, and she seemed to be in a deep enchanted sleep. The bands puzzled Ruth, and she floated closer to the comatose body, but a sharp tug pulled at her and she soared away. Steeling herself, she approached the body once more and found that the bands acted like a magnet, exerting power against her. She drew closer still, and the pull became painful, but at last she could see the shards of Blood Stone in the bands. She tore herself clear and flew to Sanctuary, her knowledge complete.

Anger welled in her, and she understood at last the truth of the Blood Stones. It was not blood or life they drank but ESPer power, the strength of the spirit.

Soulstones.

Donna Taybard's life was to flow on Abaddon's Sipstrassi, and her soul would enhance its power. Ruth's anger became fury.

A shimmering glow appeared in the corner of her study, and she turned as the image of Karitas blossomed. She relaxed momentarily as he approached smiling, but suddenly his hands became talons, his face demonic.

He lunged ... but Ruth's fury had not ebbed, and in an instant her hands came up, white fire streaming from her fingertips. The demon screamed and burned. The form of Karitas became a mottled, scaled gray under the heat of Ruth's anger, and the beast within writhed and died.

The stench of decay filled the room, and Ruth staggered back. Windows appeared all around her, and a clean breeze swept the room. She sensed the presence of Pendarric, and the king appeared, dressed in a black tunic with a single silver star at one shoulder.

"I see you have learned how to kill, my lady."

Ruth sat down, staring at her hands. "It was instinctive."

"Like Shannow?"

"I need no lessons at this time."

"The beast was not Karitas. It was summoned from a gateway by a great force, and you had no choice but to kill it. That does not negate what you are, Ruth."

She smiled and shook her head. "Had I truly the courage of my belief, I would have let it kill me."

"Perhaps. But then evil would have the victory."

"Why are you here, Pendarric?"

"Only to help you, lady. My powers in this world are limited to words—a punishment for wreaking havoc during my time here, maybe. But you have power, and you must use it."

"I will not kill again. *Ever.*"

"That is your choice, but you can end the dream of Abaddon without taking life. The Sipstrassi works in two ways: it uses power, and it receives power. It must be nullified."

"How?"

"You can find the way, Ruth. It is important that you find it alone."

"I do not need riddles."

"It is time to know your enemy. Seek him out—then you will know."

"Why can you not just tell me?"

"You know the answer to that, lady. As with your students, you do not take a child and place the power of the world in his hands. You lead him, encourage him to grow, to seek his own answers, to develop his talents."

"I am not a student."

"Are you not, Ruth? Trust me."

"If I destroy my enemies, then my life's work will have been for nothing. Everything I have believed and taught to others will have proved to be empty, devoid of truth."

"I accept that," said Pendarric gently, "but only if you kill your enemies. There is another way to restore harmony, Ruth, even if it is only the harmony of the jungle."

"And I can do that by dying?"

"It depends what manner you choose."

Ruth's head sank. "Leave me, Pendarric. I have much to think on."

Lewis returned to the tunnel, summoned the elevator, and stepped inside. At level 16 he stopped and moved out into a wide corridor. Passing the living quarters of the field men, he saw Amaziga Archer playing with her son, Luke. She saw him and waved, and he responded and walked on. He could not yet find the words to tell her that Shannow had gone, and with him the last words of her husband.

He approached control and stood outside the steel door; it opened after several seconds, and Lewis walked inside.

"You wanted me, sir?" he asked Sarento. The tall man was staring at a set of architects' plans and nodded absently, waving his hand at a chair. Lewis sat.

"You know what these are?" said Sarento, passing the blueprints to Lewis.

He scanned them swiftly. "No, sir."

"These are the original specifications for the Ark. In three days she will sail again."

"I don't understand."

"We are about to enjoy an influx of power, Lewis. With that power, to celebrate rebirth, I shall transform the Ark for twelve hours to her original state."

"The power needed will be colossal," said Lewis.

"Indeed it will, but we now have two hundred percent more energy than at this time last month, and it grows daily. The ship will be the last test. After that we will begin to rebuild the world, Lewis. Think of it: London, Paris, Rome, all rising from the ashes of the Fall. All the technology of the old world visited upon the new, with none of the errors."

"That is fantastic, sir. But where is the power coming from?"

"Before I answer that, let me ask you this: What do you make of Shannow?"

"I liked him. He is a strong man, and it took nerve to rescue Archer from Castlemine."

"Indeed it did," said Sarento, leaning back in his chair, his golden skin glowing, his eyes bright. "And I admire him for it, make no mistake. I had hoped to save his life—to use him—but he would have none of it."

"He may still succeed," said Lewis. "I would not like him to be hunting me."

"He will not succeed. I have alerted the Zealots, and even now they are closing on him."

"Why, sir?"

"Lewis, you are a fine soldier, a natural follower, a good man. But you are not involved in policy. You do not have the mantle of responsibility for ensuring the survival of a lost race. I do. When I became leader 260 years ago, how much of this . . . wizardry around you existed? We lived in the caves below the Ark; we hunted for our food and we farmed, much like the other settlements to the south. But I brought rebirth to the Guardians. I gave them purpose and long life; let us not forget that."

"I don't understand what this has to do with Shannow."

"Patience, Lewis. Archer showed the way with his records of Atlantis. The Sipstrassi was power, pure magic. But the stones soon exhausted themselves. So how did the Atlanteans build their fabled structures? Not on tiny stones, fragments, and chips. No, they had the One Stone, the Mother Stone. I searched for twelve years in the mountains, burrowing deep through hidden caverns. And I found it, Lewis: eighty tons of pure Sipstrassi in one piece. It was the great secret of the Atlantean kings, and they built a circle of stones around it below ground. It was their high altar. Pendarric, the last of their kings, hacked a section from it and used that one broken piece to carve an empire. We will go them one better. We are using it all. And now to your question, Lewis. What of Shannow?"

Sarento stood, towering over the seated Lewis. "He plans, though unwittingly, to stop the power flowing to the Mother Stone."

"Can he do it?"

Sarento shrugged. "We will never know, for he will be dead within hours."

"I asked you before where the power comes from," repeated Lewis.

"Indeed you did, and I hope you are prepared by now for the answer. Every Hellborn soldier carries a Blood Stone, and every time he kills—or even is killed—he transmits power back to the Mother Stone. When the Hellborn sacrifice their ESPers, they use Sipstrassi knives, and much of the power returns to us."

"Then the Mother Stone is no longer pure?"

"Pure? Don't be a fool, Lewis! It is merely stronger. Too

strong to create food, which is a drawback, but it can now fulfill our dreams."

"It can't be right to use the foulness of the Hellborn."

"Lewis, Lewis!" said Sarento, laying his hand on the soldier's shoulder. "We *are* the Hellborn. We created them from the dreams of the madman Welby. We gave him power, we gave him primitive guns, and he is ours, though he does not know it."

Lewis' mouth was suddenly dry. "But what of the deaths?"

Sarento sat down on the edge of the desk. "You think it doesn't grieve me? But our duty to the future is to keep alive the civilization of the past.

"You must try to understand that, Lewis. We can only keep our dreams alive for a short time in this vacuum of a colony. One natural disaster or a plague and it could all be wiped out. The past must be made to live again out there in the new world: cities, laws, books, hospitals, theaters. Culture, Lewis . . . and technology. And even the stars. For what science could not achieve, surely magic can."

Lewis remained silent, his thoughts whirling. Sarento sat statue-still, his dark eyes locked on Lewis' face.

"One thing, sir," Lewis said at last. "As we build and grow, the stone will need even more power. Yes? Do we fuel it with death forever?"

"A good point, Lewis, and it proves that I was right about you. You have intellect. The answer is yes. But we do not have to be demonic. Man is a natural hunting, killing animal. He cannot survive without wars. Think back on your history; it is a kaleidoscope of cruelty and terror. But from each war man progressed, for war establishes unity. Take Rome. They conquered the world in blood and fire, but only then could civilization take root. After conquest there was unity. With unity came law. With law came culture. But not just the Romans, Lewis. The Macedonians, the British, the Spaniards, the French, the Americans. There will always be those who desire war. We will give that atavistic need a positive purpose."

Lewis stood and saluted. "Thank you, sir, for sharing this knowledge. Will that be all?"

"No. The reason I have taken you into my confidence is a delicate one. I told you that Shannow must die. In all probability the Zealots will succeed. But Shannow is Rolynd. He may escape. He may return. I want you to find him and kill him should the Zealots fail."

Aware that Sarento was studying his reaction, Lewis merely nodded, keeping his face blank.

"Can you do this thing?"

"I'll take one of the rifles," replied Lewis.

◇ **12** ◇

FOR FIVE DAYS the riders had tried tentative attacks, but on the sixth their leader went berserk and the Hellborn mounted their horses and thundered into the pass, through the cross fire that decimated their ranks, and on to the trench where Gambion waited with ten men.

Through the cloud of dust sent up by the pounding hooves of their horses the Hellborn bore down on the waiting men.

"Fire!" screamed Gambion, and a ragged volley smashed into the first line of riders, bringing down men and horses. A second volley hammered into the horsemen; then Gambion's men broke and ran for the second trench.

Above them, with three riflemen, Janus cursed. He stood and emptied his rifle into the surging ranks of the enemy. Only Gambion remained in the first trench; his rifle empty, he tugged his pistols clear and shot a man from the saddle. Now the dust swirled above him. A horse leapt over him, then a second. He fired blindly into the dust. A hoof clipped the top of his skull, and he fell as shots hammered into the dirt beside him.

Janus screamed at the running men to take up positions, and they responded, dropping down beside the three men in the second trench. Shells tore once more into the Hellborn, and they broke and ran.

"After them!" shouted Janus, sweeping up a rifle and leaping the earthworks. Some seven men followed him; the rest hunkered down behind the relative safety of the earthworks. Janus knew the next few moments would be crucial in the battle. If they did not push the Hellborn outside into the

276

canyon, they would spread up onto the hillside and outflank the defenders. He ran to the first trench and waited for his men to join him.

"Together!" he shouted. "Volley fire. But only at my signal."

The men settled their rifles to their shoulders. "Now!" A volley shrieked through the dust clouds.

"Again!" Three times more they fired into the fleeing Hellborn. Janus led his men farther into the pass, aware that their position would be perilous should the Hellborn turn, but in the billowing dust the enemy had no idea how many men were pursuing them. At last Janus stood in the mouth of the pass itself and watched the Hellborn galloping out of range.

"Take up positions," he ordered the men around him.

"I'm out of bullets," a man told him.

"I've only got two rounds left," said another.

"Strip the dead," said Janus. "But be careful—some of them may only be wounded."

They gathered what ammunition they could from the fallen riders and returned to their positions. Janus sprinted back to the first trench, where Gambion was sitting up holding his head.

"You ought to be dead," Janus told him, and Gambion looked up at the blond youngster and grinned broadly.

"It'll take more than a kick from a horse."

"We are almost out of ammunition. We can't hold much longer, Ephram."

"We *have* to."

"Be reasonable, man. When the bullets are gone, then so are we."

"We've held this long, and we've made them pay. Just four more days."

"What do you want us to do? Throw rocks at them?"

"Whatever it takes."

"There are only twenty-two men left, Ephram."

"But we've taken over a hundred of them bastards."

Janus gave up and ran back to the pass, climbing high onto the ridge and shielding his eyes, trying to see the enemy. They had dismounted and were seated in a circle around two officers. Janus wished he had a long glass to study the situation more closely. It seemed to him that one of the officers had a pistol in his hand and that the barrel was in his mouth. The crack of the pistol drifted to him, and he watched the officer topple sideways.

Gambion joined him. "What's happening out there?"

"One of their leaders has just killed himself."

"Good for him!"

"What kind of people are they, Ephram?"

"They ain't like us, that's for sure. By the way, I done a count, and we've roughly fifteen shells per man. Good enough for a couple more attacks."

Janus chuckled. "Your head's bleeding," he said.

"It'll stop. You think they'll come in again today?"

"Yes. One more charge. I think we should take a chance on stopping it dead."

"How?"

"Line up everyone across the pass and hit them with ten volleys."

"If they break through, there'll be nothing to back us."

"It's up to you, Ephram."

Gambion swore. "I'll buy it. Damn, but I never thought to see the day when a boy would give me orders."

"And a child shall lead them," said Janus.

"What?"

"It's from the Bible, Ephram. Don't you ever read it?"

"I don't read, but I'll take your word for it."

"Do it fast. I think they're coming in again."

Gambion and Janus slid down the slope, calling the men to them. They came reluctantly for the most part and gathered in a ragged line.

"You'd better stand this time, by God!" yelled Gambion.

The riders came on at full gallop. The guns of the defenders bellowed, echoing up into the pass, and the rolling thunder of the volleys drowned the sound of galloping hooves.

The pass was black with cordite smoke, and as it cleared, Gambion watched the last of the Hellborn cantering away out of range. Fewer than fifty men remained of the three hundred who had launched the attack on the first day, while seven defenders were dead and two were wounded.

"We'd better gather some ammunition," said Janus. "Send ten men to strip the bodies."

Gambion did so, while the other defenders kept a wary eye on the retreating riders.

"We did well today," said Gambion. "You believe in God now?"

Janus cursed. It was the first time Gambion had heard him swear.

"What is it?"

Janus pointed to where, on the far side of the valley, a column of riders could be seen.

"Shit!" hissed Gambion. "How many?"

"I don't know. Five hundred, maybe."

The scavengers returned with sacks of bullets and some extra pistols. One of them moved alongside Gambion.

"They didn't have more than five shells apiece. Ain't enough to hold that bunch."

"We'll see."

"Well, I ain't staying," said the man. "I done my share."

"We've all done our share, Isaac. You want to run out on God?"

"Run out on him? He ain't doing us no favors here, is he? There must be four, five hundred more of them sons of bitches, and we ain't even got enough shells for them all."

"He's right, Ephram," said Janus. "Send a rider to Cade. Tell him he's got less than a day and he'd better speed up."

"I'll go," said Isaac, "and glad to be out of it."

The two wounded men were carried back into the pass, and Janus touched Gambion's arm. "We ought to move back, Ephram. We can't do any good here."

"We can thin them a little."

"They can afford to lose more than we can."

"You want to run, then *run*!" snarled Gambion. "I'm staying."

"Here they come!" yelled a defender, pumping a shell into

the breech. Gambion wiped sweat from his eyes and peered out into the canyon. Then blinked and squinted into the sunlight.

"Hold your fire!" he shouted. The lead rider came closer, and Gambion waved, a broad smile breaking out on his face.

"Jesus," whispered Isaac. "They're southerners!"

The troop cantered past the bodies of the Hellborn, and the leader drew rein before Gambion. He was a short, stocky man with a red mustache.

"Well, Gambion, I swore to hang you, and now I'm going to have to fight alongside you. There's no justice left in the world!"

"I never thought to be pleased to see you, Simmonds, but I could kiss your boots."

The man stepped down from the saddle. "We've had refugees streaming south for a while now, telling tales a sane man couldn't believe. Do these bastards really worship the Devil and drink blood?"

"They do and more," said Gambion.

"Where are they from?"

"The Plague Lands," Gambion replied, as if that explained everything.

"Is it true that Cade's become a prophet?"

"As true as I'm standing here. You still carrying muskets?"

"It's all we've got."

"Not anymore. We didn't have a chance to collect all the weapons from them Hellborn. You help yourself. They carry repeating rifles—damn good weapons. Ten-shot, some of them; the others is eight."

Simmonds sent some of his men to search the dead, while the rest rode back into the pass to make camp. He himself wandered up the ridge with Gambion and Janus.

"This your boy?" he asked.

"No, this is our general. And don't make jokes, Simmonds; he's done us proud the last six days."

"You shaving yet, son?"

"No, sir, but I'm two inches taller than you, so I guess that makes us even."

Simmonds' eyebrows raised. "You a brigand?"

"No. My father was a farmer, and the Hellborn killed him."

"The world's changing too fast for my liking," said Simmonds. "Repeating rifles, boy generals, brigand prophets, and Devil worshipers from the Plague Lands! I'm too old for this."

"Can we leave a hundred of your men here?" asked Gambion. "Then I'll take you to Cade."

"Sure. Is your general staying?"

"He is," said Janus. "For four more days. Then we make for Sweetwater."

"All right. What happened to your head, Gambion?"

"Horse kicked it."

"I expect you had to shoot the horse," said Simmonds.

Shannow and Batik were camped in a shaded spot near a waterfall when Ruth appeared. Batik dropped his mug of water and leapt backward, tripping over a rock and sprawling beside the fire. Shannow smiled.

"You must excuse my friend, Ruth. He is very nervous these days."

"How are you, Batik?" she asked.

"Well, lady. Yourself?"

She seemed older than when they had last seen her; dark rings circled her eyes, and her cheeks were sunken. Her iron-gray hair had lost its sheen, and her eyes were listless.

"I am as you see me," she said softly.

"Are you truly here with us?" asked Shannow.

"I am here and there," she answered.

"Can you eat? Drink? If you can, you are welcome to share what we have."

She shook her head and remained silent. Shannow was at a loss and moved to the fire. Wrapping his hand in a cloth, he lifted the small copper pot from the flames and mixed some herbs into the water; then he stirred the tea with a stick before pouring it into a mug. Batik spread his blankets and removed his boots. Ruth remained statue-still, regarding them both.

"How goes your quest?" she asked, and Shannow shrugged, aware that her question was merely the precursor of heavier words. "What did you make of the Guardians?"

"I liked Archer. Lewis seemed a good man."

"Who leads them?" she asked.

"You do not know?"

"A long time ago Karitas urged me to respect their privacy."

"It is a man called Sarento."

"Did you like him?"

"An odd question, Ruth. What does it matter?"

"It matters, Mr. Shannow. For you are a man of talent. You are a sensitive, and you have not stayed alive this long merely by being skillful with weapons. You have a knack of being in the right place at the right time. You judge men too shrewdly. In a way your powers in this respect are greater than mine. For mine have been cultivated over the centuries, while yours are latent, unchanneled. Did you like him?"

"No."

"Did you judge him to be . . . ungodly?"

"He reminded me of Abaddon—the same arrogance."

"And he offered you weapons?"

"Yes."

"Why did you refuse?"

"War is a vile game, Ruth, and the innocent die along with the guilty. I want nothing to do with the war itself; my only interest is in avenging Donna."

"Avenging? She is not dead yet."

Shannow sat very still. "Truly?"

"Would I lie?"

"No. Can I reach her before they kill her?"

"No, Mr. Shannow, but I can."

"Will you?"

"I am not sure. Something has been troubling me for some time now, and yesterday I made a discovery that frightened me, that rocked all my long-built security. The Hellborn are not the enemy. We are not dealing with an evil race; they are pawns in a game I cannot understand."

"Are you saying that the Hellborn are not at war?" asked Shannow. "That they are not butchering their way across the continent?"

"Of course not. But why are they doing it?"

"To conquer," answered Batik. "Why else?"

"I thought that before yesterday, but believe me, my friends, I have been very stupid. You are a Bible-reading man, Mr. Shannow, and you have read of possession. Demons? The Hellborn are possessed, and the power emanates from Abaddon. He is the center, but even he does not understand the source of his power; he is being used."

"By the Devil?" said Shannow.

"No . . . or perhaps yes, in another form. There is a force that I have traced that focuses on Abaddon and is dispersed by him throughout the Hellborn lands, touching the Blood Stone of every man, woman, and child. Quite simply it is hatred, lust, greed. It covers the land like an invisible fog, and it travels with his armies, bloated like a great slug."

"It will be gone, then, when I kill him," said Shannow.

"That is not the point, Mr. Shannow. The source is where the evil lies . . . and I have traced that source, and the power there is incredible."

"You speak of the Guardians," said Shannow.

"Indeed I do."

"You say you traced the source?" asked Batik.

"It is a giant stone. It feeds, if that is the word, on soul power—ESPer talents, call them what you will."

"Where is this stone?" said Shannow.

"It is lodged beneath the mountain of the Ark, and from there it draws power from every Blood Stone in the Hellborn empire. It must be destroyed, Mr. Shannow; its power must be ended or a new dark age will fall upon the world, if not the destruction of the world itself."

"Why do you come to me? I cannot defeat magic with a pistol."

"Nor can I approach the stone. It resists my power. But there is a way. The Atlanteans found a method of harnessing the energies of their stones, trapping the power. The secret is in the monolith circles around the altars. They built the Standing Stones as conduits of power that transmit and receive the energy. The Mother Stone was so powerful that special monoliths were constructed. Inset into each structure is a spool of golden wire. If the conduits are linked by gold, no energy can pass to the stone at the center. It will become drained and eventually useless."

"Why should the gold still be there?" asked Shannow. "Does Sarento not know its danger?"

"The spools are hidden within the monoliths. But yes, he may have discovered their use and removed them. That you must find out."

"I? This is not my war, Ruth."

"Do you not care that the world may die?"

"I care that Donna Taybard lives."

"Are you bargaining with me?"

"Call it what you will."

"I cannot kill, and rescuing her may take just that."

"Then you destroy the Mother Stone."

"How could you ask this of me?"

"Let me understand you, lady. You want me to risk my life against the Guardians? And yet you know they will try to stop me and that I will kill all who come against me. Apparently that sits all right with your principles. But to save a woman and perhaps kill the ungodly to do it—that is against your principles?"

"I will not argue, Mr. Shannow. I have neither the strength nor the time. What I can do is to take Batik to Donna. Will that suffice?"

Shannow shook his head. "I have no right to ask Batik to put himself in danger."

"I wish I knew what you two were babbling about," said Batik, "and I'm fascinated to know at what point you'll bring me into this conversation."

"It does not concern you," said Shannow.

"What are you, my mother?" snapped Batik. "You don't make decisions for me. Saving the world may be a horse I can't saddle, but pulling one wench from a dungeon in Babylon? Who knows? Perhaps I can tackle that without falling over."

"You know damned well it's more than that," said Shannow. "You owe Donna nothing. Why should you put your life at risk?"

"If you're looking for selfish reasons, my friend, tell me this: Ruth says the world could perish if the Mother Stone is not destroyed. If that is the case, where would you suggest I hide?"

"Let me think on it," said Shannow.

"What is to think about?" asked the Hellborn. "You want to avenge Karitas? Sarento is the man responsible. Abaddon is a pawn in his game, and you don't win wars by killing pawns."

"I will deal with Abaddon," said Ruth. "I promise you that."

"And how will you get Batik to Babylon?"

"With my own magic."

"I asked how."

"I shall dismantle his molecular structure, absorb it into my own, and reassemble him when I arrive."

"Reassemble—what's she talking about, Shannow?"

"There is little danger to you, Batik," declared Ruth. "It is how I travel."

"But you have done this before, with other people, yes?" asked Shannow.

"No," she admitted.

"Why did you have to ask her, Shannow? I preferred it when she said by magic."

"You still want to go?" asked the Jerusalem Man.

"I said so, didn't I?"

"Try not to get yourself killed," said Shannow, offering his hand.

Batik took it and shrugged. "I'll do my best. Tell me, Ruth, can you reassemble me without scars and with a less prominent nose?"

"No. Shall we go?"

"I'm ready," said Batik. "Good luck, Shannow."

"And to you. Tell Donna I wish her joy."

"Don't give up on her; her new husband's probably dead."

Before Shannow could answer, Batik and Ruth faded from sight.

And the Jerusalem Man was alone.

Batik felt no sensation of movement. One moment he was looking at Shannow, and the next he was lying facedown in the grass on a hillside west of Babylon. Ruth was nowhere in sight as he stood and took a deep breath.

He wandered to the hilltop and gazed at the city, which lay squat and dark in the distance. Covered by a pall of black smoke, it had improved little since he had fled it, and he realized at that moment that he had missed the place not at all.

Ruth appeared beside him, and this time he did not react.

"How are you feeling?" she asked.

"Well. But you look tired."

"I am weary," she admitted. "You have no idea of the energy I expend holding this body image in place. And as for carrying you across eight hundred miles . . ."

"Sadly I recall nothing of the journey. Is Donna here yet?"

"No; the wagon is half a day due west. If you start now, you should sight their camp before dawn."

"How many in the party?"

"Two hundred."

"I'm carrying only eighteen shells, Ruth."

"I am hoping you will use your brain, young man, and that there will be no need for killing."

"I might be able to get to her and untie her. Together we could run, I suppose."

"There is something else you should know, Batik."

"I don't think I want to hear it."

"She is pregnant and in a coma."

"I knew I didn't want to hear it."

"I shall pray for you, Batik."

"That will be nice, I'm sure. I suppose you couldn't conjure up one of Sarento's guns as well?"

"Good-bye, Batik."

"Farewell, Ruth," he said, and watched as she became ever more transparent.

As he set off toward the west with a jaunty stride, he pushed the problem of the rescue from his mind. The whole mission was palpably hopeless, and he decided to relax and enjoy the stroll. Wondering what Shannow would have done, he chuckled as he pictured the Jerusalem Man riding up to the army and demanding the release of his lady. And he'd probably get away with it, thought Batik. Clouds scudded across the moon, and an old badger ran across his path, stopping to squint at the tall man with the broad shoulders. Then it was gone into the undergrowth.

He came across the campsite an hour before dawn. They were camped in a hollow, having erected tents in a circle around the wagon. Batik knelt behind a screen of bushes and watched them for a while until he was sure he had placed all the sentries. Then, just as he was getting ready to move, he saw a dark shadow creep across his line of vision. Pulling his pistol into his hand, he crept out behind the watcher, moving slowly down until he was almost alongside him. The man was lean and bearded and dressed in clothes of dark homespun wool. So intent was he on the campsite that he failed to hear the approach of the Hellborn.

Batik cocked his pistol, and the noise made the man freeze, but his body tensed, and Batik knew he was about to do something rash.

"Don't be a fool," he whispered. "I only want to talk."

"You've got the gun. Talk all you want," hissed the man.

"You're obviously not Hellborn, so I wondered what you wanted from them."

"None of your business. You finished now?"

"Probably. But I do have business here, and I don't want you spoiling it."

"Well, there's a shame, sonny."

"Are you from Donna's settlement?"

The man rolled slowly to his side and gazed into Batik's eyes.

"What do you know of Donna?"

"I'm a friend of Jon Shannow. He asked me to help her."

"Why isn't he here himself?"

"He would be if he could. Why are *you* here?"

"Why do you think?"

"You want to rescue her?"

"That's the general idea, but there's a sight too many of the bastards. There's no way to sneak in; they've got seven sentries and a man inside the wagon."

"I only counted six sentries."

"There's one in that tall oak. He's got a long rifle, and I don't doubt he knows how to use it."

Batik uncocked his pistol and slid it into its scabbard.

"My name is Batik," he said, offering his hand.

"Jacob Madden," responded the other, sitting up and uncocking his own pistol, which had been concealed beneath his coat. The two men shook hands.

"We came very close to killing one another," remarked Batik.

"You came very close to dying," observed Madden. "Let's pull back to where we can talk more freely." Together they eased their way into the undergrowth and back over the brow of the hill.

There, hidden in a grove of trees, were two horses. On the ground nearby Batik saw a man lying on his side, a pistol in his hand. His face was waxen and haggard, and blood was seeping through the front of his shirt.

Madden knelt beside him. "Can't get to her, Griff. There's too many."

Griffin struggled to rise, then fell back.

"Who is he?" asked Batik.

"Donna is his woman."

Batik's eyebrows rose, and he leaned over the injured man. "Looks like he's dying," he said conversationally.

Madden swore. "Nobody asked for your opinion," he snapped.

Griffin took a deep breath and forced himself to a sitting position. "Well, I don't feel too great," he remarked. "Who's your friend?"

"His name's Batik, and he's a friend of Shannow's. Says he's been sent to help Donna."

"Do you trust him?"

"Hell, I don't know, Griff. He ain't killed no one yet, and he sure as Hades could have gotten me."

Griffin beckoned Batik to sit beside him and looked long and hard into the Hellborn's face. "What do they plan for Donna?"

"They're going to sacrifice her, according to Shannow."

"We must get to her."

"Even if we did, how do we escape? Four people on two horses, and one of the escapers in a coma."

Griffin fell back and closed his eyes.

Batik sat for a while. Then he touched Madden's shoulder, and the farmer turned. "What is it?"

"There is a festival around this time of year. I have lost track of the date recently, but it must be close. It is called Walpurnacht, and it is very holy; a great sacrifice is always made, there is dancing in the streets and wine, and all the pleasures of the flesh are sated. If it has not already passed, then that is the time when they will sacrifice her."

"How does that help us?"

"They will not have hundreds of guards around her in the temple. We must hide in the city and then attempt a rescue before the festival."

"We'll stand out like boils on a pig's backside."

"I have several houses."

"How do we know they're empty?"

"Are you always this gloomy, Jacob?"

"Yep."

"With horses we should reach the outer city just after first light. At least your friend can rest for a while and gather his strength."

Griffin reached up and gripped Madden's arm. "He's right, Jacob. Help me to my horse."

The journey took three hours, and Madden rode warily down the narrow streets of Babylon, waiting for a challenge, or a shot, or a sign of treachery. But the people they passed seemed little different from the settlers of Avalon. Women walked with children, men chatted on street corners, and few paid much attention to the riders or to Batik walking at the head of Griffin's horse. The wagon master was wearing a leather coat to shield his wounds, and he fought to stay upright in the saddle.

Batik stopped a young boy who was walking with a large gray wolfhound.

"What date is it, boy?"

"April twenty-eighth."

Batik walked on, leading them into a maze of foul-smelling tenement buildings and filth-choked alleyways to emerge at last by a high wall and a locked gate. He lifted the narrow chain and hooked his fingers around it, and Madden watched as the muscles in his forearms swelled. The central link stretched and then parted, and Batik opened the gate and led them inside. The house beyond was of white stone with arched doors and windows. Around the second story ran an open balcony beneath a slanted tile roof.

"My sister lived here," said Batik.

At the back of the house was an empty stable, and there Batik unsaddled the horses and helped Griffin into the building. Dust was everywhere, but the house was untouched by recent human occupancy.

The furniture was spartan, and Griffin was half carried to a wide firm divan by the wall beneath a window.

"I will go out and get some food," said Batik.

"Has the festival happened yet?" asked Griffin.

"No, we have two days."

"What is this holy night?" said Madden.

"It is when the Devil walks among his children."

Shannow rode into the canyon at midnight, thirty-seven hours after watching Batik and Ruth vanish into the night. As he came in sight of the ruined city, he reined in his mount and stared in awe at the ghost ship. No longer was it a rotting wreck; now it sat in colossal glory, four immense angled funnels and six rows of lights strung like pearls along its decks.

The night wind shifted, and the sound of music echoed in the canyon.

An eerie blast reverberated around the mountains, causing Shannow's horse to rear. He calmed it and watched as a trail of light shot into the sky, exploding in a cloud of colored stars that popped like distant gunshots. The sound of cheering came from the ship.

Shannow slipped the thongs from his pistols and drew a

deep, slow breath. Touching his heels to the stallion's sides, he moved down toward the ruins.

A dark shadow moved into his path . . .

"It's about time you showed yourself, Lewis," he said. "Three times now you've had me in your sights."

"I don't want to kill you, Shannow. Truly. Turn around and ride from here."

"Into the Zealots hidden in the woods?"

"You are a skillful man; you can avoid them."

Shannow sat silently, staring into the muzzle of the black rifle and feeling the tension cast by the Guardian.

"Was I wrong about you, Lewis? I took you to be a good man in the Archer mold. I did not see you as a butcher of women and children, as a bloodsucking vampire."

"I am a soldier. Don't make me kill you."

"What happened to the Ark?"

Lewis licked his lips. "Tonight we are celebrating rebirth. Every year at this time we bring some aspect of the past to life to show that what we guard is real and solid and not just a memory. Tonight the Ark sails once more in all her glory. Now leave, for God's sake!"

"God, Lewis? The lords of the Hellborn speak of God? Tell it to the wind. Tell it to the farmers nailed to trees and to the women spread-eagled and butchered. But don't tell it to me!"

"We did not create wars, Shannow. For centuries we have tried to steer mankind back to civilization, but it hasn't worked. There was no unity. Sarento says that without unity there is no order, without order there is no law, and without law no civilization. All great advances have come as a result of war. It will be different soon, Shannow. We are going to rebuild cities, and we will make the world a garden. Please ride away."

"I know nothing of your lost civilization, Lewis," said Shannow softly. "Karitas would never tell me. I don't know whether it was beautiful, but if that gun you are holding is an example of what they had then, I doubt it. Did some version of the Hellborn exist even then, sweeping across the land to bring death to thousands? Or were there weapons even more terrible than that monstrosity? Perhaps whole cities were wiped out.

And you want to bring this back? Some time ago I was wounded, and I was taken to a small village. Peaceful people, Lewis, happy people. They were led by a man who once had been a Guardian, but they're not alive now. The women were raped, and then their throats were cut. And Karitas? He was crucified. I don't doubt that if their spirits were still here, they would applaud your dream. But then, their souls aren't here, are they? They were sucked into your Blood Stone to fuel more death and despair."

"That's enough! I was told to kill you, and I've disobeyed that order. If you leave now, you'll live, Shannow. Doesn't that mean anything to you?"

"Of course it does, Lewis. No man wants to die, and that's why I am talking to you. I don't want to kill you, but I must find the stone."

Lewis lifted the rifle to his shoulder. "If you do not turn this instant, I will send you to hell."

"But that's where I want to go, Lewis. That's where it is," answered Shannow, pointing to the Ark.

In the bright moonlight Shannow saw Lewis tense, the rifle butt being drawn more tightly into his shoulder. The Jerusalem Man hurled himself from the saddle just as the rifle exploded in a thundering roar of shells. He hit the ground hard and rolled behind a boulder as chips and fragments screamed around him. Then he came to his knees with his pistol in his hand. His horse was down, thrashing its legs in the air, and a coldness settled on Shannow as he cocked the pistol and dived to the left, rolling on his shoulder. Lewis spun, the rifle bucking in his hands, shells sending spurts of earth and stone to Shannow's right. The pistol leveled, and a single shot punched Lewis from his feet. Shannow moved to the body: Lewis was dead. The Jerusalem Man walked to the dying horse and shot it through the head, then reloaded his pistol and began the long walk to the ruins.

"No man wants to die, Lewis." The words came back to him, and he felt the truth of them. Shannow didn't want to die; he wanted to find Jerusalem and know peace. He looked up at the Ark and the glowing lights, listening to the music. Then he glanced back at Lewis' body, which was merging with the moon shadows.

He walked to the rock doorway and there, drawing his pistol, stepped to the side. As the door opened, Shannow's pistol came up, but the steel tunnel beyond was empty. Keeping to the wall, he stepped inside, and the door closed behind him. There were no stairs leading down, no doorways that he could see, and he cursed softly.

The elevator door whispered open, beckoning him. Sheathing his pistol, he stepped inside.

The doors closed, and the elevator lurched slightly; when they opened again, he saw what he had expected to see: armed guards with pistols pointed at his chest. They were dressed strangely in flat dark blue peaked caps and doubled-breasted serge jackets. In their midst stood the giant Sarento in a similar suit, but white, with brass buttons and blue epaulets each bearing three gold bars.

"You really are a disappointing man, Mr. Shannow," Sarento greeted him.

The guards moved in and disarmed the Jerusalem Man, who offered no resistance. He was led out and found himself not in the shining hallway he remembered but in an enormous room filled with extravagantly carved furniture, luxurious carpets, and stained glass windows.

"Magnificent, is it not?" said Sarento.

Shannow said nothing. He stared in silent wonder at the stained glass depicting sailing ships and biblical saints, surrounded by gilded panels of exquisite carpentry.

"Why did you come back, Mr. Shannow?"

"To destroy you."

"Did you really believe you could work one of your brigand-killing miracles among the Guardians? Surely not."

People started to filter into the room; all were dressed in a curious fashion. The women wore long elaborate dresses; the men had on black coats and white shirts.

"Take him below," said Sarento. "I'll see him later."

The four guards walked Shannow to a carpeted staircase and on to a door bearing a brass plaque: B-59. Inside was a four-poster bed with velvet curtains and a small writing table inlaid with gold.

"Sit down," said one of the guards, a young man with short-cropped blond hair. "Make yourself comfortable."

They waited in uneasy silence until Sarento joined them. He removed his white cap and dropped it on the table.

"Tell me about the ship," said Shannow, and Sarento chuckled.

"You are a cool man, Mr. Shannow. I like you."

The giant sat back on the bed, and peeled off his white gloves. "Are you impressed by rebirth?"

"Of course," admitted Shannow.

"And so you should be. This was one of the largest ships ever made. It was 882 feet long and weighed 46,000 tons. It was a miracle of engineering and one of the wonders of the ancient world."

Shannow suddenly laughed.

"What is amusing you, sir?"

"Do you like parables, Sarento? It seems to me that this ship mirrors your lunatic dreams: opulent and civilized and buried by the sea."

"Except that we have brought it back," snapped Sarento.

"Yes, to sit on a mountain above the ruins of a civilization you did not know even existed. A ship on a mountain, huge and useless, like your ambition."

"A ship on a mountain? Come with me, Mr. Shannow. I would like to show you what real power is."

With the guards around him, Sarento led Shannow to the upper promenade and out onto the boat deck. The sea stretched out to a distant horizon, and the Ark glided majestically on a star-speckled ocean. Shannow could smell the salt in the air, while gulls wheeled and dived above the giant funnels.

"Stunning, is it not?" asked Sarento.

Shannow shivered. "This is not possible."

"All things are possible with the Mother Stone."

"And we are truly at sea?"

"No. The Ark sits as always on her mountain. What you are seeing and feeling is an image projected by magic. However, were you to cut a hole in the ship's side, water would pour in—salt water. For the stone would carry on the charade. And if you were to jump over the side, you would hit the sea, ice-cold and deadly. But then you would pass through it and plummet to the ruins of Atlantis. This is power, Mr. Shannow, just a fraction of the power the stone can hold. Had I wished it, the Ark would sail on a real sea. One day it will, and then I will sail it into the harbor of New York."

"How many souls will that cost?" asked Shannow.

"You have a small mind, Shannow." Sarento shook his head. "What are a few lives compared with a golden future?"

"Can we go back inside?" said Shannow. "It's a little cold out here."

"We can, Shannow. You, I'm afraid, are leaving the ship here."

"Just when I was beginning to enjoy it," said Shannow. Then, as Sarento signaled the guards forward, he crouched and whipped the double-edged hunting knife from his boot. The first guard died as the blade slashed across his throat; Shannow snatched the man's pistol from his hand and leapt at Sarento. As the big man dived to the deck, Shannow followed him, dropping the knife and hauling at Sarento's collar. The pistol was cocked, its barrel pushing under Sarento's chin.

"Be so kind as to tell your guards to put up their weapons," hissed Shannow, hauling Sarento to his feet.

The three remaining guards looked to their leader.

"Do it," he said. "I shall end this farce in my own way."

"Take me to the stone," said Shannow.

"But of course. Your infantile heroics have earned you that, at the very least."

"I congratulate you on your calm."

Sarento's eyes met his. "You may feel you have the upper hand, Mr. Shannow, but the magic that raised the Ark from the sea floor will not be undone by a madman with a Hellborn revolver."

Sarento led the way below.

And the *Titanic* sailed on through the ghostly sea . . .

◇ **13** ◇

ABADDON'S DREAMS WERE troubled, and he awoke clutching at the air. The black silk sheets were damp with sweat, and he rolled to his feet. He had felt so good three hours before, when Donna Taybard had been brought to Babylon. And tonight the reign of the Hellborn would begin in earnest; all the star charts had confirmed it. Donna was the sacrifice the Devil had been waiting for, and all the powers of hell would flow through Abaddon the moment he devoured her.

Yet now the Hellborn king sat trembling on his bed, plagued by the nameless fears that had haunted his dreams. He had seen Jon Shannow deep in hell, battling Beelzebub with sword and pistol. And then the Jerusalem Man had turned his eyes on Abaddon, and in those eyes the king had seen death.

The fear would not pass, and Abaddon moved to the cabinet by the window and poured a goblet of wine, sipping it until his nerves settled. He thought of summoning Achnazzar but dismissed that idea. The high priest had become increasingly nervous in the king's presence these last few days.

"Daddy!" The child's cry jerked Abaddon from his reverie, and he swung around, but the room was empty. He caught a glimpse of his reflection in a long rectangular mirror and stood, drawing in his belly to present a powerful profile.

Abaddon, Lord of the Pit!

"Daddy!" This time the sound came from the sitting room beyond. Abaddon ran through the open doorway only to be confronted by an empty desk and an open window. He blinked and wiped the sweat from his face.

In the streets beyond the palace walls he could hear the chants of the mob: "Satan! Satan! Satan!"

Walpurnacht was a night of beauty when the people could see their god walking among them, feel his presence in the air about them, see his image in the glow of their Blood Stones.

But this night was special. This night would see the dawning era of the Hellborn, for when Donna Taybard's powers flowed into the knives and her body was consumed by the master, the magic of hell would be unleashed on the world.

The Lord of the Pit would become the King of the Earth.

"I'm frightened, Daddy."

Abaddon whirled around to see a blond child of seven hugging a threadbare doll.

"Sarah?"

The child ran away into the bedroom, and Abaddon followed, but the room was empty. He knew it was a hallucination, for Sarah had been dead for centuries. The wine was too strong.

But so were the memories . . . He poured another glass and returned to the mirror, staring at the bloodshot gray eyes and the flowing hair that was now silver at the temples. The face was as it had been for decades—a middle-aged man, strong and in his prime.

It was not Lawrence Welby who stared back at him. Welby was dead, as dead as his wife and daughter.

"I am the king," he whispered. "The Satanlord. Go away, Welby. Don't stare at me. Who are you to judge?"

"Read me a story, Daddy."

"Leave me alone!" he screamed, squeezing shut his eyes and refusing to see the apparition he knew lay on his bed.

"Read her a story, Lawrence. You know she won't sleep until you do."

Welby opened his eyes and drank in the sight of the golden-haired woman by the door.

"Ruth?"

"Have you forgotten how to read a story?"

"This is a dream."

"Don't forget us, Lawrence."

"Are you truly here?" he asked, stumbling forward. But the golden-haired woman vanished, and Welby sank to his knees.

The door opened. "Ruth?"

"No, my lord. Are you ill?"

Abaddon pushed himself to his feet. "How dare you come here unannounced, Achnazzar!" said the king.

"The guards came for me, sire. They said you sounded . . . distraught."

"I am well. What do the star charts show?"

"Magelin says it is a time of great change, as one would expect at the dawn of an empire."

"And Cade?"

"He is bottled up in a nowhere pass where he can neither escape nor conquer."

"That all sounds well, priest. Now tell me about Shannow. Tell me again how he died falling from a cliff."

Achnazzar bowed low. "It was an error, sire, but he is now a prisoner of the Guardians, and they mean to kill him. The Jerusalem Man is a danger no longer. After tonight he will seem as a gnat in the ear of the dragon."

"After tonight? The night is not yet over, priest."

The morning of Walpurnacht dawned bright and clear, and Batik awoke filled with a sense of burning anticipation. His skin had become hypersensitive to touch, and his body trembled with suppressed emotion.

Even the air in the room seemed to crackle with static, as if a lightning storm were hovering over the city.

Batik rose from his bed and drew in a deep, shuddering breath.

The joy of Walpurnacht was upon him. His memory flashed images of past festivals when he had been filled with a holy strength and had coupled with a dozen willing women, never seeming to tire.

Remembering Madden and Griffen, he felt anger washing over him.

What link did he have with such farm-working peasants?

How had he allowed himself to become involved with their petty squabbles?

He would kill them both and enjoy the day, he decided.

He moved to his pistol and settled the butt in his palm. It felt good, and he burned with a desire to kill, to destroy.

Jon Shannow leapt to his thoughts . . .

His friend.

"I have no friends. No need of friends," hissed Batik.

But the image remained, and again he saw Shannow standing in the dark of the dungeon hall.

His friend.

"Damn you, Shannow!" he screamed, and fell to his knees, the gun clattering to the floor. His joy evaporated.

Downstairs Jacob Madden was battling with his own demons. For him it was almost worse than for Batik, for he had never experienced the surging emotions of Walpurnacht. There was no joy for Madden, only the pain of his memories, his defeats, and his tragedies. He wanted to run from the building and kill every Hellborn he saw, wanted them to suffer as he suffered.

But Griffin needed him, Donna Taybard needed him, and for Madden a duty like that was an iron chain on his emotions. It would not break for a selfish motive.

So he sat in his misery and waited for Batik.

The Hellborn dressed swiftly and cleaned his weapons. Then he moved down into the wide living area and checked on Griffin. The man's color was good, and he slept peacefully.

"How are you?" he asked Madden, laying his hand on the man's shoulder.

"Don't touch me, you bastard!" snapped Madden, knocking the arm away and surging to his feet.

"Be calm, Jacob," urged Batik. "It is Walpurnacht; it is in the air. Breathe deeply and relax."

"Relax? Everything I loved is gone, and my life is now a shell. When do we go after Donna?"

"Tonight."

"Why not now?"

"In full light?"

Madden sank back into his chair. "What is the matter with me?"

"I told you; it is Walpurnacht. Tonight the Devil walks, and you will see him. But from now until he is gone you will feel his presence in the air around you. During the next twenty-four hours there will be many fights, many deaths, many rapes, and thousands of new lives begun."

Madden moved to the table and poured himself a mug of water. His hands were trembling, and sweat shone on his face.

"I can't take too much of this," he whispered.

"I'll help you through it," said Batik. Outside in the narrow alleys the sound of chanting came to them. From somewhere nearby a scream, piercing and shrill, rose above the chants.

"Someone just died," said Madden.

"Yes, and she won't be the last."

The day wore on. Griffin awoke, and the pain from his wounds doubled. He screamed and cursed Madden, his language foul and his eyes full of malice.

"Take no notice," Batik said softly.

Toward dusk, with Griffin asleep once more, Batik readied himself for the night, smearing his face with red dye. Madden refused to disguise himself, and Batik shrugged.

"It is only paint, Jacob."

"I don't want to look like a devil. If I am to die, I'll die like a man."

Toward midnight the two men rechecked their guns and slipped out into the street, heading toward the center of the city. In the main thoroughfare they came upon a huge crowd of dancing, chanting people. Scores of men and women writhed together in the nearby doorways and alleyways. Madden looked away.

A young girl, her scarlet dress spattered with blood, was slashing at herself with a curved knife. She saw Madden and ran to him, throwing her arms around his neck.

Madden hurled her from him, but another woman took her place, running her hands over his body and whispering promises of joy. He pulled himself clear and thrust his way into the crowd after Batik.

The crowd moved on toward the temple square, and all the chants merged into a single word, repeated again and again.

"Satan . . . Satan . . . Satan . . ."

As they neared the long steps to the temple, the night sky blazed with red light and a shimmering figure appeared, hundreds of feet tall. Madden's mouth opened, and he shrank back from the colossus. It had the legs of a goat and the body of a powerful man, but the head was bestial and double-horned.

A huge hand reached down toward the crowd, and the young woman with the blood-drenched dress was lifted by the men around her and hurled into the taloned hand. It closed about her and lifted her to the gaping mouth. The girl disappeared, and the crowd cheered.

"This way," shouted Batik, pulling Madden toward an alley beside the temple. "We don't have long."

"Acolytes' entrance," said Batik as they reached an oval wooden door at the side of the temple. It was locked, but he lifted his foot and sent the door crashing open. They stepped inside, and Madden drew his pistol.

"We must get up to the temple; they will be bringing Donna out to him any moment now."

"You mean he's going to eat her?" Madden asked incredulously.

Batik ignored him and set off at a run. Meanwhile a temple guard rounded the corner, but Batik shot him down and hurdled the body, taking the stairs beyond two steps at a time.

They reached another corridor, and two more guards appeared. A shell shrieked past Madden's ear, and he dived for the floor, triggering his pistol twice. One guard pitched backward, and the other staggered but lifted his rifle once more. Batik fired twice, and the man crumpled to the floor.

At the top of another winding stair Batik paused before the door. He loaded his pistol and turned to Madden.

"This is it, my friend. Are you ready?"

"I've been ready all my life," said Madden.

"I believe you," Batik replied with a grin.

* * *

Shannow pushed Sarento into the elevator and stepped in behind him. The doors closed, and the giant smiled.

"Level G," he said, and the elevator shuddered. "You have a number of surprises still in store, Mr. Shannow. I hope you enjoy them."

"Stand against the door, Sarento."

"But of course, though your fears are groundless; there are no guards in the cavern. Tell me, what do you hope to achieve? You cannot destroy the stone."

The doors opened suddenly, and Sarento spun and dived through. Shannow followed him and opened fire, but the bullets ricocheted off a huge stalactite. The Jerusalem Man looked around at the immense cavern with a spherical roof that glistened with gold threads and shining stones. Stalactites hung like pillars. He moved into the glowing light near the center, where a small black lake surrounded an island on which stood a circle of Standing Stones, black and glistening.

"You stand at the heart of the empire, Shannow," came Sarento's disembodied voice. "Here every dream is a reality. Can you feel the power of the Blood Stone?"

Shannow scanned the cavern, but there was no sign of the giant. Walking to the edge of the lake, he saw a narrow bridge of seasoned wood on the other side of the stones. Traversing the lake, he mounted the bridge and crossed to the circle. At the first monolith he stopped to examine the sides. A deep indentation met his fingers. He pressed inside and heard a latch drop. A small section dropped away, but when he thrust his hand inside, it was empty.

"Did you think I would leave the gold there?" said Sarento.

Shannow spun to see that the giant was standing at the altar. He was dressed now in the armor of Atlantis, a golden breastplate with a golden stone above the heart. On his head he wore a plumed helm, and in his hands was a sword. Shannow fired, but the bullet screamed away up into the cavern roof. Taking careful aim, he fired once more, this time at the grinning face.

"Pendarric's armor of invincibility, Mr. Shannow. Nothing can harm me now, whereas you are defenseless. It is fitting that we should meet like this: two Rolynd warriors within the great circle."

"Where is the Mother Stone?" said Shannow, sheathing his pistol.

"You are standing on it, Shannow. Behold!"

The ground beneath his feet blurred, the covering of dank earth shimmering into nothing, becoming red-gold veined with slender black. All across the circle the ground glowed like a lantern.

"It is said that to kill a Rolynd brings great power," said Sarento, moving forward with sword in hand. "We shall see. How do you like the sword, Shannow? Beautiful, yes? It is a sword of power. Sipstrassi. In the old tongue they were called Pynral-ponas: swords from the stone. What they cut, they kill. Come, Mr. Shannow; let me cut you."

Shannow backed away toward the bridge.

"Where can you run? Back to the *Titanic* and my guards? Face me, Rolynd. Meet your death with courage. Come; I do not have much time."

"I'm in no hurry," said Shannow.

Sarento leapt forward, the great sword flashing in the air, but Shannow dived under the blade and rolled to his feet.

"A nice maneuver. It is always interesting to see an animal run for its life, but what will it gain you? A few more seconds." As Sarento ran at him, Shannow vaulted to the altar and jumped down on the other side.

"Terean-Bezek," hissed Sarento, and two stone hands grabbed Shannow's ankles. He looked down and saw the Blood Stone fingers trapping him as Sarento laughed and moved slowly around the altar.

"How does it feel to lose, Jerusalem Man? Does your soul cry out in its anguish?"

"You'll never know," hissed Shannow. As the sword came up, he looked away, down at the surface of the altar. There, engraved on the top, was the image of a sword with an upswept hilt.

The sword of the dream!

Shannow reached out. Something cold touched his palm,

and his fingers clenched around the hilt. Then the sword flashed up, and the ringing of steel on steel filled the cavern.

Sarento stepped back. Gone was the perpetual smile. Shannow lowered the blade to the stone hands gripping his ankles, and as the sword touched them, they disappeared.

"You were right, Sarento. This cavern holds many surprises."

"That is Pendarric's sword. I never could find it. I could never understand why I was unable to find it, for it was said to be awaiting a Rolynd."

"You are Rolynd no longer, Sarento. Your luck just ran out."

The smile returned to the giant's face. "We'll see. Unless, of course, you can find some armor." As he moved in, his sword slashing toward Shannow's head, the Jerusalem Man blocked the blow and his riposte thundered against Sarento's neck. It did not even break the skin.

Now the giant took his blade two-handed and attacked ferociously. Shannow was forced back, blocking and parrying. Three times more Shannow's sword thrust or cut at Sarento's armor, but to no effect.

"It is as useless as your pistol."

Sweat flowed on Shannow's face, and his sword arm was weary, while Sarento showed no sign of fatigue.

"You know, Shannow, I could almost regret killing you."

Shannow took a deep breath and hefted his sword, his eyes drawn to the giant's breastplate as Sarento stepped forward. The golden stone set there was now almost black. Sarento's sword whistled down. Shannow blocked it and risked a cut to the head. The blade bounced away, but Sarento was shaken; his hand flew to his brow and came away stained by blood.

"It's not possible," he whispered. He looked down at the stone and then screamed in fury, launching a berserk attack. Shannow was pushed back and back across the center of the circle, and Sarento's sword slashed through his shirt to score the skin. He fell. With a scream of triumph the giant slashed his blade downward, but Shannow rolled to his knees, blocking another cut and parrying a thrust.

The two men circled one another warily.

"You'll still die, Shannow."

Shannow grinned. "You're frightened, Sarento; I can feel it. You're not Rolynd—you never were. You're just another brigand with large dreams. But they end here."

Sarento backed away to the altar. "Large dreams? What would you know of large dreams? All you want is some mythical city, but I want the world to be as it was. Can you understand that? Parks and gardens and the joys of civilization. You've seen the *Titanic*. Everyone could enjoy its luxury. No more poverty, Shannow. No starvation. The Garden of Eden!"

"With you as the serpent? I think not."

As Sarento's sword lunged toward him, Shannow moved in a sidestep and plunged his blade under the breastplate and through Sarento's groin. The giant screamed and fell across the altar. Shannow wrenched the sword clear and, as the cavern shuddered, almost lost his footing. A stalactite tore itself from the roof and plunged into the lake.

Sarento hauled himself onto the altar.

"Oh, my God," he whispered. "The *Titanic*!" His blood-covered hands scrabbled at the altar top. Shannow's sword touched his neck, and he rolled slowly to his back. "Listen to me. You *must* stop the power. The *Titanic* . . ."

"What about it?"

"It is sailing an identical course to that which destroyed it when it sank with the loss of 1,500 lives. The gold . . ."

"The ship is on a mountain. It cannot sink."

"The iceberg will pierce the side, a three-hundred-foot gash. The stone will create . . . the . . . ocean." Sarento's eyes lost their focus, and his body slid to the stone. As his blood touched the glowing ground, it hissed and bubbled, and a deep red stain was absorbed by the rock. Shannow dropped his sword and stepped to the altar. Sarento's fingers had been scrabbling near a raised relief, and when he pulled at it, the top moved. Crossing to the other side, the Jerusalem Man pushed the gap wider, then reached inside. There were four spools of wire.

He dragged them free and scanned the circle. There were thirteen Standing Stones, and he ran to the first and looped the gold around the base.

Far above him the ghost ship sped through the eldritch sea, while people danced and sang in the great ballrooms. One young couple walked out onto the deck. The iceberg loomed in the night like a gargantuan tombstone.

"Isn't that incredible?" said the man.

"Yes." They were joined by other revelers, who leaned over the wooden rail to watch the ice loom ever closer.

The ship plowed on, scraping the side of the ice mountain. The revelers shrieked with laughter and leapt back as chunks of ice fell to the promenade.

Deep below the decks came a shuddering jolt, and the ship trembled as if sliding over shingle.

"You don't think Sarento has taken rebirth too far?" asked the girl.

"There's no danger," the man assured her.

And the ship tilted.

Shannow had attached the gold to six of the monoliths when a growling rumble set the ground vibrating. The vast roof trembled, and a foot-wide crack opened. Stalactites began to fall like giant spears, and water streamed from the fissure above him. Shannow grabbed the wire and pulled it tight. Below him the ground glowed ever brighter. Two more monoliths were connected when the far wall of the cavern exploded outward, as millions of tons of icy water cascaded down from the stricken *Titanic*.

The lake swelled. Shannow ignored the chaos around him and struggled on; the spool he was carrying ran out, and he swiftly tied a second spool to the wire. Water swirled around his legs, making the stone surface slippery. Then four more monoliths were joined by the slender gold line, but by then the lake had submerged the bridge and Shannow found himself wading against the current. A stalactite splashed into the water beside him, cracking against his arm and tearing the spool loose. Cursing, he dived below the water, his arms fanning out to retrieve it. He was forced to swim back to the last monolith and follow the wire down. Then, with the spool once more in his hand, he struck out. The water was rising faster now, but he ignored the peril until he had completed the golden circle.

He could no longer feel the stone beneath his feet, but the fading glow could still be seen. Water was now flooding the cavern, and Shannow watched as the roof came steadily toward him.

He searched for a fissure through which he could climb, but there was no way out. Sarento's body bobbed alongside him, facedown, and he pushed it away. As the roof loomed directly above him, he was forced to turn on his back to keep his mouth above water.

As Batik pushed opened the door, shells hammered into the frame, and the Hellborn warrior dived through the doorway and rolled. Four guards turned their guns on him. Madden came through a fraction of a second later, his pistol blazing; one guard went down, and another was stung by a bullet across the forearm. The other two opened fire on Batik, and a bullet seared through his side, while another ricocheted from the marble floor to tear the flesh under his thigh. Despite his wounds, Batik coolly returned the fire, his first bullet taking a guard under the chin and hurling him from his feet, his second hammering home into the last man's shoulder, spinning him. Madden finished the man with a shot to the head.

All around them red-robed priests were scurrying for safety as Batik grabbed Madden's outstretched arm and hauled himself to his feet.

Outside the huge double doors Achnazzar lifted his dagger over the unconscious Donna.

"No!" screamed Batik, and he and Madden fired simultaneously. Punched from his feet, Achnazzar landed hard on the upper steps and rolled to his stomach. He could feel blood filling his lungs. Clutching the knife, he crawled toward the comatose victim, but as he raised it, a giant black shadow loomed over him.

Talons as long as sabers ripped through his back. The knife fell from nerveless fingers, and Achnazzar could not even scream as the taloned hand carried him toward the dreadful maw.

Batik limped to Donna and tried to lift her.

"Christ Almighty!" shouted Madden.

Batik looked up to see that the demon, having finished with Achnazzar, was now reaching down once more. He cocked his pistol and stood, straddling Donna.

The taloned fingers opened . . .

Batik fired, and the hand jerked but relentlessly came down once more. He threw his empty pistol aside and drew Griffin's weapon from his belt. As the fingers came within reach, Batik leapt into the palm; his clothes burst into flame, but he ignored the agony as he held his gun two-handed and leveled it at the colossal face.

Eight hundred miles away the created waters of the Atlantic Ocean streamed across the Blood Stone, draining its power, blurring its energy.

Batik fell through the now-transparent fingers and plunged into the crowd below. Madden ran to him, beating at the flames on his clothing with bare hands. Incredibly, once they were extinguished, he found that Batik was still conscious. He helped him to his feet, and together they staggered back to the temple steps.

Above them the demon was fading fast, and a strange sense of calm settled on Madden.

"It's over," he told Batik.

"Not yet," replied the Hellborn as the angry crowd surged toward them.

Soon after midnight Griffin awoke. The house was empty, and he knew that Madden and Batik had set out to save his wife. Shame burned in him, swamping the pain from his wounds. He should have been out there with them.

He struggled to sit, ignoring the pull at the stitches Madden had expertly placed, and gazed from the window at the overgrown garden beyond. Never had Griffin felt so alone. He glanced down at his body and saw the wasted flesh; his shirt seemed voluminous now, and his belt had needed an extra notch, which Madden had made with his hunting knife. Anger surged, fueled by frustration and helplessness. But he had nothing on which to vent his emotion, and it turned inward as he again saw young Eric blasted from life in the doorway of their home. Tears brimmed, and he blinked them away, swinging his head to focus his gaze on the garden. The trees should have been trimmed back, for their branches were spreading above the rosebushes and blocking the light needed for good blooms.

A shadow caught his eye; something had moved in the moonlight by the gate. Griffin scanned the area. Nothing. There were no lights in the house, and he knew he could not be seen. He waited, focusing his gaze on the gate and giving his peripheral vision a chance to pick up movement. It was an old hunter's trick taught to him by Jimmy Burke many years before.

There! By the silver birch. A man was moving stealthily through the undergrowth. And there! Another crouched beside a holly tree.

Griffin's mouth was dry. He identified two other shapes as intruders and then cast his eyes about the darkened room for his pistol. But it was gone—Madden must have taken it. He lay back on the sofa and carefully eased himself to the floor, drawing his hunting knife from its sheath. He was in no condition to fight *one* man; four might as well be four hundred.

"Think, man!" he told himself. His eyes flicked around the room. Where would they come in?

The window was open, and that seemed the best bet, so he slowly moved on all fours to sit beneath the ledge. The exertion weakened him, and he felt dizzy. He took a deep breath and leaned his head against the cold stone. Minutes passed, and his mind wandered. He had once hidden like this as a boy, when his father had been hunting him to deliver a thrashing. He couldn't remember what he had done, but he recalled vividly the sense of defeat within the excitement, knowing that he was only putting off the awful moment.

The window creaked. Griffin glanced up and saw a hand on the ledge.

With infinite care he eased himself into a crouch. A leg swung into sight, the booted foot almost grazing Griffin's shoulder, and then the man was inside. Griffin rose to his feet, grabbing the long dark hair, and before the intruder could scream, the hunting knife sliced across his throat.

He began to struggle wildly, and Griffin was thrown from him. The man fell to his knees, dropping his pistol. Griffin scooped it up and crawled back to the wall, waiting for the next man.

Across the room the first intruder had ceased to struggle. Griffin cocked the pistol and closed his eyes to aid his hearing. Nothing moved . . .

He awoke with a start. His mind had drifted him into a dream, and he blinked hard, scanning the room. How long had he been asleep? Seconds? Minutes?

And what had awakened him?

The pistol butt was warm in his hand and slippery with sweat; he wiped his palm on his shirt and picked up the gun once more. Outside he could hear the sound of distant chanting, and a red glow filled the room.

A man stepped inside from the door at the far wall, and Griffin shot him twice. He stumbled and fell, then raised his pistol, and a bullet smashed into the wall above Griffin's head. Holding his pistol two-handed, Griffin fired once more, and the man fell dead. The room stank of cordite, and smoke hung in the air. Griffin's ears rang, and he could hear nothing.

He pushed himself to his feet and risked a glance from the window. A man was running toward the house; Griffin's first shot missed him, but the second took him in the chest, and he fell. The wagon master wiped sweat from his eyes as he glanced up at the night sky . . .

. . . and saw the Devil looming above the housetops.

"My God!" he whispered.

"No, mine," said a voice.

Griffin did not turn. "I wondered what had happened to you, Zedeki."

"You are a hard man to kill, Mr. Griffin."

"I am surprised you did not just shoot me down."

"I thought you might like to witness the last act in the drama. Watch his hand, Mr. Griffin. The next person you see will be your wife being carried to his mouth . . . then I will kill you."

The Devil disappeared, and Zedeki screamed. Griffin swung and fired, and the bullet punched Zedeki back against the wall; his knees buckled, and he sank to the floor, still gazing at the star-filled night sky.

Griffin sat down and watched the young man die.

Abaddon stood on the black marble balcony overlooking the temple steps, reveling in the appearance of his god, feeling his doubts swirling away from him like mist in the morning. The sound of gunshots came from within the temple, and the priests scattered. He saw Achnazzar hurled from his feet and devoured by the Devil. Then a dark-clad figure ran forward, the Devil's hand dropped, and Abaddon screamed his triumph as the warrior was swept into his palm.

But the Devil disappeared, and a pain clutched Abaddon's heart like fingers of fire. He screamed and fell back through the doorway, crawling to his bedside and the ivory-inlaid ebony box that lay there. He whispered the words of power, but the box did not open. Pulling himself to his knees, he struggled for calm and pressed the hidden button at the base. The lid sprang open, and relief surged in him as his hands pulled clear the large oval Blood Stone. The pain in his chest eased slightly. He blinked and focused his eyes on the stone; the red was fading, with the black veins growing as he watched.

"*No!*" he whispered. Brown liver spots blossomed on his hands, and the skin began to wrinkle. He managed to get to his feet and draw a silver-embossed pistol from a leather scabbard hanging at the bedside.

"Guard!" he yelled, and a young man ran into the room.

"What is it, sire?"

Abaddon shot him through the head, then carried the stone to the twitching body and held it under the pumping jet of blood coming from the man's brow. Still the power ebbed, the black veins spreading and joining.

"There is nothing you can do, Lawrence," said Ruth.

Abaddon dropped the stone and sank down beside the guard's body. "Help me, Ruthie."

"I cannot. You should have died a long time ago."

His hair glistened white, and his face took on the look of worn leather. He no longer had the strength to sit, and his body slumped to the floor. Ruth sat beside him, cradling his head in her lap.

"Why did you go away?" he whispered. "It could all have been so different." The flesh melted from his face, and his lips moved in a last ragged whisper. "I did love you," he said.

"I know."

His body fell back in her arms, and she could feel the bones beneath the skin, brittle and pointed. The skin peeled away, and the bones crumbled to the floor.

On the steps of the temple, Batik swiftly reloaded his pistol and sat facing the crowd. The roar of rage died down, and the people fell back, staring at their painted hands and looking in confusion at their comrades. At the front of the crowd a man groaned and toppled forward, and a friend knelt by him.

"He's dead," said the man. Someone else in the crowd, feeling unwell, drew his Blood Stone from its pouch; it was blacker than sin. Another man died, and the crowd backed away from the body. As other people checked their stones, panic grew.

On the steps Madden helped Batik to his feet, and they moved to Donna, ripping the silver bands from her body. She moaned and opened her eyes.

"Jacob?"

"It's all right. You're safe, girl."

"Where is Con?"

"He's waiting for us. I'll take you to him."

"And Eric?"

"We'll talk later. Take my hand."

Below them the crowd was streaming away. Madden lifted Donna into his arms as a dark-haired young man approached him.

"God's greeting," he said.

"Who are you?" asked Batik.

"Clophas. You do not know me, Batik, but I was at Sanctuary while you were there."

"It seems a long time ago."

"Yes, a lifetime. Can I help you with the lady?"

On the *Titanic* people fought with one another to climb the choked stairways and escape the rising water. The Mother Stone, unleashing all its energy, played its role to the fullest, tilting the ship to imitate the original disaster. Scores of Guardians, their wives, and their children slid below the foaming torrent, thrashing and screaming for assistance. None was offered.

Whereas in the disaster of 1912 a number of brave men had manned the pumps until the last minute, not one Guardian had the knowledge to do the same. Where the original tragedy had been enacted for three hours, this *Titanic* was sinking within minutes. Bulkheads collapsed, and hundreds died, dragged to their deaths by the seething ocean.

There was no escape. Many threw themselves from the upper decks, splashing into the sea below, only to find themselves piercing the edge of the stone's field of energy and dropping through the water to hurtle down the mountain onto the jagged marble ruins of Atlantis.

Amaziga Archer and her son, Luke, struggled through the smoking lounge and onto the A-deck foyer. The water there was waist-deep and rising. Lifting Luke to her shoulder, she climbed through a shattered window and out onto the steeply tilted deck. Luke clung to her as she fought her way up toward the stern, rearing like a tower above the swelling sea. Hooking her arm around a brass stanchion, she listened to the cries of the victims trapped below.

Slowly the dying ship slid under the waves. Cold water touched Amaziga's ankles . . . it shimmered and faded.

The Mother Stone was finished, choked by the thin thread of gold and exhausted by the disaster it had created. The ship shuddered, and the sea disappeared. Amaziga sat up and touched her clothes. They were dry. Looking around, she saw that she lay on a rusted deck and that twenty feet from her a male survivor struggled to his feet.

"We made it!" he shouted, but the rotting deck parted beneath his feet and the dead ship swallowed him and his screams. Amaziga felt the deck move beneath her and crawled carefully to the stern, where the ship touched the cliff face. The deck gave way. Amaziga's hand flashed out to grip the rail, and Luke screamed and hung from her neck. The muscles in her arm stretched and tore, but her fingers remained locked to the rail. She glanced down into the dark, empty bowels of the ghost ship.

"Hold on, Luke!" she shouted, and the boy gripped her tunic. She took a deep breath, then dragged on her arm, hauling herself upward and hooking her left arm to the rail. As her weight hit the rail, it bent outward, almost dislodging her. Swinging her feet up, she scrambled onto the hull and inched her way to the cliff. There the drop was even greater, and the ruins of Atlantis gleamed like pointed teeth. She removed the leather belt from her tunic and looped it around Luke's back, tying him to her. Then she stepped to the rock face and began the long, hazardous climb.

Shannow found a concave bulge in the rocky roof where an air pocket was trapped above the bubbling water. Death was close, and as much as he tried to prepare himself for the end, he knew he was not ready. Rage and despair tore at him. No Jerusalem! No end to the quest of his lifetime! The rising water lapped at his chin, spilling over into his mouth. He gagged and spit it out, his fingers scrabbling at the rocks as the weight of his coat and gun dragged him down.

"Calm yourself, Shannow!" came a voice in his mind. A glow began to his right, and Pendarric's face appeared like a shimmering reflection on the stone roof. "Follow me if you wish to live."

The glow sank below the water, and Shannow cursed and took several deep breaths, filling his lungs with oxygen. Then he dived below the surface. Far below he could see the Mother Stone, its glow fading fast, but ahead of him floated the ghostly face. He swam toward it, ever deeper, his lungs beginning to burn as his weary arms pushed at the water. Pendarric glided farther ahead to a black tunnel mouth near the cavern floor. There Shannow felt the tug of the current and was swept into the tunnel. His chest was a growing agony, and he released a little air. Panic began, but Pendarric's voice cut through his fear.

"Courage, Rolynd."

His body was buffeted from rock to rock in the narrow tunnel until he could hold his breath no longer; his lungs expelled the precious air and sucked in salt water. His head swam, and he lost consciousness just as his body tumbled free of the mountain. Pendarric's translucent form materialized beside Shannow, but the king was powerless to aid the dying man.

"Ruth!" he called, his plea roaring across the gulf of spirit.

Shannow lay unmoving as Pendarric called again and again.

She appeared and took in the scene in a moment. Kneeling, she rolled Shannow to his chest and straddled his back. Her hands pressed hard against the small of his back, forcing his lungs to expel the deadly liquid. But still the Jerusalem Man showed no sign of life. She jerked him to his back and lifted his head, pinching his nostrils closed. Her mouth covered his, and her breath filled his lungs. The minutes passed, and Shannow groaned, sucking in a long shuddering breath.

"He will live?" said Pendarric.

Ruth nodded.

"You are tired, lady."

"Yes, but I have found the way."

"I hoped you would. Is the pain great?"

Ruth's eyes met his, and she did not need to answer.

"You have great courage, Ruth. Hold to it. Do not let the power of the Blood Stones overpower you. They will make you dream great dreams; they will fill your heart with the desire to rule."

"Do not fear for me, Pendarric; such thoughts of conquest are for men. But as I draw the power from the stones, I can feel my soul contaminated by the evil. I can feel the hatred and the lust swell within me. For the first time in my life I understand the desire to kill."

"And will you?" asked the king.

"No."

"Can you stop the Hellborn in the south without killing?"

"I can try, Pendarric."

"You are stronger than I, Ruth."

"Wiser, perhaps, and not as humble as I was. I do not want to die, and yet you were right. I cannot live with this seething force inside me."

"Take the swan's path and know peace."

"Yes. Peace. Would that I could carry all hatred from the world with my passing."

Pendarric shrugged. "You will destroy the stones. It is enough."

Shannow moaned and rolled.

"I will say farewell here, Ruth. It was a privilege to have known you."

"I thank you for my lessons."

"The pupil is greater than the teacher," he said, and vanished.

Shannow awoke on the rocky ground a half mile from the marble ruins and found himself gazing up at the *Titanic*. Once more it was the golden, rusting wreck he had first seen. Then a great tear ripped along the hull, and the sea gushed from her like a giant waterfall, hurtling down on the ancient city below. The torrent continued for some minutes, and Shannow could see tiny bodies carried in the foaming water.

He sat up to see Ruth beside him, watching the second death of the legendary ship. Tears were falling, and she looked away.

"Thank you for my life," he said lamely.

"I bear the responsibility for theirs," she replied as bodies continued to rain down on Atlantis.

"They fashioned their own doom," he told her. "You cannot blame yourself."

She sighed and turned from the ship. "Donna is safe and reunited with Con Griffin."

"I wish them happiness," said Shannow.

"I know; it marks you as a special man."

"What of Batik?"

"He was wounded, but he will survive. He is a tough man, and he took on the Devil single-handed."

"The Devil?"

"No," said Ruth, smiling, "but a close imitation."

"And Abaddon?"

"He is dead, Jon."

"Did Batik kill him?"

"No, you did, Jerusalem Man. Or perhaps the Guardians did a very long time ago."

"I don't understand."

"Do you remember me telling you about Lawrence and how he was at peace and happy after the Fall? How he helped rebuild?"

"Yes."

"And, more important, how he came to have visions of the Devil speaking to him and guiding him?"

"Of course."

"The Devil was here, Jon, in that accursed ship. It was the stone and those who used it; they were the wolves in the shadows all along, getting Lawrence to feed them souls. They found the weakness in him and caused Abaddon to blossom and grow. They fed him power and kept him alive through the centuries. When you sealed that power, Lawrence became himself—a man long dead."

"Sarento was a man with a dream," said Shannow. "He wanted to rebuild the old world, bring back all the cities, restore civilization."

"That wasn't a dream," said Ruth. "It was an obsession. Believe me, Jon, I lived in that old world, and I can tell you that there is little I would re-create. For every blessing, there was a curse. For every joy, ten sorrows. Nine-tenths of the world went short of food, and everywhere there were wars, plagues, famine, and starvation. It was finished before the Fall, but it was taking a long time to die."

"What will you do now?"

"I will return to Sanctuary."

"Is Selah well?"

"He is fine. He has gone now, with all my people, out into the world. I sent him with Clophas; they get on well together."

"You will be alone in Sanctuary?"

"For a little while."

"Will I see you again?"

"I think not." She turned back to the wreck and saw a tiny figure climbing down the mountain. "One last favor, Jon?"

"Of course."

"That is Sam Archer's wife and son. See them to safety."

"I will. Farewell, Ruth."

"Godspeed. Seek your city and find your God."

Shannow grinned. "I'll find it."

Back in Sanctuary, Ruth lay down on her beloved sofa and drew on all the power she had amassed through the centuries. Her body glowed and grew, not only absorbing all of Sanctuary but continuing to drain the power from every Blood Stone within her considerable reach. As her strength grew, so, too, did her pain, and a war began within her as the might of the Blood Stones met the essence of Sanctuary. Rage welled in her soul, and all the forgotten moments of anger, lust, and greed flooded her being.

That which had been Ruth Welby pulsed out into the night like a glowing cloud, dispersing into the air, traveling on the currents of the night winds.

For a while Ruth fought to hold a sense of identity within the cloud, battling to subdue the dark power of the stones, establishing harmony within her strength.

At last she came upon the Hellborn army massing for the final charge against the defenders of Sweetwater. Then she surrendered to infinity and fell like a rain of golden light upon the valley.

The Hellborn general, Abaal, sat on the grass-covered crest of a hill, staring sullenly toward the Sweetwater pass while below him his army mustered for the charge. For two days now the ferocity of the defense had been weakening as Cade and his men ran short of shells. Yesterday the Hellborn had almost broken through, but Cade had rallied the defenders and Abaal's warriors had been pushed back after fierce hand-to-hand fighting.

Today, Abaal knew, would see an end to resistance. His eyes raked the entrance to the pass, where the bodies of men and horses lay bloated in the sunshine—more than a thousand young men who would never return to their homes.

The warmth of the sun made him remove his heavy black topcoat, and he lay back on the grass, fixing his gaze on the defenders. The enemy, too, had lost many men and by rights should have run. They were hopelessly outnumbered, and victory was not an option for them. Yet they stayed.

Abaal searched for the comfort of his hatred, but it was gone.

How could he hate men and women prepared to die for their homeland?

His aide, Doreval, rode up the crest and dismounted. "The men are ready, sir."

"How do they feel about the loss of their stones?"

"There is fear among them, but they are disciplined."

Abaal gestured for the young man to sit beside him. "The day has a curious feel to it."

"In what way, sir?"

"It's hard to explain. Do you hate them, Doreval? The defenders?"

"Of course; they are the enemy."

"But is your hatred as strong today?"

The young man looked away, his gaze floating over the corpses on the plain. "Yes," he said at last.

Abaal caught the lie and ignored it. "What are you thinking?"

"I was remembering my father and our parting. As he lay dying, I just sat there thinking about the wealth I would have, how his concubines would be mine. I never thanked him. Such a strange feeling."

"Tell me, Doreval, and with truth—do you want to fight today?"

"Yes, sir. It would be an honor to lead the men."

Abaal looked deeply into the young man's eyes and knew once more that he had lied. He could not blame him; the Abaal of yesterday would have killed him for the truth.

"Tell the men to stand down."

"Yes, sir," answered Doreval, unable to keep the relief from his face.

"And fetch me a jug of wine."

At the entrance to the pass Cade watched the enemy dismount.

"What they playing at, Daniel?" asked Gambion.

Cade shrugged and opened the breech of his pistol; only two shells remained. He closed his eyes, and Gambion thought he was praying and moved to one side, but Cade was merely trying to think, to concentrate. He opened his eyes and looked around at the defenders, swallowing hard. They had fought so well.

A long time before—or so it seemed—Lisa had asked Cade whether he would create an army from lambs. Well, he had, and brave they were! But courage could carry a man only so far. Now they were all to die, and Cade realized he did not have the courage to see it. He sheathed his pistol and stood.

"Pass me my stick, Ephram."

"Where are you going?"

"I'm going to talk to God," said Cade. Gambion handed him the carved stick, and Cade limped out into the entrance of Sweetwater, stopping to look at the Hellborn dead choking the grass. The stench turned his stomach, and he walked on.

It was a beautiful day, and his knee had ceased its throbbing.

"Well, God, seems like we ought to have one real chat before the end. I've got to be honest—I don't really believe in you—but I figure I've nothing to lose by this. If I'm talking to myself, it don't matter. But if you are there, then maybe you'll listen. These people are about to die. That's no big thing—people have been dying for thousands of years—but my lads are getting ready to die for *you*. And that should mean something. I may be a false prophet, but they're true believers, and I hope they don't get short shrift from you merely because of me. I never was worth much—didn't have the guts to farm and spent my life stealing and the like. No excuses. But Ephram and the rest are worth something more; they really have repented or whatever the hell you call it. I've brought them to their deaths, and I don't want to think about them lining up expectant-like outside the gates, only to be told they ain't getting in. That's all I got to say, God."

As Cade walked on toward the distant Hellborn, he pulled his pistol from his belt and hurled it onto the grass.

Hearing the sound of movement behind him, he turned and saw Ephram Gambion lumbering toward him, his bald head shining with sweat.

"What did he say, Daniel?"

Cade smiled and patted the giant on the shoulder. "He let me do the talking this time, Ephram. You fancy a walk?"

"Where we going?"

"To the Hellborn."

"Why?"

Cade ignored the question and limped away. Gambion joined him.

"You still with me, Ephram?"

"Did you ever doubt it?"

"I guess not. Look at that sky. Mackerel-black and streaked with clouds. Hell of a good day to die, I'd say."

"Is that where we're going? To die?"

"You don't have to come with me; I can do it alone."

"I know that, Daniel. But we've come this far together, so I guess I'll stay awhile yet. You know, we done pretty good against that damned army; not bad for a bunch of brigands and farmers."

"The best days of my life," admitted Cade, "but I should have said good-bye to Lisa."

The two men walked on in silence through the ranks of the dead and onto the plain before the Hellborn. There they were spotted by a scout, who took the news to Doreval; he rode to Abaal, and the general ordered his horse saddled. Gambion watched as a score of Hellborn soldiers galloped toward them and drew his pistol.

"Throw it away, Ephram."

"I ain't dying without a fight."

"Throw it away."

Gambion swore . . . and hurled the pistol out over the grass.

The Hellborn slowed their mounts and ringed the two men. Cade ignored the rifles and pistols pointed at him, watching as the steel-haired general dismounted.

"You would be Cade?"

"I am."

"I am Abaal, lord of the Sixth. Why are you here?"

"Thought it was time we met. Face-to-face, man to man."

"To what purpose?"

"Thought you might like to bury your dead."

"This is a strange day," said Abaal. "Like a dream. Is it magic of yours?"

"No. Maybe it's just something that happens when a lot of men have to die for nothing. Maybe it's just weariness."

"What are you saying, Cade? Speak openly."

Cade laughed. "Openly? Why not? What are we doing here, killing each other? What are we fighting for? A field of grass? A few empty meadows? Why don't you just go home?"

"There is an enchantment working here," said Abaal. "I do not understand it, but I feel the truth of what you say. You will allow us to bury our dead?"

Cade nodded.

"Then I agree. The war is over!"

Abaal extended his hand, and Cade stared down at it, unable to move. This man had led the massacres, causing untold grief and horror. Looking into Abaal's eyes, he forced himself to accept the grip, and as he did so, the last vestiges of bitterness fled from him and he fought back the tears welling inside.

"You are a great man, Cade," said Abaal, "and I shall be killed for listening to you. Perhaps we will meet in hell."

"I don't doubt it for a second," said Cade.

Abaal smiled, then mounted his horse and led his men back to their tents.

"Jesus Christ!" said Gambion. "Did we win, Daniel?"

"Take me home, Ephram."

As they neared Sweetwater, the defenders and their wives

and children streamed out to meet them. Cade could not speak, but Gambion swiftly told them of the peace, and Cade was swept shoulder-high and carried back into the pass.

Lisa was standing in a grove of elm, tears in her eyes, when Cade finally came to her. The sound of singing echoed through the mountains.

"Is it truly over, Daniel?"

"It is."

"And you won. Now you'll want to be a king?"

He pulled her to him and kissed her gently. "That was another man in another place. All I want now is for us to marry and start a home and a family. I want nothing more to do with war, or guns, or death. I'll grow corn and raise cattle and sheep. I just want to be with you, and I don't give a damn about being a king."

Lisa lifted his chin and smiled. "Well," she said, "now that you don't want it, you're bound to get it!"

Epilogue

IN THE YEAR after the Hellborn war Daniel Cade was elected Prester of Rivervale. He married Lisa in the biggest wedding ceremony seen in the area for thirty years. The whole community attended and the gifts were brought in several wagons.

Con Griffin, Donna, and their daughter, Tanya, returned to Rivervale and the farm built by Tomas the carpenter. Once they were clear of the Plague Lands, Donna's powers faded, though often she would be seen in the far meadow, sitting silently with her daughter. At those times Con Griffin left them alone with their faraway dreams.

Jacob Madden married a young widow and took possession of the farm adjoining Griffin's land; the two remained close friends until Madden's death eighteen years later.

Batik spent two years hunting for signs of Jon Shannow and finally tracked down Amaziga Archer, who directed him north.

As winter was approaching, he rode into a wide valley and came to a farmhouse of white stone. Near the trees were three bodies covered with a tarpaulin. The farm was run by two women, a mother and daughter, and they told him that the dead men had been robbers.

"What happened?" Batik asked the mother.

"A stranger rode in as they were attacking the house, and he killed them all. But he was wounded. I asked him to stay, but he refused; he rode on toward the High Lonely," she said, pointing to the distant snow-covered peaks.

"What did he look like?" asked Batik.

"He was a tall man with long hair and burning eyes."

As Batik turned his horse to the north and rode from the yard, the daughter, a blond girl of around fifteen, ran after him and caught at his stirrup.

"She didn't tell the whole truth," she whispered. "She didn't ask him to stay. She was frightened of him and told him to ride on. I gave him some bread and cheese, and he told me not to worry. There was a shining city just over the farthest mountain, he said, and his wound would be tended to there. But there isn't a city; it's just a wilderness. And the blood was streaming down his saddle."

Batik tried to follow, but a blinding blizzard blew up and he was forced to give up the search.

That same night Daniel Cade had a strange dream. He was walking through a mountain wood, through thick snow, yet he felt no cold. He came to a frozen stream and a small campfire that gave no heat. Beside it, his back against a tree, sat the Jerusalem Man.

"Hello, Daniel," he said, and Cade moved close.

"You are hurt."

"There is no pain."

"Let me help you, Jonnie."

"I hear you're a great man now in Rivervale."

"Yes," said Cade.

"Dad would have been proud of you. *I* am proud of you." Shannow smiled, and the ice in his beard cracked and fell away.

"Let me build up the fire."

"No. Are you happy, Daniel?"

"Yes. Very."

"Do you have children?"

"Two. A boy and a girl."

"That's good. So the wolf sits down with the lambs. I'm glad. Help me to my horse, Daniel."

Cade lifted him and saw the blood on the ice. He half carried him to the black stallion and heaved him up into the saddle. Shannow swayed and then took up the reins.

"Where are you going?" asked Cade.

"There," said Shannow, pointing to the peaks piercing the clouds. "Can you see the spires, Daniel?"

"No," whispered Cade.

"I'm going home."

THE WORLDS OF DAVID GEMMELL

Author David Gemmell is hailed as Britain's king of heroic fantasy, and through sixteen of his most famous battle-charged adventures, Del Rey brings the action to American shores.

THE DRENAI SAGA: Experience the Drenai cycle that was launched with the international bestseller LEGEND. Meet the heroes of the Drenai people . . .

WAYLANDER: He was charged with protecting the innocents and journeying into the shadow-haunted lands of the Nadir to find the legendary Armor of Bronze. But Waylander was an assassin, a slayer, the killer of the king.

LEGEND: Druss was a legend even in old age, and he would be called to fight once more, to defend the mighty fortress Dros Delnoch, the last possible stronghold against the Nadir hordes.

THE KING BEYOND THE GATE: Tenaka Khan was an outsider, a halfbreed, despised by both the Drenai and the Nadir, but he would be one man against the armies of Chaos.

QUEST FOR LOST HEROES: Among the travelers—the boy Kiall, the legendary heroes Chareos the Blademaster and Beltzer the Axman, and the bowmen Finn and Maggrig—lurked a secret that could free the world of Nadir, once and for all.

And don't miss these *new* Drenai adventures, coming soon:
WAYLANDER 2: IN THE REALM OF THE WOLF
DRUSS THE LEGEND
LEGEND OF DEATHWALKER

"Gemmell's great reading; the action never lets up; he's several rungs above the good—right into the fabulous." —Anne McCaffrey

THE STONES OF POWER: Tales of dark magic, sorcery, and conquest stemming from the Sipstrassi Stones of Power . . . a new dark age, a witch queen, a Hellborn army, and a man seeking the child born of a demon. Evil times call for bold heroes, including Uther Pendragon, Culain, and the famed Jon Shannow, the tragic figure known as the Jerusalem Man.

The Stones of Power Cycle
GHOST KING
LAST SWORD OF POWER
WOLF IN SHADOW
THE LAST GUARDIAN
BLOODSTONE

"David Gemmell tells a tale of very real adventure, the stuff of true epic fantasy." —R. A. Salvatore

"Gemmell . . . keeps the mythic currents crackling." —Publishers Weekly

Epic fantasy invades the era of Alexander the Great in tales that unite heroes of history with those of legend . . .

LION OF MACEDON: In every possible future, a dark god was poised to reenter Greece. Only the half-Spartan Parmenion could hope to defeat its evil. And so it had been foretold—Parmenion's destiny was tied to the dark god, and to Philip of Macedon and the as-yet-unborn Alexander the Great.

DARK PRINCE: The Chaos Spirit had been born into Alexander, but the intervention of Parmenion had prevented it from taking the boy's soul completely. But in another Greece where the creatures of legend flourished, a demon king sought the power of the Chaos Spirit. The demon called to the boy who would be king, and only Parmenion could hope to intervene.

"Gemmell works the reader's emotions adroitly. . . . It's a satisfying, often exciting fantasy that will thrill many readers." —*Locus*

KNIGHTS OF DARK RENOWN

The legendary knights of the Gabala had been greater than princes, more than men. But they were gone; they had disappeared through a demon-haunted gateway between worlds. But one tormented knight had held back—Manannan, whose every instinct had told him to stay. But as murder and black magic beset the land, Manannan realized he would have to face his darkest fears, ride through that dreaded gate, and find his lost companions.

"A sharp distinctive medieval fantasy. Dramatic, colorful, taut." —*Locus*

MORNINGSTAR

Jarek Mace was an outlaw, a bandit, a heartless thief. He needed nothing and no one. But Angostin hordes raged over the borders, evil sorcery ruled, and the Vampyre kings lived once again. The Highland people needed a hero, and Mace inadvertently became that hero, a legend—the great Morningstar returned. But Mace was an outlaw, not a savior. Or was he?

"It seems that every time I read a new David Gemmell novel it is better than the last—and MORNINGSTAR is no exception." —*Starburst*